D0043208

The
Outcast
Girls

BOOKS BY SHIRLEY DICKSON

The Orphan Sisters
Our Last Goodbye

SHIRLEY DICKSON

The
Outcast
Girls

bookouture

Published by Bookouture in 2020

An imprint of Storyfire Ltd.
Carmelite House
50 Victoria Embankment
London EC4Y 0DZ

www.bookouture.com

Copyright © Shirley Dickson, 2020

Shirley Dickson has asserted her right to be identified
as the author of this work.

All rights reserved. No part of this publication may be reproduced,
stored in any retrieval system, or transmitted, in any form or by
any means, electronic, mechanical, photocopying, recording or
otherwise, without the prior written permission of the publishers.

ISBN: 978-1-83888-250-1
eBook ISBN: 978-1-83888-249-5

This book is a work of fiction. Names, characters, businesses,
organizations, places and events other than those clearly in the
public domain, are either the product of the author's imagination
or are used fictitiously. Any resemblance to actual persons, living or
dead, events or locales is entirely coincidental.

To Wal and my lovely family.

CHAPTER ONE

Berlin. November 1938

Frieda

Frieda Sternberg sat on the floor in the kitchen of their upstairs apartment, behind the door, covering her ears with her hands. But she could still hear the shouts and terrifying screams from outside, and the noise of shattering glass as windows were smashed.

When they heard the mob ransacking their bakery underneath the flat, Papa herded the family down the back stairs. There was no time to take possessions.

Outside, in the twilight, feet crunching over shards of broken glass, Frieda took Grandma's arm to support her. She looked around her and was shocked at the destruction in the neighbourhood. Acrid smoke billowed from buildings; flames licked through shattered windows. Eyes stinging from choking smoke, Frieda ran, keeping to the shadows. She jumped in fright as her brother Kurt, two years younger than her, cried, 'Look, those men are setting the synagogue alight.'

Through the open heavy synagogue doors, she saw men in uniform dousing pews with petrol and setting them on fire.

'All is lost,' Grandma screamed, collapsing.

Mama took Grandma's arm and Frieda helped her, together dragging her sagging body along.

'Where are we going?' Mama asked Papa, who was leading the way.

He looked furtively around. 'To the only place I know that's safe out of the Jewish quarter. My good friend Claus Unger's.'

Papa had told Frieda many times how the friendship between the two men had begun.

'It was when we both served during the war,' he had told her. 'All men like to dream, little one, and our dream was that one day, when the conflict was over, we would own a business together. Claus had the finance and I had the business acumen. I decided bread was a necessity and therefore we'd never go out of business. Our dream came true when the war was over and we started this bakery of ours. I baked while Claus delivered and the business grew.'

'Then why did Herr Unger leave?' she'd asked.

'He met a Fräulein.' Papa had rolled his eyes. 'Gerda didn't want a husband who went out on a horse and cart delivering bread.' He tousled Frieda's dark hair. 'Even if the cart was brightly painted.' His eyes had glazed over as he smoked his pipe and remembered. 'I bought Claus out and the business became ours. Claus and I have remained good friends ever since.'

So, now the family stole away in the dark, making the six-mile journey from the Jewish quarter. past Tiergarten to the safety of Herr Unger's little house.

On a cold winter's night, weeks after Kristallnacht, Frieda was tossing and turning in the bed she shared with Kurt in the tiny upstairs spare bedroom. As the wind howled around Herr Unger's house, she could hear his anxious voice from the living room.

'…it's still too dangerous for you all to return to your apartment.'

'But isn't it dangerous for you to be harbouring us, Claus?' Mama's voice implored.

'Many Jewish men have been arrested and sent to concentration camps. It's best for us all if you aren't seen. If anyone asks, I'll say the children are relatives.'

'The troubles are getting worse. We must leave Germany,' Mama said.

'We haven't enough money to flee Germany.' Papa's voice was gruff with emotion. 'Or any connections.'

'That is why I need to talk to you, my friend. The Jewish orphanage here in Berlin was torched during Kristallnacht.' At Herr Unger's words there followed a shocked silence for a time. 'The orphanage has organised the children's emigration.'

'Where to?' Papa asked.

'I have made it my business to find out. Discreetly, of course. An old work colleague I play bridge with confided that after Kristallnacht the British government has agreed to temporarily take thousands of Jewish children under the age of seventeen. A network of organisers has been established and my friend volunteered to help make a priority list of those children who are most in peril.'

'And the children leave their parents behind?' Mama's voice sounded shaky.

'Yes.'

There was a sob.

'Who will look after them in the United Kingdom?' Papa wanted to know.

'Agencies operating under the name of "Movement for the Care of Children from Germany" have promised to find the Jewish children homes. They're also funding the operation and sponsorship so the refugees won't be a financial burden on the British.'

'Who would think our children would become refugees?' Mama wailed.

'*Meine Liebe*, it's paramount we send Frieda and Kurt to safety.' Papa's tone was firm. 'We must make arrangements for them to leave at once. First I'll make a trip to our apartment. The shop's weekly takings and a few precious possessions are in the safe.'

'Must you go?' Mama asked.

'I'll be careful, *meine Liebe*. Our children must have some kind of financial security when they leave – and a photograph as a memento of us all in happier times.'

Whatever photograph Papa chose, Frieda never found out. He never returned from his visit to the apartment. Herr Unger heard that Papa had been arrested as he left the Jewish quarter.

Now, over three months since the November Pogroms, when 'Nazi thugs', as Papa had called them, attacked Jewish people and property, Frieda and Kurt stood in the railway station, each of them clutching a small suitcase and the ten marks they were allowed to carry.

Amidst the noise and confusion, Kurt's expression mutinous, he told Mama, 'I won't go, you can't make me.' He removed his cap and ran his fingers through his raven black hair. 'Papa told me that I'm the man of the family until he returns.' To Frieda's dismay Kurt's eyes glistened with tears. 'I promised him, Mama, that I'd look after you all.'

Kurt was as stubborn as Papa's delivery horse, who wouldn't budge if he'd so decided.

Mama told Kurt, 'I know, but it was Papa who wanted you to make this trip to England.'

Though it was a calculated plan, Frieda knew it broke Mama's heart. A no-nonsense expression crossed her mother's face. 'You will do as you are told and board that train. I'll be fine here with Grandma until Papa returns. Then we will follow.' She gave an unconvincing quivery smile. 'Be good, children.' She handed them each a card. 'This is called an identity card. It allows you to enter England. It has your name, where you were born, who your parents are and where we live. Promise me you'll always keep this document safe.'

Hearing the urgency in Mama's voice, in unison they replied, 'We promise, Mama.'

Numb with shock, Frieda waited in a queue of silent children, then she and Kurt climbed aboard the train. They found seats together and looked for their mother through the window.

When the train began to move, she waved until she couldn't see darling Mama any more.

As the train chugged along the track, smoke billowing from its funnel, Frieda stared with teary eyes at the blurry scene outside. The journey was interminably long and she must have slept for hours because when she awoke it was dark and the train had stopped. Soldiers, using torches, were rifling through her suitcase.

Kurt whispered, 'We've stopped at the border – they are searching for valuables.'

Traumatised, watching her suitcase being searched, Frieda was beyond tears. Even if Papa had succeeded in his mission, the family's precious possessions would only have ended up stolen from his children.

When it was Kurt's turn to have his suitcase ransacked, by the light of the soldier's torch, she saw her brother's bunched lips and glowering expression. Unlike Frieda, Kurt could be obstinate and unruly – Mama's words to describe her son. Afraid that he would speak out, Frieda was relieved when the soldiers left and the train started up. The tense moment passed.

The train crossed the border into Holland and an older girl across the aisle shouted, 'Hurrah! We're free of the oppression of Germany!'

Finally, the train came to a halt at a platform and in the half-light, smiling Dutch women handed out milk and chocolate through the windows. It was the first thing Frieda had eaten since breakfast.

*

Later that evening, in the glare of the dockside lights, Frieda, insides quivering, followed the silent children as they filed up the gangplank, Kurt reassuringly behind. Up on deck, they made their way towards the rail. She looked below, seeing men preparing the ship for leaving the quayside.

'I don't want to go,' a young boy beside her whimpered.

Frieda, not knowing what to say, put an arm around his shoulders.

She wondered if Mama was with Grandma and whether, after saying farewell to Herr Unger, they had made their way home to their apartment. At the thought of home Frieda's pulse quickened in panic – for she and Kurt were bound for England, where they knew nobody and people spoke a different language. She shivered, not from the cold, but from apprehension.

Turning, she looked for Kurt. Her eyes searched the bewildered-looking children standing on the deck, their frightened eyes hollow with shock. But Kurt's sturdy figure wasn't amongst them.

A shout rang out and Frieda started. Men were pulling the gangplank onto the ship.

Quick as a flash, a figure ran down the gangplank. Leaping through the air and over the gap, Kurt's feet slammed onto the safety of the quayside.

Frieda stood rooted to the spot.

A man shouted in a foreign language at him. But Kurt had gone, disappeared into a throng of people working on the quayside.

At last Frieda found her voice. 'No! Please, Kurt, don't leave me!'

CHAPTER TWO

South Shields. North-East England. February 1943

Sandra

Sandra Hudson closed the coalhouse door and, hauling up the heavy coal scuttle, made her way over the concrete backyard, through the scullery and into the warmth of the kitchen. With its gleaming copper pans hanging on the walls, scrubbed wooden table, and meaty smell wafting from the coal fired range, the room was satisfyingly cosy.

Mrs Goodwin – the cook – looked up from the pan of soup she was stirring on the range top and appraised the housemaid, inspecting her black uniform dress, white apron and cap. Sandra felt self-conscious and blushed under Cook's scrutiny.

Cook moved towards Sandra and with a plump hand brushed coal dust from the bib of her apron. 'I only do it for your own good, lass. Her ladyship is in a foul mood and I don't want yi' to get the brunt of it.' She gave a broad, good-natured smile that showed a row of false teeth.

'Thanks for the warning, Cook,' Sandra replied.

It was still early morning, and Sandra hadn't crossed paths yet with Mrs Kirton, her employer and the lady of the house. She made a mental note to be on her guard when she did.

'The thing is, lass,' Cook told her, 'I know you feel awkward around Mrs Kirton but it makes you appear standoffish and if there's one thing employers can't abide it's a servant who thinks she's above her station.'

Sandra was appalled. 'Do I really appear that way?'

Cook nodded.

Sandra felt inadequate in her employer's presence – not good enough – but her upbringing had taught her that to survive you had to stay strong. Maybe she seemed more confident than she felt as a result.

'I do feel uneasy around Mrs Kirton,' she confided. 'The thing is, I live in fear that one day she will terminate me employment. You see, I've no money and no one to turn to.' She didn't add that she would end up a homeless pauper.

Cook heaved her shoulders. 'You're too sensitive, lass, for your own good. Mrs Kirton knows a good worker when she finds one. Why do you think she kept you on when war started?' She shook her head and returned to stirring the soup. 'Mind you, it would make sense if you took that blessed apron off before you brought in the coals.' She raised her eyes heavenward. 'Thank the Lord, I don't have to wear a uniform.' Looking down at her ample bosom and wide girth, she cackled. ''Cos with this figure o' mine it would have to be specially made. I cannot see her ladyship forkin' out for that, can you?'

Mrs Kirton was very particular about her staff and their station in the house. Things had changed with this war on, though. The government's Make Do and Mend scheme meant that Cook was allowed to dress in her own clothes, covered with a coarse apron. And these days the pair of them were the only staff employed in the Kirton household, which meant Sandra had her hands full fetching and carrying and doing all the housework.

Sandra had been brought up in Blakeley Orphanage with her younger brother under the hand of the forbidding Mistress Knowles, and she was used to hard work. The bleak days at the orphanage were tough and the mistress ingrained in all her charges the fact that they were worthless charity cases. Sandra had her pride and fought against the idea that she couldn't do anything right. But her childhood experience at the orphanage had left her with a crippling sense of self-doubt.

When war had broken out, all of the staff, apart from Mrs Goodwin and Sandra, had left the Kirtons' employ to do their bit for the war. Sandra had felt a certain relief when Mrs Kirton had announced, 'Mr Kirton suggests I accompany you when you register for war work and insist you stay and work for us. After all, my husband is a solicitor and we need at least one maid to help run his home smoothly.'

Mrs Kirton's plea to the authorities had worked and Sandra was granted permission to stay on as a housemaid for the Kirtons. The compromise was that she did a few hours' war work every week. So, on her afternoon off, Sandra helped out with the Womens' Voluntary Service. Her work involved standing behind a makeshift counter in the WVS clothes depot where she supplied clothes for bombed-out families or the needy. She loved seeing the kiddies' faces when she gave them a new (albeit secondhand) pair of shoes that fitted properly. With a growing need for clothes, a local paper recently appealed to readers for donations and photographed a child being fitted out with a coat. The plea had worked and clothes had been collected around the doors and the storage shelves and boxes filled.

Whenever she worked at the WVS depot, Sandra marvelled how ordinary folk could go places and do as they liked, voice their opinions even without fear of reprisal. Being brought up in an orphanage and then working in service had left its mark on Sandra. It felt like she'd been institutionalised all her life. And though she outwardly looked older, inside she was still the little lost girl from the orphanage trying to find her way in the world.

Deep down Sandra hankered for the courage to leave the household and her present life behind, because life was passing her by. The sense of *now or never* increasingly bothered her. Besides, it was her duty to do her bit for the war.

The sun was shining through the coloured glass hallway door as Sandra made her way to the front room. Entering the room, Sandra crossed the once sumptuous, now threadbare carpet, passing the gilt-framed pictures of ships that sailed the high seas, and went to the bay window. Who needed the distraction of pictures of the sea when the real thing was before your very eyes? Through the sticky paper, which had been applied to the windows to prevent them shattering if they were blown in by a bomb blast, she glimpsed the expanse of deep blue sea that met with a whitish horizon, while an eastern sun shone on glittering waters.

'Girl!' The voice made Sandra start. 'You're not employed to gawp at the view. There's work to be done. A fire to be laid. See to it now.'

Sandra turned and met the imperious stare of her employer, Clara Kirton, who sat on the chaise longue, the house accounts book in her hand. A slim woman, she wore a two-piece velvet costume with jacket to the hips and a blouse with a ruffled collar.

'Yes, Mrs Kirton. Just give us time to do the—'

'How many times, girl, do I have to tell you? The word is *me*. I don't want common language in my house.'

As she considered her employer's dissatisfied expression, Sandra wondered, as she often did, what Mrs Kirton had to complain about. After all, she had everything Sandra could only dream of. A husband, family and beautiful home.

As she moved towards the fireplace, Sandra's thoughts of family turned naturally to her younger brother, Alf, the only relative she possessed. Mam had died in childbirth and Dad, unable to cope because of illness, and with no relatives to speak of, had sent his two bairns to the orphanage. The mistress there decreed that boys and girls weren't allowed to mix, so Alf was sent to the boys' department. Both brother and sister had been desperately homesick and had pined for each other.

Her eyes blurry with the memory, Sandra became aware of Mrs Kirton's haughty expression and discontented stare. Fingers grasping the string of pearls around her neck, her employer seemed agitated.

'I want this house spotless for Duncan's homecoming this afternoon.'

At the mention of Duncan Kirton a knot of tension tightened in Sandra's stomach.

The Kirtons had two grown-up children. Miriam, who lived in Yorkshire with her husband and small child, rarely came to visit. Duncan, the eldest, had been conscripted in the forces at the beginning of the war. Sandra had been delighted and relieved to see him go.

'Stop dawdling, girl. You can start by cleaning the brasses.'

'Yes, Mrs Kirton.' As she placed the coal scuttle at the side of the mottled marble fireplace, Sandra thought to herself, *If you think I give a hoot about your precious son's homecoming, you can think again.*

'Will Mr Duncan be staying long?' Sandra held her breath. She didn't trust Duncan Kirton.

'What business is it of yours?' Mrs Kirton snapped the account book shut and stood up.

'I just thought—'

'You're here to work not think. Now set the fire and say no more. And make sure you riddle the ashes.'

There was no pleasing Mrs Kirton when she was in this kind of disgruntled mood. Sandra mentally shrugged and got on with her jobs. It was a rare occasion indeed for a fire to be lit in the front room and Sandra wondered what Mr Kirton would have to say. Probably nothing. Cecil Kirton didn't involve himself in family affairs. A partner at Carstairs and Kirton solicitors in the town, of an evening he usually sat in the small room off the master bedroom, a paraffin heater on for warmth, his office papers spread over an inlaid desk. The rest of the family used the dining room – a comfortable room with wall mouldings and painted frieze, a round mahogany table and chairs, and a pianola that Sandra secretly would have loved to have a go on – where a meagre fire burned in the grate.

Mrs Kirton made for the door. Her hand on the brass handle, she hesitated and then turned. 'My son will be staying the night. See to it that his bed is aired and a fire set in his room.'

She swept from the room, clashing the door behind her.

There was no need to guess who the favoured child was. Duncan Kirton was a year older than Sandra. When she'd begun working for the Kirton household, missing her brother terribly, Sandra had at first had a soft spot for the quiet teenage Duncan. But he had changed as he got older, became more assured – his manner sometimes bordering on arrogance. He blossomed into a handsome young man who liked to tease Sandra when his parents weren't around because they were apt to frown on him fraternising with the staff. Sandra took his naughtiness – when he would hide and suddenly pounce on her, laughing and grabbing her around the waist – all in good humour.

She wouldn't now, though, knowing what she did from Molly, the sacked scullery maid. She kept out of his way when he was home, wary of attracting his attention in any way.

Sandra missed her brother Alf terribly. She'd seen him only twice since she'd left the orphanage; he'd always been at school when she had her afternoon off and neither the mistress of Blakeley or Mrs Kirton would compromise. Alf was now in the RAF, stationed somewhere down south. They corresponded with the help of Mrs Goodwin, who'd been kind when Sandra, knowing that Mrs Goodwin liked to read romance novels, in desperation had swallowed her pride and told her, shamefaced, that she could neither read nor write.

'I skipped school when I was young,' Sandra had explained. 'Mam took in washing and I stayed at home to look after me little brother, Alf.' She didn't add that at the orphanage, too mortified to show her failing in front of the younger orphans, she'd sat at the back of the class where she could count on being ignored.

'What about yer dad?' Mrs Goodwin had looked at the girl with compassion.

'He was an invalid. He had a weak heart from when he was injured in the Great War.' In case Mrs Goodwin thought badly of him, Sandra quickly added, 'Sometimes Dad manged to cobble neighbours' worn-out shoes in the kitchen.'

'Hinny, never think you're dumb.' Mrs Goodwin's eyes gleamed. 'You're just unschooled. And you lack confidence. But tell me' – she gave Sandra a quizzical look – 'how do you manage here when you're sent for the rations and so forth?'

'I've taught myself to have a good memory.'

Mrs Goodwin was only too pleased to help. So, on Wednesdays, when Sandra needed Alf's letter to be read, or a reply to be written, Sandra called in at Mrs Goodwin's house in Wharton Street on her way back to the Kirtons' after she finished work at the WVS clothes depot. After a time, it was agreed that Sandra write and tell her brother to send his letters to Mrs Goodwin's address. Sandra thought it a good idea as she always felt uncomfortable when Mrs Kirton handed her the post, as if the woman was doing Sandra a favour.

Now, with the noise of the door slamming ringing in her ears, Sandra knelt in front of the fireplace and riddled the cinders with tongs for any lumps of coal. Like everything else, coal was in short supply and every bit had to be salvaged. She set the fire ready to be lit and, rising from her knees, wandered over to the bay where faded red velvet curtains with tie-backs framed the inset window. Through the sticky paper she looked out again at the spectacular view. The twin arms of the piers dominated the sea view, and a pilot's boat, a frothy white in its wake, bustled over to where a freighter waited beyond the harbour in deep swelling waters.

The front doorbell rang, and Sandra, startled, automatically smoothed her apron and made for the hallway.

She opened the door.

'Hi, Ma. I caught an earlier train as I… Oh, it's you.'

Duncan stood thickset and tall in his army greatcoat, cap covering his cropped black hair, and a duffle bag slung over a shoulder. His dark eyes observed her.

Sandra backed away and lowered her eyes.

'Duncan… darling.' Mrs Kirton pushed forward and, taking her son's arm, ushered him into the narrow hallway. 'Come in and let me take a look at you.'

Sandra stepped out of the way, overturning the umbrella stand.

'Stupid girl…' Mrs Kirton glowered.

Sandra took the word 'stupid' to heart. Then she thought of Cook's words: *If I was you, love, I'd take no notice. Don't let Mrs Kirton get you down.* Sandra hoped Cook's self-assurance would rub off on her one day. She pushed the hurtful word to the back of her mind.

As Duncan was led away, Sandra saw his lingering glance and recoiled.

Shaken, Sandra immersed herself in her work, setting and lighting the fires, polishing brass doorknobs, tidying and dusting rooms. Lastly, she stripped beds. When she'd finished, flushed and ready for a cup of tea, she realised now was not the time for a break as it was Monday – wash day.

Making her way into the yard, Sandra filled a washtub with buckets of steaming hot water from a boiler she'd lit earlier in the washhouse. Possing the clothes with a poss stick until her arms ached, she rinsed them in cold water in a tin bath, then hauled the mangle out of the washhouse into the yard.

The day was cold and a blustery wind rattled around the yard. Mrs Goodwin appeared wearing a wool hat, gloves and scarf. 'I'll give yi' a hand, hinny, I've time. I'll feed the clothes in the roller. You catch them and hang them on the line. Then we'll have a cup of tea.'

'Won't Mr Kirton be coming home soon for his dinner?'

'We'll make time.' Cook's voice was firm.

Later, when Sandra entered the kitchen where the heat from the range made the skin on her cheeks tingle, Mrs Goodwin handed her a cup of steaming tea.

'Why that man can't go to the Co-op café for his dinner like he used to,' she continued on from their earlier conversation, 'is beyond me. Though, if yi' ask me…' She eyed the door and lowered her voice. '…the Kirtons are skint.'

'They can't be… he's a professional man, a solicitor.' Sandra repeated the words Mrs Kirton was wont to say on occasions she wanted to impress.

'Aye, well my Tommy says with this war on folk like him are hard done by 'cos folk aren't buying and selling houses any more which brings in big money. According to Tommy, solicitors these days must make do with being executor of wills and disputes and such things. My Tommy likes to look these things up.' A glow of pride spread across her round, good-natured face.

Sandra thought that Tommy Goodwin was wasting his talents by working at Middle Docks.

Mrs Goodwin's expression was knowing. 'I reckon that's why her ladyship's keyed up… she's been doing the account book.'

She moved to the range and bent over to open the door. The meaty smell wafting from the oven intensified, and the hollow feeling in her belly reminded Sandra that she was starved.

Mrs Goodwin only worked mornings, which she professed was fine as she didn't want a full-time job. 'I've stayed at home to bring me three kids up. I first came to work to help with the finances, but now, with the bairns up and gone, I'm at a loose end. Mind you' – she folded her arms as if to verify a fact – 'I still maintain that running a home to a certain standard is a full-time job.'

Sandra was envious of Cook's life but she despaired of ever meeting a fellow herself. Sandra often experienced an overwhelming desire to turn her life around, but it was difficult to know where to start.

'The Kirtons should think themselves lucky,' Cook prattled as she prepared mashed potatoes in the pan, 'having friendly butchers givin' them joints of meat wrapped in brown paper at church. While mugs like me have to wait in never ending butchers' queues with God only knows what at the end.'

'Here, I'll do that.' Sandra, placing her empty cup on the table, took the fork out of Cook's hand.

As Sandra mashed, Mrs Goodwin picked up the meat knife. She eyed Sandra. 'Me and Tommy spoke about yi' last night. He thinks it high time you learnt to read and write. Because, lass, as he says, you're not going to get anywhere in this life without.'

Sandra, overwhelmed that the pair of them cared, was just about to say so when the front door slammed.

Mrs Goodwin's eyebrows raised. 'Mr Kirton's home and wantin' his dinner. I'll dish up in case you give them too much soup. 'Cos that'll be me starved as there's nowt to eat in the pantry at home.'

Sandra hurried from the kitchen into the passageway and almost collided with Mr Kirton as he made for the dining-room door. A lean man of average height, Mr Kirton looked dapper in his dark three-piece tailored suit and highly polished black shoes. Sandra thought there was no way Mr Kirton could be down on his luck when he could dress in such a way.

'Sorry, Mr Kirton.'

He handed over his bowler hat and umbrella which Sandra hung on the coat stand in the narrow hallway. She placed his briefcase on the floor and followed him into the dining room.

The table had been set beforehand, and Sandra had added an extra place for Duncan.

For the best part of the next hour, she fetched and carried the meal. She caught only snatches of the conversation around the table, which seemed to be mainly about Duncan.

'The fact is, Ma,' he said as Sandra put a cup of tea before him, 'word has it, I'm to be posted abroad soon.'

Sandra almost dropped the glass jug of milk she carried she was so relieved.

'That's why I'm here, to spend a night or two with the folks before I go.' He looked up and met Sandra's eyes. He gave an indolent leer.

Sandra saw her employer flush from the neck upwards. Nothing missed Mrs Kirton's sharp eyes.

CHAPTER THREE

That evening, when Sandra went into the front room to answer the call bell that had rung in the kitchen, the blackout curtains were drawn in the bay window and the twin standard lamps shed shadowy, muted light. The air in the room was a fug of tobacco smoke.

Mr Kirton and Duncan sat at opposite ends of the plush but faded settee, facing each other. Mr Kirton had changed into his blue silk smoking jacket, while Duncan, pipe clenched in his mouth, still wore his khaki uniform.

'Bring the brandy bottle and two glasses.' Mr Kirton gave her a fleeting glance.

Sandra, hurrying to the dining room to the drinks cabinet, discovered the room was empty. Mrs Kirton likely had gone to bed early. She'd complained of a troublesome headache at teatime. Making a mental note to check on her employer before she retired to bed, a sudden flash of rebellion zipped through her. Why should she? The small of her back hurt, her arm muscles ached, a stiff neck sent a shooting pain through her head, but could she go to bed? Not likely.

Fetching the half-empty brandy bottle and two crystal glasses from the almost depleted drinks cabinet, Sandra tramped back to the front room and opened the door.

'Young James is concerned about the firm's survival,' she heard Mr Kirton tell his son.

James Carstairs had taken over the solicitor's business after his father had died a few years before. Sandra had overheard

Mr Kirton and his wife discussing it over breakfast one day. James had made Mr Kirton senior partner when he'd been conscripted and Mr Kirton now ran the office alone with only a clerk to help him.

Mr Kirton continued, 'Thing is, James worries because the business has been hit hard by the war. The good fellow has written to advise me that he's arranged to send money from his pay to meet the rates and running costs. He says he wants a business to come home to.'

At times like this, Sandra thought, it never occurred to Mr Kirton she was listening in – it was as though she were invisible. She wished the same was true of his son. For Duncan Kirton's eyes followed her as she moved around the room.

'You will return to the firm?'

There was a pause as Sandra put the bottle and two glasses on the low occasional table between the men. She didn't look up as she didn't want to meet Duncan Kirton's dark eyes.

'Father, I've told you before I've no interest in the firm. The short time I worked there was enough for me to realise office work isn't for me. I don't know yet what I want to do after the war.'

'Being a solicitor is more than office work. You're throwing a fine career away.' There was irritation in Mr Kirton's tone. 'I didn't have the luxury of going to university. I was articled. And worked in the firm's office for seven years before passing the law society exam. While you could—'

'You've told me that many times before, Father. I know I could be a junior partner but that's not what I want for my life.'

There was an awkward silence.

Sandra was curious to hear more. She moved to the fire and, kneeling, she picked up a lump of coal from the scuttle with tongs and placed it on the embers. She heard a bottle opening and liquid being poured into a glass.

'How's Miriam doing?' Duncan artfully changed the subject.

'Very well, according to her last letter. She bemoans the fact she had to leave teaching when she was expecting young Arthur. She gets bored, apparently.'

'What nonsense. A woman's place is in the home.'

Sandra rose from her knees and moved towards the door. The likes of her mother hadn't had the luxury of staying at home. From what she knew of Miriam, Sandra was rooting for her. The lass had determination and made things happen. Perhaps it would pay if Sandra were more like Miriam Kirton.

As she closed the front room door behind her, Sandra felt ashamed. Why didn't she resolve to do something with her life? Because, the voice of conscience spoke in her head, she was a coward. Too scared to move out of the only security she'd known since Mam died, Sandra made no effort to change her life. Taking the flat iron from a kitchen cupboard, Sandra made a vow that things had to change.

Later, the ironing done, the sheets still damp and hanging from the ceiling pulley, Sandra placed the hot iron on the trivet on the kitchen table to cool.

Though it was past ten o'clock, she couldn't go to bed because Mr Kirton and his son were still blethering in the front room where, no doubt, they'd polished off the dregs of the bottle of brandy. Sandra had been up since six and was now flagging, as wash day was always gruelling. She was exhausted and couldn't help but feel resentful.

She was just about to collapse on a kitchen chair when she heard voices in the passageway. The menfolk were off to bed. Sandra listened at the door.

'Night, Father. I don't expect I'll make breakfast but I'll see you at lunch.'

'Good night, Duncan. Think on what I've said.'

Sandra heard footsteps on the stairs. She hurried along the passageway and into the front room, where she checked the fireguard had been put up so that no sparks could set the house alight. Picking up the empty brandy bottle and two glasses from the occasional table, she took them into the tiny scullery. She rinsed the glasses and left them on the wooden drainer. Giving a massive yawn that nearly caused her jaw to lock, Sandra checked the doors were locked then climbed the stairs in the dark – she couldn't risk waking Mrs Kirton and never hearing the end of it – hauling herself up by the polished banister rail. There were three flights up to the attic bedroom.

Wearily, she climbed the stairs to the next landing. Life was all chance, she thought, depending on who your parents were, their station in life. She thought of her mam, her lined and care-worn face, and with a shock Sandra realised that her mother would've only been a few years older than she was now when she died.

If Mam and Dad had lived in better circumstances, Dad might have stayed healthier and not had as many chesty colds. Their building had been damp and black mould grew on the walls of their flat.

'Aye, yer old man might be an invalid, but he's good at some things,' Sandra had heard a neighbour say as she patted Mam's fat belly. Too young to understand at the time, Sandra knew now what the neighbour was implying. Mam had been expecting her third bairn.

Sandra paused on the second landing. She thought of Mam skivvying away as a washerwoman to put food on the table. If her mam hadn't been so bone-weary maybe she and the baby she was carrying might have survived.

As she stood on the landing, fond memories of her parents flitting through her mind's eye, Sandra noticed the light shining from under Duncan's door. Her heart pounded in her chest.

She thought again of poor Molly, and how Duncan had been the cause of her getting the sack. Molly Hadden had arrived to work as scullery maid in the winter of '38. She was seventeen, with blonde curly hair and enormous blue, innocent eyes. She was pretty and a delight to work with as she was full of light-hearted banter. Though she was younger, Molly soon became Sandra's mate.

'These posh folks get on me nelly. They think because I'm a skivvy I'm ignorant but I've had good schooling. I can read and write and me best subject at school was history,' she told Sandra. 'If I had me way, I'd still be hairdressing.'

Molly was washing dinner dishes in the scullery sink and Sandra had brought another load through on a tray.

'Why did you leave?'

Molly turned, and heaved a heavy, regretful sigh. 'Long story but the gist is me da lost his job and me mam saw an ad for a scullery maid in the *Gazette*. So, in her wisdom' – she raised her eyes heavenward – 'she said I should apply as I was getting a pittance from the woman I worked for at the hairdresser's. Besides, it would be one less mouth to feed at home.' She made an affronted face. 'I think she wanted shot of us.'

Sandra knew this couldn't be true because Molly's family were close. She was the eldest of four and was always talking with affection about her parents and younger siblings and she went home at every opportunity she got.

'So here I am, a dogsbody. But one day I'm going to own me own hairdressing business.'

Sandra smiled. With her enthusiasm for life and her work ethic, the young scullery maid probably would achieve her ambition. And the desire to make something of her life had begun to take root in Sandra too.

Then, Sandra recalled, Molly had changed, had become pale and withdrawn, not like herself at all. At first, Sandra had wondered if she was missing home, but when she brought the subject up, Molly shook her head.

'It's nothing, I've just… got the blues.'

Which was ridiculous because Molly was such a cheerful soul.

Time wore on and when Molly didn't improve and Sandra could stand her reticence no longer, she confronted her one day as she was disposing of rubbish in the bin and Molly was hanging out the washing.

'Molly, I'm concerned. What's up with you?'

Molly's body tensed. 'Nothing,' was the gruff reply.

'You know I can keep secrets. Come on, spit it out. Have you quarrelled with your family?' Molly hardly visited with them any more; she didn't go anywhere.

The lass turned towards Sandra. She shook her head in a helpless fashion. 'You can't do nothing. Nobody can.'

No amount of coaxing would make her speak out.

'Leave me alone. There'll be trouble if I say anything.'

Sandra remembered that, to her dismay, Molly had burst into tears.

Sandra had been at a loss to know what to do. Being brought up in an orphanage had left its mark. She couldn't give Molly a hug as she found physical contact uncomfortable. If Molly wouldn't share her problem then how could she help solve it?

Sandra found out what Molly's predicament was late one night in June when she couldn't get to sleep in her hot, stuffy attic bedroom. Her tired and anxious mind was too active. Had she locked the front door? Her imagination took over. What if a burglar got in the house and stole all the silver? The thought nagged until Sandra could stand it no longer. She would have to check.

She flung back the sheet and picked up the saucer that stood on a chair beside the bed. She lit the candle with a match.

Pattering down the three flights of stairs barefoot, she moved along the passageway and, opening the inner hall door, saw the bolt on the front door was firmly locked.

Sandra knew it but she felt better for having checked. On the return journey up the stairs, she looked over the banister rail to the giddy view below. She kept to the side as the stair boards in the middle squeaked.

It was near the top landing where the carpet stopped that Sandra thought she heard a noise. It came from the attic landing. She looked up. A door squeaked open and the silhouette of a figure stood at Molly's bedroom door. Sandra held up the saucer. By the light of the candle's flame she recognised the frame of Duncan Kirton in the doorway. He looked down at her, black eyes glittering in the shadowy light.

Sandra froze.

He gave an indifferent shrug and moved into the bedroom.

The saucer in her hand shaking, Sandra ran back to her room.

The next morning, when the two of them were in the scullery, Sandra had admitted what she'd seen the night before. Molly broke down. 'I can't take it any more.'

Molly told Sandra of her distressing situation. 'It was last time Mr Duncan came home from university. He started flirting with us. He told us to call him Duncan and that he thought I was beautiful. Then he kissed us in the scullery and daft fool that I am I thought he was really interested in us. Me… a scullery maid… what was I thinking of?' Molly's distraught eyes searched Sandra's. 'Then one night I woke up to the bedroom door handle rattling as if someone was coming in.'

Sandra shivered. 'What did you do?'

'I was scared and yelled to ask who it was. Duncan's voice hissed through the doorway for me to shut up because I'd wake the household. Then I heard footsteps retreat down the stairway.' Molly wiped her nose with the back of her hand. 'He went back to university next day but not before he whispered that I'd better not play so hard to get next time.'

'Oh, Molly, how dreadful. No wonder you've been a nervous wreck all this time.' The urge to fling her arms around the young maid's thin shoulders was strong.

'I knew what Duncan was after and I couldn't sleep with the fear because I knew he wouldn't give up until he got what he wanted. I didn't dare go home because me mam would know something was up. Then I know I'd blab and say what's wrong. If me da finds out there'll be ructions.'

'You must have been sick with worry when you heard he was coming home.'

'I was. Then, when nothing happened, I started to breathe easy until—'

'Last night,' Sandra finished for her.

'I woke up and Duncan was on me bed,' Molly continued. 'I tried to yell but he covered me mouth. I bit his hand hard as I could. He got off me then and kneeled on the bed. Then I remembered what me da told us and drew me knee up and kicked Duncan hard in the groin.' She gave a grin. 'It did the trick. He cried out in pain and called me a bitch. Blood dripping from where I clawed him, he hobbled bent over from me room. But he shouted that if I said anything it would cost us me job.'

She visibly shuddered. 'I swear he'll be back to get his revenge… and next time he'll make sure he has… his way.'

They had both looked at each other. Duncan Kirton always got his own way.

Sandra was naïve about sex matters as she'd had no mam to tell her. The subject was never broached at the orphanage. In her mind it was something sacred you kept for the love of your life – not someone like Duncan Kirton.

Sandra didn't know what to say to help Molly's suffering. 'You could leave,' was the only thing she could think of. 'You've got a home and family that care.'

Molly's eyes widened in horror. 'I can't lose me job. Mam can't manage as it is. She needs the bit of money I earn to help with the bairns. And me da never gets permanent work any more at the yards.'

Sandra told Molly, 'This would never happen if us staff were given keys to lock our rooms.'

'Mrs Kirton says it's for our own safety in case there's a fire. But if you ask me it's 'cos she checks to see if we've pinched anything. I swear sometimes someone's been in me room rifling.' She squared her shoulders determinedly. 'But you've given us cause for thought. I'm going to ask Mrs Kirton if I can have a key to lock me bedroom door.'

For the rest of that day Molly's predicament whirled in Sandra's mind. As she washed the grimy walls, covered in soot – which always found its way in through the pantry grille – from the chimneys, Sandra wondered what would happen. Surely Mrs Kirton would ask Molly the reason why she wanted a key? She would be outraged at Molly's impertinence. Or maybe, by some miracle, Mrs Kirton would realise the staff needed privacy, that they weren't merely servants at her beck and call.

When nightfall came and still she hadn't clapped eyes on Molly, Sandra feared the worst. The next morning Mrs Kirton announced in the kitchen that Sandra was taking over the role of scullery maid as well as her own.

No explanation for Molly's disappearance was ever given.

When Duncan finished university and began living at home, working for Carstairs and Kirton for a while, Sandra was both wary and aloof with him. She could never forgive him for what had happened to poor Molly. He must have guessed she knew something because he kept giving her furtive looks. She remained steadfastly aloof.

At the time he had a girlfriend to keep him out of mischief. A willowy lass who had all her buttons on and spoke with a refined English accent. But no lass deserved Duncan Kirton.

Sandra had a gnawing feeling of guilt that she should have done more to help the young scullery maid and that by not speaking out she'd been a coward. Sandra vowed it had taught her a lesson. She would never be so reticent in such a situation again, even if it meant losing her job. She needed to be able to look at herself in the mirror.

She often thought of Molly and hoped the lass had found another job, and her family hadn't suffered.

One morning, a letter arrived for Sandra. Mrs Kirton, with a look that said how dare the housemaid have the audacity to receive letters, handed the envelope to Sandra as she served breakfast. Sandra was mystified. She never received post apart from Alf's letters from his base, and those were delivered to Mrs Goodwin's house. She put the letter in her apron pocket for Mrs Goodwin to read out later.

When the dishes were washed and they sat at the table having a cup of tea, Mrs Goodwin, reading spectacles perched on the end of her nose, held the letter at arm's length.

'It's from Molly. A nice lassie. I often wondered why she left, she seemed so settled here.' Cook cleared her throat and began.

> *Just to let you know you haven't to worry about me. I'm sorry it's taken me so long to write. At first, all I wanted was to put Duncan and the Curtain*
>
> – Mrs Goodwin looked up and guffawed, 'Bless the lass, she's spelt it as in "curtain" at the window.' – *household out of my mind. Then life just rolled on as it does. But I did think of you often and wondered how you're getting on. Then it occurred to me recently I was being daft, and I should just write and maybe you'd find someone to read my letter to you. So, here's hoping.*
>
> *That day when I told Mrs Curtain that I wanted a key for the bedroom. She asked what I wanted to hide.*

Me and my big mouth. I blurted that it wasn't that but I was nervous somebody might get into me room.

I knew I was in trouble. She asked who did I think would want to enter a scullery maid's bedroom? I think she knew because she went purple in the face. I just mumbled that somebody might.

Before I could say 'Bob's your uncle' I was sacked and shown the door.

Mam was great when I told her everything. She said we'd manage but I hadn't to tell anybody, especially Da, because if he found out he'd give Duncan Curtain the hammering he deserved. The good news is I'm now working in a clothes factory making uniforms and I've never been richer or happier. So, it's an ill will that does nobody any good. As I say you don't have to worry about me.

Hope Duncan Curtain rots in hell!!!

Take care of yourself,

Your good friend

Molly xx

Mrs Goodwin removed her spectacles and pulled a scathing face. 'What's this about Duncan Kirton?'

Swearing Cook to secrecy, Sandra told her the truth of the matter.

Mrs Goodwin had pursed her lips. 'I knew that lad was a bad 'un. He's got shifty eyes. If he was a son o' mine I'd knock him senseless. Poor lass, getting the heave-ho through no fault of her own. Shame on Mrs Kirton.' She folded the letter and handed it over to Sandra. A look of concern in her eyes, she said, 'You watch yerself, lass. Give us a shout if needs be.'

Her throat tight, Sandra gave a grateful nod. She'd never had anyone to rely on before. Only Alf, but as his big sister her job was to keep an eye out for him.

*

Now, here Sandra was standing on the landing, light creeping from beneath Duncan Kirton's door. He was home and pacing around inside his bedroom.

She could hear him.

Since the war started, he'd been away most of the time. In those early days he'd seen action in Dunkirk where he was rescued from the beaches by one of the brave men who crossed the channel in little boats. On his return home he was on Home Service stationed somewhere in Kent.

This year he'd only been home on leave once and that was only for a night. Sandra had managed to keep out of his way.

This time, though, Duncan was acting differently. She was aware of his dark eyes watching her too intently. He appeared troubled in some way. Sandra shivered. Maybe these were only hysterical imaginings. But this was Duncan Kirton, she reminded herself. Sandra didn't trust him.

As she gazed at his door she saw the door handle turn. Fear clutching her throat, by the light of the flickering candle Sandra took the stairs two at a time to the attic bedroom. She closed the door and stood with her back leaning against it. She blew out the candle and, clicking on the light, saw the familiar scene. The slim bed, rickety chest of drawers, wooden chair. The sloped ceiling, sash window that despite being covered with a thick blackout curtain let in the cold night air. At the foot of the bed, her few clothes hung on string that crossed the room.

Her room, and security for the past ten years.

Not any more.

Sandra lifted the bedside rug from the floor and placed it behind the door. Then, taking hold of the wooden chair, she wedged its arched back beneath the door handle – something she'd seen in a film at the cinema. With a trembling hand, she switched off the light and climbed back into bed.

A strong wind outside buffeted the window and Sandra, staring into the darkness, burrowed down in the chilly bed. Though tired, she couldn't sleep and it felt like an eternity before her eyes started to droop. Then a noise alerted her and she was wide awake.

The bedroom door handle was rattling. Sandra sat bolt upright.

Someone was trying to get in and Sandra knew who it was. Pulling the blanket up to her neck, she lay shaking in the bed.

Please, God, don't let Duncan get in.

The door handle rattled again.

Please keep me safe.

The rattling went on longer this time, then there was a sound as if someone had heaved against the door.

I'll do anything.

The noise stopped. The silence in the room was deafening.

After a time, the enormity of what might have happened overwhelmed Sandra. She sagged with relief. She wasn't safe here any more, but unlike Molly, who had family, Sandra had nowhere to go. A tidal wave of nervous anxiety washed over her and she was frozen with terror.

Afterwards she'd swear she never slept but she must have dozed, for the noise from outside brought Sandra back to sleepy consciousness.

The sound of the air raid siren.

CHAPTER FOUR

Galvanised into action, Sandra leapt from the bed and, switching on the light, shrugged on her coat and slipped her cold feet into her shoes.

She heard aeroplanes, like a swarm of bees, droning in the distance. They sounded as if they were coming closer. As Jerry planes roared overhead, the noise of guns blazed from the ground. There was a descending scream as a bomb plummeted to the earth. A moment's silence when the house appeared to shudder, then a terrific explosion that cast powdery dust in the air. Sandra, momentarily frozen to the spot, could taste it.

Please, God, don't let this house be hit.

She removed the chair and opened the door. She clicked the switch on the wall and mercifully harsh yellow light flooded the now dust-ridden staircase. Sandra's intention was to make her way down to the garage shelter in the back yard that had two layers of concrete to reinforce it and had been passed by a council man's inspection.

As the roar of the first wave of bombers faded into the distance, Sandra prayed that would be the end of the raid – though she doubted it.

Her legs trembling, she reached the second landing and was just about to descend the next flight of stairs when someone grabbed her by the arm from behind. Sandra let out a scream. She pulled away with such force that it took all her agility to stop herself toppling down the stairs. Strong hands grabbed her around the waist and hauled her backwards. The stench of alcohol wafted up Sandra's nostrils.

Duncan Kirton.

He dragged her, kicking and screaming, through his bedroom doorway, a wave of raiders thundering overhead drowning out the noise. He heaved her onto the double bed and, straddling her, pinned her down with the force of his body. He ripped her coat open.

Sandra, sitting up, pummelled him with her hands. With a strength she never imagined Duncan could possess he took her wrists in his hands and with the mass of his body pinned her down. Suffocated, she felt helpless. Duncan let go with one hand and, undoing the buttons of his trousers, jerked them down. As planes shrieked overhead and bombs whistled and exploded on the ground, Sandra willed the house to be bombed; she'd rather die than face this.

A picture of Molly came to mind and Sandra's thoughts blazed: *I will not allow this to happen.* With all her might she writhed, kicked and clawed at Duncan. With brute strength, he took her hands in his and restrained them above her head. His face bent close to hers so that she could smell the stench of his breath, and she saw his intentions in his dark, resolute eyes.

Realising her fate, Sandra's mind raged with fury. Molly had kicked him in the groin but Sandra was trapped and helpless to do anything. She wouldn't let Duncan have the satisfaction of putting her through torment. If she could distance her mind then he wouldn't win. Sandra focussed on something she held dear, something that no one, not even Duncan Kirton could interfere with. Her memories. As Duncan wrenched up her nightdress, she willed her mind to detach from the present situation and be transported to a happier place, to her beloved family when she was young and still lived at home. *Dad was cobbling shoes and Mam was handing him a cup of...*

At that moment the light switched on, blinding Sandra.

A figure stood in the doorway. A figure that made Duncan, when he looked up, falter, then release her hands. He slid from the bed.

Sandra turned her head. She looked into the horrified, grey eyes of Mrs Kirton. Even in her distress, Sandra couldn't get over the sight of her. Gone was the immaculate lady of the house. Mrs Kirton wore a full-length dressing gown and her hair, done up in iron curlers, was covered with a hair net, her feet ensconced in fur-lined slippers. Her lips pursed, Mrs Kirton stretched out an arm and pointed first to Duncan and then to the door.

Duncan pulled up his trousers and, fastening the buttons, walked to the door and disappeared.

Somewhere in Sandra's dream-like mind she registered that planes were thundering over the rooftops, as bombs fell and guns blazed. Then came a shrieking noise. Automatically she held her breath. For a moment the room went deathly still, then the walls trembled – and everything went black.

The next morning Sandra woke up on the chaise longue in the sitting room with Mrs Goodwin kneeling on the floor beside her. Sandra's head hurt like blazes.

'Here, lass, get this down you.' Mrs Goodwin passed her a cup of tea she held in her hand. 'They say you were out for the count for a while. If I'd been there, I'd have given yi' smellin' salts. But the main thing is, lass, you survived all the masonry falling down on yi'. Though you'll be sore for a while.' She nodded to the bruising on Sandra's hands and arms below the sleeves of her nightdress. 'If you ask me the Kirtons want their heads examining. Anyone with common sense would've taken you to the infirmary to be checked out.'

Sandra took a sip of the sickly tea. 'What happened? Did I pass out?' She could only remember bits of the night: Duncan on top of her, Mrs Kirton in the doorway. Why was she there? Had she heard Sandra scream?

She stared into the space in front as the scene played in her mind. Shadows on the wall, the stink of alcohol. The feel of *it* on her skin, harder, bigger than Sandra had ever imagined.

She began to shake and Mrs Goodwin took the cup of tea out of her hand. 'What is it, lass?'

Sandra swam back to reality. Mrs Goodwin's kind face looked at her in concern and the sight made Sandra well up. Too over-wrought to speak, she shook her head.

'It's that lad, isn't? I wondered what you were doin' in his room…'

Sandra tensed. She felt guilty somehow, as if what had happened was her fault.

'The bugger tried it on, didn't he?'

'Yes.' The word tore from Sandra. 'But he didn't succeed.'

She told Cook how Mrs Kirton had come into the room. 'I've been thinking, maybe she was checking to see if Duncan had made it safely out of the house.'

Mrs Goodwin shook her head in disgust. 'Thank God she did. I hope that bugger has been given his marching orders. But I doubt it. Though there was quite a rumpus this morning.'

'What was the rumpus about?'

Mrs Goodwin paused while she collected her thoughts. 'Her ladyship and Duncan were upstairs in her bedroom. I happened to be getting some laundry from the cupboard.' She pulled a mock innocent face. 'Mrs Kirton was going hammer and tongs at Duncan. Then he rushed out of the room – nearly knocking me over, mind you – and hurtled down the stairs and out of the house. Thing is, he didn't take his duffel bag or his coat.' She sniffed. 'Mark my words, he'll be back and all will be forgiven.'

'D'you think so?' Sandra heard the unease in her voice.

Mrs Goodwin smiled, reassuringly. 'Rest assured, hinny, his mam will keep a close eye on him. She won't want a hint of disgrace, especially about her precious son and a housemaid.'

Sandra fervently hoped Cook was right. Sandra didn't feel strong enough yet to make any big decisions about what she should do about her plight.

Mrs Goodwin went on, 'Mr Kirton told me about the blast while I made his breakfast. He's not a bad sort when his wife isn't about.' She made a knowing face. 'Typical! He diddled off to work as usual. I think he knew there was going to be trouble. He turns a blind eye if you ask me. Anyway, a bomb hit the house next door and it seems the after-blast caused the roof and part of Duncan's bedroom ceiling to collapse. You're a lucky lass, escaping with such little injury. You could have been killed.'

Sandra remembered wishing that would happen as Duncan held her down. She shivered.

'Did Mr Kirton carry me downstairs?' The man was puny and thin.

'No, hinny, the warden turned up and a fireman.' She bristled. 'I hope Duncan Kirton doesn't show up while I'm here. It'll be hard to keep me mouth shut. The rotter.'

Mrs Goodwin handed her the cup back and Sandra took a sip of the sweet tea. 'Is there much other damage upstairs?'

'The top landing is a mess with rubble. Your room too. And apart from the two bedroom windows at the front of the house being blown out, that's the lot.'

Mrs Goodwin moved towards Sandra and examined her face. 'That's a right shiner on your brow and your eye's gone black and blue. You've had a shock, lass. I'd take some time off if I was you.'

'It's not up to you, Cook.' Mrs Kirton's shrill voice spoke from the doorway. Dressed in a velvet pleated skirt and pristine white blouse, her hair coiffed to perfection, she showed no sign of being affected by the night's drama. She pinned Mrs Goodwin with a stare. 'Cook, I'll take breakfast in the dining room. Perhaps a slice of bread and jam.' Her eyes wandered to Sandra. 'You, girl, can get dressed in your uniform.'

Mrs Goodwin struggled to stand up.

Sandra, staring at Mrs Kirton, saw only haughty coldness in her glare. No apologies for the suffering caused by her son, or concern over how she was faring after part of the ceiling had fallen on top of her.

Sandra stood up from the chaise longue, her head held high. 'I'm not ready to continue work after… what happened to me. I feel shaky and fragile.'

'I beg your pardon.' Mrs Kirton appeared to double take. 'You'll do as you're told, girl. Get changed at once.'

'Maybe, Mrs Kirton, it would be best—' Mrs Goodwin began but Mrs Kirton raised a hand and stopped her.

'Enough, Cook! I know what's best in this household.'

All the years of being submissive in the orphanage under the rule of the mistress, and now another tyrant lording it over her, Sandra saw red. It was high time she stood up for herself.

'I know what's best for me, Mrs Kirton. I need to rest for a while.'

Mrs Kirton, infuriated, spluttered, 'I… think, young lady… you should pack your bag. You are no longer employed in this house.'

There was a stunned silence. But Sandra couldn't back down now.

Cook said, 'But Mrs Kirton, she has nowhere—'

'The girl should have thought of that before she answered in such an impudent manner.' She turned to Sandra. 'After you've packed meet me in the hallway. I want you out of the house at once.' She swung on her heel and was gone.

'Ahh! lass, I feel bad about this, it's my fault for encouraging yi' to take time off.'

'No. I was standing up for what was right. I was nearly raped by her son. Then I was nearly killed. The woman has no morals or compassion.'

Mrs Goodwin shook her head despairingly. 'In my opinion this is what her ladyship has wanted all along. It suits her to have you out of the house, out of the sights of her precious son. What's the bet the next housemaid is as old at the hills?'

Despite the graveness of the situation the pair of them laughed.

Then, as reality hit, Sandra's newfound bravado faltered. She'd been sacked. From now on she'd have to make her own way in the world.

Sandra, carrying a small brown suitcase packed with few belongings and a box that held a gas mask, had her winter coat draped over a forearm. Most of her clothes on the line weren't worth salvaging but she found a skirt and blouse that would do until she manged to wash them through. She closed her mind to when that might be.

It was true, she wasn't as fit and well as she imagined. As she descended the stairs, legs wobbly, head aching, left eye still in pain, all she wanted was to lie someplace in the peace and quiet.

But Sandra wouldn't beg, she decided. She made her way to the hallway, and, looking at Mrs Kirton's unyielding face, Sandra knew with certainty that even if she had wanted to it wouldn't have done her any good.

Mrs Kirton held out a brown envelope that rattled with money. 'Your employment here is terminated.' She drew herself up but didn't meet Sandra's gaze. 'My son tells me you led him on—'

'Pardon me? Duncan told you that?'

'It would pay you to remember, girl' – there was real menace in Mrs Kirton's tone – 'Mr Kirton is a solicitor. If you tittle-tattle about any of the goings on in this house it will be you who will be disgraced. If you understand my meaning.' She moved towards the front door and opened it. 'Shame on you, girl.'

'I never—'

'You will leave the property now.'

Again, Sandra felt a cold shiver of fear. She stepped over the threshold, and the door slammed behind her.

What had she done?

She had nothing; no place to live and no one to turn to. Numb with shock, she stood at the top of the five stone steps. All she could think was that the front steps were scruffy and needed scrubbing and she'd left the sheets on the kitchen pulley.

But none of this was her problem any more.

From this high vista, Sandra looked out over the stretch of lacklustre grass to the road and the sea beyond, where a fishing boat made its way over harbour waters. It was raining, she realised. A large dog barked as it bounded over the sodden grass, seagulls squawked as they soared and swooped like miniature aeroplanes overhead. She must move on, but where to?

She moved down the steps, turned right for no other reason than the pavement ran downhill. There was an acrid smell in the air. She looked around. Houses were without windowpanes and piles of broken glass and debris were heaped on the ground. A man wearing a cap and boiler suit stared out of a broken window. He smiled and gave her a thumbs up as if to say he was glad to be alive. That was the British way, Sandra thought. The enemy can take our homes but not our pride.

She must buck up. All she'd lost was her job – and the roof over her head, the voice of insecurity told her. She was a good-for-nothing maid without a reference. Who, in their right mind, would employ her?

Sandra squared her shoulders. She remembered Mrs Goodwin's words that she wasn't dumb. She couldn't afford self-pity, she told herself sternly, she must find a job and somewhere to sleep tonight.

But despair, as ever, won, and Sandra's spirits plummeted. An impossible task, the doubting voice in her head told her.

Sandra continued to the end of the block and, looking along the street where broken chimney pots looked ready to topple, she saw the top floor of a house which was a burnt-out shell. People were milling around looking shocked as they tried to take in the damage. A mobile canteen was parked at the far end of the street where WVS women dressed in grey-green uniforms handed out tea to the workers.

A movement at the lane end a few yards away caught Sandra's eye and she was surprised to see Mrs Goodwin's large frame, apron flapping in the wind, hurrying towards her.

'Eee, lass, I'm glad I've caught yi'. That bitch had no right to do what she did. I don't know' – she looked scandalised – 'treating folk like that. It's a disgrace.' She pressed a large metal door key in Sandra's hand. 'Here, take this, lass. It's for me front door. Make yourself at home till I get back from work and then we'll figure something out.' She gave a warm smile that made her plump cheeks rise and creased her eyes into a slant.

Without another word she turned and hurried back along the street.

Making her way to Mrs Goodwin's two-bedroomed flat, Sandra walked past the town hall along the busy high street towards the Westoe bridges. She noticed some of the of the shops had sandbags stacked against the windows. Thinking of bombs led her to remember the raiders last night, but not wanting to dwell on the incidents that followed, Sandra's train of thought diverted to Alf flying in bombers.

Automatically, she fingered the necklace she always wore beneath her clothes, lingering on its round stainless-steel identity disc with her name inscribed on it. Dad had given one to each of his children when he left them at the orphanage.

With sunken cheeks and grey face, he'd told them, 'I'm sorry, kiddies, for what I'm doing. I hope when you're older you'll understand and forgive us. Be good and make your mother proud.'

Months later, the mistress of the orphanage had sent for Sandra and Alf. Sandra wondered what they'd done.

'I've been informed,' she told the two children, 'that your father's heart gave out and he's passed away.'

'Passed where to?' Little Alf wanted to know.

'Died.' The mistress's tone was without a shred of sympathy. 'Which means the two of you are orphans. You'll stay here with the master and I until you're fifteen.'

Alf's face crumpled but he didn't cry.

Outside the mistress's office, when they had a few minutes alone together, Sandra pulled out the identity disc from beneath Alf's jumper. 'Remember Daddy giving you this?'

Alf nodded.

'Whenever you're sad or lonely, hold on to it and think of him and Mam. It'll make you feel better. Always remember they love you, Alf.'

Face serious, he nodded. 'I promise I will.'

Now, as she handled her own identity disc, Sandra thought how long it had been since she'd last seen her brother.

If it hadn't been for the help of Mrs Goodwin they might have lost touch completely. Alf, by the age of ten, was proficient at both reading and writing and his big sister was proud of him for achieving what she had never managed.

When it came to Alf's turn to leave the orphanage, Sandra had been greatly relieved when he wrote to say that the mistress had found him a job at a local factory that made parts for aeroplanes. He lived in a room in a nearby lodging house. At the time, Alf had told Sandra not to worry as the owner of the lodging house, a Mrs Ivy Robinson, though outspoken, was the kindest person. Her husband, though, was a cad, as all he did was spend his time in the bay window, a jug of ale at his side. They had a daughter, May, who was employed in the factory canteen where Alf worked and she always gave him an extra-big portion of dinner.

The last time Alf and Sandra had been able to see each other was when Alf's shift work coordinated with her afternoon off. He took her to Colmans' New Central Café on the seafront. They'd sat in one of the long rows of tables covered with pristine white tablecloths while a palm court orchestra played in the background.

Alf had insisted he treat his big sister to fish and chips with his earnings.

When the waitress, wearing a black uniform, apron and frilly cap, brought them a pot of tea and china cups, Sandra whispered, 'I'm not used to being waited on. I feel like a lady.'

'Sis, you'll always be a lady to me.'

Sandra proudly regarded her brother who, seventeen by then, was tall and, with his sandy-coloured hair and twinkling green eyes, rather handsome.

Alf announced, his young face aglow with excitement and happiness, 'You'll never guess what? I've been accepted in the ADCC.'

'The what?'

'The Air Defence Cadet Corps. I'm to be trained so that I'll be ready when the time comes to join the Royal Air Force. That's what I want to do, sis.'

Sandra was devastated but didn't show it for Alf's sake. She'd known the time would come when he'd have to join the war effort but she still hadn't been prepared for it.

Alf's attitude changed and he couldn't meet her eyes. 'The downside is lots of the instructors have been called up into regular service, and buildings taken over for government war work. Sis, I might be sent to work on a RAF station.'

He'd looked awkward, as though he longed for her approval. 'When?'

'I don't know. Maybe I'll do basic training first. I'll have to wait and see.'

Sandra had struggled with her emotions but she didn't want to let Alf down. 'That's wonderful, Alf. I'm so proud of you. So would Mam and Dad be.'

Alf beamed. 'I'll miss you, Sandra.' She felt quite emotional as he said her name. 'Try and get letters written to me as often as you can. I'll have this to remember you by.' He held up the stainless-steel identity disc Dad had given him.

'Big softie,' Sandra said, her throat tightening, but she refused to cry.

Sandra realised now it had been two years since that day. Alf had left when he was eighteen and joined the RAF as a Wireless Operator Air Gunner. He'd done his initial training on the west coast (Alf couldn't say where because of censorship) and sent a black-and-white photograph of him standing proudly in his RAF uniform. After he became a qualified wireless operator, he started a course at gunners' school. Finally, he was posted to his squadron somewhere down south where he began operational duties.

In his recent letters Alf talked of his squadron and life at the base. He didn't fool his sister because she knew missions were dangerous but he also didn't want to worry her.

Sandra was thrilled with all Alf had achieved and prayed at night for him to be kept safe.

Her footsteps took her past the butcher's where a notice was displayed in the window. She stopped and stared, wishing as always that she could read.

'Hinny, you could do worse these days than working in a butcher's,' a diminutive woman with a wrinkled face and a turban-style headscarf told her.

Sandra chose her words carefully. 'That's what the notice says.'

'Aye, it does. Think how over the moon your mother would be if she didn't have to stand in never-ending queues. 'Cos her daughter would get first dibs at any meat.'

Chuckling to herself, the woman moved away.

A bubble of excitement rose within Sandra. She didn't have to be a housemaid any more. But her optimism deflated as quickly as it had arrived. How could she be a shop assistant when she couldn't read? What if someone handed her a note or she had to read instructions? She was useless. All at once the worry of independence, of not managing, terrified Sandra.

Surely there was something she could do with her life?

CHAPTER FIVE

Mrs Goodwin's two-bedroomed upstairs flat had a bay window and, at the entrance, a small forecourt garden bounded by a low stone wall. The wall's handsome black railings had been carted off earlier in the war to be melted down to make weapons.

Sandra turned the key in the lock and, pushing open the door, stepped inside the tiny lobby. Picking up the mail, Sandra opened the lobby door and climbed the stairs. Houses had their own smell and Sandra always loved the aroma that emanated from Mrs Goodwin's home when she came to visit: furniture polish mingled with a cleaning agent, and a fruity smell Sandra associated with the cook's famous fruit scones permeated the air.

Although it felt odd being there without Mrs Goodwin, Sandra relaxed once inside the kitchen-cum-living room with its saggy but comfortable couch, fireside chair and polished dropleaf table. The room was homely and the only concession to the war was the bay window, elegantly draped with tied-back blackout curtains and the obligatory sticky tape attached to the panes.

With one of Mrs Goodwin's favourite sayings playing in her head – *Home is where the heart is* – Sandra put the suitcase on the floor with the mail on top, the required gas mask in its box alongside.

She stepped into the minuscule scullery and, turning on the cold-water tap – the only tap – she filled the kettle. She found the box of matches on the drainer and lit the gas ring, putting the kettle on to boil.

Back in the kitchen she removed her coat and hung it on a peg and then sat on the lumpy couch. Accustomed to the flat being filled with the sound of the Goodwins' rowdy chatter, Sandra found the eerie silence uncanny. Mrs Goodwin had two children. Herbert, the eldest, whose wife was pregnant with their first bairn, lived two streets away. The youngest, Kenneth, had been conscripted last year to the horror of his mam.

'He's posted abroad somewhere in North Africa,' Mrs Goodwin had whispered with big agonised eyes. Furtively, Cook had looked around the kitchen as if she expected to see a spy listening in. 'Tommy and me looked Africa up on the map. Fancy Kenneth going all that way when the farthest he's ever been is Whitley Bay on a Sunday School trip.'

Sandra's heart went out to Mrs Goodwin, who she knew lived in fear of the telegram laddie in the street.

She'd once told her, 'It's murder when yi' see the lad turn the corner on his bike and cycle up the street. Womenfolk, at their front doors, stop gossiping and watch as he rides by.' She crossed her arms tightly over her chest. 'Everybody holds their breath. But satisfaction is short-lived if the lad stops at some poor soul's door.' Cook shook her head in sorrow. 'The howl as he hands over the telegram is unbearable. Out of respect everybody goes inside.' Expression resolute, she continued, 'But folk rally round if needs be. For folk are good at heart and I've seen it demonstrated many a time in this war.'

Mrs Goodwin, with her kind and maternal heart, no doubt would be the first in the queue to help.

Thoughts of her own mother came to Sandra's mind. To remember hurt, but memories were all Sandra had and she could never forget Mam. The smile that lit up her weary face, the hugs she gave when Sandra felt Mam's sticky-out bones through her clothes. Mam never sat down, hauling pails of steaming water from the boiler into the tub, pegging out other folk's washing.

She gave so much time to everybody else she never had any left for herself. There'd been a time when Sandra loathed the baby who'd killed Mam, then she'd felt bad because the poor mite didn't get to have a life.

What had Sandra done with her life? Dependant on security, she'd settled for serving other people – watching them live out their lives. That was not an option any more. Sandra had to carve a life out for herself now and the knowledge scared her.

Her head aching with all these disturbing thoughts, Sandra felt woozy. She realised what the matter with her was; she was still suffering from last night's events. But she couldn't escape the fact she had some serious thinking to do, and choices to make.

Being brought up in an orphanage – where decisions were made for you and you didn't have to fend for yourself – didn't help. Mam's example came to mind. She'd taken in washing so the family would survive. She kept her bairns in clothes (albeit secondhand) and sometimes they didn't have shoes but Mam always made sure there was food on the table. Mam never gave up. But the pitiful, unsure voice in Sandra's head, ready with excuses, said, *Mam wasn't institutionalised.*

Sandra peered into the scullery where steam from the boiling kettle billowed in the confines of the room. She'd known the time was coming to have the courage to take control of her life, to find employment, a home of her own – to start living. Sandra shivered. Who knew, the next time a bomb dropped, Sandra mightn't be so lucky.

Sandra found the makings for a cup of Ovaltine in the scullery. Coming back into the kitchen, she noticed the two letters perched on the top of the suitcase. She bent to pick them up and, seeing the handwriting on the top one, her heart raced. She recognised Alf's loopy scrawl. Placing her cup on the floor, she tore the envelope open. As she removed the sheet of paper, a photograph dropped out.

She picked it up, and looked at Alf, handsome in his uniform. She thought, *My little brother has become a man.* She stared at the black-and-white photograph, taking in every detail of his features. His thin face, awkward smile that showed the gap between his upper two front teeth, the wistful gleam in his eye that had been there since he was a little boy. Sandra could identify with that loneliness; the feeling of wanting someone you could call your own.

We have each other, she thought. An inescapable urge made her tell the photograph, *I will forge a life of my own and make you proud.*

The front door banged, giving Sandra a jolt, and she heard footsteps on the stairs. Mrs Goodwin, cheeks plump and rosy, bustled through the kitchen doorway.

'I don't know, that woman gets worse.' She shrugged out of her coat. 'Her ladyship only wants me to be doin' your job as well as me own so she won't have to pay anyone else. If she thinks I'm going to shift the muck after last night's raid, the woman can think again.' Taking out her hat pin, she removed her black felt hat. 'After the way she treated you, lass, I've a mind to hand in me notice. These days, there's plenty of work for women.' Sandra's ears pricked at this. 'Tommy's always telling us the Kirtons don't appreciate their staff and I should go somewhere where they do.'

Flouncing her dark brown hair with her fingertips, she glanced at Sandra. 'Eee! Sorry. Here's me tellin' you me woes when you're in such a pickle.' She glanced at the letter in Sandra's hand. 'Is that a letter from your Alf?'

Sandra nodded.

Taking the single sheet of paper out of Sandra's hand, Mrs Goodwin removed her spectacles from her handbag and placed them on her nose. 'This is just what you need to cheer you up. Let's see what it says.' She plonked on the couch beside Sandra.

Dearest Sandra,

I do mean to write more often but, to be honest, not much goes on here except much of the same and I don't wish to bore you to death.

I'm here in the mess with Harry Stokes (who I've previously told you about) and the rest of the crew, who are mostly playing cards and darts or just staring, like me, out of the window at planes landing and taking off and the personnel painting the underside of aircraft black in readiness for operations at night.

An aircraft is being loaded with fuel which makes me think there is a trip on for tonight and I'm wondering if I'll be on it. Dear girl, I know you'll get down in the dumps when you think of me on a mission but remember that it's what I like doing best and that I wanted to join in the fight for my country.

This was unusual for him as Alf rarely mentioned missions. He concluded by asking about her work at the Kirton household and how her war work was going.

Then Mrs Goodwin, eyes shining, looked up at Sandra. 'Listen to this.'

Sandra, good news. I've just heard that I'm due rest from ops. Dare we hope this is so. And if it happens I'll hitch a ride to see you in the north-east. I'll let you know if I have further news.

Meanwhile, affectionately, Alf

Excitement surged through Sandra at the thought of seeing her brother again.

Mrs Goodwin folded the letter and handed it to Sandra. 'Aw! That'll be lovely. Just the tonic you need. There'll always be a bed for your brother here.' Laughing, she added, 'Even if it is in the makeshift bed in the attic.'

Her eyes darted to the other envelope perched on the suitcase. 'That might be from Kenneth.' She picked up the letter and read the writing. 'It is.' Her eyes brimmed with tears. 'I don't care what's he's got to say' – her voice cracked – 'as long as he writes. It means…' Her chin wobbled and she couldn't go on.

Sandra understood.

'I'll make you a cuppa while you read it.' Sandra moved through to the scullery and boiled the kettle for a fresh brew.

When she returned, cup in hand, Mrs Goodwin waved the letter and shook her head. 'Twerp that me son is… tells me nothing except how he's starved and what good mates he has and he's got a bloody corn on his big toe. I ask yi'?' She raised her eyes skyward. Then she beamed with pleasure. 'But he does send his love to the family and two lovely kisses for me and his dad.' She placed the precious letter on the mantelpiece. Sandra knew it would be read many times.

Mrs Goodwin took the cup of tea and settled back on the couch. 'Now, lass, what are wi' going to do about you? You can stop in our Kenneth's room as long as you like. And don't worry, you'll get a job in no time.'

'Mrs Goodwin… I've decided I'm not going to be in service any more. I want to do war work.'

The idea had struck Sandra when she heard what Alf had said in his letter. That he wanted to fight for his country. Sandra knew that was what she wanted: to do her bit too.

'First of all, pet, now you're shot of that dratted place, you can call me Olive. Secondly, good for you, lass. What d'yi' want to do? Factory… join the forces?'

For the second time that day excitement surged through Sandra.

*

That evening, after a tea of thick slices of fried Spam and chips, as she sat around the put-you-up table with the Goodwins, Sandra couldn't believe she'd only been there half a day. The Goodwins treated her like family.

Olive told her, 'I'll air that bed and put Kenneth's stone hot water bottle in it.'

Her husband Tommy stood up. 'I'll go and see if I've got a light bulb. That last one in the room has had its day.' A skinny man, all bones, Tommy had a face creased with worry lines and large hands that were calloused.

'He's got a bit of a bad chest,' Olive told Sandra, concern in her eyes, 'I'm convinced it's with workin' all weathers at the docks.'

'Take no notice of her.' Tommy turned and looked at his wife with adoration in his eyes. 'It's only a bit of a cold.'

Later, their son Herbert and his wife popped in on their way home from the early showing at the pictures.

'You want to be careful going out in the black of night in your condition,' Olive told her daughter-in-law as she sat in the fireside chair, knitting needles clicking as she made what looked like baby's mittens.

Sitting the other side of the fire on a dining chair, Tommy told her, 'Olive, there's a full moon to see by.' He pulled a long face. 'I only hope it doesn't mean Jerry will give us a pasting tonight.'

They all went silent for a time, gazing into the fire. Then Olive told the others about Sandra's predicament and how she was now looking for employment.

'Leave the lass be.' Tommy put a pipe in his mouth and, lighting the tobacco with a match, clouds of smoke belched from the bowl. His face contorting in anxiety, he told Sandra, 'From what I hear about your job, likely you're due a rest. Take all the time you want, it's fine by us, isn't it, Olive?

Their kindness was too much for Sandra to bear and she felt quite teary. But she didn't want to be a burden.

Polly, sitting next to Herbert on the couch, her hands resting on the enormous mound of her abdomen, turned towards Sandra. 'If you're thinking of work you should watch the feature on the Pathé news. It's about Land Girls doing their bit. It was interesting, wasn't it, Herbert?'

Sandra pricked up her ears.

Polly turned to her husband, adding, 'Didn't the lasses look as if they were having a ball, laughing and joking as they went about their work in the fields? The newsreader said they were thoroughly modern women doing their bit to feed the nation.'

Herbert butted in. 'It's not my cup of tea being way out in the middle of nowhere.'

His wife gave an impatient shake of the head. 'Take no notice of him. He's a grouch because he starts the six till two shift tomorrow morning at the mine.'

Herbert checked the clock on the mantlepiece. 'Aye, and it's time we made tracks so I can get some kip.' He stood up and addressed Sandra. 'I suppose you could do worse. I mean think of all the grub, with all the hens and pigs and the like.'

Olive stood up and cuffed the side of her son's head. 'Away with you. Always thinkin' of your belly.'

Later that night as Sandra stood in Kenneth's bedroom, littered with paraphernalia from when he was a lad – toy aeroplanes that hung from the ceiling, his football card collection – she felt disorientated. So much had changed in the last twenty-four hours.

She unpacked on the single bed and she gazed at her pitiful few belongings: a Sunday best frock that had survived the blast, knickers, vest, pair of lisle stockings, a greyish bra, gloves, cardigan and alarm clock. An inkling of an idea formed in her mind. But then doubts came crowding in. The plan would mean responsibility. Sandra likely would foul up and folk would see her for the fool she was. As negative thoughts scuttled her mind, a sound from outside made her freeze.

The wail of the air raid siren.

Someone banged on the door. Tommy shouted, 'Get yerself in the shelter.'

Sandra hurried from the bedroom and made for the makeshift shelter in the washhouse in the yard. Cold and dank, the shelter had no heating and only benches against the walls to sit on. Light was provided by the paraffin-smelling hurricane lamp that stood on a card table in the corner.

'Here, put this on.' Olive bundled a blanket into Sandra's arms, then sat beside her, placing a flask and plate of homemade biscuits between them.

'Ginger snaps,' Olive told her. She turned to her husband next to her. 'Have you brought the playing cards?'

'Aye,' Tommy's croaky voice replied. 'By God, I'm getting weary of this malarkey. But who am I to grumble? I could be dead.'

As bombers droned in the distance and blasts from bombs could be heard as they exploded, Sandra felt nervy and jumpy. It was too soon after escaping death the night before. The events replayed in her mind: Duncan's hairy arms chafing her skin, the smell of alcohol on his panting breath, the noise of exploding bombs. Her thoughts grappled with the enormity of what could have been.

Rather than be overcome by these thoughts, the knowledge that she'd escaped both being raped or killed made a new-found optimism wash over her. She realised that dwelling on what had happened with Duncan Kirton would mean that he'd won, after all. From now on she would banish him from her mind. She had a future, more than could be said for a lot of unfortunates in this war.

She made up her mind. Tomorrow she would go to the early showing at the cinema and see for herself the Pathé news about Land Girls.

CHAPTER SIX

Leadburn. Northumberland. March 1943

Frieda

Frieda Sternberg stood behind the counter in the village post office. She had replaced Aunty Doris, the postmistress, who was upstairs doing the mail for the Home Comforts Fund. The fund, organised by Leadburn villagers, was set up to send a few essentials and goodies to the men and women serving away from home. Items such as knitted socks, gloves, cigarettes, chocolate and writing paper were packed and sent through the Special Services Mail.

Aunty Doris had volunteered after she'd attended a Comforts Fund meeting in the village hall. Returning home, Frieda's aunt had declared, 'What was I thinking of? Volunteering to take on another responsibility when I've plenty to do here.' She let out a harassed sigh. 'But I suppose, everyone's got to do that extra bit these days.'

Frieda, nearly fifteen, still attended the village school even though the official leaving age was a year younger. The reason was that when she had been evacuated to England, despite having studied English at school in Germany, Frieda still struggled to understand sometimes, especially the local accent. The headmistress of the school thought it best if Frieda stayed down a year until she'd mastered the English language.

Frieda couldn't wait for the day she finished at the school and she skived off as often as she could. The school turned a blind eye because it was only a few weeks until the Easter break when Frieda would leave for good.

'Have you any idea where you'd like to work?' Aunty Doris had enquired that morning over breakfast. 'There's a part-time job as a waitress up for grabs at the village store teashop. Mrs Curtis says it's yours if you want it.'

Frieda, chewing on a mouthful of bread and jam, considered Aunty Doris. Slim, with short, blonde hair, she had a forthright outlook on the world.

Frieda vehemently shook her head.

'Why ever not?' Aunty Doris had asked, bemused.

When Frieda hadn't answered, Aunty Doris, with a worried little frown, didn't press the matter but did what she always did in such a case as this. She went over and gave Frieda a hug. 'You will tell me, won't you, if there's something bothering you?' Physical affection didn't come easily to her but where Frieda was concerned, she bent the rules. For, after four years of living together, a bond had grown between them.

Frieda nodded.

She often wondered if Aunty Doris suspected the torment she'd experienced at school but Frieda doubted it. She was good at keeping secrets. The truth of the matter was the girls who bullied her all through school frequented the village teashop. She couldn't tell that to Aunty Doris because Frieda felt ashamed; the bullying must have something to do with her inadequacies.

Now, Aunty Doris called down the stairs to Frieda. 'Are you managing all right? Don't forget to holler if you need any help.'

'I'm fine. Hardly anyone has been in this morning.'

'I thought I hadn't heard the bell. I'm making your favourite pea soup for dinner.' Aunty Doris giggled.

The soup, made from dried peas, was Frieda's least favourite meal. Though, in these times of war, when food was scarce, she shouldn't grumble. Frieda was forever in her aunt's debt. For that was how Frieda considered her after all these years – as a real aunt. Not only had she provided a home for Frieda but she'd taught her how to understand English.

The day Frieda had arrived in England was forever etched in her mind. She'd stood on the quayside, chaotic with crowds of weary children. Knowing no one, Frieda experienced a horrible panicky feeling. She thought her racing heart might stop and she might die. The shock of leaving Mama behind and seeing her brother jump the ship had traumatised Frieda and the equilibrium she'd once known could never fully be regained.

Once in England, some of the children were told they had sponsors and were to travel by train to London. Frieda and the others who had no foster families waiting were taken to a place called Harwich, and then to a nearby holding camp by the sea. Here she stayed until arrangements were made for her to be fostered. The weather was perishingly cold, she remembered, and snow was on the ground, but the main hall where she ate her meals and where a German teacher taught lessons, did have heating. Frieda, understanding the distress of the little ones who, like her, were parted from their mothers, comforted them by reading stories from books written in her own language.

There was entertainment at the camp, board games and the occasional trip to the pictures, but, reserved and rather shy, Frieda hadn't mingled with the others. Though she couldn't deny the English were most friendly. With smiles of welcome, they treated her to chocolate, lemonade and occasionally sweeties.

One day, she was given a postcard by one of the teachers from the camp who had escorted the children to England and spoke the language. The kindly lady spoke to her in German. 'You must write to your parents and tell them you have arrived safely. Then they will not worry.'

But when it came to writing, Frieda sat thinking for a long while. What could she say? She was homesick and worried about Papa? Had Kurt found his way back home? No. She would send the kind of postcard Mama would be happy to receive.

> Dear Mama,
>
> I am so happy here in England. Everyone is kind and I am given hot food, chocolate and cake. Hopefully, Papa is back with you and Grandma and you are making arrangements to come to Britain. I am looking forward to meeting the people I will be staying with in England. Please don't worry about me. Hundreds of kisses.
>
> Love from your Frieda

She never got a reply. The next day, accompanied by the same German teacher, Frieda and six other refugees made a long two-train journey up north, arriving in a pretty place called Hexham. The journey didn't end there. Twilight falling, the children were herded onto a bus that rumbled along twisty roads. Frieda, who couldn't see out of the window because of the darkness, hurt her neck when she nodded off, her head jerking up and down.

At her journey's end, Frieda alighted and was ushered into a low-roofed, large echoey hall where lots of people were waiting. Exhausted from the journey, she couldn't stop the tears welling. In a strange place, foreigners milling around, she didn't know what was expected and wanted the reassurance of Mama.

A lady came towards her with an understanding little smile on her milk-coloured face. She said something that Frieda didn't understand. She then stretched out an arm and handed Frieda a book. On closer inspection the gift was a dictionary.

Frieda had returned a shy smile. The lady, taking her by the hand, took Frieda to her new home. The lady, Frieda found out much later when she had a grasp of the English language, was called Mrs Leadbeater.

'But you can call me Aunty Doris, if you like.' Her face lit up in a grin. 'I've never been an aunty before.' Then she sobered and added, 'I know your parents are kosher. But Frieda, I've read up on the subject and you don't need to worry. I'll abide by your wishes.'

'Abide?'

'Roughly means I'll do as you wish.'

But the first time Aunty fried bacon, savouring the smell, Frieda couldn't resist. She felt bad about eating the delicious food later – but Mama wasn't there to be disappointed.

Gradually, she began to live the British way but somewhere in her being she'd always belong to the old ways. She pined for home and sometimes at night Mama and Papa stole unbidden into her dreams while she slept.

Frieda came out of her trancelike reverie as the post office bell tinkled. Mrs Nichol from the nearby farm entered.

'Your aunt not in?' she asked in that breathless way of hers.

Mrs Nichol wasn't a storybook farmer's wife – robust and jovial with a heart of gold – she was wiry and pale-faced with lines etching her face and an abrupt manner. But Frieda always found Mrs Nichol fair-minded and at least she never referred to her as 'that German girl'.

'Aunty Doris is upstairs sorting the Comfort Fund mail.'

Mrs Nichol's face softened in a rare smile. 'My son said in his letter that he'd received a parcel from home. He swapped the cigarettes for chocolate.'

The villagers knew Mr and Mrs Nichol's son was away in the army serving his country. But then, everyone in the village always knew everyone else's business.

'Tell your aunt she's doing a grand job.'

Frieda was taken aback at this warm request.

Mrs Nichol brought out her purse. 'Two tuppence halfpenny stamps, please.'

Frieda passed the stamps over the counter. Mrs Nichol, rifling in her purse, handed her the pennies, which Frieda rang up in the till.

Mrs Nichol studied the stamps before putting them in the wallet of her purse. 'If they print them with any less ink the king's head won't show at all. Never mind, His Majesty would be the first to condone such saving in an effort for the war.'

Frieda was surprised at Mrs Nichol's comment; usually she was a woman who kept to herself.

'Why are you not at school?'

Freda felt accused. Embarrassed to say her age, she improvised by saying, 'I'm leaving in two weeks and I've been allowed the day off.'

'I know you're leaving. I heard from Mrs Teasdale.'

Nobody in the village called Peggy, the post lady, Mrs Teasdale except the children, who were respectful of adults.

'If you're looking for a job there's work to be done at the farm.' Mrs Nichol placed the handle of the wicker basket over her arm. 'Good day.' She moved to the door and with a tinkle of the bell she was gone.

Frieda turned and checked the large round clock on the wall behind her. One o'clock. Dinner time. She thought of the pea soup and wrinkled up her nose. It was better, she supposed, than being at school.

The first day she'd walked into the classroom at Leadburn school, in the autumn term of '39, she'd seen hostility in the children's faces. It had reminded Frieda of the hatred she'd experienced at school in Berlin. She'd once overheard a mother warning her daughter, *Don't use the toilet after that dirty Jewish girl.*

In the English school, Frieda was considered different – a foreigner; the enemy. The children stared from behind their desks. She'd escaped from one country's hatred to be confronted with the same here.

The teacher, with caring blue, intelligent eyes, spoke to the class. She must have explained the situation that Frieda was Jewish and fleeing Germany to come to the safety of their country, because most of the children, though they weren't exactly friendly, left her alone after that.

Not so Dulcie Irwin and her gang. Dulcie had a way of making her gang obey whatever she said. Frieda was picked on both verbally and physically and life became a misery. When the headmistress of the school decided that it was best to send her down to the class a year below, the bullying intensified. She was labelled *stupid dunce* as well as *that bloody German girl*. Dulcie and her gang taunted her with those words throughout school.

But there was a part of Frieda that was ashamed she'd fled Germany and survived the horrors of her homeland, and felt this was her punishment.

In the early days, Aunty Doris had set time aside every night to teach her the English language. Frieda was encouraged to build words into phrases. 'Brush' became 'That is my hairbrush'. 'Teeth' became 'I clean my teeth every morning'. The method worked and as she progressed, her aunt made learning fun by making up silly rhymes to repeat. Frieda easily got frustrated when she couldn't speak as quickly as she did in her own language or when she made the same mistakes: 'I goed' instead of 'I went' or, 'zee stamp' because she couldn't say 'the stamp'. Aunty Doris told her not to be so hard on herself and to laugh it off. Which was easy with Aunty Doris but not at school with Dulcie Irwin around. So, Frieda became even more reserved and was considered by everyone at school as standoffish.

With no sign of any more customers, Frieda locked the post office door and followed the smell of pea soup up the stairs. As she did so, memories of when she first saw the house came flooding back. She'd awoken early that first day in her sunlit bedroom at the back of the house. The lady (as Frieda thought of her then) who'd brought Frieda to this home was busy making breakfast in the kitchen and gestured for Frieda to take a look around. Frieda had descended the stairs and gone into the passageway. When she unlocked the front door, she had been stunned at the lovely village that appeared before her, with its attractive honey-coloured stone houses with long front gardens. A snaking stream ran through the village, a wooden bridge with white handrails built over it. Birds tweeted in the still and tranquil early morning air, soothing Frieda for the first time since she'd left Mama. And hope sprang in her young heart for the future.

'Was that Mrs Nichol I heard downstairs?' Aunty Doris was buttering delicious-looking homemade bread to accompany the pea soup. Baking was another of her aunt's talents and probably the reason why Frieda had grown so large. The discussion they'd had the other day when Frieda had broached the subject that she was fat played on her mind.

'You're not plump,' Aunty Doris had assured her. Then she'd regarded Frieda with a suspicious look in her eye. 'You're not being teased at school, are you?'

Of course Dulcie and her cronies had been tormenting her – about what she wore, how she looked, how she spoke – but she knew it wouldn't do to worry Aunty Doris. *Besides,* the voice of guilt in her head had told her, *this is your punishment for fleeing your country.*

'You're gorgeous the way you are.' But Aunty Doris was biased, Frieda knew. 'I was like you at your age and the puppy fat dropped off me when I got older.'

So, there was confirmation. She was fat! The problem was it comforted her to have a full tummy. Frieda had banished the upsetting thoughts from her mind until today.

Aunty Doris looked quizzically at her while she waited for an answer.

'Yes, it was Mrs Nichol. She bought stamps.'

'She seemed quite talkative.'

'She was.' Frieda began to wash her hands under the cold-water tap, putting the plug in the sink so she wouldn't waste water. She turned the tap off and dried her hands. 'It seemed like Mrs Nichol was offering me a job at the farm.'

Her aunt smiled and put her hands on her hips. 'So, what d'you think?'

'I rather like the idea.'

What Frieda liked was the fact she wouldn't have to mix with company.

'Then go ahead. There's nothing to stop you.' Her aunt gave a beaming smile as she put thick green soup in a bowl.

After breakfast the next morning, as thoughts of Mrs Nichol offering her a job buzzed in her mind, Frieda collapsed on her bed and picked up *Anne of Green Gables*, the book she was reading. She had another quarter of an hour before the post office opened.

The knocker banged on the front door. Aunty Doris's footsteps could be heard descending the carpeted stairs.

After she'd read the same sentence three times, Frieda laid the book down on the patterned eiderdown. She sat up and gazed out of the bedroom window, looking over the fields dotted with sheep to the stone-built farm with its peaked roof and smoke billowing from the chimney pots. Soon she would be free of school and able to work at the farm. Her first job, besides working for Aunt Doris in the post office. Frieda wondered what she would do at the farm.

She heard voices downstairs. One was male.

'Come on up.' Aunty Doris's voice.

Footsteps came up the stairs. Voices came through the bedroom wall from the kitchen beyond. Frieda strained to hear.

'It's good of you to call.'

'Not at all. I've decided to introduce myself to the parishioners personally.'

Aunty Doris laughed. 'The ones that don't turn up at church on Sundays, you mean.'

The new curate from the local church, Frieda thought. The villagers were agog for news about him.

'Would you like tea?'

'I would, thank you.'

There were tea-making noises from the kitchen, then general discussion about the village.

Frieda had seen the curate – Mr Carlton – last Saturday outside the church after he'd officiated at a wedding, when the bride and groom were having their photographs taken. The bride wore a flowing, long-sleeved, white dress, nipped in at the waist, and a sparkling tiara headdress and veil, while the groom looked smart in his khaki army uniform. The curate stood behind, dressed in an ankle-length cassock. He was quite young, Frieda had thought, tall and slim with an earnest but pleasant face. His brown liquid eyes looked both attentive and empathic. Instinctively, Frieda knew that the new curate was the kind of man you could tell your troubles to. If only she could tell him about her cowardice the day the boat left for England, perhaps then the self-loathing she experienced would go away. But shame wouldn't allow her to.

She tuned into the voices coming through the wall.

'Where did you hear about the Jewish children's evacuation?' The curate's soft mesmeric voice spoke.

'On the BBC Home Service radio station. Viscount Samuel appealed for foster homes. I volunteered, then someone came to inspect the house to make sure it was suitable. It didn't matter that I wasn't Jewish.'

'It was kind of you to take Frieda in.'

'Someone had to. She's such a lovely girl. It's what Jack, my husband, would've wanted. He had a soft heart.'

In the poignant silence that followed, Frieda was surprised as Aunty Doris hardly mentioned her husband. Frieda had been told that he'd died. On the sideboard there were photographs of their wedding day and on the mantelpiece another one of him standing beside a motorcycle.

'It's very difficult when you lose a loved one.' Mr Carlton's tone was gentle.

'I find I can't talk about him. But I think about him all of the time.'

'May I ask, was it in the Great War?'

'Good Lord… erm sorry, no. We weren't married then. It happened eight years ago. Jack was riding his motorcycle home from a farm up the shire. He'd been helping a friend with lambing. It was night-time and Jack wasn't going fast by all accounts. He couldn't on these twisty roads. A lorry was taking a bend the same time as him and…' She didn't finish the sentence. Another silence – longer this time. 'They say Jack died outright and he didn't suffer.'

'It's good you found each other and had happy years together.'

'What a lovely thing to say, I'd never thought of it like that before. I am fortunate in that we were so very happy if only for a short time. Some people never find the right person, do they?'

Frieda was so glad her aunt had found the right one. She hoped someday the same would happen to her. Mama had told her there was someone for everyone out there.

'Has Frieda got siblings?' The curate's voice again.

Frieda's ears pricked.

'A brother. He jumped ship just before it left Holland. I try to keep her mind off the past but I wonder if I'm being fair. Maybe we should talk about it more. But like me, she bottles things up.' A big sigh. 'Ever since I heard the foreign secretary condemn what's happening to Jews in the camps, I've feared for her family's safety.'

'God help them. I shall pray for them all.'

She had survived. Guilt and self-loathing washed over Frieda.

Frieda stared unseeing at the ceiling. Never had she faced the fear of what might have happened to her family before. All through these past four years when she hadn't had any communication from them – no replies to all the letters she'd sent – she made up explanations. The apartment had been bombed and the family had moved and Mama didn't know where to write to her. They didn't have the money to travel to Britain and were in hiding. Even if they were in a camp some of what was being said might only be rumours. People survived in… *Gefängnis*… she searched her mind for the correct word in English… jail, why not in camps?

That moment a strange thing happened. The smell of Papa's bread flooded the bedroom – a long-forgotten aroma but one that was as real as the air Frieda breathed. Transported back to the family's oval dining table at home, she imagined Mama, Papa, Grandma and Kurt all sitting around eating, chatting, happy to be in each other's company.

A rush of adrenalin made her dizzy. Was this an omen?

Frieda slid from the bed and looked at herself in the standard mirror. She thought about how everything in her life was out of control and had been since the day she'd left Mama in Berlin. She turned sideways and gazed at her tummy, which made her look as if she was having a baby. The tops of her legs, so disgustingly fat, rubbed together when she walked.

She could do something about this, Frieda told the reflection in the mirror. She banished the distressing thoughts she couldn't cope with back to the recesses of her mind. Aunty Doris insisted she was exaggerating but Frieda could see for herself the evidence in the mirror. This was something she could take control of.

From now on Frieda would stop eating until she was willowy thin.

CHAPTER SEVEN

South Shields. April 1943

Sandra

That first night at the Goodwins', sitting in the shelter as bombs rained down on the town, Sandra had made up her mind to buck up and follow her dream to change her life. The following night she'd gone to the pictures to watch Land Girls at work on the screen. Sandra was elated as she watched girls like her laughing in the sunshine as they worked together in the fields, while boisterous, uplifting music played in the background.

The next day she'd sought out the Women's Land Army Headquarters and enrolled.

She'd passed the medical, when the doctor had asked if she could do manual work. Thinking of all the coals she'd shovelled from the coalhouse and then hauling heavy bucketfuls up and down the Kirtons' stairs, she vigorously nodded and agreed that she could.

She was then requested to attend an interview where a panel of mature-looking ladies fired questions at her: present occupation, experience of country life, if she had a bicycle, her figure size. Afterwards, Sandra, certain she hadn't impressed, was convinced she'd failed the interview.

When the form had arrived at the Goodwins' house asking her for two references, Sandra, initially ecstatic at passing the interview, had been at a loss at first to think who to ask. But of course, one could be Olive. For the other, she asked a respected WVS lady at the clothes depot where she'd worked, who was only too pleased to give Sandra a reference.

Then one morning, a week later, an official-looking letter plopped through the Goodwins' letterbox. She spent the morning on tenterhooks in her room, frustrated beyond measure that she couldn't read the writing on the envelope while waiting for Olive to arrive home from work.

As soon as she heard Olive's key in the lock, Sandra hurried to the top of the stairs. She waved the letter in the air. 'I can't wait to hear if this is from the War Agricultural Committee and if I've got the job.'

'All right, lass.' Olive held the bannister rail and lumbered up to the top stair. 'Wait till I get me breath back and we'll see.'

Before she took her outdoor coat off, Olive sank down in a dining chair in the kitchen and put on her spectacles. She tore open the envelope Sandra handed her and scanned the sheet of paper. Beaming, she looked up. 'It is. It's from the War Ag Committee. The top of the letter reads in bold letters, *Remember your ration book and Identity Card.* Beneath is your Women's Land Army number.'

A burst of excitement exploded in Sandra as Olive continued.

> *It has been arranged for you to start work in the district of Leadburn arriving on Sunday, 11th of April for The War Agricultural Executive Committee. Living accommodation will be provided at Leadburn Hostel. Your nearest bus stop and travelling instructions are overleaf. Your starting wage will be seventeen shillings per fifty hours (overtime extra) with board and lodging. Ten pence deducted for Health and Pensions, one and a halfpenny for Unemployment Insurance contributions. Uniform will be sent to your home address.*

On receipt of this notification write without delay to The Warden W.L.A. Miss E. Roberts, Leadburn Hostel, Northumberland.

Olive looked up and handed over the letter. 'A space has been left for your address on the enclosed card to return. Congratulations, Sandra!'

Sandra's heart soared with joy. She'd done it. Then negativity set in. What if she fouled up? She didn't have a clue about either the countryside or animals. What if she didn't make friends with the other lasses? At the orphanage everyone kept to themselves except for her good friend Dorothy Makepeace and her younger sister, Esther. The day Sandra left the orphanage she'd promised to write to them. She'd managed once with Molly's help. But Molly didn't have the time to help correspond with both Alf and the orphan sisters and so, regrettably, Sandra hadn't been in touch again. But she often thought about the sisters and hoped that life was treating them well. Apart from Molly and Olive she'd never had cause to make friends since then.

That night, Sandra shared her fears over a cup of Horlicks with Olive. They sat in flannelette nightgowns in front of the fire's dying embers.

'You're beaten before you start.' Olive shook her head sorrowfully. 'That's what life's done to yi'. The thing you don't realise is that you're strong-willed, a fighter, and that's what will see you through. Many a one would have settled for goin' back into service. Not you, you want to improve yourself. Good on yi', lass.'

With a lump in her throat, Sandra told Olive, 'I'm going to miss you so much. I consider you as close as family.'

*

A week later, as the bus rattled along, Sandra gazed at the scene outside the window. Sheep grazed in the field, farmhouses nestled in the distant hillside, and her thoughts turned to her hometown that held a special place in her heart. After all, that was where her happy memories of her parents and Alf were.

Mam had had dreams for her children. At night, when she tucked her children in bed, their legs wrapped around each other for warmth, Mam sang lullabies and songs, and always ended with the favourite, 'Happy Days Are Here Again'. Then Mam would tell them, 'When you're grown you can do anything you want if you set your mind to it.' Alf's usual reply was, 'I want to be a train driver.'

Mam would've been so proud of her son, at what he'd achieved, Sandra thought. Her heartstrings pulled in sorrow at the thought that Mam hadn't lived to see Alf grow up.

As the countryside flashed by, Sandra made a pledge to the Almighty, *I promise I'll visit church every Sunday if you keep Alf safe.*

The one time Sandra had gone along to the church the Kirtons attended every Sunday, she had been put off by the vicar ranting from the pulpit about sin. For a week after, she'd been riddled with guilt that she couldn't shake off. So, Sandra felt reserved about going back to church regularly; she couldn't abide a whole service but she would at least stop by once in a while to say a prayer for Alf's sake. She only hoped the village would have a church so she could keep her promise and pray for Alf's safekeeping.

The enormity of what she was doing made her heart palpitate. This was madness. What good would she be on a farm, when she didn't know the first thing about animals? As anxiety rose, blind panic followed and the urge to ring the bell and leap from the bus overcame her. She took deep calming breaths and thought of Alf, what he'd done with his life. He must have experienced the same anxieties.

Alf's letters were to be forwarded by Olive to Sandra's new address. If she couldn't find anyone to read them, then Sandra would keep the letters safe until she next visited South Shields. Goodness only knew how long that would be.

Olive had seen her onto the train to Newcastle, where another train ride followed to Hexham, a pretty market town with narrow streets and attractive stone buildings. At Hexham bus station she had asked a bus driver if his bus went to Leadburn village. He nodded and Sandra boarded and sat on the first vacant seat by the window. The bus trundled along twisty roads and Sandra took in the vast landscape of trees, fields and rolling hills that stretched to the horizon.

An elderly woman sitting next to her turned towards her. 'I see you're a Land Girl.' She spoke with a cultured voice and was dressed in a two-piece tweed costume and green felt hat.

Sandra, after being in the employment of Mrs Kirton, was suspicious of folk who spoke with posh voices; and the lady was stating the obvious, as Sandra was in uniform: gabardine breeches that finished at the knee, thick long stockings, greatcoat, cream shirt, brown jersey and brimmed hat.

Sandra nodded. 'Yes, I'm… new.'

'You should be proud. You'll be doing the nation a great service by providing food. Where are you from, dear?'

Sandra warmed to the lady. 'South Shields.'

'Such a way… I know some Land Girls live locally while others are billeted.'

'I'm at Leadburn Hostel.'

'I know it well. I live in the village.'

They lapsed into silence while Sandra gazed out to the now misty countryside where she could just about make out stone-built walls meandering up the hillside.

'I hope you qualify for free transport,' the woman continued.

'Not that I've heard of.'

'Shameful. Though I have heard the WLA is the Cinderella of the services.'

The bus began to slow and the woman collected her black umbrella as she readied to go.

'Who's for Leadburn?' the conductress shouted.

'Our stop, dear.'

Sandra peered out of the window, where nothing was to be seen but more fields and a bus shelter with a wooden seat.

The lady stood up and told Sandra, 'I've been a traitor to Leadburn church this morning, even though I wanted to meet the new curate. I've just been to the abbey with a dear friend who lives in Hexham. A historical treat, my dear, you must go.' She gave a friendly smile and then, holding onto seat backs, made her way down the aisle.

So, there was a church, Sandra thought, delighted. Her superstitious mind had worried that if she didn't keep her word and anything happened to Alf – God forbid – his misfortune would be all her fault. Sandra made the decision to visit the church that very day to be on the safe side.

Carrying her small brown suitcase and wellington boots in a sack, she smiled at the conductress then alighted from the bus.

A girl stepped off behind her. 'Hiya… I had hoped to sit beside you but the old dear beat me to it.'

'Sorry I didn't notice you.'

'I'm Evelyn… I'm new.'

'So am I. Sandra Hudson.' Sandra, feeling inadequate, blushed.

Two girls wearing the WLA uniforms cycled by as rain started pattering on the ground. Disorientated, Sandra went in the direction of the two cyclists as they rounded a corner and disappeared up an earthen path, Evelyn following. Sandra checked her wristwatch. One o'clock. It was over three and a half hours since she'd left the security of Olive's home and Sandra felt a million miles away from her friend.

'Where did you train?' Evelyn asked. 'I was sent to Newton Rigg farm school in Cumbria. I had a jolly time.'

'I haven't done any training,' Sandra admitted, suddenly alarmed by the fact.

'Strange.' Evelyn looked puzzled.

Sandra noticed the fashionable dent in Evelyn's uniform hat and felt silly as hers stuck up in a great mound.

'Should I have?' she asked.

Before Evelyn could answer, a woman wearing an overcoat around her shoulders appeared from the earthen pathway ahead and hurried towards them.

Thin, with grey hair, she looked flustered. 'Welcome to Leadburn. I'm the hostel's resident warden, Miss Roberts.' She turned and headed back up the path, telling them as they walked, 'Mrs Sanderson, my assistant, who lives in the village, usually does the welcoming honours but she's arranging help for Cook as the girl whose job it is hasn't arrived back after a weekend spent at home.'

As the lady bustled ahead of them, Evelyn pulled a long face and whispered, 'I hope that isn't a bad omen for what the place is like.'

'Jessie, the forewoman, who has been with us for a long while,' Miss Roberts prattled as she led the way, 'allocates Land Girls to farms each morning and gives out wages. Then, of course, there's Mrs Sanderson's husband, who helps with the maintenance of the hostel and gardens.'

They followed her around a corner where a large piece of land was surrounded by tall trees. To the right was a long, low red brick building with a row of white-painted windows at intervals along the walls. In front of the building was an allotment garden with a fenced-off area where scrawny hens scratted in the soil. Miss Roberts approached the building's porch and pushed open the door.

'Follow the rules and you'll get on fine,' she called as she stepped inside.

The door closed behind her.

Left outside in the rain, Evelyn muttered, 'Nice to meet you, too.' She raised her eyebrows at Sandra. 'I hope the others aren't as impolite.'

Taken aback, Sandra thought Miss Roberts had been quite civil, seeing as she'd ventured out in the rain to greet the new arrivals. But maybe being in service had left Sandra with a different point of view.

She looked sideways at Evelyn. Willowy tall, with crinkly eyes when she smiled, Evelyn had an air of assurance that Sandra could only envy. The lass didn't seem fazed at the prospect of meeting new folk or worried about what to expect next. Maybe, one day, Sandra could aspire to such self-assurance.

The rain was easing now. She looked around her. Apart from the hens, not a thing moved nor was a sound to be heard. Sandra was in a different world to the one she was used to, where traffic blared and streets of terraced houses, with tall chimneys belching grimy smoke, marched into the distance. Unnerved, Sandra followed Evelyn as she opened the door and entered the building.

Inside, a corridor ran along the back of the building while a door to the left had a notice pinned on it. A hubbub of voices and music came from inside.

Evelyn read the notice: '*Remove muddy boots.*' She obligingly added, 'I assume we're supposed to go in here.'

As Evelyn opened the door, the noise got louder. The large common room had a peaked ceiling with wooden beams, on which a couple of small suitcases were precariously poised. A row of tables and chairs lined one side of the room, a piano nearby, while comfortable but shabby-looking couches and a table tennis table took up the space on the other. Halfway down the room a group of girls huddled together on chairs in front of a tiled fireplace where a coal stove burned merrily.

Evelyn dumped her case and sack on the floor and headed towards the fireplace. Making her way through the group, she sat on a vacant chair. 'Blimey, this is more like it,' she told the lass next to her. 'It's so very damp and cold outside.' She smiled around at the lasses. 'I'm Evelyn Chalmers, by the way.'

Sandra cringed. She worried if the others would be offended by Evelyn's forward ways.

To her amazement, the girl next to Evelyn smiled back. 'I'm Ruby, where are you from?'

'Gosforth. I'm here to escape the parents, who insist they plan my future. Mummy wanted me to stay and help with the WVS which she started in the area. No thank you! I want some adventure.'

The group of lasses laughed. Sandra, who wished she wasn't so awkward in company, hung back as one by one they introduced themselves.

After the introductions, Evelyn said, 'I'm surprised – I thought there'd be more of you here.'

'There are,' Ruby said. 'There are twenty-seven of us now counting you two. Some have gone home for the weekend and aren't back yet. We' – she looked around the small group – 'unfortunately didn't get the weekend off and had to work.'

Evelyn removed her heavy greatcoat. 'Is there anything to eat? I'm starved. I've had nothing since breakfast.'

'Dinner was at twelve, but it was only sandwiches. There's some left for latecomers on the hatch over there,' a lass with round-rimmed metal spectacles told her, pointing to the far end of the room. 'It's Sunday, so tonight's meal is cold mutton as it gets cooked the day before. There'll be taties—'

'I hope it's not wild nettles again,' another piped up, then groaned.

'The spring cabbage looked ready in the garden.' The lass with the spectacles looked eager.

Ruby laughed, then eyed Sandra. 'All anyone thinks about – apart from lads, that is – is food.'

Sandra, standing like a mute dummy in the background, worried the others thought her aloof.

Evelyn appeared to notice her discomfiture. 'This' – she nodded towards Sandra – 'is Sandra Hudson. We travelled on the bus from Hexham together.'

All eyes turned on Sandra and she forced a smile. 'I'm pleased to—'

The kitchen door opened at the back of the room beside the hatch and a plump, middle-aged woman appeared. She had a no-nonsense air, and not a strand of her black hair, streaked with grey, was out of place. A wraparound pinafore covered her clothes.

She looked around the group of girls. 'Miss Roberts says the new arrivals are here.' Her eyes rested on Sandra then Evelyn. 'I'm Mrs Sanderson. I'll show yous around.'

Evelyn stood and the two of them accompanied Mrs Sanderson back into the main corridor, the chatter from the lasses resuming behind them. Sandra wondered if they were talking about her.

Following Mrs Sanderson, Sandra discovered the building was formed like a letter U. To the left was the common room that extended to the kitchen and, further still, the warden's accommodation. On the right-hand side were three large bedrooms, each with bunk beds to accommodate ten girls. Across the bottom, joining the two sides, was a corridor with communal washroom with baths and toilets.

'These will be your bunk beds.'

Mrs Sanderson stepped inside one of the bedrooms and pointed to the bunks farthest away from the door. Sandra looked outside the window to the courtyard in the middle of the two lengths of the building, where a boardwalk led to a patch of grass and more garden planted out with rows of greenery.

'Work will start any time between five and half six in the morning,' Mrs Sanderson told them. 'Farmers are apt to come and collect the number of hands they need first thing. Collect a bait tin from the hatch in the common room and a lemonade bottle filled with tea. If you're lucky it will be reheated at the farm where you work. When you return it's first come first served in a shared bath, but mind' – she gave them a warning glare – 'remember to keep to the regulation five inches of water.' She pointed to a notice pinned to the back of the door. 'That's the drill for a raid but fortunately Jerry isn't interested in cows and sheep. We are near the aerodrome, though, so there's always the worry he'll mistake the buildings.' She addressed Sandra. 'You are allocated to help Cook in the kitchen. Be there sharp at half five in the morning. Townies find it difficult to fit in without the amenities they're used to.' She sniffed. 'There's no cinema in the village or shops with the latest fashions. Only common folk that know the countryside. If a bird flies overhead, they know its name and they can forecast the weather. We know the ways of every plant and wild creature. So, don't you go thinking we're mere country bumpkins.' As the woman glowered at her, Sandra squirmed, thinking, *It's like the old days back at the orphanage.* 'Furthermore,' Mrs Sanderson went on, 'if you're wise, you'll try and fit in with the villagers any spare time you've got. Join the WVS, start knitting or volunteer to be one of the fire watchers. And don't go smoking in the stackyard where there's a crop of hay.' She was about to turn, then thought better of it. 'If you get homesick don't come snivelling to me.'

'We do know,' Evelyn's tone was haughty, her stare imperious, 'the Land Army motto… which is to stick it out through thick or thin.'

Mrs Sanderson went the colour of beetroot. 'Further,' she emphasised as if she wanted to get the last word in, 'the hostel curfew is ten o'clock and the door will be locked. Saturdays you can have a pass till eleven. But only at my discretion. Lights out half an hour after the curfew.' Having had the last word, she turned and her footsteps could be heard clattering down the corridor.

Evelyn, heaving her suitcase onto the bottom bunk, said, 'Blimey it's like being back at boarding school. If Mrs Sanderson thinks I've escaped from home to sit and knit, then she can think again.'

'Do we really have a motto?' Sandra wanted to know.

Evelyn chuckled. 'I haven't a clue but I think we should.'

Sandra laughed. She hauled her suitcase onto the top bunk, took off her hat and made a dent in the middle. But then she thought about reporting to the kitchen in the morning. *After the relief of escaping being in service*, she thought, *here I am back where I started.*

CHAPTER EIGHT

When they'd unpacked their possessions into lockable boxes beneath the bottom bunk bed, Evelyn declared, 'That's me off back to the common room to grab a sandwich and hear the gossip.' She headed for the door. 'Are you coming?'

Sandra agonised at the thought of joining in. She'd started to find herself at ease with Evelyn, like she could open up to her. But the anxiety of being in front of the group and how she might not have anything interesting to say about her past dull life threw her. She'd feel inadequate. How could she tell them about her deprived childhood, the orphanage and how she'd been a servant?

Sandra seriously questioned what she was doing here. The other lasses appeared so worldly-wise. But she knew she was tired from the journey and the wrench of leaving Olive behind was probably the reason why she felt so insecure about meeting people. What she needed was to be alone, and to get some fresh air where she could gather herself. Despite herself, she smiled as she imagined herself like a jigsaw with scattered parts. Could she piece herself together again and perhaps even one day think of this place as home and the girls her family?

'What's the joke?' Evelyn asked, looking prepared to be amused.

'Nothing. Just a thought.'

Evelyn shook her head as she opened the bedroom door. 'I can tell you're the interesting type. You run deep, as Mummy would say.'

That Evelyn thought she was interesting cheered her. Maybe there was more to herself than Sandra thought.

'I think I'll take a walk and have a look around. I'm not quite hungry yet.' This was true, as nerves had stifled any appetite she otherwise might have felt.

'Ta-ta, then. See you later.'

Outside, the sky had begun to clear. Sandra, walking back down the path towards the main road, saw white cotton wool clouds floating in the sky, and the sun breaking through, shafts of yellow light drenching the faraway hilltops like a sign from heaven. With a jolt she remembered her quest to find the church.

In the eerie silence, as she inhaled the smell of the earthy countryside, Sandra reflected how she'd always wanted to change, to do something different – and now she had the chance.

She turned to her right and, following the road, was surprised when she passed a herd of cows in a field. The nearest cows raised their heads and as they chewed grass their watchful eyes followed her. Sandra marvelled at their size. Apart from mongrel dogs and cats in the town and the occasional milk-delivery horse, she was unaccustomed to animals.

She came to a road and, looking to the right along it, Sandra saw a row of houses either side. The village of Leadburn, she guessed. She turned and followed the road, passing more quaint stone-built houses with long front gardens. After a while, the road opened up to reveal a picturesque village. A stream meandered through the middle, where tall trees grew from grassy banks either side. A white wooden bridge was built over the stream's flowing waters.

Sandra's heart rose as she saw, up ahead and over the houses' peaked rooftops, a tall church steeple that pointed towards the blue heavens. Hurrying towards the church, the sun warm on her back, Sandra passed a long low building with notices pinned to the windows. She stopped and, peeking in, saw a long hall with a raised stage at the farthest end. Beyond the building, beside a wooden seat that looked over the village green, was a red postbox beside what appeared to be the village store. Sandra looked in through the window at the rows of wooden shelves which were mostly bare, apart from a few stacked tins and sweetie jars which were practically empty.

Reaching the church's wooden gate, she unhitched the latch and walked up the moss-covered path. In the arched entrance Sandra marvelled at the stonework. That moment, the heavy-looking wooden door squeaked open and a girl stepped from the doorway.

Staring at each other, they both moved the same way.

'Oops!' Sandra found herself smiling.

The girl looked to be about fourteen and was rake thin with black hair, an elfin face and huge eyes.

'I am sorry.' The girl moved aside.

She had a foreign accent but Sandra couldn't detect what country she came from as she'd never been out of her hometown until now.

'Am I intruding?' she asked. 'Is there a service on inside?'

The girl looked hesitant. 'There is nothing happening, I just came to...' Whatever the girl had just come to do, she didn't disclose it. Turning her head left, then right, as if looking for someone, she gave a heavy sigh. 'There is no one in the church.'

Sandra didn't know if it was her imagination but the girl's face appeared to sag in disappointment. 'Thanks, I hoped that would be the case.'

There was a silence as if both waited for the other to speak. Then, saying goodbye, the girl took off down the path.

Sandra, opening the heavy door, went into the surprisingly light and airy atmosphere of the small and welcoming church. Inside was a dazzle of red: carpet, hassocks, seat covers; and at the end, the intricately carved pulpit and an organ raised on a plinth. The church had a holy atmosphere, as if all the prayers of worship over the centuries had soaked into its thick stone walls.

Making her way down the aisle Sandra went to sit in a pew facing the three arched, stained-glass windows at the front. In the silence, she thought of her brother, flying in a bomber up in the heavens. She imagined guns shooting from enemy territory below like she'd seen on the Pathé news, flak exploding around his aeroplane. There was a dropping sensation of dread in her stomach. She kneeled on a red kneeler and, putting her hands together, prayed, *Please, God, keep Alf safe.*

What else was there to say?

A door squeaked open. A movement at the front of the church caught her eye. At the top of a few stairs on one side of the pulpit was a door that Sandra hadn't noticed before. A figure emerged. A clergyman dressed in his cassock. A shaft of sunlight shone through a stained-glass window and gave him an ethereal appearance. He looked around the church and then spotted her. Making his way down the steps, he moved to the hymn board. She watched as he changed the numbers.

This was probably the new curate the woman on the bus earlier that day had referred to. The curate, slim and tall with sandy-coloured hair and broad shoulders, had a graceful bearing. He made his way up the aisle but avoided eye contact with her.

'Am I in the way?' she asked when he was level with her pew. 'D'you need to lock up or anything?' She felt daft asking such a silly question but how was she to know?

'I've disturbed you.' His voice was soft and mesmeric, and it encouraged her to relax. 'Please continue with your prayers.' He cupped his hands before him and bent forward in a way that suggested he was here to help however he could.

She stood up. 'I'm not much good at praying.' That was an even dafter thing to say.

His smile was gentle and there was an air of shyness about him. He seemed very different from the bible-bashing clergyman breathing fire and damnation in the Kirtons' church.

'Pray as if talking to your best friend. Say what's in your heart.'

It seemed simple, put like that.

'I did, only it was short and sweet.'

Caring brown eyes met hers. 'It's not the quantity of prayer that counts.'

She decided she liked this curate. She blurted, 'I promised I'd attend church every Sunday to keep me brother safe.' The curate didn't answer but waited as if he knew there was more. 'His name is Alf and he's an air gunner.' Should she be talking about guns and killing in a church? 'I haven't seen him for two years. But he writes and I look forward to receiving his letters.' She felt foolish as her throat constricted and tears welled in her eyes, but it didn't prevent her from continuing. The curate was easy to talk to. 'D'you think God will be angry that I'm bargaining with him?'

'He knows a good heart.'

Another simple answer.

Her chin trembling, Sandra realised past events – being sacked, finding a home with Olive, applying for a job – had taken their toll. 'Alf's all the family I've got.'

'Would it help if you told me about your brother?' The curate looked a little self-conscious, as if that was uncomfortable for him to say. For an instant she saw the man behind the cloth.

Sandra sensed the natural wall of protection begin to build as talking about herself didn't come easily. But the curate genuinely seemed to care. Tentatively, she began telling the curate everything. About her poverty-stricken childhood, Dad being an invalid, Mam working every God-given hour doing washing. She and Alfie being institutionalised and how she felt responsible, and yet couldn't protect her little brother. As she talked a sense of wonder overcame her. 'I've never thought before but that's how I feel inside. That it's my duty to look after Alf.'

He nodded, his quiet reserve reassuring. 'What I think, Miss…?'

'Sandra. Sandra Hudson,' she prompted.

'Miss Hudson, is that Alf is a lucky fellow to have such a loyal big sister as you.'

Her chest swelled with pride at his words.

'You're at the hostel?'

The sudden change of focus surprised her. 'Yes. I've just arrived today.'

'Give yourself time to settle in and just *be* for a while.'

Such an easy-going attitude, it made Sandra smile. The idea of letting go, without the expectation of complications that might arise, was tempting. But life could never be that simple, could it?

She changed the subject. 'I had the impression you were looking for someone earlier.' Then, she had a thought. 'If it was a young girl, she's just left.'

He looked preoccupied. 'No matter.'

CHAPTER NINE

Frieda

Frieda was woken by the sound of aircraft flying over the house. She leapt out of bed and drew back the blackout curtains. Wave after wave of raiders blocked out the moon and it was as though a tremendous thunder rumbled overhead. She blocked her ears with her hands and, heart racing, stood rooted to the spot – but mercifully no black bombs fell from the planes.

Her window looked out over flat countryside to the far-off vicinity of the aerodrome. As bombers droned in the distance, she didn't hear explosions but saw a crimson glow spread the sky from fires below.

Shaken, Frieda drew the curtains and crept back into bed, pulling the blanket up around her neck. Staring into the darkness, scenes played again in her mind's eye of the night at home in Berlin when she'd listened to the horrifying events outside. She relived the acrid smells of raging fires, the screams from the street down below and crescendo of falling glass as windows broke.

At times like this in the apartment in Berlin when she couldn't sleep, Frieda would creep into her parents' bed and the security of Mama's arms. But Mama was gone, as were the rest of the family, and Frieda's mind shied away from the thought as to where they might be.

The last time she'd had these worrying thoughts, she'd decided to ask the nice curate if he knew about these camps in Germany. She'd even gone to the church the previous Sunday but as she sat in the pew, Frieda realised she couldn't face whatever the truth was of what Jewish families were suffering in Germany. She wanted to keep up the pretence of imagining her family going about their daily lives. This helped ease her conscience and ward off the guilt and shame she felt for not looking after her little brother and leaving him behind when he'd jumped ship in Holland.

The next day, after Aunty Doris had locked the door to the post office, the pair of them sat at the table eating tea. Bleary-eyed having been kept awake by last night's raid, she seemed to be watching Frieda like a hawk while she ate.

Frieda toyed with the slice of bread in her hand, wondering how she could get rid of it.

'You need to eat. It's not right that a young lass like you should be lolling about the house listening to the wireless every night, then be in bed before nine. That's what old people do.' A look of remorse crossed Aunty Doris's expression. She shook her head in exasperation. 'I'm sorry, pet, for being so sharp, but it's because I'm worried about you.'

Frieda accepted that her aunt's annoyance was born out of frustration and that she was responsible. She felt ashamed that there was nothing she could do as, these days, the thought of food obsessed her – not what she ate but how to avoid eating in front of others.

Frieda did worry about what she was doing to herself. She tried to think what to eat to give her body the sustenance and energy she so desperately needed without putting weight on. Her body was exhausted to the point that even doing the most mundane activities was taxing. Since she'd left school, she'd begun working at the Nichols' farm, but she found milking the cows such an effort.

Tea today was bread and the dripping from yesterday's Sunday joint – made especially to titillate her appetite.

Aunty Doris, apparently unable to sit still, stood and took her empty plate over to the sink.

Desperate to rid herself of the food in her hand, Frieda squished the soft bread with its crisp crust and dropped it on the floor. Taking a white handkerchief out of her slacks pocket, she bent over and covered the bread. She was just about to pop the handkerchief package in her pocket when the eerie silence in the room made her look up.

Aunty Doris, arms folded, stood watching her. A worried frown creased her brow. 'Lass' – her tone was weary – 'what are we going to do with you? I've never heard the like before, starving yourself till you're so skinny the clothes hang off your body.' Her chin quivered but she quickly recovered.

Frieda felt bad for causing her aunt distress. But when she looked in the mirror all she saw was a fat waistline and big hips.

Aunty Doris continued, 'I don't usually give a damn what people think but folk are starting to comment and I'm worried they think I'm not feeding you properly. The authorities might take you away.'

A cold shiver ran down Frieda's spine. She'd grown to love her over the years. She was kindness itself and the thought of losing her new aunt as well as her family terrified Frieda. But the wilful voice inside that ruled her life and didn't allow her to eat wouldn't give in – even for Aunty Doris.

How could she explain, when she didn't even understand why she had this starving problem? All she wanted was to be normal and eat without thinking. Frieda despised herself. For when it came to food, she'd turned into this secretive deceiver and barefaced liar.

'How about we go to see Doctor Shepherd?' Aunty Doris, ever diligent over her responsibility towards Frieda, appeared to know her very thoughts. 'Maybe he'll know what to do.'

Frieda desperately wanted to change as she knew she must be damaging herself, but she couldn't ignore the powerful will that seemed to take over. Perhaps she should give the doctor a try. She did want to conquer this dread of eating, didn't she?

She looked Aunty Doris in the eye and nodded.

Her aunt gave a relieved sigh. 'We'll go to the surgery tomorrow after work.'

As they sat waiting in the queue at the surgery in the basement of Doctor Shepherd's house, Frieda regretted her decision. She would rather have a broken leg or disfiguring spots on her face like some boys had at school, than what troubled her. She was afraid Doctor Shepherd would class her insane and have her put away.

She was distracted from her thoughts as Doctor Shepherd hurried out of his surgery, black bag in his hand. Without looking up he rushed out of the basement doorway and up the outside flight of stairs.

'An emergency call,' Betty, the nurse who came out of the surgery's disinfectant-smelling dispensary, told the waiting queue.

After three quarters of an hour, the doctor returned and resumed his surgery.

When it was their turn to be seen, Frieda took a seat on one side of his large inlaid desk, Aunty Doris next to her.

Doctor Shepherd was elderly-looking, with grey hair and a bald patch on top of his head, and wore a black suit. Aunty Doris waited until the doctor had finished writing and looked up, before she said, with an anxious face, 'As you can see, doctor, Frieda's lost a lot of weight. I'm at me wits' end what to do. There's nothing physically wrong with her but she just won't eat. She's becoming skin and bone.'

Both Doctor Shepherd and her aunt stared at Frieda and she felt like a specimen in a glass bottle they used at school.

He sat back in his chair and, resting his hands on his chest, entwined his fingers. His expression looked faintly amused. 'Now then, what's all this about? You must eat to stay healthy.' He went on to tell her the benefit of certain foods and recommended she drink milk for healthy bones.

Frieda saw that Aunty Doris was getting irritated, but didn't interrupt the doctor. For like the clergy, doctors were held in high respect.

'So, enough of this nonsense,' he finally ended. 'Do you promise to be sensible and eat properly?' Doctor Shepherd raised an eyebrow.

To please him, Frieda nodded.

The consultation finished, Aunty Doris stood up, her expression bemused as she made for the door. Frieda followed.

'Frieda,' the doctor called from his chair, 'remember, boys prefer a girl to have a bit of beef on them.'

Aunty Doris tutted in fury and slammed the door.

'Well, are you going to keep your word and eat?' Aunty Doris wanted to know as she closed the doctor's front garden gate and they started to make their way home.

Frieda studied the stream gurgling beyond in the allotments. She wanted desperately to say yes to make her aunt happy but the voice, still objecting, was firm. *You'll get grossly fat.*

An idea struck her. She could find out which foods didn't put weight on and give that a try.

'I will try,' she hedged.

Aunty Doris let out a sigh of relief. 'Then I suppose the visit to that old fool was worth it in the end.'

CHAPTER TEN

Sandra

As time went by, Sandra fell into the drudgery of doing kitchen duties and serving up meals at the hatch. She hardly ever saw the other lasses as by the time she'd finished tidying up after the evening meal, most of the others had gone to bed. She felt alienated, and not at all like a proper Land Girl.

The day was one long round of chores that started at half five in the morning when Sandra washed, dressed and folded her blanket on the bed. She felt like she was back in the orphanage. At quarter to six she knocked on bedroom doors to waken everyone and then she rang the bell at six o'clock for breakfast. Sandra helped Mrs Parsons, the kindly but demanding cook, make cheese or beetroot sandwiches for the Land Girls to take to their respective farms for a makeshift dinner, and prepared and served breakfast at the hatch for those who wanted it. Breakfast at the hostel rarely deviated from lumpy porridge and a slice of fried bread. Land Girls who helped with milking left earlier and had breakfast later at the farm when the work was done.

There was a roster for mealtime duties and one of the eight girls that sat at each table waited on the others, then helped wash the dishes after the meal. The common room was always filled with either tired or high-pitched, excitable voices – depending on the time of day – and Sandra, rather envious, wished hers was one of them.

Her working day was spent clearing and tidying the common room and kitchen, cleaning the bathroom and toilets, scraping vegetables, then helping Mrs Parsons organise and cook the evening meal. Generally this was meat stew, potatoes and greens, followed by milk pudding or the favourite suet pudding and custard. The Land Girls were always starved after working in the fresh air.

At six thirty, after they all returned, Sandra rang the bell for the evening meal. When the dishes were done, she again tidied the kitchen and common room, washed the pantry floor and set tables for the morning. Finally, Mrs Sanderson came to inspect and after a nod of approval, Sandra, exhausted, was only fit to collapse into bed.

Mrs Parsons told Sandra one morning, as she stirred a pan of porridge, 'Living in the country is a different world to what you're used to. My sister is a townie like you and she's only got a concrete back yard. How, may I ask, can she dig for victory like the ministry wants?'

Thin but wiry, Cook was one of those women of indeterminate age. She liked nothing better than to talk while she worked.

She clicked her tongue in annoyance. 'Would you believe, the Nichols up at the farm have to apply for permission to the local Ministry of Agriculture offices for permission to slaughter a pig? You'd be surprised how many pigs have accidents in the area.' She chortled. 'But you have to watch out 'cos the powers that be have eyes everywhere. I read in the local paper someone was brought before the magistrate's court for pinching food from a scrap bin for the pigs. Poor soul, they must've been starved.' Sandra surreptitiously smiled because Cook entertained her with her gossiping.

Sometimes, Cook told Sandra to take the scraps along the road to the Nichols' farm during her dinner break. 'In the hope we'll get some of the end result when a pig's slaughtered,' she cackled, reminding Sandra of her dear friend Olive.

Though the Nichols' farm was a good stretch of the legs along the main road, Sandra found it therapeutic to be out in the fresh air. Carrying the sack and avoiding the cowpats on the path leading to the farmhouse, she went to the back garden and emptied the sack of scraps into the bin.

Making her way back to the hostel, Sandra passed fields where diminutive figures in the distance helped with lambing. Sandra wished she was working alongside them. They were doing a vital job like the posters said, to help feed the nation. While Sandra was… just a skivvy slaving in the kitchen in a job any numbskull could do.

'You're such a bore,' Evelyn, yawning, had told her one night as they were getting ready for bed after Sandra had complained about her lot working in the hostel kitchen. The others were still in the common room, so they had the bedroom to themselves. 'You'll be telling me next you ending up in the kitchen is to do with people looking down on you.' Evelyn folded her jersey and laid it on the bed. 'Don't you realise you're as good as the next? It's believing it that counts.'

Sandra realised with shock that what Evelyn said was true; she was still convinced that she couldn't do anything right.

'Though, I should talk,' Evelyn went on. 'I've always felt second best to my eldest brother. Eddy is the son and heir and can do no wrong. And he's a scoundrel, especially where girls are concerned. He gets away with it because he's only, according to Daddy, sowing wild oats.' Evelyn snorted. 'If I acted the same way I'd be sent to a convent sharpish. The thing that gets me is I'm not allowed ambition because apparently, education is wasted on girls.'

Sandra was amazed at Evelyn's confession. She assumed that Evelyn, with her strength of character, could do anything she wanted and with her family's approval.

'I bet you think you're in the kitchen helping Cook because of your working-class Geordie accent or some such thing.'

Sandra did.

'Has it never occurred to you it's purely because your previous employment was on your application and mentioned in your interview? It's because you're so experienced that they'll have decided you're best suited in the kitchen where you're proficient.'

Sandra hadn't thought of this.

'Whereas, well… I have to prove myself because, as far as the locals are concerned, I'm just a spoiled good-for-nothing townie who is frightened to get her nails dirty.'

This was news to Sandra. That someone like Evelyn, who came from the middle classes, had problems asserting herself in life.

'If you're not careful, you'll end up an inverted snob… and in my book that basically means scorning someone just because you consider them posh.'

Sandra flushed. Her friend was right.

'The thing is' – Evelyn's tone changed, became gentler –, 'we all have choices and what you decide makes you the person you are. I'm going to prove to Dad and those cynical locals they're wrong. I'm intelligent and strong and can pull my weight. While you… what you can do is simply to tell Jessie you're not happy and you'd prefer working on a farm. She's an understanding sort under that tough exterior.'

So, taking Evelyn's advice, that's what Sandra had done.

'Have you trained at agriculture college?' Jessie wanted to know when Sandra, hesitantly, had requested she work on a farm.

'No. Should I have?'

Jessie shrugged. 'It's a four-week course that incoming Land Girls are required to do.'

If that was the case, Sandra thought, she was destined to work in the kitchen forever.

Jessie shrugged, resignedly. 'The reality is for most of the recruits in Northumberland, training is a rarity. They have to make do with the farmer or his foreman to show them the drill. And usually that never happens either.'

'So, how do I get trained?'

'You'll learn as you go along.' Jessie smiled and winked.

A few days later, after breakfast, Sandra stood with the rest of the Land Girls outside the hostel where a hazy moon, sailing across the sky, shed the only light. She was wearing dungarees, a jerkin, and a turban-like scarf covered her hair. She carried a yellow waterproof and sandwiches in a bait tin.

Jessie stood in front of them. A robust woman, she appeared to be bursting out of her clothes. 'Those of you already allotted work on a farm, off you go.'

A group of Land Girls made off to the bicycle shed and were seen, cloaked in the half light, to pedal their way along the earthen path. Sandra had never learnt to ride a bicycle and she worried it might hinder her travelling to work.

Jessie continued, 'The Ministry of Ag has sent notice they need a gang up at Tyler's farm.' She peered into the semi-darkness and called out some of the girls' names. 'You six know where it is, you've been there before.'

'What's ahead?' one of them asked.

'Clearing fields.'

'Of stones?'

'Correct.'

There were groans.

'What does that mean?' Sandra asked Ruby, who stood next to her. Ruby Todd slept in the opposite bunk bed. She came from Sunderland and Sandra felt an affiliation because the lass was northern.

'They'll toil all day picking stones and filling buckets and then probably they'll chuck them the other side of the farmer's field.'

'Why's that?'

'A stony field means the ploughshares get destroyed. Picking stones is a soul-destroying, back-breaking job of work made a hundred times worse if it's raining. I'm glad it's not me.'

Sandra thought the same. 'What's a ploughshare?'

Jessie, hearing the conversation, piped up. 'Blimey! Save me from townies. It's the main cutting blade behind the plough.'

There was a lot of activity as farmers arrived in cars or sent lorries to pick up Land Girls to work on the farm. When all the vehicles had left, only Sandra, Evelyn and a girl called Enid – who had long manicured nails and wore a hint of lipstick – were left standing. A forlorn group, they stood waiting until an old Morris car came up the earthen path and the shadowy figure of a famer loomed from the front seat and came striding over. He peered at Sandra and she smelt stale, beery breath.

He bellowed to Jessie, 'Is yon lassies all that's left?'

'It is.'

He pointed with the stick he carried to Evelyn and Enid. 'I'll have to make do with you two.'

The car made off with the two girls in the back and Sandra, the only one left, felt rather dejected – and yet relieved.

Jessie told her, 'Take one of the bicycles and get yourself to the Nichols' byre. They have a device you can use to learn how to milk cows. I'd show you but I've got to check on a gang planting seedlings.'

'I can't ride a bike.'

'Then walk. You've got legs.'

The morning was cold and the sky, with its orange glow on the horizon, shed enough light to see dew sparkling on the grass and dandelions growing in the hedgerows. These April days were deceiving – sunny and bright one minute but the threat of lambing storms when the skies darkened the next.

Sandra walked along the country road past the village until she reached the opening that led to the Nichols' farm. Making her way up the track, she passed the peaked roof farmhouse with its white front porch that looked over the main road to the fields beyond, all owned by the Nichols. She continued past the back garden where washing hung on the line. A dungy smell Sandra now associated with the area permeated the air. Making her way to a sprawling shed covered by a tin roof, she could hear cows mooing.

Inside, by the light of hurricane lamps, her eyes acclimatised to the scene before her. Cows, tails swishing, were tethered to stalls either side of the passageway. They looked huge and Sandra was wary as she'd never seen a cow this close up before. The stalls were raised with a channel running in front filled with cows' muck and urine. The reek of cattle manure made Sandra wrinkle her nose.

An old man with an unlit clay pipe dangling from his mouth sat on a three-legged stool milking a cow, while a ruddy-faced man with an air of authority stood talking to him. The man who stood sighed and shook his head in a burdened sort of way.

Sandra looked in the next stall and her eyes widened in surprise. Sitting on a three-legged stool milking a cow was the girl Sandra had bumped into at the local church the other Sunday.

The ruddy-faced man, thickset, with muscled arms protruding from the sleeves of his checked shirt, walked towards her.

'Bob Nichol.' He gave a curt nod. 'The hostel sent you?'

'Yes. I'm Sandra.'

Mr Nichol looked her up and down. 'You been on a farm before?'

'This is the first time.'

He heaved a laboured sigh. 'You'll be from the town I expect?'

'I am.'

He pulled a disgruntled face.

A sense of not being good enough washed over Sandra. Her confidence dipped and she was transported back to her time with the Kirtons – a dogsbody. Then she remembered the new life she was making for herself. She was in the WLA and proud to be doing a vital job.

She pulled back her shoulders. 'I'm here to work,' she reminded her apparent employer.

'It was yesterday I needed help when Antonio didn't show.' The timbre of the farmer's voice held a strong Northumbrian burr. 'Have you been shown how to milk?'

Stiffening at his attitude, Sandra shook her head. 'No.'

With an air of impatience, Mr Nichol scowled at Sandra as if all his ills were her fault. He rolled his eyes. 'Then why have they sent you? I haven't the time for novices.'

'To learn,' she volunteered.

Mr Nichol nodded at Sandra. 'See that?' He pointed to the other end of the byre where a contraption of make-believe udders filled with water hung across a beam that was between two wooden uprights.

'You can practise on that. Frieda,' he called to the girl in the stall, 'you can show her.'

He turned and made his way back to the old man.

The girl stood and, removing a bucket from beneath the cow she was milking, placed it outside the stall. She moved into the passageway between the stalls, gesturing for Sandra to follow. Passing the cows' huge hindquarters and aware of their swishing tails, Sandra felt the hairs on her neck stand up. The animals were enormous. *What if they break loose? Or kick out?* The urge to flee overcame her but she told herself to buck up. She meant to prove herself and make a success of the job.

Past the stalls now, the girl turned and addressed her. 'How d'you do? I'm Frieda. I've only been here a few weeks.'

She spoke with the same unique accent Sandra had noticed during their first encounter at the church. Sandra took in her slight figure and pale but attractive face and wondered if the lass was unwell.

Frieda sat down on a stool and, picking up a galvanised bucket, clasped it between her knees. She stretched out her arm and grasped a fake teat. 'This is how milking is done.'

Sandra watched for a while and then had a go herself.

Once Sandra seemed to get the hang of it, Frieda told her, 'I have to get on.'

After an hour, Sandra's fingers, forearms and wrists ached and all she had to show for her effort was no more than a thimbleful of water.

She despaired as yet another squirt of water missed the bucket and hit the byre floor.

'Real thing's trickier.' Sandra turned and looked into Mr Nichol's woebegone expression. 'If that there was milk' – he eyed the puddle of water on the floor – 'it would do a family for a day.'

Sandra hadn't thought of it that way and accepted she must try harder. She made to grasp the udder.

'Not now, lass.' Mr Nichol gave an exasperated shake of the head. 'You'll be far more use up at house giving Mother a hand with the workers' dinner. I'll help here.'

Did she have *I'm no better than a skivvy* written on her forehead? Sandra wondered. In that moment Sandra questioned the wisdom of leaving the cosy kitchen with the good-natured cook. She'd heard gossip from the lasses as they gathered at night around the supper table about how some farmers and labourers treated Land Girls. Apparently, they thought lasses were incapable of doing a man's job and gave them menial tasks around the farm. Their dander up, the Land Girls set out to prove the biased farmers wrong. Sandra remembered the earlier conversation with Evelyn, when she'd said people's choices affected their lives.

So, her chin jutting, she told the farmer, 'I'm not a housemaid. I've been sent to work on the farm.'

Mr Nichol looked at her in surprise. Taking off his cap, he scratched his head. 'I never said you was.' His eyes twinkled. 'I like a bit of spunk in a lass… Mother was the same way when she was your age.' Then, as though he'd said too much and time was of the essence, his attitude changed. 'After the milking's done, help clean up. The muck is to be tipped in the midden, pigs are to be fed and cleaned out, stables mucked out and, if you've time after that, I can find yi' plenty more work… on the farm.' A hint of a grin played on his lips.

Whistling a tune, he marched up to a stall and sat on a three-legged stool.

Sandra felt she'd passed some kind of test.

The milking done, Sandra's forearms and fingers ached like mad from practising. She stood in the byre doorway watching the old man, the clay pipe still dangling from his mouth, herding the cows head to tail up the uneven track towards the gate and the field beyond.

'That's Mr Jeffries,' Frieda said. 'He lives in the village. He only works here when Mr Nichol needs an extra pair of hands. He's been here all the time since I've started.'

She went on to explain what happened once the cows were milked.

The milk had been poured over a cooler contraption and put into ten-gallon galvanised churns which stood at the bottom of the track at the farmhouse gate waiting to be collected, apparently, by a Co-op society lorry that, according to Frieda, would take it to the dairy in a place called Stocksfield.

Frieda then showed Sandra how to hose the cow shed and sterilise the milking equipment.

'What's next?'

'Breakfast at the farmhouse if you want.'

'Are you going?'

Frieda shook her head. 'It is porridge and I've already had some.'

Sandra, although always ready to eat, decided to skip traipsing to the house where she didn't know anyone or what to expect.

'Where's Mr Nichol?'

Sandra wasn't afraid of the farmer exactly, but in her short lifetime she'd learnt to treat all figures of authority with respect. They had the means to change life in a heartbeat.

'Out with the horse and cart delivering milk to villagers.'

'Are his moods always so changeable?

Frieda shrugged. 'Mr Nichol speaks his mind,' she said non-committally. 'He's always been good and fair with me.'

Sandra felt there was more that Frieda wasn't telling.

Being with Frieda, who was also reticent, brought Sandra out of herself. Determined to make Frieda talk, she leant on the handle of the sweeping brush she was carrying and enquired, 'What's your full name?'

Frieda brushed a strand of black hair behind an ear. 'Frieda Sternberg.'

'What accent is that?'

'German.' Frieda looked unsure, as if she expected a reaction. She went on, as if preventing any further comment on the subject, 'Normally, Antonio mucks the stables out. He helps the horseman, apart from doing other jobs around the farm.'

'Antonio?'

Frieda's features softened and she gave a shy smile before responding. 'He is a prisoner from the camp in Ponteland. He comes from the island of Sardinia and was captured with his platoon by the British in Tobruk. He's never fired a shot at the enemy,' she put in as if to prove Antonio was a decent man. 'He was sent to England by boat as a prisoner.'

She appeared to know a lot about this Antonio, Sandra surmised, having noticed the sparkle that came into the lass's eyes when she spoke about him. 'How does he get to work?'

'Mr Nichol phones the Ministry offices in Hexham when he needs help and Antonio is dropped off by lorry the next morning, then collected at night. Only he didn't arrive yesterday or this morning.'

The nosy side of Sandra longed to ask Frieda about herself, why she was here and where she lived. But she held back, knowing that she too would be reluctant to share her past with a stranger. She would make do with being friendly. She had warmed to this young German girl. Instinctively, Sandra knew there was a story behind Frieda's reserved manner.

'Frieda, can I be truthful?' The girl looked nervous. 'I'm new to all this. A townie. Could you help show me the ropes? I mean, tell me what's expected as I don't have a clue.'

A smile – of relief? – split Frieda's face, then, her expression turning thoughtful, she said, 'As I told you I am quite new here myself. I live at the post office with my… I think the word is… substitute… aunt and she encouraged me to work here after I left school. I too had to practise milking cows on that.' She pointed to the contraption where the rubber dangled from the beam. How silly it looked.

Merriment bubbled within Sandra, sparked by relief that she'd found someone she could relate to, and she burst out laughing. Frieda hesitated, then, as though a bolt of understanding struck her, eyes sparkling, shoulders shaking, the lass joined in the hilarity.

When the laughter had subsided, Frieda told Sandra, 'Don't worry, I will show you these ropes.'

'I must say, Frieda, you have an excellent command of English.'

A shadow seemed to fall on the lass. 'I got… teased is the word?' Sandra nodded. 'At school… so then I learnt to speak perfect English.'

Sandra knew by Frieda's solemn expression there was more to it, but she decided not to pursue the matter in case it upset her.

*

The rest of the morning was spent traipsing after Frieda around the farmyard and Sandra was glad of the wellingtons she'd been supplied with. She filled the pig trough with a bucketful of small potatoes. A rather scary job as she worried the huge, coarse-skinned creatures might knock her over in a frantic scramble to get the food.

As Sandra watched the snuffling pigs eat their food, she thought they probably ate better than half the population. Then, thinking of the end result, she averted her eyes guiltily as she changed the straw in their sleeping quarters. Lastly came the job of mucking out the stables. Tired and worn out after a morning's work, Sandra finished by collecting eggs from the hen house.

At one o'clock, dinner time, the two girls stood on a fenced-off piece of land, hen houses surrounding them. Hens clucked and walked in that peculiar stiff, head-jabbing way. A lone plane soared low overhead and two geese spreading their wings let out an ear-piercing screech and gave Sandra such a fright.

Shading her eyes with a hand, she saw the plane was a Lancaster. 'It's one of ours.'

Frieda let out a sigh of relief. 'Thank goodness.' She nodded to the eggs she carried in a bowl in her arms. 'I'll take these up to the house.'

'Are we allowed in the farmhouse for dinner?' It was nippy outside, and Sandra didn't fancy eating in the byre.

'Mrs Nichol provides soup for the workers but she won't spare any tea.'

Sandra wasn't surprised. Loose tea was a prized commodity and the weekly allowance was only four ounces.

'The hostel provides sandwiches and cold tea,' Sandra told Frieda as she followed her up the field. 'A bowl of hot soup would be sorely appreciated. How about you?'

Frieda's body tensed. 'I... You go on without me.' She turned and handed the bowl of eggs over to Sandra. Without another word Frieda made her way to the top of the field then hurried out of sight around the side of the farmhouse.

Taken aback, Sandra watched her go. With her slight figure and bony wrists and ankles it looked as though a gust of wind would blow her away.

Sandra thought of her mother who, with her poverty-stricken life, had been the same way. She fervently hoped the lass wouldn't suffer the same fate. But why, if Frieda was starved, would she refuse a bowl of warming soup?

CHAPTER ELEVEN

'Take your wellies off or you'll have Mother after you.' Mr Nichol greeted her at the farmhouse back door.

Sandra removed her wellingtons and left them upside down on the rack outside with the rest, then stepped inside, bait tin in hand.

Mr Nichol went over to the sink and, turning on the cold-water tap, began washing his hands.

Two farm labourers in dungarees sat at a sturdy-legged table in the middle of the room where more places were set. Unsure what to do, Sandra surveyed the large cluttered kitchen with its stone floor and meagre fire in the range by the far wall, a black-and-white collie curled in front of it. The dark wood dresser standing in an alcove was messy with ornaments, papers and photographs. Sandra inched forward to take a better look.

'That's me lad, Wilf.' Mr Nichol, drying his hands on a cloth, approached, following her gaze. 'He didn't want to stay on the farm and couldn't wait to do his bit for the war.' His chest expanded. 'That's Nichol men for you. Won't shirk when duty calls. Least, that's what I keep telling Mother.'

At that moment a woman scurried in, an efficient air about her. She darted to the range and stirred a pan on the hob. With grey hair and a forehead riddled with worry lines, she was a head shorter than Mr Nichol.

'How many times have I told you, Mother? There's no rush. That heart of yours won't stand for it.'

She turned, a wooden spoon in her hand. 'It's you harping on about me heart I can't stand. You cause me palpitations.'

Mr Nichol shook his head. He turned to Sandra. 'Meet the wife, who' – he stared pointedly at Mrs Nichol – 'no matter what the doctor says, denies she should look after her dicky heart.'

Comprehension dawned on Sandra. 'Your wife?' Sandra spoke without thinking.

'Silly old fool…' Though Mrs Nichol looked scornfully at her husband, Sandra detected a fondness in her tone. 'Still calls me Mother, long after our lad's grown and… left home.' Her voice faltered.

Mr Nichol, with a concerned look, said quickly, 'We're mighty proud of him, aren't we, Mother?'

The woman shook the wooden spoon at him. 'You, with your talk of how we won the Great War… It spurred that lad on and the farm wasn't enough for him any more.'

There was an awkward pause before Mr Nichol said, 'Let's not start that again, Mother, we have company here.'

The workmen sitting at the table were listening, agog.

Mrs Nichol looked Sandra up and down. 'Sit yourself down, you make the place look untidy.'

Sandra knew from the lasses' chatter at the hostel that farmers' wives could be prejudiced against Land Girls. 'They're worried we might steal their husbands,' Ruby Todd had whispered to Sandra one night in the dark when neither of them could sleep. 'Fat chance. The old farmer I worked with today was old with yella teeth and a beer belly. Ugh!' Sandra inwardly smiled at the memory.

She volunteered, 'I've brought sandwiches.' Part of her wished she'd stayed in the cowshed, anywhere rather than here, to eat them.

'Why? Isn't my soup good enough?'

'Of course. I just didn't realise you'd provide lunch.'

'Now, Mother, don't take your frustration with me out on the lassie here. Just think, it'll save on bread.'

'Hmm!'

While Mrs Nichol began ladling the soup into bowls, her husband surreptitiously winked at Sandra.

The kitchen door opened and Mr Jeffries walked in and, with a nod to both the Nichols, he took his cap off and sat down at the table.

'You locked the gate in the field, Joe?'

Joe Jeffries – as Sandra thought of him now – looked affronted. *He must be forgetful,* she thought.

'I have. You know I always do.'

'Except that time the bull got out,' Mrs Nichol added.

The two workmen guffawed as they sat down at the table and the collie padded over to sit by the side of his master's chair.

'No point in opening old wounds,' Mr Nichol consoled.

Mrs Nichol put their soup in front of them. By the grim look on the woman's face, she didn't like to be corrected.

'Jim, Ralph,' Mr Nichol addressed the two workmen, 'this here is Sandra Hudson.' He turned towards Sandra. 'They're labourers come to help with lambing.'

Introductions over, Sandra ate the thin chicken soup. Silence reigned in the room, apart from slurps of soup.

'Where does Frieda go for dinner?' she blurted, unable to bear the quiet any longer.

The Nichols looked up and then at one another.

'There goes a mystery,' Mr Nichol volunteered. 'Mother thought she might go back to the post office for a bite to eat with Doris but on further investigation that isn't the case.'

He took a thick slice of homemade bread from the plate and spread butter on it. Sandra marvelled at how in the countryside food wasn't a main preoccupation. All her life – at home with Mam and Alf, then the orphanage and even with the Kirtons in town with the war on – food had been an obsession. She took a mouthful of sandwich, gazing longingly at the dish of butter that she hadn't tasted in months as at the hostel they made do with margarine.

His cheek bulging with bread, Mr Nichol told them, 'When I delivered the milk, Doris said she'd taken the girl to see Doctor Shepherd but he was useless. Apparently, the lassie won't eat and Doris is worried sick.' He shook his head. 'The lassie's probably fretting about her family in Germany.'

Mr Jeffries spoke up. 'She's as thin as a chip. Half the village are talking about her. I wouldn't have thought in this modern day a lass would want to look that skinny. I mean all the pin-ups – Betty Grable, Rita Hayworth – have hips on them.' The workmen looked at him incredulously. He was defensive. 'I go to Hexham pictures now and then.'

'Nobody is asking you, Joe.' Mrs Nichol, as though she'd heard enough, stood up. 'As for you' – she glowered at her husband – 'kindly don't speak with your mouth full. And what happens at the post office is none of our business.'

'You were only just saying how we should encourage the lassie…'

'It was a private conversation, Bob.' Mrs Nichol collected the soup bowls.

'Didn't you say in this war we have to look after—'

'No more, I tell you.'

Mr Nichol stared at his wife in bafflement. He stood up and took the bowls from her. 'Let me help you with those.'

Sandra rose to go, wondering if avoiding food was the only reason Frieda didn't eat at the farmhouse.

Mr Jeffries brought the cows in again that afternoon. As they followed their leader into the cowshed, Sandra marvelled at their beefiness and deep cherry red colour. She noticed their engorged udders and wondered if they were painful.

She went back to the pretend udders. Her fingers ached like blazes and only a thimbleful of water at the bottom of the bucket was to show for her effort.

Then the morning's routine was repeated. The cows milked, floor scrubbed and swilled, muck taken to the midden.

When they'd finished, Frieda turned to Sandra. 'Antonio isn't here…' She paused, then blushed before quickly carrying on. 'So our last job of the day is to groom the horses.'

Sandra noticed the awkward expression when the lass mentioned the Italian's name, as if she had something to hide.

Frieda also looked done in, and so was Sandra, for that matter. She'd worked a ten-hour day and was so overtired the thought of horses felt like a step too far. It was one thing to see horses at a distance as they'd clip-clopped by in the cobbled street; to be only a hair's breadth away from them was something that Sandra could do without. But she was a Land Girl, she reminded herself, this was her job. She recalled the talk at the hostel about farmers being scathing about women doing a man's job.

Sandra, like the rest of the Land Girls, would prove them wrong.

'Let's go,' she told Frieda.

Later, on her way back to the hostel, the late sun was setting, making the vast scene of countryside look like some glorious painting. The wind softly ruffled Sandra's hair and she was filled with a sense of wellbeing. She whistled a tune like she'd heard Mr Jeffries do when he took the cows back to the field.

Before leaving the farm, Sandra had looked for Frieda. She wanted to thank the lass for all the help on her first day, but she wasn't to be found.

Sandra wondered about Frieda's life in Germany. Why was her family not here with her? Sandra remembered that earlier in the war Mr Kirton had mentioned something about Jewish children being evacuated from Germany. Maybe this was the reason Frieda was here. Poor lass, no wonder she didn't want to talk about her home life. Sandra made a mental note never to press her.

Later, back at the hostel, after being the third one in the same bath water, which barely covered Sandra's buttocks, she found Evelyn sprawled on the bottom bunk in their bedroom. Already changed from her work clothes into her dress uniform ready for supper, she was reading a copy of *The Land Girl* magazine.

The room was empty, apart from Ruby who was busy collecting toiletries to go into the bath.

'How was your first day?' Evelyn wanted to know.

'Not so bad.'

Before Sandra could go into details, Evelyn pulled an expression of disgust.

'So much for posters of carefree, smiling Land Girls carrying fluffy lambs. My first job of the day was hoeing rows of turnip seedlings until my back ached. The farm labourers were there and I refused to let it show. That was mild compared to what came next.'

'Why? What did you have to do?'

'I think the menfolk might have set me up, but who knows.' Evelyn made a face. 'I helped castrate a pig.'

'What?'

'You know, cut off his male thingies.'

Sandra was horrified, but laughed at the description. 'Goodness. I don't know if I want to hear the details.'

'Suffice to say it involved me holding a can of Jeyes Fluid and the man doing the deed with a sharp knife, then blood everywhere and pigs squealing.'

'Ugh! Enough.'

'I never winced. Though, I did go rather jittery and thought I was going to faint. It was the expectation in the pig man's eyes as he looked at me that kept me strong.'

Sandra was truly impressed at Evelyn's nerve, and told her so. Being frightened of cows and horses paled into insignificance.

Evelyn laid the magazine down on the bed. 'Daddy reckoned I won't last long here.' A stubborn look crossed her face. 'I'm determined to prove him wrong and that I'm as good as any man.'

A sudden surge of empathy for Evelyn washed over her. Even if she did come from a comfortable background, Evelyn had problems to contend with. Sandra decided she wasn't keen on Evelyn's father. By escaping to become a Land Girl, Evelyn was showing her dad she had grit. Good for her.

Evelyn picked up the magazine. 'By the way, did you see you've got a letter?'

Letters were left on an occasional table in the corridor and Sandra usually checked when she went by.

Sandra rushed to the corridor. Only one letter lay on the table; picking it up, Sandra recognised Alf's handwriting. Back in the bedroom, she placed the letter surreptitiously, while Evelyn was reading, in the lockable wooden box beneath her bed. Although she liked Evelyn and considered her a friend, Sandra felt too shy to tell her about her illiteracy.

But all through the evening meal of rabbit stew, and later, as she only half-listened to the group of lasses who sat around the stove, rage simmered inside Sandra. Here she was with a precious letter from Alf and she couldn't read the damn thing. Unlike Evelyn, who came from a family with the means to send their children to a private school and university. She was ignorant, but through no fault of her own. Oblivious now to the chatter all around, Sandra admitted to herself her stupidity, that she hadn't known there was such a thing as universities until Evelyn told her.

She saw Evelyn watching her over a few girls' heads, with a concerned expression. 'Are you all right?' she mouthed.

Sandra nodded, abashed. The lass could no more help her heritage than Sandra, and they were both products of their past. Sandra sighed in disgust; she'd had enough of this self-pitying attitude. She should take a leaf out of Evelyn's book and let nothing stand in the way of achieving what she wanted.

A memory emerged from the distant past – what Dad had said when he put the necklace with the stainless-steel identity disc around her and Alf's necks. 'You're master of your own destiny, always remember that.'

At the time she hadn't fully understood what he meant.

With sadness she realised she'd never really known her father, his thoughts on matters, whether he was angry at serving in the war that left him unable to provide for his young family. Sandra remembered that Dad always had his nose in a book. She could never ask why he hadn't taught her to read. She realised her parents were a mystery to her. What had their family life been like? How was their childhood spent? All their experience was gone, buried with them in the grave, and Sandra had no one to ask.

Her attention gradually tuned in to the voices around her. One of the lasses was relating her day.

'...Wait till you've cut thistles with a G-bow stick... It was no joke, I'm telling you. Afterwards, Damson the horse was frightened to go through gates and nearly tipped the cart. What a palaver. The clever dick farm labourer said this was Damson's way and if I didn't want to be thrown on my backside, I'd have to lead the damn horse through the gate myself.'

Laughter followed and the room was filled with a happy atmosphere of camaraderie. Sandra liked this crowd of lasses, she decided. Though whacked from a heavy working day, they still had time for each other and were always ready for a laugh. It felt like they were all part of the same... family.

A warm sensation spread through Sandra's chest.

She was fed up with taking a back seat in life. In future, she'd involve herself more with what went on here. Even more importantly, she resolved, she would educate herself and learn how to read and write. After the war was done Sandra could, perhaps, become a teacher – she'd ensure that every child she taught would become literate so that they would be prepared for the future.

Sandra gave Evelyn a friendly smile. She wondered who she could ask to teach her to read and write, to enable her for the future.

An idea formed in Sandra's mind.

'It's not fair,' Sandra heard Ruby say as the lass entered the bedroom, 'I'm being penalised because I'm not going home this weekend.'

'Why aren't you, by the way?' Evelyn asked as she followed Ruby in.

It was six o'clock on the last Friday night in April and Sandra, lying on the top bunk, was waiting for supper time. The two Land Girls, just out of the bath, had skimpy towels wrapped around them.

Ruby went on, ''Cos Mam and Dad are in Yorkshire looking after Grandma; the poor soul's ill. I'd have to do all me own cooking so I decided to stay here where we have it done for us. I was goin' to go to Hexham to buy a dress I'd seen in Robbs department store window. I'd even saved the seven coupons. Now I'll have to wait till next week.'

'I'm not happy about working tomorrow, either,' Evelyn's piqued voice said.

The weekend was supposed to be time off but for those who didn't go home to their families that rarely happened. Cows didn't know it was the weekend and still needed milking so Sandra, who never went away, didn't get time off.

She asked, 'Why, what's happened?'

Evelyn's head appeared as she stood on the lower bunk. 'Jessie collared Ruby and me as we came in from work. She'd heard Ruby wasn't going home this weekend—'

'And knowing I can drive,' Ruby interrupted from the area of her bunk bed, 'I was told to take the van and attend a machinery maintenance course at Berkeley Hall.'

Evelyn groaned. 'I tried to escape but I was told to go with Ruby.'

'The course must be necessary,' Sandra intervened, 'because with the shortage of petrol the hostel van is only used on important occasions.'

Evelyn pulled a disgusted face. 'What is important was my appointment to meet up with a certain sergeant tomorrow afternoon.'

'Ooo! Who is this sergeant?' Ruby, getting dressed, wanted to know.

'He's in charge of the prisoners at the local camp. I met him at the village hall dance last Saturday. You should've come. There were heaps of people, lots of army and RAF.'

Sandra had heard that units from the Welsh and Lancashire Regiments were based at nearby Matfen and in Leadburn. Servicemen were billeted in homes and farms in the area. The Leadburn villagers were accommodating and helped out when they could, opening up their homes and offering tea and warm water for the soldiers to wash and shave. To thank the villagers, servicemen were generous with spare rations from the NAAFI, who were set up in a large tent on the village green.

'The sergeant isn't special. But he's a hoot and jolly to be with.' Evelyn stepped down from the bunk. 'But my heart belongs to another.'

Sandra sat up and swung her legs over the side of the bunk. 'And who might that be?'

'My boyfriend, Gordon, who's overseas. So, you see...' She gave a squinty-eyed grin. 'Daddy is right. My life is mapped out.'

'You've never mentioned this Gordon before.'

'Gordon lives local to me. He's a plumber by trade. I met him at the Theatre Royal. He sat next to me. Daddy wouldn't approve if he knew.'

Before Sandra could answer, Ruby interrupted, 'My Roy's special. He's a local from the village. He hasn't been called up because he's an apprentice at the coal mine. I met him the first week I was here at the local pub. I knew Roy was a gentleman when he stood up to give us his seat... His sister's none too keen on me, though. She never speaks, just glares. Same as his mam. They think I'm gonna spirit Roy off back home to Sunderland... which of course I am.'

While Ruby prattled on about her love life, Sandra's mind wandered. She was determined this Sunday to pluck up the courage to meet with the curate. She planned to ask him to help on her journey towards literacy and the thought filled her with nervous excitement.

CHAPTER TWELVE

Frieda

It was Sunday morning and Frieda surveyed the bedroom from beneath the thick woollen blanket. She slipped from the covers and opened the dense blackout curtains. The sun, rising from the dark tips of the faraway hills, shed radiant crimson light through the sash windowpane.

Frieda was always cold, and even on the warmest of days the sun's rays didn't warm her. Nothing did. Except when she had thoughts of Antonio and then a cosy glow spread through her. She imagined him now, in the tack room, sleeves rolled up, the muscles in his upper arms flexing while he worked.

'Your being so cold is because you've got no meat on your bones,' Aunty Doris had told her.

Collapsing back on the bed, Frieda shivered and pulled the blanket up to her neck. Lying in a dazed stupor, her gaze wandered the room, the only movement she felt capable of. She took in the aged walnut wardrobe and chest of drawers, the floral-patterned wallpaper and the threadbare carpet. She found the familiar surroundings of her room comforting, for they gave a feeling of permanency; the sense that between these four walls everything stayed the same, while the world outside was frighteningly unpredictable.

'Frieda, you know I'm here if you need to talk to someone. It might help,' Aunty Doris had repeatedly told her when she first came to Britain.

Frieda didn't need help. She knew what her problem was and telling anyone wouldn't put it right. She was homesick and pined for her family; she wanted life back to how it was before the troubles began in Germany.

But Frieda felt bad about the worry she was causing Aunty Doris.

'You're like the daughter I never had,' her aunt had once confided when she'd had more than one glass of sherry at Christmas.

Frieda did love Aunty Doris but in a different way to Mama. She belonged to Mama.

Usually, Frieda was obedient. So obedient that when the boat pulled away from the quayside taking her away from Mama to a foreign land, she didn't think to follow Kurt as he ran down the gangway and disappeared.

'Little girls must do as they are told,' Mama had told Frieda ever since she was little. For she had been wilful and Mama had despaired. 'That stubbornness of yours will get you into trouble, *meine kleine*.'

Not any more. Frieda couldn't summon the energy to be wilful. Besides, her willpower now concentrated on forbidding her to put on weight. This was the only way she could describe what went on in her head.

The obstinacy she had no control over stopped her eating and was bigger than any warning from Mama, or need to please Aunty Doris, or even the fear of what would become of her if she carried on starving herself. At all costs she must stay thin.

She calculated what day it was. Sunday, the day she could leave work after milking was done. Frieda checked her wristwatch. Half past six. She was late.

Hauling herself out of bed, she took off her winceyette pyjamas and, pulling on a pair of grey slacks, noted with satisfaction the sizeable sag of material at her waistline. Shivering, she pulled on an Aran sweater, which Aunty Doris had knitted reusing the wool from a man's jersey she'd discovered in the local second-hand shop. For in these frugal times even clothes were rationed and Aunty Doris was an earnest supporter of the Make Do and Mend policy.

Frieda, brushing her hair, called through to Aunty Doris who was still in bed, 'Aunty, I'm off to work. I'm late.'

'What about breakfast?'

'I haven't time.'

'Frieda, it's nice you're raring to go to work but having a slice of bread won't make any difference to the time you get there.'

These past weeks Frieda had looked forward to going to work at the farm even if it did sap her energy. The reason was her new friendship with Sandra. Though Sandra was older, she had a certain naivety that made her seem the same age and Frieda felt she'd met a kindred soul. There was also a reticence about Sandra when she was with others that Frieda understood. It was as though Sandra too felt she didn't belong and wasn't good enough. It was different when they worked together; they were comfortable in each other's company and could be their true selves, cocooned in the byre.

In the kitchen, Frieda turned on the tap and washed her face with a sliver of soap. The house didn't have a bathroom and the toilet was an earthen closet down the back garden. A bucket under the sink behind a curtain was used for emergencies at night.

Just as she was about to leave for work, Frieda saw a jar of homemade blackberry jam on the table. She remembered her plan to find out what foods didn't fatten but still nourished the body. Tired before she started the day, she knew she couldn't go on like this. She needed sustenance to give her the energy to carry out a morning's work. All there was at hand was jam. She had to eat properly at some point if she was to avoid getting weaker. Why not start now?

Taking a loaf out of the bin on top of the bench, she cut a slice off with a bread knife, then sliced it in half, then quarters. Buttering a quarter, she spread black jam thinly on top.

Staring at the bread in her hand, the obstinate voice in her head spoke. *Bread is fattening and Aunty Doris puts heaps of sugar in the jam.* Tears rolled down her cheeks.

Frieda couldn't do it, not even to save her life.

That afternoon, the congregation long gone, hymn numbers removed, and red hassocks replaced on footwells, Frieda sat in the front row pew hoping for Mr Carlton to appear.

In the peace she asked to be healed. But the voice in her head nagged that if she were healed and ate properly, she would become fat again. In despair that she couldn't get the obsessive thoughts out of her mind, she closed her eyes and tried to think of something pleasant. Mama's face swam behind her closed pink eyelids. Why had the family never followed her as Mama had promised? Why did they never get in touch? Frieda had written her forwarding address on all the letters she sent.

Maybe, she told herself, the family had been stopped by the authorities from leaving Germany. They might have moved out of the area for some reason and never received her letters. There could be a number of reasons why they hadn't contacted her. Frieda's mind snapped shut at the unthinkable – the terrifying thought she could never bring herself to explore.

Not knowing what had happened to her family was hard to bear. Then the thought occurred to her that knowing might be even more heart-breaking.

Sitting in the stillness of the church, Frieda felt her eyelids droop. She jerked awake. She was always tired, not from starvation but because of the recurring, frightening dreams that made her too afraid to sleep.

Her thoughts turned to the curate, who she could trust, not just because he was clergy but because of the sincerity she saw in his caring brown eyes. Frieda had confidence in such a man. She would tell him everything... maybe not quite everything. She might lose his respect if she told him about her reaction when her brother jumped ship, and the cowardly thoughts that had prevented her from following him.

The door by the pulpit squeaked open and the curate walked down the stairs and came to sit beside her.

Maybe, she thought, if she told Mr Carlton the whole story, beginning with the night of the riots when she heard terrible screams, smelt acrid smoke and all the windows were shattered, she would be released from the nightmares that plagued her.

They sat in silence for a while.

Then, like water dripping from a dam, the words leaked out.

Patiently, as though he was a statue, Mr Carlton listened. When she had finished, he gave a gentle smile. 'You're very brave to withstand what you've been through.'

'Mama said she would follow as soon as Papa came home. Mama always keeps her word. I'm afraid they've been arrested like Papa.'

The curate didn't say the expected, that God worked in a mysterious way and she must pray and ask to keep her family safe. Mr Carlton didn't say anything but closed his eyes for a time and kept so still that Frieda thought he might have nodded off.

He opened his eyes and they brimmed with gentleness. 'I suggest you speak to God, as you've spoken to me. Tell Him what is in your heart. Fear, anger, confusion, whatever the case may be. Tell Him of your distress for the family. Speak to Him as a friend and tell Him everything.'

'Then what?' Frieda wanted to know.

'Trust in Him.'

In the silence that followed, Frieda desperately wanted to tell him about her problem with food. The guilt and sadness she felt every mealtime when she caused Aunty Doris such unhappiness.

To tell him about the power of the voice in her head that ruled her life.

'I have this—' she began, but a noise from behind stopped her and, turning, she followed the curate's gaze.

The church door opened and Sandra stood there.

Frieda wiped her eyes with the back of her hand. She didn't want Sandra to see her like this. And today Frieda had neither the energy nor inclination for social chatter with her friend.

The intimacy of the moment of confession over, she told the curate, 'I must go.'

His knowing eyes understood. His smile was generous. 'I'm here if you need me.'

Frieda made her way up the aisle and, nodding acknowledgement to Sandra, she heaved the church door open and went into the cold outside.

*

Sandra studied the curate as he walked towards her, seemingly immersed in thought. He stood level with her.

'Did I interrupt something?' she asked.

With a distant look in his eye, he gazed at her, but then he gave a welcoming smile. Sandra was reminded how easy it was to confide in him.

'You work with Frieda at the Nichols' farm, I believe.' His reluctance to address her question made him go up in Sandra's estimation a thousandfold. Confidences were safe with him. It gave Sandra the courage to tell him why she was here.

'Yes,' she replied. 'We get on well together.' She didn't add that she'd become close to the lass in the few weeks they'd known each other and she felt a protectiveness toward her.

Everyone needed a listening ear and Sandra was glad for Frieda's sake she'd chosen Mr Carlton to tell her troubles to.

Nervous, Sandra braced herself, then plunged in. 'I've something to ask you. It's more of a request, really.'

He stood aside and indicated towards a pew. 'How can I help?'

She moved past him, sat and brought the two letters from her pocket. Then, the disgrace of her illiteracy made the words she wanted to say dissolve in her mouth.

'Are those letters from your brother?' he helped.

She was amazed that he remembered, and it gave her confidence. 'Yes. One of them is. The other is from a good friend I used to work with, Mrs Goodwin. I wondered if… you would read them to me. You see…' The burn of shame made it difficult to go on.

'Whatever it is, you're in God's house and your secret's safe.'

His words, like a balm to her troubled spirit, gave her courage.

'The thing is, I've never learnt to read or write. In the past I've always found someone to read me letters but here I don't like to… Oh, it's difficult. Not that I think anyone would judge me. I get along with everyone…'

There, she'd spoken the words out loud and the heavens hadn't caved in and neither did the curate look shocked.

'I understand.' Whether he did or not, Mr Carlton put Sandra out of her misery. 'Would you like me to read the letters to you?'

'If you'd be so kind, I can't wait to know what Alf has to say.'

His smile was understanding. 'One thing. If you can't read how d'you know who—'

'The letters are from?' she finished for him. 'I know Alf's handwriting and me friend has a code so I know it's her. See…' Sandra pointed to where the envelope was sealed. 'Those four kisses are to let me know the letter is from her.'

'Good idea,' he approved. His expression solemn, he turned his attention to opening the first envelope. His eyes travelled to the end. 'It says it's from Olive.'

'That's me friend – Mrs Goodwin. She lives at the coast.'

The curate began reading, and as Sandra listened, Olive's voice rang out through the words.

Dear Sandra,

I'm glad you're hearing this because it means you've found someone to read your letters.

I hope they help you to reply because I can't wait to know what it's like where you live and what working in the country's like. I never thought I'd say this but after another raid last night and no sleep in that blooming draughty shelter, I could fancy a stint of country life meself. You're missing nothing here, lass, except queues at the shops which are getting worse. The daft thing is no matter how long they are, folk join in and hope for something worthwhile waiting for them at the end.

That b— woman, Mrs Kirton, has gone too far. She thinks I'm a skivvy. All I hear is, 'Mrs Goodwin, the steps need scrubbing, the beds haven't been changed, the ironing needs doing.' Who does the b— woman think she is! I've only got one pair of hands! My Tommy insists I leave. He says, 'You're a cook and I won't have you scrubbing floors, not with your bad legs.'

So, I'm thinking of working in the clothing factory canteen in John Clay Street, where I might be appreciated. I'd feel I'll be doing me bit and having a bit of chinwag with the other workers at the same time.

Last night, after midnight, it was murder with a raid going on. We heard that the bombs were dropped over the Cleadon and Boldon area but no real damage was done. The poor souls in Sunderland got the worst of the raid. There's tell of folk killed and injured but the woman up the street said some of her family were rescued from their buried indoor shelter. Thank the Lord! Aye, hinny, you're best off where you are, and no mistake.

*We haven't heard from Kenneth in a while but like
Tommy says, no news is good news. And like the rest of folk
I keep me spirit up because right will conquer in the end.*

*Hope you find someone to write back and remember
there will always be a welcoming bed here if needs be.*

Ta-ra, lass, your loving friend,
Olive xxx

'Your friend sounds a cheerful soul… colourful but jolly.' He folded the letter and handed it to Sandra.

He was nothing like any clergyman she'd known before, Sandra decided, as she returned his smile. Not that she'd met many. The two that stuck in her mind were the vicar at the Kirtons' church who'd preached about mortal sin and damnation and the priest who came to the orphanage who'd frightened Sandra with his sermons about going to hell if you weren't good. She'd prayed for forgiveness at her bedside that night, her knees aching from kneeling so long on the wooden floor.

Gazing into the curate's earnest expression, Sandra felt obliged to tell the truth. 'I don't go to church. I only visit on Sundays to say a prayer for Alf. I can't abide sermons when you're not allowed to ask questions after, when you don't understand. You just have to sit in silence and listen.'

Mr Carlton's lips twitched. Then, his eyes focussed on the second letter. A bubble of excitement rose in Sandra's stomach as he began reading.

Dearest Sis,

*I trust you are well. I feel I must write to tell you my
latest news. Along with one of my crew, I've been transferred
to a different bomber command (can't tell you where) and
my 'rest' has been cancelled for now. My biggest regret is
I won't be able to visit you as promised for a while, which*

I had looked forward to sorely. But this war has intervened in everyone's lives. And so, if you don't hear from me in a while don't worry. I promise I'll visit on my next leave come what may.

It's the thought of seeing you that keeps me going.
Your loving brother,
Alf Xxx

The curate folded the letter and handed it to her, a questioning look of concern in his eyes.

'I'm fine,' she fibbed. 'Mad that Alf refuses to stay safe and out of harm's way but that's a luxury no one has these days.'

He nodded in agreement.

It was peaceful to have someone who neither butted in nor wanted to tell about their experience, someone who simply listened.

Sandra didn't want to betray the overwhelming fear she had for her brother and she didn't want him to offer for them to pray. So, her anguish drove her to be flippant. 'I mean, you don't have to be in a bomber to be in danger, you could be anywhere. In a shelter knitting, in your bed asleep, then next minute a bomb's dropped and you're gone.'

If she'd thought he would look shocked, she was mistaken. Again, the curate just listened. She had expected him to spout some religious pearl of wisdom.

She goaded, 'I thought you might quote an apt passage from the bible.'

He smiled passively. For some reason that fuelled the anger that boiled within her.

'Aren't you going to say anything? Aren't you supposed to comfort?'

Shocked at herself, Sandra's inner voice told her to be ashamed at the way she was treating someone in his position.

'I'd rather try to understand.'

'What's there to understand?'

'What drives you to react in such a confrontational manner when that's not your way. But maybe I would too if it was my brother courting such danger.'

Her anger turned to curiosity. 'Have you got a brother?'

For a moment he looked unsure, as if as he didn't know if he should answer. Then his clerical poise slipped and she saw him as an ordinary man, probably with the ups and downs of life like everybody else.

'Yes. Older. He's a vicar in a Yorkshire parish.'

'Your brother's a man of the cloth too?'

A reticent expression crossed the curate's face as though he was considering if this conversation was appropriate or not.

'So is our father. I've always wanted to follow his path and mapped my life accordingly.'

Sandra didn't know how the curate did it but the anger within her now dissipated, she felt comfortable sitting here beside him, as if she could breathe easily for a while. She thought of the outside world, Alf somewhere, perhaps, on a mission over Germany. The constant gnawing worry in her stomach about her brother was wearing her down, she admitted. But everyone was suffering the same way.

She thought of Olive's words when she had talked about her son, Kenneth, away serving his country. 'In me selfish moments I think how much easier it must be to have no one to fret about. Then I come to me senses and realise life would never be the same without Kenneth.' She'd given a heartfelt sigh, adding, 'Loving someone, lass, always holds the heartache of losing them but if you've no family, what's... Eee, sorry, lass.' She'd almost welled up. Sandra knew that what Olive had said was true. If she didn't have Alf, life would be impossible. The thought of losing him was too unbearable even to contemplate. But then, she was lucky to have such a close brother to hold in her heart.

She was aware of the curate as he gazed intently from beneath thick, dark, perfectly arched eyebrows.

'Your mam must be proud at having three clergy in the household.'

It occurred to Sandra that she had changed. Not so long ago, when she was a subdued housemaid, she would never have dared to ask such a bold question.

'Mum is not the type—' He looked startled, as if he didn't know how they'd arrived at such a conversation. 'You haven't come here to talk about me.'

She took a deep breath and dived in. 'I have another request.'

The curate nodded his consent for her to go on.

'I want to learn to read and write. I wondered if…'

At this point Sandra did lose her nerve. She thought, *Fancy having the audacity to ask Mr Carlton such a favour.*

The curate looked unsure. 'In such a matter it's best if I speak with Mr Fairweather, the vicar here at Leadburn Church.'

'I shouldn't have bothered you. I'll find another way to—'

'It isn't a question of bother. It's a matter of propriety. I would need Mr Fairweather's permission for such a request as this.'

'It was cheeky of me to ask. Please don't trouble yoursel—'

'Miss Hudson, if it was up to me, I wouldn't hesitate to say yes.' Again, his expression was uncertain, as if he had spoken out of turn.

CHAPTER THIRTEEN

May 1943

Frieda

Frieda sat alone at the kitchen table, listening to the news on the wireless. The newscaster reported, in a typically English voice – posh, was how Aunty Doris described it – that German troops in Tunisia had surrendered.

Frieda stopped eating the porridge in front of her.

She'd found that if she made the porridge oats with water and didn't add milk, sugar or treacle, she could eat a small bowlful and she didn't put on any weight. The energy the porridge gave her made it possible for Frieda to work for the rest of the day at the Nichols' farm, something she desperately wanted, as she longed to see Antonio when he returned. A shiver of excitement surged through her at the thought. It seemed forever since Antonio had last worked at the farm and she'd met him in the tack room.

Frieda wondered if the news meant that the end of the war might be near. Her thoughts turned to her family. Were they still in Berlin?

She'd seen on the map in the butcher's shop window illustrating RAF targets, that Germany and Berlin were amongst them. The British had targeted only areas of military significance so far, but the raids on Berlin had, so it was reported, infuriated Hitler and he'd retaliated by ordering the Luftwaffe to target British cities.

While some villagers favoured the RAF doing the same, Frieda's concern was for the neighbourhood she'd grown up in and the people she'd known. It was harrowing to think what might have become of them and the family she held so dearly in her heart.

Her mind in turmoil, she willed her brain to think of something else. Her thoughts diverted to a more acceptable subject. Antonio. Today might be the day when the lorry carrying prisoners would arrive. Frieda envisaged his thickset figure stepping down from it and her heart rate quickened.

Her tummy uncomfortably full, she washed the bowl and left it on the wooden drainer so Aunty Doris would see proof that she'd eaten breakfast.

Later, sitting on the three-legged stool in the stall, Frieda saw Sandra as she entered the byre.

A beaming smile on her face, she walked up to Frieda's stall. 'Morning, Frieda, did you sleep well?'

'Well enough, thank you.' Another fib. Her empty stomach and the nightmares prevented sleep and Frieda had tossed in the bed thinking about the morning when she could eat her bowl of porridge.

'What a beautiful clear day. You can see over to the hills.' Sandra was so enthusiastic it made Frieda smile.

Frieda now considered her a friend. Sandra hadn't flinched that day when she'd told her she was German, and neither did she speak in that foolish way pronouncing words as though Frieda didn't understand English. She treated Frieda as an equal.

'I was hurrying and didn't notice.'

'You're kidding me. How could you miss the dawn? It was so spectacular!'

Intent on getting to work to see if the lorry carrying prisoners had arrived, Frieda hadn't noticed the weather.

Apart from Aunty Doris, Sandra was the only person Frieda felt totally at ease with since she had left Berlin. They talked to each other as they milked the cows, something Sandra was now competent at after all the trials she'd experienced learning. Mainly they discussed the different characters in the village and farm life and giggled like schoolchildren at the silliest things.

Frieda recalled the time they'd taken the cows back to the field together. Sandra, afraid at first to be amongst a herd of cows, had kept to the outside. She'd been whistling then suddenly stopped. Frieda, the other side of the cows, looked over the top of the large beasts but couldn't see her friend's head. Mystified, she waited till the cows passed then saw Sandra sitting on the field on her bottom.

'Damn and blast. I slipped on a cowpat!' Her look of disgust had been comical and made Frieda laugh. An indignant look on her face, she stood and viewed the damage on the seat of her dungarees, then pulled a disgusted face. 'It's not funny,' she told Frieda, who stifled a giggle.

As their eyes met, Sandra's lips twitched and they had both dissolved into giggling wrecks.

Sandra, by now, had disappeared into the next stall where Gertie was tethered. Frieda grimaced. Gertie was not Sandra's favourite cow. Last week, Gertie had moved one of her hooves and tipped over the galvanised bucket with the precious milk. Frieda suppressed a smile; her friend didn't have much luck with cows.

As Frieda worked with the hypnotic splash of the milk hitting the side of the pail, she found herself speculating what Sandra would think if she knew what a coward she really was.

The self-loathing returned. She wasn't the brave girl the curate imagined.

The scene that day on the ship replayed in her mind's eye. The men shouting in a foreign tongue. Kurt, quick as a flash, running down the gangplank. Frieda, standing frozen in fear. She hadn't even attempted to follow him.

The voice of guilt told her: *Kurt was your little brother; it was your job to protect him.*

Frieda had tried to make the shame go away by telling herself that even if she had acted and run after Kurt she could never have caught up.

Deep down, she knew that wasn't the reason she'd stood rooted to the spot on the ship that day.

She'd wanted to be on the boat. She hadn't wanted to go back to Germany where people were attacked for being Jewish, their homes ransacked, innocent people arrested and sent to goodness knew where. Frieda had been glad to have arrived in England, where she wasn't reviled or spat on. And though, because she was different, she'd experienced being bullied here at school, Frieda still didn't want to go back to her homeland.

And if her family knew, could they ever forgive her?

*

Sandra stared up at Gertie, whose wide-apart eyes looked back with a ponderous gaze of aversion. 'I don't like you either, especially after you spilt the milk and got me in trouble with the boss,' Sandra told the cow.

'You'll be in trouble again, lassie,' Mr Nichol's voice piped up, 'if you don't get on with your work.'

Crikey, Sandra hadn't seen Mr Nichol in the byre.

Bucket clasped between her knees, Sandra washed the teats with a cloth and then with a thumb and index finger – her other fingers around the teat – she gave a gentle but firm squeeze. She squirted the milk into the bucket and after a good ten minutes – it took the others less time than this but Sandra wasn't that accomplished – with the bucket satisfactorily full, Sandra carefully removed it from beneath Gertie.

'Thanks,' she whispered, 'for behaving this time.'

For her trouble, Sandra got a painful swipe across her face from the swish of Gertie's tail.

'Ow!'

'Are you all right?' Frieda called from the next stall.

Her cheek smarting, Sandra picked up the bucket and moved to where she could see Frieda. 'Gertie's just swiped me. But I'm fine.'

'She certainly has it in for you.' Frieda's voice sounded restrained, as if something was troubling her.

Sandra liked it best when her friend laughed – even if it was usually at her expense. For Frieda seldom looked carefree. She didn't appear to have any other friends, Sandra thought, though she'd noticed that Frieda must have a soft spot for Antonio.

Sandra made a mental note to do something fun together with Frieda. A trip to the pictures or some such thing – but when did they ever get the time?

On Sunday when Sandra visited the church in the early afternoon, Mr Carlton was busying himself by the font at the back of the church. He greeted her in his usual kind and attentive way. He wore a dog collar, cassock with surplice and black scarf with a hood.

'The Roberts family are celebrating the christening of baby Joseph this afternoon,' he explained.

'Oh, I won't stay long.'

'Take your time – everyone is welcome.' He looked directly at her. 'Apologies for taking so long but I've now had a word with Mr Fairweather about the matter of teaching you to read.'

'Thank you. What did the vicar say?'

'Mr Fairweather has agreed I may help in this matter but on one condition. That he is present.'

Blimey, she thought, what did Mr Fairweather think they were going to get up to? She blushed.

The curate quickly put in, 'It's only a matter of protocol.'

The Roberts family, dressed in Sunday best attire, started entering the church.

'Are you free tomorrow night?' he asked.

'Yes.'

'Good. Come to the vicarage at seven.'

He moved away, smiling a courteous welcome to the new parents and baby Joseph as they entered the church.

The next night after a bath and evening meal, Sandra headed in the direction of the church. The vicarage, with its peaked roof, porch and attic windows, was a big detached house only a few yards from the church's side entrance.

Sandra walked up the driveway and knocked at the door. She felt nervous but when Mr Carlton appeared his calm expression helped her relax.

'Come in, it's good to see you,' he welcomed.

She entered the hallway and followed the curate into the dining room. The room boasted an enormous speckled grey marble fireplace, with a wooden-framed mirror that reached to the corniced ceiling above it and reminded Sandra of the one at the Kirtons' house. She shivered at the memory of that place.

Mr Carlton's easy-going manner put her at ease, but it wasn't so when she met Mr Fairweather, who was inclined to be rather formal and abrupt.

The vicar, sitting in a wing-backed leather chair, spectacles perched on the end of his nose, looked Sandra up and down.

'Good evening,' he greeted her, 'if you're staying please talk quietly as I can't read a word if people chatter.' Without another word he opened the book he held and started reading.

Mr Carlton moved over to a large sideboard where a shelf was stacked with books. He pulled one out and brought it over to the table where Sandra sat and put it down before her. 'It's called *Just William,*' he told her. 'A favourite of mine when I was young.'

The book's pages were yellow with age, and on its cover was the picture of a boy who had a mischievous grin and wore a peaked cap. Sandra would have preferred a more girlish book but she was that grateful to the curate for taking the trouble to help her, she would have persevered to read the bus timetable if he'd requested it.

The first lesson didn't go well. Struggling because of her inadequacy to read even the simplest word, Sandra found it difficult to relax and concentrate. Aware that reading wasn't going to be as easy as she'd hoped, she vowed there was no way she would give in.

The next Monday, determined to overcome the nagging doubts in her mind, Sandra made her way to the vicarage.

As she passed the village store, Mr Curtis, who ran the shop, called, 'How do, lass?' He was cleaning the front shop window with a cloth. A slight man, with a perpetual worried-looking expression, he wore round spectacles, and a three-piece suit. 'Been meaning to do this all day but the shop's been heaving.' He scratched his head. 'You're the lassie that sometimes helps Bob Nichol do the milk round.'

'Yes, but only when Mr Nichol's knee plays up.'

Sandra's job was to hop off the cart, run ahead and collect the next jug waiting on a front step, fill it from the churn, then return it to the step where the owner would come out and collect it.

'Aye, that knee of Bob's has never been right since the Great War. All that mud.' Mr Curtis grimaced and his expression became bleak. 'We were the lucky ones, Bob and I. Never thought I'd live to see another war, though.'

Sandra had never imagined that Mr Curtis served in the Great War. She respected him and Mr Nichol all the more now.

She had high regard for all the villagers. There were one or two of the lasses from the hostel who thought them small-minded busybodies with nothing else to do but wag tongues. But it couldn't have been further from the truth, what with the war effort, the comforts fund, knitting for the boys at the front, organised dances in the village hall with the takings towards 'packages from home', salvage drives to save cardboard and rags – the list was endless. Many of the villagers had known each other since childhood, been to school together, attended each other's weddings and family funerals – and they looked out for one another.

Sandra's thoughts turned to her brother and the pining to see Alfie welled within her and grew like a sickness.

Tongue-tied as to what to say to Mr Curtis about surviving the Great War, she thought it best simply to pass the time of day. 'The shop's always heaving when I'm in,' she agreed.

Sandra sometimes walked to the store in her dinner hour and had a mooch around, not that there was much on the shelves to see.

Mr Curtis warmed to this conversation; she could tell. 'I tell you, lass, the sweetie jars are all but empty, these days kiddies mostly have to make do with liquorice. And since the Ministry of Food recommended households have an emergency supply of food, all the flour, treacle and condensed milk has flown off the shelves.' He gave a beleaguered sigh and scratched his balding head. 'We all just took food supplies for granted before the war.'

Sandra didn't divulge that never in her life before had she taken anything for granted.

'Good day, Mr Curtis, I've got an appointment and must be off.'

'Aye, that'll be to the vicarage.' Cloth in hand, he began polishing the window. 'No doubt, the curate will be waiting for you.'

Sandra, smiling, shook her head. It was difficult keeping a secret in the village.

*

Sandra walked up the driveway and knocked on the vicarage door. Mr Carlton answered. She noticed his sandy hair had been neatly combed back and he wore slacks and a jersey over his dog collar.

'Come in, I've got a surprise for you.'

He stood aside as she stepped into the large musty-smelling hallway – an odour Sandra would always associate now with the vicarage. She followed him into the dining room, wondering what his surprise could be.

The vicar was in his usual worn wing-backed chair, a heavy tome in his hands.

Mr Carlton told him, 'It's Miss Hudson, remember, Mr Fairweather? She called last week and I helped her with her studies.'

'Ahh, yes, you read from that infernal *Just William* book. Never could get on with William Brown.' He peered at Sandra. 'My first book was the bible. I mastered reading it when I was six, so Mother told me.'

Sandra guessed that Mr Fairweather had had a very different childhood from her.

She decided she did like the vicar, though, if only because he was different from anyone she'd ever met before.

'I hope you've been practising, Miss Hudson.'

She smiled politely. 'When I have the time.'

'Excellent.'

The curate pulled out a chair from beneath the dining table, where condiments from the previous meal sat in the middle.

'Our housekeeper, Mrs Bertram, tries to keep the vicar and me tidy but it's a thankless task.'

The curate moved over to a large sideboard where a shelf was stacked with books. He pulled one out and brought it over to the table and put it down before Sandra. She gazed at the front cover, the large title and diminutive people below in old-fashioned attire.

'It's called *Gone with the Wind*. I thought you'd have had enough of *Just William*.' His tone was hushed as he glanced across, a conspiring expression on his face.

'A real grown-up book.' Sandra flicked through the book's pages. She too whispered so as not to disturb Mr Fairweather, who was immersed in his book.

'It's my mother's favourite. Her own copy, in fact.'

'Then, why is it here?'

Mr Carlton looked somewhat abashed. 'I telephoned Mum and asked her advice about a suitable women's novel to encourage you to read. She offered this.' He gestured to the book. 'My brother brought it with him when he visited for lunch last Friday.'

Sandra was touched by his mam's generosity – and by the effort Mr Carlton had gone to. 'Please thank your mam for me.'

Mr Carlton nodded.

'Does your brother live far?' she asked, more to fill the silence than any curiosity she had.

'He lives near my parents in a village outside Durham.'

The curate took the book and opened the first page. Sandra could tell by the tender look on his face that the book was special to him.

'How long d'you think it will take me to read?'

'I asked a teacher from the congregation and he thinks it would take an adult approximately six months.'

Sandra was overcome by a mixture of happiness and frustration. Why hadn't she learnt to read before? Because she hadn't had any encouragement. Now at least she had Olive and the curate.

'Let's get started.' He placed the book before her on the table.

The curate pointed at simple words from the first page and, painstakingly, she pronounced each letter separately, then she combined each letter to sound a word.

They carried on like this and after an hour and a half the curate called a halt.

'You did remarkably well.' He grinned and she saw a dimple in his right cheek. He placed the book back on the shelf. 'How about tea and a biscuit? Homemade by Mrs Roberts as a thank you for the christening of her grandson.'

A snore came from the direction of the fireside. The vicar sat with the book open on his lap, his head bent forward on his chest.

Sandra felt it was indecent somehow to stare at him, a man of the cloth, while he slept. 'I don't want to keep you any longer.'

'It isn't a problem. My pastoral visits are done. I'm finished for the day.'

'Then, tea would be lovely, thanks. Won't we be disturbing Mr Fairweather?' Sandra never, in these days of rationing, refused a cuppa. Besides, there was something she else she needed to ask the curate.

Mr Carlton smiled affectionately at the older man. 'I think not. He refuses to retire. The church is his life.' He pulled a sorrowful face. 'He sorely misses his wife.'

Later, when he brought two cups of tea in and set one before Sandra, she said, 'As you know I'm working at the Nichols' farm, I work with Frieda from the Post Office. She told me she's German.'

He nodded. 'Yes.' He hesitated. 'It's no secret. Mrs Leadbeater from the post office volunteered to foster Frieda some years ago. She is a German Jew, escaped to Britain just before the start of the war. She left family behind.'

Sandra sipped her tea and let this sink in. It was as she thought, the poor lass had had to flee her homeland.

She continued, 'I worry about her because she's so thin and I never see her eat.'

'You're very observant.' Then he was silent and drank his tea. A muscle clenched in his jawline as he considered the matter, and Sandra could imagine him being unwavering in his conviction when the situation arose.

'I can only tell you this: the child is a concern to her aunt. Mrs Leadbeater has spoken in the village of her concern. Like everyone who cares I'm baffled to know what can be done about Frieda. I'm telling you this in the hope you're in a position to be of help to her.'

'This is why I've brought the subject up. There's nothing I'd like better. But I've never heard the like before.' She put her china cup on the saucer and looked the curate in the eye. 'I hoped you could advise me. Maybe Frieda could do with some fun to take her out of herself.'

'Good idea. What kind of fun?'

'That's the problem; I can't think of anything. Just the pictures in Hexham and that isn't exactly riveting.'

They sipped their tea in mutual bemusement.

Mr Carlton spoke. 'Any more letters from your brother?'

'Unfortunately, no.'

'Or that colourful friend of yours?'

At his words, a marvellous idea struck Sandra. She now knew what to do about Frieda.

She told the curate, who thought it a good idea and assured Sandra that he'd help in any way he could.

CHAPTER FOURTEEN

The curate saw Sandra off the premises with a look of regret, as if he'd enjoyed the evening and was sorry it was over.

It was still light at this time of evening. Sandra thought it a treat. With the blackout, the winter months seemed to be lived continuously in the dark, but the start of the spring had brought with it a sense of hope for better things to come.

Olive would be impressed with Sandra's philosophical attitude these days. It was living in the country, with Mother Nature all around, that did it.

Walking back to the hostel, she wondered how to approach Frieda with her idea, without scaring the lass off. After all, they hadn't known each other that long and Sandra was some years older. Not that age mattered. Look at her and Olive; they'd clicked from the start and had been firm friends ever since. Then again, Olive was a one-off, with her kind heart and plain speaking, she got on with everyone.

Instinct told Sandra that if anyone could help Frieda, it was Olive.

Back at the hostel, Sandra opened the front door then went into the corridor. She stopped and listened. A piano played in the common room and voices sang – male voices too. She opened the door and a blast of jolly atmosphere hit Sandra.

RAF men in uniform and lasses were grouped around the piano singing 'You Are My Sunshine'. Sandra felt the urge to join in.

Why not? Throwing off her inhibitions, she joined in and with gusto. The lass next to her linked arms and they swayed together as they sang.

Evelyn, standing behind the piano, waved at Sandra to come over. A sensation of belonging washed over her and she nodded. For an instant she thought of the young foreign girl who didn't have any friends and Sandra's kind heart was saddened. For everyone needed a friend to share the highs and lows of life. At least Frieda had found a caring home.

Strains of 'Home Sweet Home' then filled the room. The hilarity stopped and the mood in the room became sombre.

With a shrug of regret to the girl she'd linked arms with, Sandra moved over to where Evelyn and Enid were standing.

Sandra asked, 'What's going on? Why are the RAF here?'

'They sent a lorry from their camp to take us girls over but typically, Mrs Warden wouldn't allow such a thing. She insisted the RAF had to come over here.' She pulled a face.

Enid chipped in, 'She probably thinks we'll get up to hanky-panky at the camp. And she wants to keep her beady eye on us. More's the pity.'

A rush of mortification overwhelmed Sandra. She'd had no dealings with the opposite sex. What would the two girls think if they knew? Sandra's newfound assurance floundered.

She realised the piano playing had stopped and the common room held an eerie silence. Sandra looked around and saw everyone had turned to look at the doorway. She did the same.

Jessie stood there, an arm around Ruby's shoulders. Ruby's face was white and gaunt, her eyes like saucers, her body trembling.

'The County organiser has been in touch. Ruby's had some bad news,' Jessie told them.

'There's been a raid at home,' Ruby blurted, tears leaking from her eyes. 'Our house took a direct hit. Me mam and dad've been killed.' Her voice went squeaky. 'There's only a space left where our house was.' She was reduced to shoulder-heaving sobs.

Later that night, as Sandra lay in bed staring out into the darkness, her last thought before she dropped off to sleep was for poor Ruby – her boyfriend would never get to meet her parents now.

On Monday morning at the farm, Sandra got a surprise. Approaching the byre, she saw Frieda talking, all dewy-eyed, to a foreign-looking lad who had large red circles on his clothes indicating he was an Italian prisoner. The lad looked in his early twenties.

'Sandra, this is Antonio.' Frieda's lips parted and her expression when she looked at him was one of adoration.

An alarm went off in Sandra's head. 'Pleased to meet yi'.'

Antonio, burly with dark curly hair, wore an open-necked shirt, brown trousers and stout boots, which must have annoyed the villagers as, with the shortages, sturdy boots were in short supply.

'Hello, they ask me at the camp if I am ready for work and I say no. I am still sick but they send me still.' He shrugged.

An uncomfortable silence followed.

For something to say, Sandra told Antonio, 'You speak English well.'

'I learn myself when I first came. The book is called *The English in Three Months.* I take longer.'

Sandra was impressed. It gave her hope to be able to learn to read in a short time.

'I go now.' He sauntered away but not before giving Frieda a lingering look.

'Antonio seems nice.' Sandra tested the waters.

'He is.' Frieda pressed her lips together as if she felt uneasy about discussing Antonio.

That was the end of that particular conversation.

Still feeling gloomy after Ruby's disconcerting news yesterday, Sandra spent the morning in reflective silence as she milked the cows.

At dinner time, she searched for Frieda because this was the day, Sandra had decided, that she'd put her plan into action. She intended to invite her friend for a day out at the seaside and to meet Olive.

Though Sandra looked everywhere, Frieda wasn't to be seen.

'That Italian lad is bone idle,' Mr Nichol told his wife as she doled out soup at the dinner table.

Only Mr Jeffries and Sandra joined them today. The three Land Girls from the hostel helping in the fields had chosen to eat their sandwiches outside as it was a sunny day.

'I find Antonio charming,' Mrs Nichol told her husband.

'I don't know why you defend him.' Mr Nichol clicked his tongue. 'I've to keep an eye on the lad and I haven't the time.'

Sandra, eating a slice of homemade bread spread thinly with butter made at the farm, knew by now that if Mr Nichol said something was black his wife would insist it was white.

Mr Nichol took another slurp of his soup. 'And I don't like the way Frieda hangs around the Italian prisoner. I've just caught them in the tack room together.'

No wonder Sandra hadn't been able to find her. She would never have thought to look there.

Mrs Nichols looked appalled. 'What did you do about it?'

'To be fair the girl was helping. She was cleaning Rosie's saddle.'

'Hmm!'

'The one good thing I'll say about the lad...' Mr Nichol gave a positive nod. 'He's willing to work on the farm. It's said the other prisoners consider co-operators traitors.'

'Or maybe they're afraid of retribution when they get back home,' Mr Jeffries put in.

'I've had enough talk about war and prisoners.' Mrs Nichol, slamming the pan on the range top, disappeared into the pantry, not before she'd straightened the photo of her son on the dresser.

Mr Nichol raised his eyebrows at Sandra. 'Mother is sensitive about war talk.' He glanced towards the photo.

Spattered with muck from cleaning the pig houses earlier, Sandra approached Frieda, who was washing her hands at the cold water tap in the yard.

A wobble of apprehension overcame Sandra. What was she doing? It was none of her business. Why would Frieda want to spend time with her?

Deep down Sandra knew why. Frieda had no family to speak of and appeared lonely for a friend. But how to broach the subject?

Frieda smiled and made to move away.

Sandra blurted. 'I'm glad it's nearly knocking-off time. I'm famished for me supper.' Sandra could have bitten off her tongue. Of all the stupid things to say.

Frieda turned, her elfin face curious. 'What food do you eat at the hostel?'

The best thing was to be natural, Sandra decided. 'Mostly stews but my favourite is cheese dreams.'

'What are they?'

'Leftover cheese that's made into a sandwich and fried in lard.'

'I do not think I'd like that.' Frieda shook her head.

'It's delish and my favourite.'

'Delish?'

'Delicious.'

'Ahh!'

'You speak English well too.' Sandra remembered the conversation with Antonio.

'I now think of English as my mother tongue. I think my pronunciation sometimes is not good and people don't understand.'

Hurrah! Sandra thought. *A way in.* 'Where I come from – which is South Shields – folk speak broad Geordie. Nobody outside the area understands anything they say.'

Frieda, listening intently, nodded.

'I'm hoping to go soon. I'm allowed time off at weekends but with milking still to do, I've never bothered.' With no family to visit there was no point, Sandra added in her head. She acted surprised. 'I've had a thought. Why don't you come with us? The town's by the sea and it'll be lovely to share a day out with yi'. Only if you want to, of course. No need to rush. Think about it first. Talk it over with your Aunty Doris.' *Enough*, she told herself. *Don't make it sound like you're trying to convince her.*

Frieda looked startled. 'The coast is a very long way…'

*

Frieda opened the door with the latchkey.

'Hello, I'm home.'

There was no welcoming *yoo hoo* from Aunty Doris.

Climbing the stairs, Frieda felt dragged down by weariness. She entered the kitchen and saw the note on the kitchen table beneath the pepper pot.

> *There's a salvage drive at the village hall tonight. I'm helping out. Your tea's under the tea towel. I know you like hard-boiled eggs so I saved you mine. The bread's freshly baked this morning. I surprised myself by having the time. See you about nine. Love Aunty Doris*

Frieda moved to the sink and looked under the tea towel covering a plate on the wooden drainer. She considered the boiled egg, two thick slices of bread smothered with butter – no doubt obtained from the farm – and a little glass pot that contained jam.

The egg she could eat because it didn't put on weight. It was permissible to leave the jam. Spying the paper folded on the table, she tore a page out of the middle and wrapped the slices of bread in it. Frieda would dispose of the package in the bin later.

The deceit of duping Aunty Doris and getting rid of precious food rendered Frieda guilt-ridden and she loathed herself.

As she sat at the table eating the hard-boiled egg, she stared out of the kitchen window, to where distant, undulating hills were in shadow from the sun. It was such a lovely night, she wondered what Antonio was doing. He'd described the camp the first time she went to see him in the tack room in her dinner hour. He told her how he lived in a round Nissen hut and that there were no restrictions on how many times he could write letters home. Frieda could tell this pleased Antonio. She liked the fact that family was important to him.

'But my family not see the letters for the month.' He'd upturned his hands and shrugged. 'I get the cigarettes allowed once a week and I spend my five pennies' pay at the… how you say the name of the shop that moves?'

Frieda was baffled then she realised. 'Mobile shop.' She laughed and couldn't remember when she last felt so carefree.

She loved being with Antonio. She knew by the intense way he looked at her that the feeling was mutual. He was charming and different and she longed for the sight of him. When she'd first started at the Nichols' and felt like the new girl at school, it was Antonio who'd befriended her, bringing her dried fruit and sometimes an apple every day from the prison camp rations.

Frieda soon got over her shyness and reserve. Antonio was handsome in a rugged sort of way and, with his mischievous grin and twinkle in his eye, he was fun to be with. Though he did have a serious side too, when he talked of matters of war or the large family he loved so much back home in Sardinia.

When Frieda was with Antonio, she felt light-hearted, something she hadn't known in a long while. It wouldn't do to let others at the farm know how she felt, as he was a prisoner and a lot older than her. So, she told no one, not even her good friend Sandra.

Now, as she stared out of the window, she thought about whether Antonio would prefer her figure to be curvier. Her stomach tensed at the thought.

Antonio had told her, 'I like to be with you. You are *bella*. But you are too…' He sucked his cheeks in. He'd looked silly and Frieda had laughed. But she worried that maybe he really did think she was too skinny.

Why did Frieda have this strict code of conduct, the need to be perfect in every way, to be thin, to be the best student, the perfect older sister, even? Was it a German trait or something her parents had instilled in her or something that she was born with?

Her thoughts turned again to Antonio, his happy, uncomplicated expression. She was determined to change if only for his sake.

The first step was to forget rules. Frieda immediately felt alarmed, but she pushed on telling herself she was doing this for Antonio. She would act impulsively. When was the last time Frieda had been out of the village? The first step towards her new way of life, she decided, was to consider the outing to South Shields with Sandra.

But only consider.

*

Although Doris knew that she and the curate were the only two people in the post office, she looked left and right to check before she spoke.

'The bread was scrunched up in newspaper in the bin. I don't know what to do, Mr Carlton, Frieda's disappearing before my very eyes. When she's not working, her life revolves around sleeping.' At his questioning expression, Doris confessed, 'I feel bad spying on her, rummaging through the bin. It was after I saw the page missing out of the *Courant*. I had to know if the lassie was still starving herself. I'm always on guard where Frieda's eating is concerned. I can't help myself.'

Mr Carlton looked as troubled as Doris felt.

At first, when he had entered the post office on an errand, they'd discussed village news. How well baby Joseph's christening had gone. That Mrs Connor couldn't get about and needed villagers' help as her daughter and family lived down south.

All the while Doris was tormented inside until finally she'd explained her worries about Frieda, in the hope that the curate might be able to help her resolve the problem.

She continued, 'Then last night, when I got home after the salvage meeting, Frieda took my breath away by saying she's thinking of going to South Shields, of all places, with a friend from work.'

'I know who you mean.' The curate's answer surprised Doris. 'She's a Land Girl from the hostel. Take my word for it, Miss Hudson is thoroughly reliable. I think they've become good friends. She'll only have Frieda's best interests at heart.'

'The lassie's never set foot out of the village for an age. So, if this new friend is willing to take her on an outing she's got my blessing. I'm hoping the change will do Frieda good and she'll find her appetite.' Her voice wobbly, unaccustomed tears prickled Doris's eyes. 'My only worry is the bombing. Most folk are trying to get out of coastal areas.'

The curate nodded, sympathetically. 'I understand.'

But Doris believed in the philosophy, *live your life to the full*, especially after the sudden death of Jack, her darling husband. She told the curate and he gave a non-committal nod.

'Thing is, Mr Carlton, I don't know how Bob Nichol will react when Frieda asks for time off, especially if her friend works at the farm too. Bob's got a lot on now that the Ministry has commandeered his land for more food production.' Doris shook her head in a helpless fashion, then she looked expectantly at him.

'What are you asking, Mrs Leadbeater?'

'Bob will listen to you. Though he doesn't go, he's got respect for the church.'

'I'll see what I can do.'

'Thank you.'

CHAPTER FIFTEEN

As she made her way to work the next morning, Sandra saw Frieda waiting at the farmhouse gate.

'I'd like to join you when you visit your hometown. If I still can,' she told Sandra, without preamble.

'Of course. But why the change of heart?'

Frieda looked startled, as if she didn't want to answer.

'Never mind, I'm just pleased you've decided to come. I can't wait to show you the sights. We've got a fair, and the walk along the coast road up to Marsden Bay is spectacular with the sea views.'

Frieda nodded enthusiastically.

Then Sandra's hopes were dashed as she realised. 'Oh, but Mr Nichol won't be pleased if we both want time off together. He'll have to arrange for replacements.'

'I thought the same and when I told Aunty Doris, she said, "You won't get anything if you don't ask." So, I did and guess what?'

It was the first time Sandra had seen Frieda's face so animated, and it pulled at her heartstrings. She so badly wanted this scheme to work and for her friend to have a good time. For her to meet Olive, who, perhaps, might talk some sense into her.

'Come on. Don't keep me in suspense.'

'Mr Nichol agreed to both of us having time off. He's going to ask your forewoman for replacements for a couple of days. It's all arranged for the twenty-third and twenty-fourth of this month.'

'Two days!' Sandra couldn't believe their luck. She had been worrying it was a lot to do in a day.

'Yes. Mr Nichol said it was to his advantage for us to be fit. Neither of us have had a day off in an age.'

'Wonders never cease.' Sandra was both thrilled and dumbfounded.

The next Monday when Sandra arrived at the vicarage for her reading lesson, the curate, as soon as he opened the door, asked her, 'Have you had further news about your visit to the coast.'

Sandra told him the news, adding, 'The Lord works in mysterious ways.'

The curate's broad grin made him look quite boyish.

Sandra knew then that there'd been a conspiracy at work.

'I'm thinking we could stay the night. Then Frieda can have the whole seaside experience.'

'Good idea. Your friend said in her letter there'd always be a bed for you. We'll write immediately.'

So, they composed a letter between them, with Mr Fairweather looking on, a faintly bemused expression on his face.

The curate thought it necessary they tell Olive a little about Frieda's background to save misunderstandings or embarrassment. Sandra wholeheartedly agreed. Olive was wise and would pick up on the nature of things.

'Thank you,' she told the curate when they'd finished. 'For everything.'

Sandra didn't know how but she knew with certainty that the curate had had a hand in persuading Mr Nichol. That was the village way, to look out for each other and give a helping hand if needs be. She was pleased to be part of such a tight-knit community. The villagers treated her decently, but like most small communities where everyone minded each other's business, it could be difficult if you were a private person or had a secret to keep. Fortunately, neither applied to Sandra.

Don't tempt fate, a little voice in her head said.

Mr Curtis at the store had told her, 'Lassie, you have to be born and bred here before you fit in.'

Nevertheless, Sandra felt she belonged.

The next day, Jessie caught up with her as Sandra made her way to breakfast.

'The War Ag's been in touch and sent word that the Land Girl at the Dobsons' farm in the shire has bunked off home.' Jessie's expression showed disgust. Giving up, like being a shirker, was not the Land Girls' code of behaviour. 'You've been assigned to take her place until a replacement has been found.'

The only good news about this information was that Sandra wasn't being reassigned permanently. Sandra enjoyed working at the Nichols' farm, where she saw all different aspects of farming life. If she was in a gang, she'd go around the different fields mostly doing the same job. Besides, she'd grown used to, and liked, the people at the farm. Apart from her brother, they were the closest thing Sandra had to family.

'Why am I being sent?'

Jessie heaved a *who knows* shrug. 'I just carry out orders.'

'Who will replace me?' It seemed an odd situation, but as Jessie implied, who could understand the powers that be?

'One of the women from the gang who works in the top field, apparently.'

'Can they spare her?'

Another shrug. 'Ours is not to reason why. Can you ride a bike yet?' Jessie changed the subject.

'Not proficiently. I practise as much as I can but the front wheel still wobbles.'

'Take the bus, then, to the Dobsons' farm. I'll give directions. Mind, if there's any bother at this farm, get in touch. There've been cases where farmers or their sons have been randy buggers.'

Sandra, taken aback, felt a stab of worry in her stomach.

Despite her reluctance, she asked, 'When do I go?'

'Straight after breakfast.'

Three quarters of an hour later, Sandra, standing at the roadside, saw the Hexham single- decker bus appear from around the bend in the road. She stuck out a hand.

Climbing aboard, the conductress, Elsie Turnbull – a married lady from the village whose husband was serving abroad – greeted her.

'Morning, Mrs Turnbull.'

'Morning. Where you off to?'

'The Dobsons' farm up Rookdale way.'

'That's a bit far to travel, isn't it?'

The bus pulled away from the grass verge and Sandra found a vacant seat and looked out of the window.

When Mrs Turnbull came to take the fare, she told Sandra, 'Time you saved on bus fares and learnt to ride a bike properly. I've seen you wobbling along the road.'

Sandra couldn't help but grin; nothing escaped the eagle-eyed Mrs Turnbull.

The bus station in Hexham was situated in the main street and it occurred to Sandra, as she got off the bus, that she should visit this picturesque town more often. She asked a passing gentleman where the bus stand for Rookdale was. Giving her a puzzled frown, he pointed to a stand.

When the bus bound for Rookdale arrived, Sandra boarded and sat again by the window.

The conductress (known as a 'clippy' to the villagers) came to take her fare, and Sandra politely asked, 'Could you tell me when we reach the Dobsons' farm, please.'

The clippy nodded.

With menfolk away fighting for their country, there was a shortage of bus conductors and women were relied upon to take their place. Looking out of the window to the town's narrow, bustling streets, Sandra found herself thinking how life had changed for women. No longer tied to the home, they were sent out to the workforce. The worry was, Sandra knew, that when the menfolk returned triumphant from war and wanted employment, would this state of affairs last for women? And if it did would it be a good or bad thing?

Sandra grinned at the idea that, with all this reading and these fresh ideas, she was becoming a thinker.

The bus had left the town by now and as hedgerows passed, aglow with white hawthorn, trees reborn in vibrant green splendour, Sandra thought how therapeutic it was to live in the country.

The bus trundled along the narrow and twisty road, and the scene outside the window changed to soaring countryside. In the distance the moors, with rugged elevations, where once lead mining was a lucrative industry, had farmsteads nestling in the hollows.

After a time, the clippy called, 'Who's for the Dobsons' farm?'

Stepping off the bus, Sandra stood in what she could only describe as the middle of nowhere with only two farms in view. One of them, accessed by a track a hundred yards or so away, was positioned way up the far hillside where Jessie said it would be. The other, nestled out of the wind, was at the bottom of the hill, far away in the distance.

Sandra watched as the little bus, wending its way up the road, disappeared over the hill and a sense of isolation crept over her.

She was being silly, she told herself. It was a new adventure. But peering again at the building way up the hillside, her stomach seemed to plummet. She pulled back her shoulders and made for the track.

The farm, when Sandra eventually came to a plateau where it stood, was depressing. It stood a lonely sight, surrounded by open grassland. Slates were missing from its roof, one of the upper windows was boarded up, and all the paint had peeled off the windows.

A long, low barn stood at the rear of the building while at the front was a drystone wall where bracken grew through the gaps. Hens strutted in the foreground while somewhere beyond the farmhouse she heard the squeal of a pig. Sandra shivered as she recalled Evelyn's sickening tale.

Approaching the farmhouse gate, Sandra saw a face appear at one of the downstairs windows. The front door opened. A man wearing blue dungarees, grey shirt, and a red neck scarf, appeared at the door. A black-and-white dog pushed past him and bounded up to her, barking a greeting. The man gave an ear-piercing whistle and the dog stopped in its tracks and, tail drooping, ran back to its master and sat alert by his side.

The man squinted in the sun. 'Have you come from yon hostel? The last one run away. Young 'uns.' He clicked his tongue in annoyance. 'No backbone.'

A woman appeared. Thin, with high, sun-bronzed cheekbones and lines etching her skin, she had slate grey hair and all-knowing eyes. She wiped her hands on the coarse apron she wore.

'Take no notice of him. The lassie was scared stiff and I for one don't blame her. Living here in the wilds of the countryside, in a mould-ridden house with only us from company. And her a townie.'

Sandra shuddered. Matters were getting worse by the minute.

The woman turned to, presumably, her husband, 'You've been up here far too long on your own.' She cuffed his shoulder. She turned her attention back to Sandra. 'I'm Sadie, and this is my older brother, Joe, but he'll want you to call him Mr Dobson.'

Sandra remembered her manners. 'Pleased to meet you both. I'm Sandra Hudson. I don't mind if you call me Sandra.'

'What kind of farm work are you used to?' Mr Dobson's gruff voice asked her.

'I've mostly just milked cows so far.'

'We've only got two,' Sadie told her.

'I do general work about the farm too.'

Sadie looked at her brother. 'I suppose she'll do for now.'

Mr Dobson heaved an exasperated sigh and went into the house.

Sandra wondered why the two of them seemed so dissatisfied with her. Maybe it was life in general they were disappointed at and there was no pleasing them.

Sadie ushered Sandra into the house, jabbering as she went along. Sandra supposed the woman was lonely with only her uncommunicative brother to keep her company.

'Good job lambing's over. Probably why the other lass ran away. She couldn't take the long hours and toil. Working dawn till sunset sometimes. One of the farm labourers comes to stay and there's always folk from Rookdale happy to help if needs be.' Sadie heaved a heartfelt sigh. 'It's a busy time and no mistaking.'

'Are there many sheep?'

'A small flock but it's enough to keep Joe going. He's getting on and labour is hard to come by with all the young menfolk gone.'

Sandra was shown around the house and then taken to see the animals: pigs, a goat, geese. Lastly, she was shown an earth closet toilet with two wooden seats. Sandra smothered a smile as she had visions of the two Dobsons sitting on the 'throne' side by side. The farm was primitive and remote. The wind whistled continuously around the farmhouse and Sandra's mood plummeted further. Sandra wasn't cut out to live this isolated, she realised. For all that, she couldn't deny the magnificent view from this high vantage point.

In the kitchen, where a kettle sang on the hob and the dog slept curled up in front of the range, Sadie told her, 'Catch me living here if me old man was still alive.' Her eyes went pink and watery. 'He was a labourer and we lived in a tied cottage. When he passed on, I was shown the door.' She sniffed, stood tall and looked around. 'But it's a decent life. We have milk from the cows and I make me own butter and cheese and Jerry leaves us alone, apart from flying over. Sometimes I feel like waving.'

Sandra smiled politely at the attempt at a joke.

Sadie continued, 'I've got a wind-up gramophone that I listen to every night when it's dark and I can't see to read.' She looked squarely at Sandra, a hint of hope in her eye. 'I was thinking, by the time you get back to the hostel at night it'll practically be time to get back. You could stay here in the bedroom upstairs for the time you're here, if you like?' Sadie's tone sounded as though she was trying to convince her.

'I'm... the forewoman expects me back at the hostel,' Sandra stammered, feeling cornered. Though she felt sorry for the woman, there was no way she wanted to stay. 'The nights are lighter now and travelling is no problem. Thank you for the kind offer.'

The next day Sadie showed her the ropes. From that time on Sandra's working day felt never-ending.

By the third day Sandra struggled to get out of the bunk bed at the hostel. She seriously wondered if she should take up Sadie's offer and stay at the Dobsons' farm. What stopped her was the thought that if she did, she'd be kept there for the duration.

One night, as she travelled back to the hostel on the bus, Sandra had a dreadful thought.

'Excuse me,' she said to the fresh-faced but startled youth who sat next to her, 'what day is it?'

He looked uncertainly at her. 'Monday.'

She blurted, 'That means yesterday was Sunday. I've missed going to church.'

The youth's expression suggested he'd decided that a mad person was sitting next to him. He stood, stretched his arms over his head, then moved to another seat.

Fear grabbed Sandra by the throat. She'd made a promise to God and hadn't kept it. As apprehension for Alf's safety washed over her, Sandra's limbs became shaky.

She longed to speak with the curate. He would know what to do. But by the time she arrived back at the hostel it would be too late to call on him.

That night in the silence of the common room, as Sandra ate the shrivelled meal Cook had left in the range's oven, she prayed.

I'm sorry I didn't keep me promise. Please keep Alf safe.

CHAPTER SIXTEEN

The next morning, after a sleepless night, Sandra caught the two busses and turned up at the farm, tired and miserable. Determined to have the grit to plough through the day, she told herself to buck up. Some had it far worse – but the thought didn't help.

Her body active, Sandra's mind, with nothing to occupy it, worried throughout the morning about Alf.

At dinner time she decided to forgo Sadie's soup and sit outside and eat the cheese sandwiches Cook had made at the hostel. Land Girls got an extra allowance of eggs, butter and cheese as they did manual work and needed energy. The hostel always made sure the women got their fair share.

Mr Dobson was away; he'd taken the battered van with the bonnet tied down with string to the cattle market in Hexham earlier that morning.

'The only time he sets foot off the place,' Sadie had grumbled.

Sadie didn't look too pleased when Sandra explained her intention for dinner. But Sandra wanted to be alone as thoughts of her brother had put her in a melancholy mood.

'Before you start' – Sadie's tone was piqued – 'take this pail of swill to the pigs.'

Carrying the swill bucket, Sandra made her way up the field behind the farmhouse and headed for the tumbledown shed that housed the pigs. The shed was small with an opening at the side where the pigs could trot out and dig up the earth with their shovel-like snouts. It had rained torrents during the night and the hole the pigs had dug had filled with water. Sandra smiled as she saw one of the pigs wallowing in it.

Then she froze. The drone of aeroplanes sounded in the distance. The hair on Sandra's neck prickled. She stood an exposed figure in the open countryside, she realised. From her vantage point she had a perfect view of the four aeroplanes that flew along the valley, seemingly at eye level. Sandra shaded her eyes with a hand. *They're ours*, she thought in relief. They flew in tight formation and were fighters as they only had one engine.

Watching them as they flew past, for a heart-stopping moment Sandra would swear two fighters' wing tips appeared to touch. One soared away, the other one, Sandra saw in horror, looked to be going out of control. With a feeling of helplessness, she saw the fighter plummet, screaming on its way, to the grassy land below.

The spectacle was over in seconds. There was a sense of unreality about the incident and Sandra stood paralysed on the spot.

The rest of the planes thundered away but not before she saw the white five-pointed stars of the American insignia on the side of their fuselage.

She stared stupidly at the heap of aeroplane on the ground. She thought of Alf. *Someone's loved one was in that plane.* Galvanised into action, she dropped the swill bucket and, heart thumping in her chest, ran pell-mell down the hill's uneven ground in the direction of the wreckage.

Gasping for breath, she reached the aeroplane. Sandra's mind was calm and still as she made sense of the scene before her. The plane was on its belly with wreckage strewn all around on the ground. The far side wing was missing, the fuselage snapped in half, the tail broken off a few feet behind.

Sandra could see the pilot's head in the cockpit. There was no sign of movement. The nearside wing low enough to reach, she clambered up. She peered into the cockpit at the ashen-faced pilot wearing his leather flight helmet. Anger rose within Sandra. She was too late; the pilot was dead. She hammered on the cockpit.

No movement. She tried again. The pilot's head twitched. She banged again. This time he turned sideways and his eyes opened and met hers.

'Open the cockpit.' She gestured frantically with her hands to show him.

His arm moved. Slowly, he reached up and, unlatching the cockpit, opened the canopy.

She stared at him as blood ran from a nasty gash in the middle of his forehead beneath his helmet.

'Can you move?'

His startling blue eyes looked dazed. 'Can't,' he breathed. 'Legs won't move.'

He is conscious and aware.

Sandra thought of what the Red Cross person had said about accidents when he came to the hostel to give a talk. *Assess the situation. Are you or the casualty in any danger?*

The risk of fire occurred to her.

There was no way Sandra's slight frame could heave the man out of the cockpit. Even if she could, she'd never get him down the wing. She tried to think if there was anything she could do. Surely all she'd learnt from the Red Cross was useless in this situation, except *get help*. She was torn. She didn't want to leave him.

Keep the casualty talking, they're probably in shock.

The pilot's eyes closed again, but Sandra was relieved to see the rise and fall of his chest.

'I'm Sandra,' she told him.

His eyes blinked open. 'Sandra…' His voice was barely audible. 'Hudson.'

He mumbled her surname.

'You've been in a plane crash.' She checked the fuselage but there was no evidence of fire. She must go for help. What if

something happened while she was away? Sandra didn't know
if a fire could start long after an aeroplane had crashed. What
should she do for the best?

'I remember,' he told her. 'Wing touched beneath mine... I'd
no chance...' He began to cough and winced.

Alarmed, Sandra's thoughts turned to chest injury.

'Don't think about it now. Conserve your energy.'

A movement caught Sandra's eye. A black vehicle moved along
the track from the distant farm. She watched it turn into the main
road and continue. A truck. Her heart lifted as saw it turn into
the track and head in their direction.

'You're in luck, airman,' she told him. 'Help's coming.'

Again, he'd closed his eyes. Again, she checked he was
breathing.

As the truck got closer, she could see two heads over the
dashboard – both male.

Her breathing came easier. *Airmen can survive a crash,* her
anxious mind told her, thinking of Alf.

'You never did tell me the details about the crash,' Evelyn said
to Sandra as they sat on deckchairs outside their bedroom in the
sun, though the tall silver birch cast a shadow over them at this
time of day.

Neither did Sandra want to. She was permanently back at the
Nichols' farm now and having finished work for the day she was
at the hostel, waiting her turn for a bath.

It had been five days since the crash and Sandra was still in a
peculiar state of mind. All she wanted was to sit and stare at the
four walls. Her mind was blank and she couldn't concentrate.

She turned to Evelyn. 'I told you all there was. I waited with
the pilot till help arrived.'

Evelyn gave her an odd look. 'Is everything all right?'

'Yes, why?'

'It's just you seem preoccupied lately.'

Before Sandra could reply, Ruby burst into the room. She was wearing a floral dressing gown and a towel was wrapped around her head.

'Your turn for the bathroom. Be sharpish or somebody else will nip in.'

Everyone had been worried about Ruby since that night she was told of the tragedy. While on the surface she seemed to be managing, Sandra and Evelyn knew differently.

She confided to them one night when they were alone in the bedroom, 'I don't know who to turn to. Mam was me best friend. Roy is sympathetic but he thinks I should be getting on with me life. But I'm still not fit for anything and cry at the smallest thing. Roy's mam says I can stay at their place for a while but I'm not sure. What do you two think?'

Sandra didn't know and was nervous of saying the wrong thing.

Evelyn, however, had no inhibitions. 'If you don't know you should stay here and keep busy. You don't want to be hanging around your boyfriend's house with no purpose. Wait till you're positive you know what you want.'

So that's what Ruby was doing.

Sandra realised that Evelyn's advice was sound and she decided to follow suit. She'd keep busy and hope this strange state of affairs she was experiencing would soon pass.

Ruby, drying her hair with the towel, said, 'By the way, did you know there's a letter on the table for you?'

Sandra observed Ruby's strained face and reproached herself. Here was Ruby struggling with tragedy, while Sandra couldn't handle a plane crash in which no one was killed. Ashamed of herself, she vowed to buck up.

'No I didn't notice, thanks.'

It was Ruby's turn to look oddly at her. Letters were generally the highlight of the day.

Making her way to the front corridor, anxiety burned in her stomach. She still feared the outcome of forgetting to go to church that Sunday and hoped the letter was from Alf so she'd know for definite he was safe. She approached the post table and her eyes swept the envelopes. Sandra saw four kisses on the seal of one of them. Olive. Sandra was disappointed the letter wasn't from her brother, but she longed to hear what Olive had to say. The problem was today was only Wednesday.

She made up her mind. Though it wasn't her night for visiting the vicarage, she'd try her luck and see if the curate was in.

She hadn't seen Mr Carlton for two weeks.

When she arrived, Mr Fairweather answered her knock.

He looked bemused. 'Is it Monday already?'

Sandra assured him it wasn't. 'I haven't come for a lesson. I'm here to ask if Mr Carlton would read a letter I've received.'

'In that case you'd better come in.' He stood aside. 'Go through to the dining room. I'll tell him you're here. I'll be in the sitting room, there's a programme I want to listen to.'

Sandra smiled. Waiting in the dining room, she felt like a small child who wasn't to be trusted left alone.

Mr Carlton's face lit up as he came into the dining room.

'Miss Hudson, w-what a welcome surprise. I heard you'd been sent down Rookdale way to work on a farm. How was it? Oh… sorry, I'm forgetting my manners. Please, sit down.'

She sat on the wing-backed chair. The curate sat opposite. He seemed oddly flustered. His usual well-groomed hair was mussed, and his features were soft, as though he'd just awoken.

'I hope you don't mind me calling.'

'Not at all. Mr Fairweather told me you'd received a letter. Is it from your bother?'

'No. My friend in South Shields. I couldn't wait till Monday. I hope I'm not disturbing yi'.'

'We were just listening to *In Town Tonight* on the wireless. One of Mr Fairweather's favourite programmes – goodness knows why. I'm afraid I dozed.'

Sandra brought the envelope out from a pocket and handed it over to the curate.

Olive's letter, as Mr Carlton read it, with all the goings on in her life and her sense of humour, was a tonic.

The letter ended:

> *Of course you and your friend from the village can come. Me and Tommy are delighted. Hopefully I can wangle a day off work. I'll expect you late morning, all being well. I've got plenty of spare beds now the family have gone, more's the pity! Silly lass, you don't have to ask. Tell your friend she'll be very welcome. I'm looking forward to hearing all about country life.*
>
> *Your good and loving friend,*
> *Olive xxx*

'A good friend, indeed.' The curate folded the letter and handed it back. His brow furrowed as he scrutinised her. 'Is everything all right?'

'Why shouldn't it be?' As soon as the words were spoken, she regretted the defensiveness in her tone.

'You just seem rather quieter than your normal self.'

'In other words, I talk too much.' She grinned.

'That's more like you.'

The seriousness took hold again. 'I…'

'Yes, go on.'

'I witnessed an accident. An aeroplane crash near the farm.'

'Yes, I heard. News of the sort travels fast. He was an instructor based at the airfield. He was out on a training flight. It was a miracle he wasn't killed, by all accounts.'

'D'you know what happened to him?' She realised she had a feeling of lack of completion about the whole affair.

'Only that he was in a bad way and taken to a Newcastle hospital.'

'So, you don't know if he survived or not?'

'I'm afraid not.'

They sat in meditative silence for a while, the atmosphere calming. Sandra felt that Mr Carlton seemed to have this aura of inner peace about him, as if everything in life would sort itself out.

He leant forward, as though he wanted to say something but couldn't find the words.

She decided she could trust him.

She stood and moved to the chair next to him. He seemed startled, and there was a tension about him, as though their proximity made him nervous – and the feeling was mutual. As their eyes met, Sandra forgot what she'd meant to say.

'Ahem!' Mr Carlton sat up straight and the moment passed.

'Since the crash I haven't been myself,' she admitted.

'Do you want to tell me about it?' His soft tone was encouraging and she knew he was the only person she could talk to.

So, she did – about how there had been no one else there to help, how she stayed calm throughout, how thoughts of Alfie's safety had plagued her then and since.

As she spoke the curate nodded as though every word was of vital importance and Sandra experienced a sense of self-assurance she'd never known before.

She finished, 'I went to pieces after the accident.'

'You've found something out about yourself you didn't know before.'

'I did?'

'You can be relied on to cope in a crisis.'

'I'm not coping now. I feel terrible about my grumbles when there's folk far worse off.'

'You wouldn't believe how many times I hear the same thing. This is your problem. Worrying about other people's predicaments won't help. You're in delayed shock. And who wouldn't be? You didn't know what you were going to find in that aeroplane. It was your responsibility to keep the airman alive till help came. No wonder you went to pieces afterwards. I'm used to all kinds of troubles but I hope I never have to meet a life or death situation such as that.' His words rang with sincerity and were comforting. 'On top of everything else, it brought out all the fears about your brother that you'd buried and didn't want to think about.' He gave her a reassuring smile. 'I think you're allowed to go off the rails for a while.'

'I feel better already, thank you.' She realised she really did.

She darted a look at him and, seeing the set of his firm jaw, her fingers tingled with an impulse to touch his soft skin. Shocked, Sandra looked hastily away and concentrated on the marble fireplace.

The weight that had been dragging her down had lifted. How did he know so much? Did the clergy get trained to give such sound advice? But she knew in her heart that the curate was genuine and wouldn't have needed to be taught sympathy or understanding.

'My pleasure, Miss Hudson. In my experience it's better to share worries. It takes courage to do that.'

'I can't thank you enough.' It was wonderful to voice her fears to someone so considerate. She rose to go.

'You're leaving so soon?' He stood too.

She was conscious of his lanky frame towering above hers and, looking up, she saw something she couldn't quite discern in his eyes.

'I've wasted enough of your time.'

His gaze held hers, then he appeared to collect himself. 'But of course, you'll be tired after work.'

'Yes.' In truth she wanted to stay and gaze into those appealing brown eyes.

But he was a clergyman, for goodness' sake.

CHAPTER SEVENTEEN

Frieda

The train, billowing steam, chugged over the bridge. Looking out of the window, Frieda saw a street below with plentiful shops and teeming with people going about their everyday lives. But for Frieda this was no ordinary day; she was overcome by a mix of nervous excitement and dread: the excitement of attempting a new venture, dread of the unknown.

'Are you all right?' Sandra asked. 'You've gone pale.'

'I feel nauseous.'

'We're nearly there. Hopefully you'll feel better when we get off the train and you get some fresh air.'

Frieda wasn't lying; the apprehension churning in her stomach made her want to vomit. It served a purpose, though, because she could use this excuse to avoid eating over the next couple of days. The idea of being cooped up in a stranger's house, her every move, especially at mealtimes, being watched, was terrifying. Her fraught mind tried to recall why she'd put herself in this disagreeable position. Because she felt pressured, she remembered. Everyone had agreed – Aunty Doris, the curate, Mr Nichol even – that a holiday would do her good.

'This might be just what you need, love,' Aunty Doris had told her, smiling with delight. 'A breath of sea air to stimulate your appetite.'

The thought that this outing might be the first step to putting normality back in her life clinched the matter. And so, wanting to please her aunt, and Antonio, Frieda had agreed to make this trip.

The thought of Antonio diverted Frieda's mind for a time. Over the past weeks she'd spent break time with him in the tack room and she never tired of seeing him.

He'd told her in his endearing accent, 'You are only person understands me.'

And her heart ached for him.

His handsome face had creased into a small frown as he explained, 'I tell you only. You are same as me. I too miss family and wanna go to my home. I hope for you to come and meet them some day.'

He'd looked so sad and dejected that Frieda was tempted to kiss him but she'd resisted as it wasn't done for girls to take the lead in these matters.

'Nearly there now.' Sandra's enthusiastic voice interrupted Frieda's thoughts. Sandra stood and hauled their luggage down from the rack. She placed the suitcase at Frieda's feet. 'I can't wait to see Olive. Honestly, Frieda you'll love her. She's a card.'

'Card?'

'Means witty… eccentric.'

The train lurched, causing Sandra to unbalance. In high spirits, she laughed.

Sandra was a good and honest person, and true friend. Someone Mama would approve of, Frieda knew.

As she stood up Frieda decided to make the most of the visit. But when she opened the carriage door and stepped onto the steam-filled platform – where shrill whistles blew, bustling porters pushed trolleys filled with suitcases, and servicemen looked frantically for relatives – despite her good intentions, she was engulfed by anxiety.

Sandra led Frieda down a busy street where they found a bus stop and climbed aboard a trolley bus. It was heaving with people, and the pair of them had to stand in the aisle. As the trolley made its way up the hill and through the town, Frieda saw evidence of bomb damage – a gap in a row of houses, buildings reduced to a shell with roofs, windows, walls missing – and she was overcome by horror at what the townspeople must have to go through. She realised how lucky she was to be living in the countryside.

When the trolley stopped and they alighted, Sandra led the way over a busy main road, up past a row of terraced houses. She stopped at a house with a little forecourt surrounded by a low brick wall and a front door with gleaming brasses.

'Here we are. This is Olive's house.'

She banged the knocker. Frieda's nerves, as she waited at the front door, got the better of her. She didn't know what to expect.

*

Sandra eyed her friend standing beside her at Olive's front door. The poor lass looked scared stiff, and no wonder, coming to a strange place when she'd hardly stepped foot out of the village since she came to this country – and that, according to Frieda, had been only to the little market town of Hexham.

A moment of indecision washed over Sandra; she hoped she'd done the right thing bringing Frieda here.

The door opened and Olive stood there. Seeing her friend's wide, welcoming smile, Sandra relaxed. Olive would work her magic and soon put Frieda at her ease.

'Lass, hello! It's good to see yi'. Let's have a look. My, how bonny you are with your tanned complexion. And your hair's all glossy and shining. Country life's doing you the power of good.' She turned to the girl who stood next to Sandra. 'You must be Frieda. Welcome! Make yourself at home. If there's anything you need just shout. Lordy, where's me manners, come in the both of yi'.'

Sandra smiled affectionately as she followed her friend up the stairway. With her plump face, rosy cheeks and wearing the obligatory apron, Olive never changed. But a hint of uncertainty lurked in Olive's eyes and Sandra hoped nothing was wrong.

'I've managed to get some skirt of lamb,' Olive gabbled, 'and made a casserole, then it's a nice, filling jam roly-poly pudding for afters.' She led the way into the kitchen-living room.

The aroma of delicious food mingling with the smell of furniture polish that Sandra associated with Olive's house comforted her and she was so pleased she'd decided to bring Frieda.

Olive's face radiating happiness, she told the pair of them, 'I'm putting you, Sandra, in Kenneth's room. Frieda, you're upstairs in the attic. I wish I could say you'd get a nice view but all you can see is rows of rooftops. Do you want to see your room?'

'Yes please.' Frieda's voice was barely audible.

Olive took her visitor upstairs and then returned alone. She eased down beside Sandra on the couch. 'I've left the lass to herself for a while. Me and me big mouth. I think she's overwhelmed. Tommy told me after we read the letter yi' sent us not to overpower her with me chatter.' She looked stricken. 'D'yi' think I have? Poor lass, after all she's been through, she doesn't need me to put me foot in it.'

Sandra squeezed her friend's arm. 'Don't worry, Olive, you didn't. You spoke naturally and that's the best way to be. Frieda will detect it if you're overanxious around her.'

'She's got a good friend in you, Sandra, and, no doubt, she's poured out all her troubles.'

'Not really. I only know the basics but there's a curate at the local church who I suspect Frieda has confided in. She thinks highly of him.' Sandra, lost in thought for a moment, imagined Mr Carlton's dear face, his glistening brown eyes gleaming with sincerity.

'I'm pleased you told us about Frieda's eating problem.' Olive's voice broke into Sandra's thoughts. 'I've never heard the like.

I hope I didn't upset the lass by talking about all that food. It's a failing o' mine because I do like to see folk enjoy their grub. Which reminds us, I'm sorry, hinny, but I've only got a few hours off then I must go to work. The canteen's short-staffed and I've to help with the dinners and tidyin' up but I might be able to get off early.'

'That's fine by me, Olive. It's kind of you to have visitors when you're so busy working.'

'You're not a visitor. You're family. Anyway, help yourself to food – it's all in the cooker, the plates are warmin', the table's set. Anything left over I'll give to Tommy tonight for his tea. He's always starved.' That look of uncertainty clouded her eyes. 'Poor man, he's worried to death because it's been over seven weeks since we've had a letter from our Kenneth. Though his letters do take some time arrivin', it's never this long.'

Ahh, so she was right. Olive did have a worry on her mind. Feeling inadequate, she put her arm around Olive's shoulders. 'I don't know how you cope; you must be out of your mind with worry too.'

Olive's chin worked and her eyes swam with tears.

In the silence, Sandra reflected that men like Alf and Kenneth were doing a dangerous job; their luck could run out at any time. She couldn't bear the thought of what Olive must be going through.

Olive sniffed and wiped away the tears with the back of her hand. 'Tell you what,' she said over-brightly, 'why not show your friend the sights of South Shields this afternoon? It's a pity I can't come with you, but before you can turn around twice, I'll be home.'

Dinner was a lonely affair. Sandra sat at the table with places set for two. She'd been up to see Frieda in the attic room under the eaves where she found her friend lying on her bed.

'I just need to lie down for a while. I still feel queasy.'

'Can I make you up a plate of dinner and you can eat it later?'

'I couldn't face a big meal, thank you.' She looked abashed. 'I've brought cream crackers. I'll eat them later.'

What could Sandra do? She decided for the next two days she'd abide by the lass's wishes. But it was heart-breaking that she couldn't help in some way.

Later, after Frieda had appeared and had eaten some crackers thinly covered with margarine, the pair of them set off to explore the town.

They took the trolley from the bottom of the street to South Marine Park, by the beach. Frieda was entranced by the Victorian bandstand where they were thrilled to find that a colliery band was playing. People sat in rows of metal chairs in the late afternoon sun. In a rare moment of nostalgia, Sandra wondered if her parents had trodden the same path and listened to music in the bandstand. She felt a pang of sadness for her loss.

They walked for a while along the promenade where blue horizon met with glittering waters and golden sands stretched for miles.

'Are those rolls of barbed wire?' Frieda asked, looking out over the sands.

'It's to prevent invasion from the sea,' Sandra said.

They went for a cup of tea in a small and cosy seaside café. Frieda refused anything to eat and Sandra worried because the lass hadn't had a substantial meal all day. But she wasn't the lass's keeper and it wasn't her place to interfere.

Afterwards, back at Olive's, their host was bustling about making tea. She told the two friends, 'I'm always starved after the fresh sea air. I've saved eggs so that you can have one each and I've made some of me home-made fruit scones. Only I'd no dried fruit to put in them.' She hit her forehead with a hand. 'How daft can you get? How can they be fruit scones?' She cackled, but stopped when she caught Sandra's warning eye.

'Course, after such a big dinner yi' mightn't be hungry. It's your choice.'

That evening, when Tommy arrived home from working at the docks, Olive introduced her husband to Frieda.

'It's a pleasure, pet, to meet yi'.'

As the pair of them chatted, Olive took Sandra to one side and said under her breath, 'Don't mention Kenneth because the silly sod is worried to death about the lad.'

'How are you coping, Olive?'

'I just go on believin' what Tommy usually says, that no news is good news…' But her eyes told a different story.

Later, when they all were sitting around the table, Frieda ate the egg and managed half a slice of bread but refused the scone.

Olive raised her eyes at Sandra, sympathy written all over her face. In return, Sandra gave a slight *there's nothing we can do* shrug of the shoulders.

The evening finished with them all sitting around the put-you-up card table with the green felt top, having a game of whist. Olive explained the rules.

Afterwards, when the card table was put away, Olive asked, 'Who's for a cup of Ovaltine? I think there's enough milk.'

They all wanted one, surprisingly, including Frieda. She'd become more animated since Olive had asked what she'd like for breakfast.

'I don't suppose you have porridge?'

'Aye, lass, we do and you can have as much as yi' want – depending on how hungry you are, of course.'

Olive was really trying, Sandra thought. And Frieda was beginning to seem more relaxed, so it was paying off.

When they'd drunk the hot, comforting drink, it was time for bed.

'You'll be tired after your long day, Frieda.' Olive's tone was motherly. 'Off you go up to the attic to bed.'

When Frieda had left for bed and Tommy took the cups through to the scullery and checked the doors were locked, Olive turned to Sandra. 'I've been wondering how you really are. By the sound of the letters you're happy enough, but letters can be deceiving.'

'At first I thought I'd made a big mistake…'

'And now?'

'I've got to know people and they've become good friends and I feel settled at Leadburn.'

'I'm so pleased, lass. You've done yourself proud since you left the Kirtons and it's grand to see.' She gave Sandra a probing look. 'What about a fellow? Is there anyone special?'

Sandra pulled a face.

'I hope you're not still feeling the aftershock of your last night with the Kirtons.'

'To be honest I've been so busy there's not much time for thinking. Anyway, nothing really happened.'

'Praise be to God. All the same, something like that leaves its mark. *And* you could've been killed.'

In the pause that followed, Sandra sensed there was more Olive wanted to say.

'What?' she asked her friend.

'A man like Duncan Kirton can put you off for life; there are some rotten buggers like him out there. But there are lovely ones too. Take my Tommy. The man drives us crackers at times with his finicky ways but I wouldn't swap him for the world.'

Afterwards, as Sandra switched off the light and snuggled down in her bed, she found herself thinking of the last night she'd seen Mr Carlton. Closing her eyes, his face swam behind her lids. And she realised then what the look he'd given her had been when she'd told him it was time to leave: a look of disappointment.

*

Frieda unpacked her case and folded her clothes neatly on the back of a wicker chair. She changed into her flannelette nightgown and, switching off the light, hopped into the cold bed.

In the claustrophobic darkness – the blackout curtains were so thick no moonlight could shine through – she stared up towards the ceiling. Antonio's handsome face came into her mind's eye – his easy-going expression and lopsided grin. An overall warmth of happiness cascaded through her.

Her hand, automatically travelling over the top of her nightdress, felt protruding hip bones and a stomach that caved in. Satisfied no roll of fat could be found, Frieda ignored the ever-increasing hunger pangs. Turning on her side, exhausted, she went straight to sleep and the repetitive dreams of the past years, which were vivid and felt real, played in her mind while she slept.

Running figures, screams, shattering glass.

One of the screams awoke Frieda. Unnerved, for a moment she couldn't recall where she was.

The piercing noise in her head wouldn't stop.

She had to get out; it was dangerous here.

Papa's voice called to her. 'Frieda, we must go.'

Frieda threw back the covers and leapt from the bed. Slipping her feet into shoes, she put on her dressing gown and groped in the darkness for the bedroom door.

'I'm coming!'

Papa would take them to the safety of Herr Unger's place.

*

'Frieda,' Tommy called again, 'we must go. Be quick about it.' He turned towards Sandra, who was standing on the landing. 'Welcome to South Shields. Jerry's hotspot at the minute for raids.'

Although his words were jokey, Tommy's expression, as he waited at the bottom of the attic stairs, was deadly serious. Dressed in trousers and braces over his striped pyjama top, Sandra noticed that he was barefoot.

Olive, wearing a dressing gown and iron curlers in her hair, came to stand next to him. 'Take these.' She bundled blankets into his arms. 'I'll go fill the flasks.'

Frieda appeared then, around the bend in the stairs. The lass looked dozy with sleep. She looked around as if she couldn't believe what she was seeing. 'I dreamt that—'

'There, pet.' Olive took her arm and led her away. 'Everything's all right. Come with me and we'll make tea.'

'Can you hurry, then,' Tommy told his wife, 'wi' haven't got all night.'

Tommy was agitated, Sandra could tell. Though she tried to stay calm, anxiety got the better of her. She thought of the curate telling her she was strong in an emergency. He should see her now.

When they were all assembled at the top of the back stairs, the wail of the siren piercing the air, Tommy made a checklist.

'The lamps and heater are in the shelter—'

'So's the bucket and cards. I've got flasks and the first aid kit,' Olive breathlessly interrupted.

'I've got blankets. Right, I think that's everything. Hang on, what about matches?'

His wife told him, 'Tommy, man, just go. They're in me dressing-gown pocket.'

The three women trooped down the steep and narrow staircase following Tommy into the semi-lit back yard.

The siren, which sent cold shivers down Sandra's spine, now mercifully stopped.

'Aye, Jerry picks his night, all right.' Tommy turned up his face and glared at the moon sailing high in a clear sky. He led them to the brick-built shelter beyond the washhouse.

It was cold, dark and dismal inside and the stench of damp and disinfectant assaulted Sandra's nose. Tommy pulled out a match and, lighting the wick, set the oil lamp down on the table. Eerie shadows leapt up around the red-brick walls. On a shelf nailed onto the far wall, Sandra spied books and games of all kinds. *Perhaps it could be a good idea to play a game and distract ourselves,* she thought.

'For the neighbours' kiddies downstairs,' Olive told her. 'Only they don't use it now as they prefer to shelter under the stairs.'

Sandra thought them wise; if she were going to cop it, she'd prefer to be in the relative comfort of a house.

She noticed Frieda standing, a bleak figure in the doorway.

At the same time Olive did too. She took Frieda's arm and guided her to a deck chair.

'Bonny lass, have me chair and put this blanket around yi' to keep warm.' She placed the blanket around Frieda's shoulders.

'Thank you.' Frieda's voice was small. 'I'm sorry—'

'No apologies necessary. I'm scared out of me wits as well. Though, I'm mad at Jerry choosing this night to make a call. Why don't you have a cup of tea to settle your nerves?'

Sandra smiled. Olive's cure all for everything was a cuppa.

'You were mighty quick making the flasks,' she told her friend.

Tommy gave his wife a gentle tap on her bottom. 'She has everything ready before she goes to bed. Don't you, love?'

In the distance came the drone of aeroplanes. Guns fired incessantly from the ground and Sandra could imagine the criss-cross beams of light searching the sky. Bombs exploded as they hit the ground.

Frieda covered her ears.

'Crikey, it's a full-scale raid,' Tommy said.

Planes droned terrifyingly nearer and mighty explosions made the earth beneath them shake.

A scream pierced the air. At first, Sandra thought it was Frieda, but then her blood ran cold when she realised it was Olive. She had never before seen her friend lose composure.

CHAPTER EIGHTEEN

The deep drone of the planes thundering overhead reverberated in Sandra's heart.

As guns blazed at the enemy from the ground, Sandra thought of Alf. In the distance she heard an aeroplane scream to the ground and explode, and the thought occurred that that could be someone's beloved brother.

Tommy told the group, 'We're all right in 'ere, they're after the docks tonight.'

As he spoke bombs rained down, and there was a sudden flash, then a terrific explosion that shook the shelter walls so that Sandra feared they'd fall down. As a nearby building toppled, dust and mortar trickled from the cracks in the building, filling their mouths and nostrils, making them cough and gasp for air.

'Damn and blast!' Tommy raised a fist at the shelter ceiling. 'Don't they know they're flying over a civilian area?'

The raiders passed and were heard to drone off into the distance.

'Tommy, man, sit down and be quiet.' Olive had, by now, collected herself but Sandra detected a wobble in her voice. 'You'll frighten the lassies here.'

As if we aren't scared enough, Sandra thought. But it wasn't British to show your fear in the face of the enemy.

Then, in the distance, the bombers sounded again and Sandra braced for what was to come. Bombs shrieked to the ground – thuds and explosions could be heard all around – and this time, as the shelter walls shook, the paraffin lamp went out, plunging the four of them into darkness. Then a bomb exploded, it seemed, in the lane, and for a second there was absolute silence then a long crescendo of splintering glass.

'Stop it! Make them stop!' a voice screamed. 'This is my nightmare.' Frieda dissolved into high-pitched, hysterical sobs.

Olive hugged the young German girl against her large bosom, until at last the noise died away and the all-clear sounded.

Tommy, with the aid of a torch, fixed the paraffin lamp, which now shed light upon them.

'There, there, pet.' Olive stroked back Frieda's hair from her forehead. 'It's all over now, Jerry's turned tail and gone home.'

Frieda's thin body shook as she clung to Olive.

Sandra thought, *Who better than Olive to cope with such a delicate situation.*

Tommy stood. 'Aye, well, I'll go and make us a strong pot of tea.'

'You do that, love.' When he left, Olive told Sandra, 'Tommy's not good with emotions, especially not now when he's worried about his son.'

Sandra wondered who looked after Olive when she was down.

'Will she be all right, d'you think?' Sandra glanced at Frieda, who, eyes glazed, was staring at the space in front of her. She felt guilty for bringing her here to this hellish situation.

Olive whispered, 'It's best we keep her here for now. The lass has something in the past that still troubles her. I believe troubles should be shared and not bottled up where they can fester and make you ill. That's what happened to Mam when Dad was killed in an accident at the mine. She never spoke his name again. Mam's life stopped too the day of the accident.'

Sandra decided she'd be a happy woman just to have a quarter of Olive's wisdom; and the thing about her friend was that she was modest and unaware of her qualities.

'Frieda, hinny,' Olive's voice crooned. She helped the lass to sit up. 'What ails you? Get it off yer chest, lass. You're amongst friends.'

Frieda stared trance-like at Olive. 'They broke the windows and I heard screams. We ran for our lives. Papa was taken away. Karl jumped ship… I should have…' She shuddered and tears spilled from her eyes and rolled down her cheeks. 'I am a coward.'

Olive and Sandra looked at one another.

'Why?' Olive asked. 'Don't bottle your troubles up, love. Tell me from the beginnin'.'

Frieda's eyes gazed into Olive's. She took a deep breath and started talking. As the tale unfolded about her last months in Germany, she appeared less dreamlike and more in the present.

'So, you see,' she concluded, 'I am a coward. Even if I could have caught up with Kurt, I had no intention of following him. The awful thing is, I love my family dearly but I'm relieved that I've escaped my homeland.'

Olive stroked her hair. 'Of course you are, pet. It's only natural. Who wouldn't feel the same way? Believe me, your mam only wants what's best for yi' and she'll have peace of mind knowing you're safe and sound.'

Frieda looked surprised. 'Do you really think so?'

'I know so. It's what any parent would want. Furthermore, I'd be furious if Kurt was my son, jumping ship like that when I thought he was safe and out of the thick of it in England.' She nodded. 'But your mam won't tell him that and make him feel bad.'

Olive's words seemed to do the trick because Frieda's eyes widened in wonder. 'I never thought of it like that.' Her young face lit up in an appreciative smile.

Sandra sat quietly listening in; her respect for Olive knew no boundaries.

*

The plan for the next day was for the two visitors to leave early afternoon so that they'd be home in Leadburn in time for tea.

Sandra's idea had been to take Frieda on a return trip on the little ferry over the River Tyne to North Shields in the morning. Frieda then could see the mighty shipyards on the Tyne crammed with ships. But, after the raid and the aftermath of their emotional night, the pair were content to have a lie-in and late breakfast, making a mid-morning start.

Olive had to go to work but she promised to try and see them before they left.

After a breakfast of a bacon sandwich – a rare treat these days and Sandra could imagine the wait in the butcher's queue Olive must have had – and porridge for Frieda, the pair of them packed their small attaché suitcases and were ready for the off.

As they descended the sunlit stairs, the front door opened and Olive stood there. 'I pleaded with me supervisor,' she told them as she took the key out of the lock and put it her coat pocket, 'for an hour off to see me company away as I didn't know when I'd next see them. The canny woman said the time I worked overtime, she thought she could spare an hour.' She moved into the lobby and, peering up the stairs, noticed their suitcases. 'The Lord be praised, I'm just in time.'

The goodbyes at the front door were difficult. True to form Olive pasted a smile on her face and Sandra followed suit.

Olive couldn't hide her emotion. 'Now, lass, you know you're welcome any time. Don't make it so long. Tommy and me love having yi' to stay.' Then it was Frieda's turn. 'You too, lass. Tommy and me consider you one of the family.'

Frieda's chin trembled. 'Thank you for everything. You have been very kind. Especially…' She couldn't go on.

A tightness came into Sandra's throat as she watched the pair of them hug.

As Olive pulled away her gaze wandered into the street where the telegram boy rode his bicycle up the hill. Sandra saw her friend gasp then hold her breath. He pedalled closer and it seemed an age before he passed in the road. Olive, her face turned ashen, clutched Sandra's arm for support. The boy pedalled further up the street then, stopping, he dismounted and stood his bike by the kerb. He rummaged in his bag and brought out a yellow envelope.

The threesome, as if transfixed, watched on.

The post laddie looked at the door numbers and moving two doors up the street, knocked on the doorknocker.

A small cry escaped Olive. 'Oh! It's Mrs Burton, it'll be her husband. Poor soul, she's got no family. I'll have to go to her.'

The two of them sat in perturbed silence in the train compartment and it was as though they didn't have the words to convey their feelings. Sandra wanted to make sure Frieda was all right before they went their separate ways.

She ventured, 'It's been an eventful time.'

Frieda turned, and gazing out of the window gave a tentative look. 'I'm sorry if I spoilt your time with your—'

'Don't be silly. I'm glad you got things off your chest.'

'Your friend is one of the nicest people I've ever met.'

'Olive's a treasure and no mistake.'

Frieda looked bashfully from beneath long dark eyelashes. 'I revealed things I have never told anyone.'

Sandra hesitated then decided to go on, 'It must be terrible for you not knowing about your family.'

'That is the worst part.' Frieda's face contorted in sorrow. Sandra understood how wretched she must feel. Frieda then asked, 'Where is your family?'

What could she say? Sandra decided to tell the truth. 'This is something I have rarely revealed either.' She told her friend about how she came from an impoverished but loving home. 'After Mam died, Dad put me and Alf in an orphanage because he couldn't cope.'

'Alf?'

'Me brother. He's in the RAF.'

'What is an orphanage? I don't know that word.'

'It's a place children are sent to when both parents are dead or can't look after them. There was no other family who could take us in.'

'What happened to your papa?'

'He died soon after.'

'That is sad.'

Frieda listened in wide-eyed horror when Sandra described her time at the orphanage and how she and Alf were separated from the beginning.

Frieda confessed, 'I worry about my family. That they have been taken away and that… I too am an orphan.'

Sandra knew the courage it took for Frieda to voice her greatest fear. The train was slowing down and as it pulled into Newcastle central station, Sandra did something she'd never done since her mam had died: she turned towards her friend and hugged her.

'Can you see the bus stop for Hexham?'

'Sandra, I think you need spectacles. It is right here – look!'

When they sat themselves on the bus, Sandra looked around to see if anyone could listen in. In fact, the bus had few passengers and they were seated further down the aisle.

As the bus started up, she revealed, 'I have something else to confess… I couldn't see the sign because I can't read.'

'Oh, how dreadful for you. However do you manage?'

Sandra told her about Olive helping her in the past and Mr Carlton teaching her to read.

Frieda's smile heightened her cheeks and, in contrast to her usual gaunt appearance, she looked young and pretty.

'He is a good and kind man. Mr Carlton knows about my problems too.'

Sandra imagined the curate's opaque, intent brown eyes as he listened to Frieda. 'Your secrets are safe with him.'

They sat for a long while, content to stare out of the window where the suburban scene changed to that of rolling countryside where sheep and black-and-white cows grazed. The bus meandered through villages and small towns with honey-coloured stone houses gracing the roadside.

Suddenly Sandra felt brave; she reckoned this was the time to broach the subject she'd purposely avoided. She spoke in a hushed tone. 'Frieda, why is it you eat so little? Are you ill?'

Frieda flushed and her eyes brimmed with tears. Her lips firmly pressed together, she turned again to stare at the view.

As the bus left a busy little town called Prudhoe, the view outside the window changed. Looking out over the valley to distant countryside, Sandra found the scene breathtaking.

Frieda, sitting in the window seat, turned to face Sandra. 'I can't help the way I am.' She spoke in a small voice and Sandra had to strain to hear.

For an instant Sandra wished she hadn't brought the subject up, especially now when Frieda had been through so much in the last few days.

The lass turned and faced Sandra, eyes pleading for understanding. She swallowed hard. 'It's difficult for me to talk about. At first, when everything seemed out of control, I decided I could do something about my figure. I wanted to be thinner. I had always been teased at school.'

By the look of her friend's clenched jaw, Sandra knew she'd suffered more than teasing but she decided not to interrupt.

'Then… it got complicated. I couldn't eat.'

She was getting somewhere, Sandra realised and a surge of anticipation washed over her. 'Why couldn't you?'

The conversation stopped as the bus drew up to the kerb at a bus stop in the quaint village of Corbridge. Sandra watched as passengers stepped down from the platform onto the pavement and continued with their daily lives.

The bus started up again and as it travelled over the seven-arched bridge over the River Tyne, Frieda's voice spoke up. 'I don't expect you to understand, Sandra, because I don't either. Normal eating is impossible for me. I fib rather than say I haven't eaten and hide food too. I am amazed that I'm telling you these things. I haven't even told Aunty Doris.'

Sandra was concerned for Frieda and gratified that she had opened up to her. 'Can you explain what happens?'

Frieda pondered. 'A force in my mind I can't control won't let me because I have this morbid fear I might get big again. I'm scared if people knew, they would think I am… what is the word?'

There were so many horrible words to describe illness of the mind, Sandra didn't want to choose. The bond she had now formed made Sandra want to gain her friend's trust. To be completely truthful was the only way. 'Minds are peculiar things. Have you seen a doctor?'

'Yes. Aunty Doris took me to see Doctor Shepherd. He was no help. I don't think he has come across a case like this before.'

'Frieda, you know you can't go on like this. You'll become very ill. Is there nothing you think you can eat? What d'you consider safe?'

'Food that doesn't put on any weight. Plain porridge and vegetables like cabbage and carrots. Other food too… eggs… fruit, but it is so difficult with rationing. I don't like to trouble

Aunty Doris…' Her face crumpled. 'I do so want to get better. I… have another secret. And Mama isn't here to tell.' Her voice had become barely a whisper and Sandra had to concentrate hard to hear.

'Your secret is safe with me.'

'I don't… you know… bleed any more.'

'You mean your monthlies have stopped?' This was an uncomfortable subject for Sandra. Discussions about how a baby was conceived and born were taboo at the orphanage. To this day Sandra was naïve on the subject.

Frieda, acutely embarrassed, flushed from her neck to her cheeks. They were a pair, thought Sandra.

Frieda went on, 'Nothing has happened for two months. My teacher at school once discussed… *meine tage* with me at school. I know that if you don't have one you can't have a baby. I'm scared, Sandra.' Her voice cracked and her face looked bleak. 'What if I have damaged myself? What will happen when I get married?'

Sandra's heart ached for Frieda. What a state she was in. Hopeless at such a topic, she racked her brain for how to help.

'I know I'm older than you but I'm ignorant about such things. I'd advise you to tell your aunty. She's a good sort and like Olive she'll want what's best for you.'

'I know that. I just couldn't bring myself to tell Aunty Doris. Now, though, after speaking with you and your friend, talking about it doesn't seem so difficult any more.'

'I've got an idea,' Sandra ventured. Frieda's wide, innocent eyes looked hopefully expectant. 'One thing we could try would be to try different foods from the ones you feel safe eating. Small bits at first, then experiment with more.'

Frieda's expression was unsure, but Sandra took her silence as a good sign; at least she hadn't said no. It was a start.

CHAPTER NINETEEN

As she stepped from the bus in Hexham, the events of last night sat heavily on Sandra's mind. The outing was supposed to lift Frieda but because of the bombings, Sandra feared the opposite was true. She wanted the trip to finish on a high note and she had a brainwave.

'D'you fancy a shopping spree in Hexham?'

Frieda hesitated.

'I've saved two coupons to buy a pair of sandals,' Sandra went on. 'I've never owned a pair before, there was never any need. I'm hoping in the summer months I'll find an occasion to wear them.'

Frieda appeared unsure.

'Go on! You'll be a big help reading the labels and prices.'

Sandra didn't add that because of her illiteracy, she'd never had the nerve to go shopping in town before.

'All right, then,' Frieda replied with a smile.

They made their way into the picturesque town's cobbled main street and then entered Robbs department store. The next half hour was spent pleasurably browsing the store's wares, before Sandra tried on sandals in the shoe department.

She couldn't make up her mind up. 'I like both the brown and the white pairs,' she said.

'If it helps madam to decide,' the shop assistant replied – her face set in a noncommittal mask –'I would suggest considering which is most comfortable.'

'They both feel like I'm wearing slippers.'

The assistant, sniffing, pursed her lips.

'The white ones with the ankle strap look summery,' Frieda commented.

Sandra nodded. 'The white ones it is, thank you,' she told the assistant.

Outside, a rather relaxed Frieda told Sandra with a mischievous grin, 'I think madam was testing the assistant's patience.'

'Madam thinks so too.'

With a hoot of laughter, Sandra linked arms with Frieda, guiding them to the marketplace where they browsed the stalls. Then, after sharing a pot of tea in a rather select lounge at the Beaumont hotel, they made their way back to the bus station.

Sandra, glancing at their reflection in a shop window, gave a satisfied sigh. For Frieda finally wore a somewhat carefree expression. But more, there was the sense that the afternoon's adventure had helped bond their friendship.

Later, as she walked up the path to the hostel, Sandra mulled over the conversation with Frieda on the bus. She tried to think of foods her friend might eat.

The thing about the diet during this war – mainly potatoes, bread, suet puddings and suchlike – though it helped fill you up, unfortunately, it wasn't the best for the figure. For all Sandra's work on the farm, she found the waistband of the slacks she wore was tighter than before.

Opening the door to the common room, a wall of voices met her. The Land Girls in dress uniform, ready for the evening meal – some lounging on couches, others at the table, impatient for the meal – talked animatedly to one another. Cigarette smoke fogged the air.

Sandra didn't feel like an imposter any more and felt that she belonged. She could approach a group of women without feeling awkward. She moved to the lasses sitting on the wooden seats by the stove. No warm glow came from the stove and Sandra wasn't surprised as the evening was mild and fuel had to be conserved whenever possible.

'Hi, Sandra.' Enid gave a little wave.

'It was a lone bomber.' Enid's eyes were wide as she continued with her conversation to the others. 'The villagers reckon it had been damaged and the pilot jettisoned his bombs to help him get home.' She checked her nails, as she was apt to do on numerous occasions, to see if any were broken. 'Mercifully, no one was hurt.'

'It's left a huge crater,' a lass listening in at the table called over. 'One of the villagers told me this morning when I delivered the milk.'

She looked directly at Sandra as if to say, *Yes, I had to do your job.*

Sandra asked Enid, 'When did this happen?'

'Late last night.'

Sandra thought of the terror the townspeople of South Shields had gone through the previous evening. She felt glad to be back in the relative safety of the countryside. Then immediately felt guilty for having such thoughts. She wondered if this was the cause of Frieda's illness; the guilt of turning her back on her homeland was making her punish herself. Tired after the events of the past days, Sandra decided that the main thing was to help the lass to get better.

She checked her wristwatch. Quarter to six, enough time to unpack and change for supper. She moved towards the door, hearing snatches of conversation on the way. Enid was saying, '…did anyone hear what the newscaster said on the wireless last night? That women are getting muscles with all the work they do. I hope I don't. It's bad enough having rosy cheeks that no amount of powder will hide. Wait till my Dan comes home from abroad and sees me now…'

Sandra, opening the common room door, almost collided with someone.

'Oops! Sor—'

Frieda stood there, breathing heavily – a yellow envelope in her hand.

Sandra's mouth went dry. 'For me?'

Frieda nodded. 'Aunty Doris met me at the door. I ran all the way to give it to you.'

Sandra took the envelope from Frieda and stared at it in shock. 'Not here…'

They went outside the front door into the soft evening air.

A wild impulse to throw the envelope into the dustbin overcame Sandra. But that was a coward's way of doing things. She ripped the envelope open then handed the telegram over to Frieda.

The light of understanding dawned in her friend's eyes. She took the telegram and began reading.

We regret to inform you that your brother Alfred Hudson has been reported missing in action. If further details or information are received—

Sandra's legs threatened to buckle and she couldn't listen any more. She reached for the hostel wall to steady herself. Fury overcame her. 'I hate the bloody Germans for starting this war,' she cursed, shaking her fist at the sky.

Frieda handed her a handkerchief. 'I think it is best I leave you alone.' Shoulders drooping, she made towards the path, a forlorn figure.

Sandra, numb and without emotion, let her go.

An image of Alf when he was a kid came into her mind's eye. His clothes unkempt, little Alf had a broad grin on his face, two square upper front teeth, a tuft of hair that wouldn't comb down, and shining, eager eyes.

Fear for her brother clutched around her chest and Sandra couldn't breathe. She gasped in some air. *Missing*. Did that mean there was hope?

She needed to talk to someone.

The curate was the first person she thought of.

Mr Carlton answered the door, his expression concerned.

'I know it's late but I wonder if I can possibly talk with you. There's no one else.'

If he did have misgivings, the curate didn't show them. 'Of course, come in.' He led the way to the front room. 'Mr Fairweather is upstairs in bed nursing a cold. We can be private in here.'

He gestured towards the couch and Sandra sat down, then immediately wished she hadn't because she felt strung up inside. Mr Carlton stood facing her, hands cupped before him in that posture of patience Sandra found calming.

'It's Alf. I've had a telegram. It's says he's missing. His plane didn't arrive back from a mission.' Her voice had gone squeaky; she couldn't hold the tears back any longer. She dissolved into great shoulder-wracking sobs which came from deep within her stomach and hurt. Finally, taking gulping gasps and sniffing hard, she turned her face up towards the curate who stood still as a statue. Sandra was glad that it was he who witnessed her distress, and she was struck by the peacefulness he exuded.

He handed her a white handkerchief. 'The telegram says *missing*.' His tone was reassuring. 'There is hope yet. Your brother may have bailed out or the pilot could have landed because the plane was hit and damaged.'

A new thought came to Sandra. 'Alf might be taken prisoner.'

But she didn't want her brother a prisoner someplace in Germany. She wanted him safe here where he could visit like he'd promised. Then the voice of sanity took over. *Far better a prisoner than the alternative.* Powerless to do anything about her brother's state, her ribcage tightened and Sandra thought she was going to faint.

'He might be.' The curate gave an encouraging smile. 'I'll pray for Alf's safekeeping. You can join me, if you wish.'

If she wished. Sandra would have run around Hexham marketplace naked if she thought it would keep her brother safe.

She told the curate about how she'd missed going to church to pray for Alf one Sunday. 'I was working at Dobsons' farm and got mixed up with the days. Maybe this is my punishment.'

He spared her the sermon she expected. 'Don't make Alf's captivity your fault, Miss Hudson. The nation is at war. Whatever's happened to Alf isn't your fault.' He didn't pursue the matter. 'Who read the letter to you?'

'Frieda. I'd confessed beforehand that I couldn't read.' Sandra remembered the rant about Germans. She pulled a regretful face. 'I was shocked and not very pleasant. I vented my anger at the Germans. Poor lass, she's had a rough time of it recently and didn't need me adding to it.' Sandra was too fraught and exhausted to explain about the recent visit, but the curate seemed to understand and didn't press.

'She's a sensible girl.' His voice soothed Sandra's frayed nerves. 'Frieda will understand your anger wasn't meant towards her.'

She knew he was right.

She stood up. 'Thank you.'

'I didn't do anything.'

'You made me feel better.'

As their eyes met, she saw uncertainty in his, as though he didn't know what to say or do. Glimpsing his vulnerable side, the inner man, Sandra felt drawn towards him.

He cleared his throat and seemed to recover his poise. 'Miss Hudson, your brother is reported missing. Have faith. Hold onto that.'

As she left the vicarage and walked home, golden rays of sunshine broke through grey and dark clouds.

A sign for the future? Sandra's broken heart hoped so.

One thing was for sure, she'd visit the church every Sunday and pray for Alf's safe return.

*

Matthew Carlton watched Miss Hudson as she walked down the vicarage drive. Closing the door, he wandered into the hall, picturing her distraught face as she told him about her brother. Like an open book, she couldn't hide a single emotion.

Matthew had strived to heed his calling; his job was to be of help to the troubled in their time of need and not to get emotionally involved. This wasn't the case where Miss Hudson was concerned. Feelings of gladness and that the world was a happier place overpowered him whenever she was close, ever since that wonderful moment when he first saw her in Leadburn church. The attraction ran deep in his soul and was against everything that he'd mapped out for his life. The plan was to finish three years of training and then, when he became a vicar with his own parish, he could think of settling down and having a family.

When he was in Sandra's company – he dared to call her by her first name in his head – Matthew was unsure how to behave. The trouble was he didn't feel like Matthew Carlton, the curate, but an ordinary self-conscious man in the presence of a pretty woman for whom he had feelings.

Matthew walked into the front room and, distractedly picking up the parish magazine from an occasional table, he reclined on the settee to read. But thoughts of Sandra's tear-stained face came into his mind's eye and he couldn't concentrate. He couldn't bear to see her cry. Matthew ran his fingers through his hair. There was something different about her; a mixture of vulnerability and determination shone in her eyes. The set of her jaw was resolute;

she let nothing stand in her way to accomplish what she wanted. She'd swallowed her pride and asked for help to achieve her ambition of learning to read, and he was glad to be of service.

Over time, he knew, despite self-denial, he'd grown fond of Miss Hudson. The only time he'd felt this strongly about something was when he'd entered the ministry and done his first curacy as a military chaplain. Matthew's eyes glazed as he remembered the scenes he'd witnessed: men in despair, suffering colossal injury; the stark fears of those that lay dying. The faces of those brave men still invaded his dreams.

Opening his eyes, Matthew willed his mind away from the past. Here he was ordained and in his second curacy at Leadburn where he was committed to serving God and his parishioners.

He picked up the magazine where it lay open on the couch. He wanted what was best for Miss Hudson – a life of freedom to do as she pleased, not one of duty serving in the community. He paused. Didn't he?

CHAPTER TWENTY

Frieda

The next morning, Frieda was rather nervous as she waited in the farmyard for Sandra to appear.

At first, Frieda had been shocked at Sandra's outburst. Then she felt anger that Sandra had turned her rage on innocent Germans such as her. Fraught by the events of the past twenty-four hours, Frieda had fled the situation and sought the reassurance of Aunty Doris.

Her aunt, seeing her distress, had made a pot of tea and the pair of them sat at the kitchen table. Frieda, calmed by the cuppa, had sought her aunt's advice.

'Love, why do you think your friend reacted in such a way?'

Looking into Aunty Doris's caring eyes it dawned on Frieda what she was getting at. 'Sandra didn't mean me, did she?'

Aunty Doris shook her head.

'She lashed out in distress, didn't she?'

Her aunt had smiled and nodded.

Now, as Sandra walked up the farmhouse track, Frieda noticed her friend's guilt-ridden face.

Sandra came straight up to her. 'I'm sorry, Frieda, that was unforgivable of me yesterday. I didn't—'

'It's all right. I did feel hurt at first,' Frieda cut in, 'but I understand. Truly, I don't hold any ill feelings towards you.'

Sandra's cheeks burned in shame. 'That's good of you to say but I still feel bad about my reaction.'

'You realise,' Frieda continued, 'I would probably react the same way if it had been Kurt missing.' As comprehension dawned in Sandra's eyes, Frieda smiled. 'Let's forget about the incident, shall we?'

Gratefully, Sandra nodded. She brought out her lunchbox from the rucksack she carried and opened it. 'As promised, I've brought a morsel of food so you can try different kinds of food each day.' She brought out a piece and put it in Frieda's hand. 'It's oat biscuit from last night's supper at the hostel.'

Frieda, realising this was a peace offering, couldn't refuse. Closing her eyes, she took a deep breath and, popping the biscuit in her mouth, gulped it down.

'Well done. See, the heavens haven't caved in.'

When Frieda opened her eyes the pair of them smiled at each other – a somewhat relieved smile.

Their friendship was intact.

CHAPTER TWENTY-ONE

June 1943

A week had passed since Frieda's visit to South Shields and the traumatic night in the shelter. She was sitting at the breakfast table with Aunty Doris. It was still early morning and she had time to eat something before she left for the Nichols' farm.

Telling Mrs Goodwin about her last months in Germany and leaving her family behind had lifted a weight from her mind. Just before she'd left the flat, Mrs Goodwin, giving Frieda a bear hug, had whispered in her ear, 'Remember, lass, a problem shared is a problem halved.' It must be true because ever since she'd confided her troubles, the nightmares from the night of the broken glass had miraculously stopped, to Frieda's immense relief.

Though, if Sandra hadn't been so good and kind as to take her to stay with Olive Goodwin this peaceful state of mind would never have happened. Sandra was a caring friend and Frieda was pleased the pair of them had made up.

'You've plenty of time to eat your porridge before you leave for work.' Aunty Doris's voice broke into her thoughts.

Picking up her spoon, thoughts of Antonio filled Frieda's mind. She was worried that he might not be on the lorry from the prison camp as he'd heard he might be allocated to a different farm.

'D'you know' – Aunty Doris looked up from the newspaper she was reading – 'I really do have high hopes we're going to win this war.'

The German and Italian troops had surrendered last month in North Africa and Aunty Doris was excited at the notion that it might mean the end of the war. Frieda, though joyful that at last she would be able to search for her family, couldn't deal with the ramifications – Would she be sent back to Germany? How would she find her family? Were they alive? – and so she buried her head in the sand.

She regarded her aunty and thought how lucky she'd been to be sent here. When she had first arrived Aunty Doris had spoken to her in a crooning voice as if Frieda had understood every word. When she did understand the English language properly, her aunt told her, 'I'll borrow you until your own folk turn up and find you.'

Frieda knew when that time came, it would be with great sorrow that she'd leave Aunty Doris and the home where she'd felt secure during the war. Then it struck her that when she did return home, Aunty Doris would be left all alone.

An impulse to please her aunt overcame Frieda.

'Shall I make you a cup of tea, Aunty?'

Her aunt's face lit up with pleasure. 'Why, thank you, that would be lovely.'

Frieda knew what would make her aunt really happy: if she ate a substantial meal.

But it was still a step too far, even to please Aunty Doris.

The weather, after earlier storms, had changed to a few days of brilliant sunshine now that the balmy June days were upon them. With so much work to be done though and the threat of more storms, the Land Girls worked in gangs till nine o'clock at night – even on Sundays.

Only Frieda, Mr Nichol and Mr Jeffries – who had said he'd forgo attending church this morning for Holy Communion – were there for milking. Sandra wasn't in that morning to milk the cows, because Mr Nichol wanted her to help with haymaking in one of the fields across from the farmhouse.

Then, to Frieda's absolute delight, the lorry full of prisoners arrived at the farm and, as Antonio climbed down, his eyes locked on hers with a slow smile.

'I help with horses in the field,' he told Mr Nichol.

'Indeed, you will not. There's milking to be done. You've done it before. I've plenty of people in the fields.'

Frieda didn't think Antonio looked very pleased because he preferred messing in the stables or tack room, especially on Sundays when he got paid overtime from the prisoner camp. She knew this from the numerous times she had visited him in the tack room.

Frieda, exhausted before she started, thought milking would never end. She was kept on her toes by the fact that Antonio's stocky body was never far away. These days, what preoccupied her thoughts was food *and* Antonio. Smiling like an idiot, she gazed into his glittering eyes whenever he addressed her; then, forever self-conscious, as his eyes roved her slim figure she blushed to the roots of her hair.

'That's it. Breakfast,' Mr Nichol called as he came into the byre. All the work was done, the cows taken to the field.

'Mr Nichol, you no understand I bring the food. I eat outside in sunshine.' Antonio surreptitiously winked at Frieda.

A shiver of excitement running up her spine, she nearly dropped the empty pails she was carrying.

Mr Nichol left and made his way up to the farmhouse to join Mrs Nichol for his Sunday morning breakfast of bread and dripping topped with a fried egg.

Frieda, collecting the last pail, was conscious of Antonio's closeness as he came up behind her.

She turned.

He smiled, flashing brilliant white teeth. 'I go to the field. You come with me, we eat the breakfast together. It makes me very happy. I like your company when we are together.'

Frieda was taken aback. 'Erm… I had porridge for breakfast earlier on.'

She saw a spark of irritation in his eye. Perhaps he thought she was giving him the cold shoulder?

She quickly put in, 'I could keep you company if you like while you eat yours.'

He flashed his smile again and, gazing adoringly at him, Frieda felt her legs weaken. He led her up the uneven path to the field where sheep and cows grazed, then through the gate. In the field beyond he patted a grassy spot beside him in the seclusion of a drystone wall.

'Come, sit beside me, Frieda.'

They had met, the first time, in the stables where she hid every morning when the others went to the farmhouse for breakfast. It was cold on those mornings back in April, but it was the only place she could think to go. Antonio, discovering her one morning shivering in the shadows, hadn't asked questions but had taken her by the hand to the tack room and put one of the horses' blankets around her shoulders.

Frieda had met him in the tack room whenever she could after that, to help Antonio with his work and chat with him. Though shy at first, she soon relaxed in his company, with his gregarious and hilariously funny attitude to life, and willed the time to pass every morning so she could meet with him. Each time she saw him, her heart hammered in her chest.

Here in the field, sitting this close together, Frieda smelt a sweaty and curiously manly odour emanating from him, sending a pleasurable thrill throughout her abdomen.

Antonio, crunching an apple and licking juice from his lips, threw back his head and belly laughed as if he understood what she was experiencing. 'You like the corned beef sandwich. I brought you some to enjoy.'

She didn't want to offend Antonio. 'No. It's for your—'

'I share it with you.' He broke the sandwich in two and handed her half.

Luckily, since the other day, when Frieda had eaten the piece of oat biscuit, she'd been experimenting with morsels of food that Sandra brought her. Yesterday's token was a small piece of ginger and date cake. Frieda had eyed the cake with suspicion. 'It'll have loads of sugar in it.'

'Only a smidgeon.'

'I can't,' she had wailed, defeated.

'You can. You've been doing so well.'

'Imagine if someone tried to make you eat poison?'

Sandra had taken the cake from her and snapped it in half, handing it back. 'How about this? It's no more than a crumb.'

They had looked at each other and the silliness of the size of the cake made them both giggle. When she'd calmed, Frieda took the morsel and with a swift movement put it into her mouth and swallowed.

'Well done. Only next time why not enjoy the experience instead of wolfing the food down. It makes no difference how quickly you eat.'

Staring now at the half-sandwich, Frieda closed her eyes and took a small bite. She did this for Antonio, she told herself. Chewing slowly, she swallowed.

Antonio, lying back in the sweet-smelling grass, clasped his hands behind his head then, turning his head towards her, gave a somnolent smile. 'This is good. We do it again, yes, and have more of the… conversation.'

Frieda would like nothing better. She nodded, enthusiastically. 'Yes.'

*

That morning, when Mr Nichol had told Sandra she was to work in a gang haymaking in the fields, he'd looked up at the heavens.

'Aye. Best get finished early tonight. There's a thunderstorm brewing.'

Sandra, following his gaze, had looked up to a clear blue sky and wondered what she was missing.

When Sandra reached the field, it looked like a war recruitment poster. The field swarmed with Land Girls holding long wooden tools in their hands, hard at work in the brilliant sunshine.

Evelyn's words came back to her from last night in the bedroom, when Sandra was inwardly fretting because she'd still had no news about her brother and was in a state of limbo. She hadn't shared her worries as her superstitious mind warned that if you voiced your fears some universal force might hear and act upon them. But Evelyn could tell she was agitated and sought to soothe her.

'Work is the ticket, my father would say,' Evelyn had told her, pulling a long face. 'And for once, I think he's right about something.'

So did Sandra.

Sandra's job was to rake hay, which had already been cut and turned, into small heaps. The next day, weather permitting, four heaps would be raked into pikes. When the pikes were completely dry, a chain was wrapped around them and they were winched onto the hay bogey pulled along by a Clydesdale horse who plodded the well-trodden route back to the stack yard.

The best part of the day was when Mrs Nichol arrived in the afternoon with a tray filled with tea and doorstep sandwiches. The lasses, sitting with their backs against the drystone wall in the sunshine, had a singsong after they'd eaten. 'Show Me the Way to Go Home' was Sandra's favourite.

That night, as Sandra made her way back to the hostel, bone-tired, her arms burnt by the sun, there was an eerie silence like just before a storm. Suddenly, lightning flashed, followed by a rumble of thunder that climaxed into an almighty crash, giving Sandra a fright. As she made a run for the hostel, the heavens opened.

'How did Mr Nichol know?' she asked Evelyn as she arrived soaked and dripping in the bedroom.

'It's called country lore,' Evelyn told her. 'By the way, a letter came for you this morning. It's on your bed.'

Sandra's heartrate quickened. She reached up to the bed and tore the envelope open. She tried to read what the letter said and she could pick out a few simple words, but she couldn't get the sense of the letter. Highly frustrated, she looked at the single word at the end and presumed it was the sender's name.

She spelt the word out under her breath as the curate had taught her. 'B-RA-D'.

'Brad.' She spoke out loud.

Evelyn looked puzzled. 'Who's Brad?'

That's what Sandra wanted to know.

When Sandra arrived at the farm wearing a yellow waterproof the next morning, Mr Nichol gave a frustrated sigh. 'Seeing how it's wet, you'll be back on milking today. Though, you would have been anyway, Mr Jeffries can't make it in.'

In the byre, the cows already in their stalls, Frieda was sitting milking. 'Hello, Sandra. I missed you, yesterday.'

'Me too,' Sandra replied.

The farm, village life, was her home now and Sandra doubted she'd ever want to leave the area. Days like yesterday, as she sat in the sun with the rest of the gang singing, she felt she was making memories to last a lifetime. Hopefully, one day such memories would help eradicate the memories from the orphanage and the years of servitude at the Kirtons'.

'Yesterday I ate a piece of corned beef sandwich,' Frieda told her proudly.

'Did you bring it to work with you?'

'No, Antonio gave it to me.' A dreamy look crossed the lass's face.

When she didn't embellish, Sandra answered, 'Good for you.' She didn't pry, though she wanted to.

It occurred to Sandra how close she'd become to Frieda, how she thought of her as more of a younger sister than a friend.

She moved over to the stall where Frieda was milking Daisy. 'I have a favour to ask.'

'I am happy to help.'

'I've received a mystery letter. I can only pick out a few simple words and I'm dying to know what it says.'

'You have it with you?'

'In my pocket. I've spent all night worrying that the letter might have something to do with Alf. I've been cursing myself for not being able to read yet. D'you think you could read it out at breakfast time?'

'I'm… sorry but no, I'm…' She blushed, and seemed flustered, but then she paused with her head to one side before speaking again. 'All right, then. I will. But I have to go straight after.'

Sandra, at first mystified at her friend's reaction, decided Frieda was allowed to have a life she didn't know about. She suspected her response might have something to do with the Italian.

When the cows were ready to be taken back to the field, Sandra's suspicion was confirmed as Antonio appeared from the area of the stable.

'Mr Nichol, he say that I walk the cows to the field. I tell him I have done it before.'

Frieda's look of absolute adoration when she looked at Antonio said it all.

*

In the byre, sitting on two upturned pails, Sandra handed over the letter to Frieda.

Frieda opened the envelope.

Dear Sandra,

I expect you'll get a surprise but I wanted to get in touch to thank you for saving my life.

A puzzled frown creased Sandra's brow, then it dawned on her. 'Why, it's from the airman whose plane crashed.'

Frieda nodded then went on.

The situation that day when I saw the earth hurtling towards me, was that I thought I was a goner. After the plane crashed, I was unconscious. Then I heard a voice and I thought an angel called out to me. But it was you insisting that I opened the cockpit. When I turned and saw your face, it brought me back to earth. I knew I had to make the effort to pull through. You kept me going until help came.

They tell me I'm in a Newcastle hospital all busted up and they say I'm getting better by the day. The farmer who brought me here told the staff that the girl who found me made them aware of what happened and that he'd heard she was a Land Girl from a hostel in Leadburn.

No one knew who you were, but I remembered your name. So, that's it. I sure do hope I'm able to thank you in person one day but who knows where I'll be posted next. I was on 'rest' from operations.

Forever grateful,
Brad

Frieda looked up. 'He seems nice. What was he like?'

Sandra shrugged. 'I only saw the top half of him but I seem to remember he had blue eyes. Come to think, he seemed older. Perhaps that was because of the accident.'

'Do you think he will come and see you?'

With heavy heart, Sandra realised her brother never had the chance. 'A serviceman's time isn't their own in this war.'

'Are you thinking of your brother?'

'Yes.'

'Kurt is always in my thoughts too. What became of him? My biggest fear is he got caught and sent away.' She groaned. 'It's the not knowing that is the worst. I cope by imagining them all in our apartment in Berlin getting on with their lives. Of course, that isn't so. Or else, why don't they answer my letters?'

The unspoken words that Frieda might be an orphan too hung in the air. She looked a bleak figure sitting on the upturned pail.

When she spoke, Sandra's voice was thick with emotion. 'D'you know, we're two of a kind. Our lives mirror each other.'

'I have never thought of that. But it is true.'

Sandra, unable to bear the lost look in Frieda's eyes, changed the subject. 'Honestly, you don't need to answer this if you don't want to. But what's this with Antonio?'

Frieda's face changed, became startled. 'What do you mean?'

'I see the way you look at him.'

Frieda's head lowered and she looked up nervously. 'I sometimes meet with him in the hay barn when everyone is eating at dinner time. It is not what you think. Antonio is a gentleman.'

'Frieda, tread carefully. He's older and might take advantage. Besides, he's a prisoner and I've heard they make all kinds of promises.'

'Alf might be a prisoner of war too. He fought for his country. Neither of them had a choice.' In the silence that followed, Frieda looked shocked at her outburst. 'I'm sorry, Sandra. I shouldn't have said that.'

'You're angry.' Sandra was reminded of when she did the very same thing. 'You've every right to be. It's none of my business.'

'But I want you to know my business.'

Her words eased the tension and they both looked at one another as if wondering how they'd got to this point.

Sandra knew there'd be no reasoning with Frieda. She was young and impressionable. And who was Sandra to judge? She'd never had a romantic relationship – more's the pity – and didn't know what she was talking about.

Sandra wondered about the relationship between Antonio and Frieda. But it would seem just a flirtation on Antonio's part. Where was the harm? Let Frieda have fun while she was young. An infatuation didn't do anyone any harm and it was all part of the growing-up process.

If this were true then why did a sense of unease grip Sandra?

*

Frieda was lost in thought as she made her way into the hay barn to meet with Antonio at dinner break. She felt bad about the way she'd reacted towards Sandra as she knew she only had her best interests at heart. But Sandra was wrong about Antonio. Yes, he had enlisted in the Italian army, but that was before the war started, when he was a labourer.

He'd told Frieda days before when they were in the hay loft, 'You understand I never wanted to follow Mussolini.' All he'd done was basic training apparently. When the war started, his inexperienced and untrained platoon was captured in Libya at their very first battle. Antonio was sent to the POW camp in Northumberland. He finished in his appealing broken Italian, 'The little man, he no has a choice – he no start the war but he has to fight, yes?'

Frieda had nodded her agreement because Antonio was wise and made so much sense. If only Sandra could listen to his views, she would change her mind.

Frieda would never forget that day because, as they lay on the fragrant hay, Antonio had confessed he loved her. Then he'd leant forward and kissed her and Frieda didn't resist. The sweet kiss transported her to a happier place; it was wonderful to forget her troubles, to just *be* for a while.

When they pulled apart, Antonio asked her, 'You no tell me how old you are? I think you look seventeen.' He gave an odd, cautious kind of look.

He thinks I'm older.

She had been worried he thought her a kid as most people took her for younger than her years. She hadn't contradicted him.

'One day when this war is over, I take you back to Italy. We marry and have babies together.'

Frieda had laughed, shocked but delighted that he would say such a thing. He made life sound so simple and perhaps it was. Mama, Papa and Kurt were so far away and maybe there were good reasons for them not to be in touch. When the war was over, her parents would search for her.

All she knew, she thought as she now approached the hay barn, was that Antonio made her happy and complete and she wanted to be perfect for him. And she found whatever it was that stopped her from eating left her alone for a while when they were together.

And once Sandra got to know Antonio properly, and saw how charming he was, she wouldn't help but like him.

Antonio was already in the hay barn when she arrived and Frieda was shocked to see him smoking a cigarette. He dropped it on the floor and stubbed it out with the toe of his boot.

'*Amore mio*,' he whispered as he came closer.

She didn't understand the words but, by the burning desire in his eyes, she knew Antonio was telling her he loved her.

He came towards her and took her in his arms. While they kissed, his hand slid into the open neck of the white blouse she was wearing and fondled her breast beneath her bra. Frieda felt uncomfortable when he touched places she considered private but she was too afraid to say because she would die if he stopped loving her.

She pressed his shoulders and he pulled away. She saw the deep need in his eyes. Frieda knew forevermore the aromatic smell of hay would remind her of Antonio.

Two days later was a hot and sunny day and with her afternoon milking done, Sandra was lending the gang a hand in the field. Everyone was expected to work late to get the hay in while the weather was dry and the longer summer days meant hours of toil.

Suddenly, a thin, reedy voice could be heard from the vicinity of the farmhouse. Looking in that direction, Sandra could see Mr Nichol with someone at his side. Her spirits took a nosedive. Peggy Teasdale, the post lady.

Mr Nichol shouted again, 'Saaandra!'

Her legs went to jelly.

'I'll come with you.' Frieda linked arms with her. Side by side, they walked over the field to the front gate.

Peggy wordlessly handed Sandra the telegram.

Trance-like, she passed the yellow envelope to Frieda. She had to know one way or another. Sandra held her breath.

Frieda opened the telegram and read.

> *Report just received through the international Red Cross… your brother Sgt. Alfred Hudson has been interned by the Swiss government. If further details or information are received you will be notified at once.*

No *deep regret* or *killed.* Sandra sagged.

Then, euphoria changed to doubt as her natural anxiety for her brother's welfare took over. Was he injured? What did 'interned' mean, exactly? Furious at her ignorance, she wondered who she could ask.

And then she thought of her friend, Mr Carlton.

To keep her mind occupied, she'd worked the rest of the day, but asked Mr Nichol if she could leave at eight o'clock.

No one answered at the vicarage when she knocked. Standing at the door, wondering what to do, Sandra noticed young folk emerging from the church doorway. She made her way over.

'Excuse me. D'you know where the curate is?' she asked Bobby Teasdale, who delivered the post when his mam was unwell.

'Inside.' He jerked his head towards the church. 'We've been takin' communion lessons.'

By the look on Bobby's face Sandra guessed he was forced to go by his mam, a keen churchgoer.

Sandra found the curate sitting in the front pew, sifting through papers. When he turned at her footsteps, he jumped up, scattering the papers on the stone floor. She helped him pick them up. They stood facing each other.

'Miss Hudson, I… What are you… Is something wrong?'

'It's Alf. He's been interned in a Swiss camp. What does that mean exactly? Aren't they a neutral country?'

She realised she must look a fright: her hair blown all over, mucky trousers; she hadn't had a bath. There were no niceties, she'd just charged in and bombarded him with questions.

He didn't flinch but looked hard at her, deep concern in his eyes. He thought for a while.

'I'm not an authority on such matters, but to answer your questions' – his soft voice and tranquil manner were a tonic to her barbed nerves – 'Switzerland is a neutral county, though I've heard tell they've stopped American and British aeroplanes flying over their airspace. I would think your brother's bomber came down somewhere over or around the Swiss border. Far better internment in a neutral country, than be a prisoner of war in Germany. He may well be interned for the duration of the war.'

And he'll be safe, Sandra thought.

'Try not to worry too much. I think everything considered, he's a lucky man. I don't know the formalities, but the Swiss will abide by the Geneva Convention and Alf will be allowed to send letters home.'

Three days later, a postcard arrived. Sandra gave it to Frieda to read.

> *Hi Sis,*
> *I'm safe and well. Plane went down the favourable side of Swiss border. Being transported to be interred in ski resort!! Supposed to stay till war ends. Will send letter. Loving brother Alf*

Sandra burst into tears with relief.

CHAPTER TWENTY-TWO

July 1943

July brought the news that the Allies had taken the island of Sicily.

'Aunty Doris is positive that we have tipped the scales towards the end of the war,' Frieda told Sandra as the pair of them sat eating their dinner beneath the shade of the oak tree to escape the hazy and muggy heat. The weather had been roasting for the past few days. Hot and sweaty working in the heat, Sandra kept her dungarees rolled up to her knees, her shirtsleeves up to her elbows.

As she watched Frieda taking bites of her food, Sandra realised how far she had come with her eating problem. While she by no means ate with a hearty appetite and still was wary of consuming anything sweet or stodgy, Frieda ate enough to sustain her health and she appeared to have put on some weight – something Sandra wouldn't risk telling her as it might tip her over the edge to starving herself again.

Sandra still brought in titbits of food for Frieda to build her confidence on her road to normal eating. Today's offering was a piece of rhubarb pie from last night's supper at the hostel. Frieda had eaten a tiny portion but left the crusty edges of pastry.

Sandra also encouraged Frieda to speak about Antonio so she could keep an eye on things, despite having sworn not to get involved. Frieda was vulnerable and Sandra worried about her. She felt the kind of protectiveness an older sister might have for a younger sibling.

'These crushes are quite normal at her age,' Evelyn had told Sandra, when she'd asked advice on the matter. She trusted Evelyn and knew she wouldn't repeat the confidence to anyone. 'Would you believe I had a crush on the arithmetic master at school.' She laughed. 'Believe me, this infatuation will pass. Some servicemen and prisoners never miss a chance with a bit of flirting. As long as there's no hanky-panky involved she'll be fine apart, perhaps, from a broken heart. That goes with the territory, I'm afraid, and only helps to make us fussier and stronger. I should know.'

The talk had left Sandra worrying about what Frieda got up to in her dinner time. So it had come as a great relief when the Ministry offices in Hexham assigned Antonio to the Robsons' farm for a spell. But it hadn't stopped the lovebirds. According to Frieda, who met up with him one night, his job was to dig drains in the fields where he lived. He was allowed out at night within the limit of five miles and he and Frieda had cycled to the pictures in Hexham.

If her aunt knew about Antonio, Frieda didn't say, but Sandra didn't think that was the case.

She didn't know what she thought about Antonio's apparent freedom to come and go. She wondered if Alf got the same kind of leniency. Frieda, lying down now beneath the rippling leaves of the oak tree, told Sandra, 'Antonio doesn't listen to war news and so he won't know Sicily's been taken by the allies.' She sat up and hugged her legs. 'He doesn't get involved if there isn't anything he can do. I agree with him, why worry if there is no need?'

'Are you seeing him again?' Sandra kept her voice light as if it were just a question, not an inquisition.

Frieda's face lit up. 'We're going for a bike ride when I finish work on Sunday.'

'Where?'

'I don't mind. As long I'm with Antonio.'

*

One summer's evening at the end of July, Mr Carlton and Sandra were sitting at the dining room table as Sandra read passages from *Gone with the Wind*. The sash window was open and the curtains billowed in the soft breeze. Mr Fairweather was outside, sitting in a basket chair with a newspaper over his face.

Sandra, head bent as she stumbled over a long word, sensed Mr Carlton's pride.

When, finally, the passage came to an end, Mr Carlton exclaimed, 'Well done. You should be proud of yourself. You've done remarkably well. You can read short sentences without any help.'

'Oh, I love reading about Scarlett O'Hara,' Sandra enthused, 'she is such a feisty character. Ashley is weak. I do so hope Scarlett and Rhett Butler get together.'

'Ahem,' Mr Carlton interrupted.

Sandra, carried away by the story, felt embarrassed. But was there a gleam of amusement in Mr Carlton's eye?

'Mum was right. She assured me you'd fall in love with the story and it would encourage you to read.'

Sandra was flattered he'd told his mum about her. 'Please, thank your mam for me.'

'It won't be for a time. I don't get to see my parents as often as I'd like.'

'Oh, that's a pity.'

'I try to make it down once in a while. The last time... was for Mum's birthday. I went by train.'

'Yes, getting petrol can be a bother, I've heard.' She hated these formal talks and felt daft as she didn't know if the curate even owned a car. But it was nice seeing him talk freely about his family. He looked rather awkward when he spoke about personal things, but Sandra felt she glimpsed the lovely private man he was; a man whose family was important to him. He lost his reserve and looked happy – and handsome. Caught off guard by the thought, she blushed.

There was a lull in the conversation. Sandra found she didn't want to leave quite yet.

She ventured, 'Do your parents come by train when they visit?' As he hesitated, she thought she'd gone too far prying into his private life. She babbled, 'There are so many servicemen travelling these days, it's probably difficult for them finding a seat in a compartment.'

He thought for a moment then made a decision. 'It's not that… Dad had a stroke some time ago and is wheelchair-bound.'

'Oh, I'm sorry—'

'Don't be. The old man is perfectly happy sitting with the bible on his lap making notes, the newspaper at the ready… Mum fussing and supplying copious cups of tea. They have lots of company, both friends and from the clergy.' Surprisingly, he went on to tell her a little about his background, how he and his brother had the happiest upbringing. They'd lived in various vicarages, 'with huge gardens with trees for us boys to climb against our parents' wishes.'

'What a wonderful childhood. If I ever have kids that's what I'd want for them too.'

In the silence Sandra was embarrassed that she'd spoken her thoughts out aloud.

Mr Carlton gazed wonderingly at her. 'What a lovely thing to say.'

Then it was his turn to look abashed. 'Forgive me, I forget myself, you want to be away.' The clerical mask was in place again.

Sandra found herself thinking about Alf, and how he was faring being cooped up in a foreign country. Every day since the postcard she'd searched the table for another letter from Alf, growing increasingly anxious when one didn't arrive. Her brother had been in touch, she told herself, and she'd just have to be patient; as the curate had said they didn't know the formalities.

To be truthful, part of her was glad Alf was interned in Switzerland out of harm's way till the end of the war. But she knew her brother would be like a caged animal and being held in captivity would remind him of the orphanage.

She felt the urge to say something to Mr Carlton before she lost the chance. 'I still haven't heard from my brother.'

The curate's brow furrowed. 'That must be difficult. But you've told me that he's been in touch. That will have to suffice for now, I'm afraid.'

'I know I'm impatient.'

'Perfectly understandable.' His neck went crimson for some reason.

There came an unsettling moment when neither of them appeared to know what to say.

She stood up ready to leave. 'Again, thank you.'

Outside the window, Mr Fairweather removed the paper from his face.

'Till next time.' Mr Carlton smiled. 'Soon you will be proficient and won't need any more reading lessons.'

'You'll be glad to be rid of me.'

She realised her jocularity was to hide the disappointment at his statement.

Matthew watched Miss Hudson make her way down the vicarage path, then closed the door.

Perfectly understandable, foolish man. What a *perfectly* starchy thing to say to a young lady. She thought he wanted rid of her, when nothing could be further from the truth. Monday nights had become the highlight of his week. She kept cropping up in his mind and he couldn't concentrate. Matthew ran his fingers through his hair. All he knew was his step was lighter since the day he'd met Miss Hudson.

This wasn't the time for him to get involved with someone. Besides, as an ordained priest what did he know about women? When he'd been accepted for ordination training, he'd been thrilled to go to theological college. Above all else, Matthew wanted to please his parents, in particular his father whom he admired. Now he must see where his calling led him.

He could end up anywhere and it wouldn't be fair to Miss Hudson... Sandra. Not that she'd be interested in a formal, stuffed shirt such as him. What was he thinking? Sandra showed no interest in him that way. Besides, he would need the bishop's permission to court Miss Hudson...

Calm down, Matthew told himself, as his jumbled thoughts raced. *Take one step at a time.*

What was his first step? As for his feelings for Sandra; what were they?

Matthew's heart melted when she gave that sweet little frown of concentration when she got stuck on a word while reading *Gone with the Wind*. The book was not to his taste but for her sake he'd persevere because he would do anything to make her happy.

His mother's words played in his mind; what she had advised him and his brother when they were both still young men setting out in the world. 'When true love comes, grab it with both hands. Don't listen to anyone, especially your parents. Look at your father and me. Everyone was against us marrying so young... yet here we are twenty years later.'

His mind was made up on the matter. He didn't know how Sandra felt about him but to approach her when he hadn't been given permission would be downright foolish. Especially when the bishop, for a number of reasons, might disapprove.

The first thing Matthew would do in the morning would be to make an appointment to see the bishop.

He felt better already.

CHAPTER TWENTY-THREE

August 1943

Sandra

Sandra could contain her anxiety about the lack of correspondence from her brother no longer. At her last meeting with the curate, she'd confided that she must do something or she'd go insane with worry.

'I would think that if you contact the Red Cross they might be of help,' was his useful suggestion. 'I know they run a department for prisoners of war.'

Sandra duly attended the next Red Cross meeting in the village hall and asked a kind lady there where to send her enquiry letter about Alf.

Later, she dictated the letter to the curate.

All Sandra could do now was wait.

Today, like every other day, Alf was the first thing Sandra thought about when she woke up.

After breakfast, she left the hostel and made her way to the farm where the Clydesdale horses were ready in working gear for ploughing. The weather was unseasonably wet for August, and unsettled Sandra, who wore her yellow waterproof as protection against the occasional showers of rain.

The Ministry of Agriculture's directive was that more pastureland was needed to grow corn and so Mr Nichol had appointed Sandra to help plough one of his fields over the road from the farmhouse. Mr Jeffries had been assigned to show her how to plough.

'First thing yi' have to learn is to speak to the horses. Tell them left and right.'

Sandra had inwardly laughed but it was true; the Clydesdales seemed to know what she was saying and obeyed accordingly.

This morning, the two Clydesdales pulling the plough, Sandra guided the wheels in a straight line following the furrow, the blade turning the pastureland. Concentrating on the job, she was distracted when an aeroplane began to drone in the distance. As the plane drew closer, Sandra recognised that it had only one engine. Shading her eyes, she looked towards the sky and was relieved to see a Spitfire. The wings of the plane, as it roared overhead, waggled and Sandra couldn't help but raise an arm and wave in recognition. As the Spitfire sped away, she watched until it had disappeared over the rim of a hill.

That night, as she wearily plodded in the rain back to the hostel, body aching, blisters on the heels of her hands, dungarees wet and clinging to her knees, Sandra looked forward to a bath and the relative comfort of her bunk bed.

She had missed the evening meal and found a plate of congealed macaroni cheese waiting in the kitchen oven. Starved, she sat at a table and devoured the plate of food, listening to the chatter going on all around in the common room. Some of the girls looked over, giving her a welcoming nod or smile.

These days, fully at ease now with the others, Sandra joined in with conversations and had a laugh – she even surprised herself sometimes by expressing an opinion.

'Apparently, the Yanks call them rubbers…' Enid held court on the couch and the wide-eyed lasses listening savoured every word.

'That's true,' Trudy, a lass with silvery blonde hair Sandra had befriended, piped up. 'I come from Worcestershire and we have an American unit there. I heard tell of an American who asked in the local pub where he could get a rubber. He was sent to the nearest stationer's shop.'

There were hoots of laughter.

'You're having us on.'

'No, I swear.'

Sandra was puzzled. She had no idea what they were talking about.

Enid laughed. 'You can be assured our boys have a French letter in case of an emergency.'

'And you would know?' the blonde girl asked with a smirk.

Enid threw a cushion at her.

It was after she'd washed her plate and cutlery in the kitchen sink that Sandra, on her way to the bedroom, worried. *Why would a soldier carry a French letter around with him? And in what kind of emergency would he need it? And what if he couldn't read French?*

She found Evelyn in the bedroom, lying on her bed staring into space, her eyes swimming with unshed tears. Evelyn was one of the most emotionally strong girls here, or so Sandra had thought.

'Whatever's wrong?'

Evelyn swung her legs off the side of the bunk bed and sat up. She brought a handkerchief from her jodhpurs pocket and blew her nose noisily into it. 'It's just the news got to me.' A pained look crossed her face. 'The local newspaper reported a cargo ship was torpedoed and sunk with a loss of the crew. When I think of those poor boys in their watery grave and the suffering of their families back home' – her voice had gone weak and high pitched – 'I imagined how I'd feel if it was Gordon and I couldn't bear it for them.'

Sandra went over to the bed and, sitting beside her friend, she automatically put an arm around her.

'You're tired, that's all. You've been slogging away in the fields all week.' Sandra knew the lass went out of her way to prove herself. Not that any of the other girls or farmers doubted Evelyn's abilities. 'You can't worry about everyone's heartache. You're down, that's all, because you haven't heard from Gordon in a while.'

Evelyn sniffed. 'You're right, I do feel bushed. The trouble is when I fall into bed my mind won't stop thinking and I can't get to sleep.' A rare look of bashfulness overcame her as she met Sandra's gaze. 'The thing is, I'm in love with Gordon and can't bear the thought of anything happening to him.'

Sandra gave a sympathetic nod.

Evelyn brushed away her tears with her hand. 'How selfish am I when you've got your own troubles about your brother to contend with.'

They lapsed into silence for a while.

Sandra asked, 'Why do some servicemen carry a French letter?'

A smile twitched at Evelyn's lips and her eyes crinkled. 'Don't tell me you think it's an actual letter?'

'Isn't it?'

Evelyn explained.

'Oh!' Sandra felt the heat of a blush. 'I feel daft.'

'Don't be. How were you to know if you'd never heard the expression before?'

'But at my age!'

'I think it's lovely you're innocent about... such matters.' A twinkle of fun came into her eye. 'You'll know when the time comes not to expect a letter.'

The scene played in Sandra's mind's eye, and as she met Evelyn's playful stare, they both burst out laughing. They laughed and laughed until tears rolled down their cheeks.

'It's Saturday tomorrow,' Evelyn said, wiping her face as they calmed down.

'So?'

'The dance will be on in the village hall. Let's go. It's time we had some fun.'

'I can't dance.'

'We can easily fix that.'

Tiredness forgotten, Sandra found herself waltzing around the bedroom, tripping over Evelyn's feet.

'Now, how about I show you the jitterbug?'

Try as she might, Sandra couldn't master the lively dance.

'Stop worrying,' Evelyn said, as Sandra smoothed the skirt of her borrowed dress for the umpteenth time while approaching the village dance. Sandra wouldn't have had time to go to the shops in Hexham even if she had had the eleven coupons necessary to buy a frock. The borrowed dress was blue with exaggerated shoulders and flared skirt. Sandra was taller than her friend, and the frock's hem came only to her kneecaps – hence the constant desire to keep smoothing the skirt down. The finishing touch was the white sandals with a strap at the ankle that she'd found in Robbs department store.

As she entered the village hall, a wave of heat and noise greeted Sandra. The room was full of servicemen and women who were in uniform, while the local lasses wore frocks. Couples swirled around the room, dancing to music provided by a band on stage that consisted of three elderly men playing, respectively, a fiddle, an accordion and drums. Tables and chairs were scattered around the wooden floor and a window at the far end was open as it wasn't yet blackout time.

'Here they are, the sodbusters.'

Sandra turned to see where the female voice came from. She saw soldiers sitting with ATS (Auxiliary Territorial Service) girls at a nearby round table which had a jam jar filled with flowers on top. She looked into the cheeky face of the girl who had spoken and wondered how the lass knew they were from the hostel. Probably their rosy cheeks and suntanned faces, which no amount of powder could hide, gave the two Land Girls away.

'You'd notice if we weren't here to put food on the table,' Evelyn quipped.

The ATS lass didn't turn a hair but the man beside her looked somewhat uncomfortable and abashed. As their eyes met, Sandra raised an eyebrow. There was something familiar about him. He wore an American air force uniform. Sandra took in his strong jaw, watchful eyes, salt-and-pepper hair.

His bright blue eyes lit up as he saw Sandra and his broad smile showed a row of brilliant white teeth.

Sandra gasped in both pleasure and surprise. It was the airman who had crashed in the fighter plane. She couldn't help but be pleased to see him.

Before Sandra had time to react to the airman's smile, Evelyn pulled her by the arm and threaded them through the dancing couples. At the far side of the room they stopped at a table where Ruby and two other girls from the hostel were sitting.

Their friends moved round to make space for them. Above the din of the music, Evelyn yelled to the others, telling them what the ATS girl had said.

'Cheeky beggar,' Enid snorted. 'They think they're above us. It makes me livid when I think of the hours we work and in all weather, and what thanks do we get?'

'None. Just disgruntled farmers,' Ruby put in.

'I don't know, though.' Another lass Sandra didn't know well joined the conversation. 'Farmers are surprised at the manual work we do. They know they can't do without us.'

'That's true,' Enid agreed. 'You never know, one day we might get a medal for our service to farmers.'

There were hoots of laughter around the table.

'You lot are terrible.' Ruby put on a mock face of disapproval.

Sandra was glad the lass was having a nice evening, her grief forgotten for a time.

The band had stopped playing. The man who played fiddle spoke up. 'How about the "Palais Glide"?'

A cheer went up in the hall. Sandra looked around the eager, jovial faces. For a few hours they could forget the austerity, the danger of war. Who knew what tomorrow might bring? She shivered.

'Ooo!' Enid stood up. 'Let's have a dance.'

As one, they all stood up from the table and joined the rest of the crowd in separate lines on the dance floor. Trudy, sitting next to Sandra, took her by the hand.

'Don't think you're going to shy out of this one,' she said.

She pulled Sandra onto the dance floor. Sandra didn't have a clue what to do but Trudy, insistent, linked arms with her. When the motley band started up Sandra copied the other dancers as they started heel to toe in time with each other. Face flushed and lips aching from grinning, Sandra didn't want the dance to end.

'That was great fun,' she told Trudy when the music stopped.

'Now take your partners for a waltz,' the man with the fiddle announced.

A step too far for Sandra, she escaped before Trudy could catch her. But she needn't have worried as a local farmer asked Trudy to dance. Sandra made for the table, sitting down and preparing to watch as the others partnered up.

She looked over to where the American had been sitting at his table, but he was gone. Then she saw his figure, walking with the aid of crutches on the outskirts of the room, moving towards her. He only wore one shoe as his left foot – and presumably leg – was in a plaster cast. Anticipation coursed through her and Sandra momentarily felt weak. The airman stopped at her table and he towered over her.

'Ma'am, have you been rescuing any more airmen recently?' His lazy, wide grin was infectious.

Flummoxed how to reply, she grinned stupidly up at him.

'D'you mind if I sit, Miss Hudson?'

'Call me Sandra. Please, sit down.'

'Brad Carter.' He held out a hand. 'I knew it was you the minute you entered the room.'

He had a mature look – Sandra guessed he was somewhere in his early forties – and with his warm and sparkling blue eyes and angular face, she found him attractive.

The touch of his hand, as she shook it, sent little electric shocks throughout her skin.

He swivelled round on one leg and sat, leaning the crutches against the table. She caught sight of his left hand and checked to see if he was wearing a wedding ring.

Why had she done that? She'd never thought to do it with anyone before.

She couldn't help being nosey and found herself wondering about him. A man of his age and as good-looking must have a history. Though Sandra was too polite to enquire.

There were all kinds of questions she wanted to ask, but she settled for, 'How come you're here at the dance tonight, Brad?'

'To find you.'

That flummoxed her.

'As I said in my letter, I wanted to thank you in person. You did get my letter?' His voice had a Southern drawl she'd heard about and found rather appealing.

'Yes.'

'After I was discharged from the hospital in Newcastle, I was sent to Hallington Hall. The old boy who owns the place has turned his home into a hospital for wounded servicemen. I asked around about the hostel at Leadburn and decided I'd look you up.'

'I didn't know Americans had a unit up here?'

He nodded. 'It's all under wraps as everything is these days. What I can say is, I was sent as an instructor to train fighter pilots low-flying techniques. You're probably aware of them.'

Sandra thought of Mr Nichol's assumption and nodded. She had the good sense not to ask what kind of mission they were training for. She wondered if it was the invasion of Europe that everyone talked about. She knew Brad wouldn't say even if she asked.

'Were you stationed down south before?'

'Cambridgeshire.' He pulled a wry face, deftly changing the subject. 'Boy, it's so good to meet you at last.'

'How did you know I would be here?'

'I didn't. My buddy over there' – he nodded to the table he'd vacated where an American in uniform, holding a glass in one hand, waved with the other – 'knew there was a dance on in this here village and he thought I could do with a change and some fun. We were dropped off in a jeep.'

Sandra marvelled that both the RAF and these Americans alike didn't seem to have trouble finding petrol, even though it was rationed and used only for essential needs and essential war work. Not folk gadding about the country to dances and such like.

'Imagine the surprise I got when you showed up. I remembered your face. I would have known you anywhere.'

Sandra changed the subject. 'I was so pleased to hear you were recovering. I...' His gorgeous blue eyes, watching her, left her lost for words.

'Yes, for a while back then I wondered if I'd ever be mobile again.'

'Was it that bad?'

'Bad enough.' He pulled a rueful face. 'Broken leg, arm. Concussion and chest injuries. But hey, I survived. By the way, Mom and Pop send you big thanks and blessings for help saving their only son.'

Embarrassed, she nodded.

'Thing is, Mom's shook up. She's kinda superstitious by nature and thinks bad luck comes in threes; I guess she's waiting for the second one.' He chuckled. 'It sure is hard being an only child.'

To have a parent worry over you was a dream Sandra could only imagine, but you only know your own experience.

The music started up and they watched on as folk began to swirl around the room with their partners.

'Y'all have a great fun time at these dances.' He hummed along to the music for a while. Then he turned towards her. 'Hey, Sandra, how about you and me going to the cinema? I hear there's one in Hexham.'

'Together?' she replied, then felt foolish.

He gave an audacious grin. 'Yep. How about Sunday?'

'That's tomorrow.'

'All the better.'

She really wanted to. 'I… don't think that would be manageable.' She cringed. Why was she speaking such rot? 'The pictures probably won't be open then… some families don't even allow their children out to play in respect of the day of rest.'

'We could think of something else to do.'

She thought of Ruby's parents. Gone in the blink of an eye. 'How about we make it Monday? I'll ask Mr Nichol if I can finish early. I never ask a favour so with luck he'll agree.'

'What time?'

'Can you manage a bus?'

'If it's to see you I can.'

'I'll meet you on the half six Hallington-to-Hexham bus.'

'That's handy to know there's a local bus to Hexham.'

'Just stick your hand out and it'll stop.'

'Y'all have such cute ways… and narrow roads.'

Sandra found herself wanting to imitate his drawling twang when she spoke. Then, the thought occurred to her that she might not be able to get away from work in time. 'What if I can't make it?'

He brought from his pocket a pack of cigarettes and offered her one.

'Thank you, but I don't smoke.'

Putting a cigarette between his lips, he lit it with a lighter. Exhaling, his warm gaze studied her through the smoke. 'Sandra, you're not going to get rid of me that easily.' His eyes as he squinted looked sincere. 'I'll catch the bus every night until you do.'

CHAPTER TWENTY-FOUR

On Monday morning, Jessie collared Sandra as she got ready to leave the hostel for work.

'Hudson, the war ministry's been in touch. The gang at the Robsons' farm have finished in the fields. Some of the women are being sent to the Nichols' farm. So, you can get back to the job of milking.'

Sandra didn't like the idea of being replaced but the thought of finishing work in time to meet Brad appealed.

All that day Sandra felt nervous and excited. The sky looked bluer, the leaves on the trees greener, the countryside surrounding the farm – its array of patchwork fields and hive of activity with workers – wondrous to behold. She even had a passing word of greeting for the hefty bull in its stall of whom normally she was terrified.

Later, back at the hostel, after a rushed meal of yesterday's cold mutton, fried taties and cabbage from the hostel garden, Sandra scraped back her chair from the table and stood up.

Evelyn, sitting beside her and still eating her meal, looked up. 'Why the rush?'

'I'm off out.'

'Who with? Not that dreamy man you were talking to at the village dance?'

'Actually, yes.'

Evelyn pulled a mock disgusted face. 'You're a sly one, Sandra Hudson. Pretending to be the innocent when you attract the best-looking fellow in the room. An American at that.'

Sandra, by now used to girlish banter, grinned. 'You're only jealous.'

A shadow passed over Evelyn's face and Sandra knew she was thinking of her sweetheart. Sandra was in a hurry, but she couldn't leave her friend like this. 'Sorry, I wasn't thinking... Still no word from Gordon?'

'No. It's happened before. I go forever without a letter and then a bunch of them arrive from him all at once.' She shrugged as if to convince herself. 'He is at sea, after all.'

Sandra could tell Evelyn was trying to be brave.

'The American at the dance was the one in the crash I told you about. He's convalescing nearby.'

'He came to find you?'

'We both just happened to be at the dance.'

Evelyn gave her a questioning look. 'Go on, then, toddle along. But Sandra, judging by the way the man looked at you I'd say he's gone on you.'

With Evelyn's words ringing in her ears, Sandra ran to change and then made her way to the bus stop at the bottom of the hostel path. Waiting for the bus, the idea that Brad would be peering out of the window for the sight of her gave her goose bumps.

When the bus came into sight and rattled towards her, Sandra put out a hand.

What if Brad had changed his mind? And what was she doing agreeing to see him after only meeting him once? Because she was attracted to him, she knew.

Brad was the first person she saw as she boarded the bus. He was sitting on the front seat by the window, crutches between his legs.

Sandra's stomach seemed to somersault.

The clippy was Elsie Turnbull from the village.

'Good evening, Mrs Turnbull.' Sandra, feeling awkward, reverted to being formal. 'What time is the last bus to Hallington?'

Mrs Turnbull looked at her as though she'd lost her senses. 'The usual time of half past nine these lighter nights. Though, the boss is seeing how it goes passenger-wise.'

Sandra nodded and, conscious of other passengers staring, took the seat beside Brad.

He looked incredibly handsome in his khaki uniform and military-style peaked hat. His bulky figure appeared to dwarf the seat.

He gave an approving whistle. 'Hi, Sandra. Boy, am I glad you made it.'

Elsie Turnbull approached, ticket machine at the ready, and with an intrigued expression.

Devilment took hold of Sandra. She turned to Brad and said in an unnaturally loud voice, 'It's so nice of you to ask me out.' She gave a surreptitious grin. *Sandra Hudson, these days, you're getting above yourself.* But it was worth it to see the satisfaction at getting first-hand gossip on Mrs Turnbull's face.

Sandra paid her fare and, when the clippy moved up the aisle and out earshot, Brad leant towards her. 'I take it she's the local gossip?'

Embarrassed at being caught out, Sandra replied, 'Something of the sort.'

She realised Brad had seen it all before and nothing would escape him.

They chatted as the little bus wove its way along the country roads, past clipped, dense hedges. When the bus pulled into the market town of Hexham, Brad asked, 'D'you know what film's showing? Did you look in the local paper?'

'No, I never thought.'

It was at that moment that Sandra remembered she was supposed to be at her reading lesson with the curate. She should have got in touch to tell him she wasn't coming. She hadn't seen him yesterday when she visited the church, then it simply slipped her mind.

Because your thoughts were full of Brad, she admonished herself.

Why did she have this sense she was being disloyal to the curate? *Because you have feelings for him,* the voice in her head told her. But Sandra knew the feelings weren't reciprocated. Mr Carlton had shown no regret the time he'd told her that she was proficient in reading, effectively telling her they wouldn't be meeting up for lessons any more. *But would the curate allow his feelings to be revealed?* What was she thinking? Mr Carlton was a man of the cloth and married to the church. Hadn't he once told her his life was mapped out?

But Sandra felt bad about her thoughtlessness. Mr Carlton deserved better.

*

Matthew heard the church clock strike the quarter hour: quarter past seven. Sandra was never usually this late. He hoped she wasn't ill. Working in the rainy weather in the fields, she might have caught a cold. Disappointed at the thought he wasn't going to see her tonight, Matthew picked up *Gone with the Wind* from the table.

He hadn't seen Sandra yesterday because he was tied up all day until after evensong. Last Monday, she'd informed him that she was working in the fields till late. So perhaps that was the reason she hadn't turned up this week for her lesson.

But it wasn't like her not to tell him.

He fingered the piece of paper in his pocket with the pointers for the speech he'd noted down earlier. He'd been anxious all day and the words he wanted to say kept vanishing from his mind. How could a little speech make him so jittery when he could deliver a whole sermon with a sea of faces staring up at him?

Because so much depended on Sandra's answer, he knew.

Even the meeting with the bishop hadn't been so nerve-wracking. After a discussion with Mr Fairweather, who'd given his blessing, Matthew had managed to have an audience with the bishop the previous Friday and he'd made his request.

After many probing questions, the bishop gave his consent for Matthew to officially court Miss Hudson. Though he stipulated the couple had to court discreetly until the engagement was announced, as gossip about a curate was reprehensible. Matthew omitted to say that at this point the young lady in question had no idea of what his intentions were. As he made his way home after the meeting, Matthew admitted to himself that he was overjoyed that the first hurdle had been accomplished.

Over the next two days since his meeting with the bishop, Matthew's emotions had swung from joy that finally he was going to voice his love to her, to despair at the thought of Sandra declining his offer. The next step was up to Sandra and Matthew had no idea how she felt about him.

Now, as the church clock struck the half hour, Matthew realised that Sandra definitely wasn't coming and that all his preparation and nerves that day had been in vain. He took the book over to the sideboard.

There was always next week, a voice in his head reassured him.

*

They stood in front of the cinema reading the billboard – Sandra pretending to read as she'd rather die than face the shame of Brad knowing she was illiterate, even though her reading was improving.

'*Casablanca*,' Brad, leaning forward on his crutches as he scoured the billboard, helpfully declared. 'Ingrid Bergman and Humphrey Bogart. It's a good cast.'

He looked in exasperation at the long queue that snaked down Market Street. 'D'you think we should wait?' His eyes darted back to the billboard. 'It looks somewhat mawkish to me.' He checked his watch. 'We've missed the B film, but *Casablanca* starts shortly.'

'Go on. Give the young lass a treat.' A rather plump, mature-looking lady wearing a wool coat – which looked as though it was made out of a blanket, often the case in these days of shortages – stood at the front of the queue and winked at Sandra.

The woman shuffled back a little. 'Here, soldier, go in front of me. It's the least a body can do to say thank you. And with that gammy leg of yours, standin' for long periods will be purgatory.' She addressed the queue behind her, 'Nobody minds, do they?'

The folk behind, unsure about the bossy woman, nodded their consent.

'I think the decision's been made for us by this kind lady here,' Brad said to Sandra. With a friendly twinkle in his eyes, he turned towards the older woman. 'Thank you, ma'am.'

The woman's features softened and Sandra would swear she became coy as she gave Brad an adoring smile. 'Any time, young man.'

Sandra realised this was probably the reaction Brad got from all women.

At that moment the cinema doors swung open and a horde of people swarmed through the doorway as they left the cinema.

'Champion,' the older woman told Brad. 'That lot must've seen the feature film. More seats for us.'

The couple went in, Brad bought tickets at the kiosk and they took their seats. The houselights went down, the curtains swished open and the news began.

Brad fidgeted and put something in her hand. By the beam of the overhead projection light, she saw a wrapped oblong bar.

'Is it chocolate?'

'Yes.'

Sandra had heard that Americans had access not only to gum and chocolate but stockings too.

On the big screen a review of the year so far was delivered by the urgent voice of the newscaster. Sandra broke a square off the chocolate and put it in her mouth. Silky and creamy, it was delicious. She relaxed and pretended she came to the movies and ate chocolate all the time – but still she savoured every bite.

Then the word *JANUARY* blared from the screen in big letters and she was thrust back into reality again. A grave-looking President Roosevelt was delivering a speech. The newscaster continued to report that the first step to this desirable end was the President's meeting with Prime Minister Winston Churchill at Casablanca to discuss plans for the year; terms for the enemy were to be unconditional surrender.

A thrill of elation ran through Sandra. They were already talking about the end of the war. The thought was amazing. She'd forgotten what real life was like without always thinking about food. To be able to eat a banana again, or hear an aeroplane without a tight knot of tension in the stomach, was something she couldn't imagine. The fact that the two influential men had met in Casablanca made Sandra experience a déjà vu moment. It seemed that in some universal scheme, she was meant to be sitting here alongside Brad. He must have felt the same way too as, stubbing his cigarette out in the metal ashtray on the seat in front, his warm hand slid into hers.

The feeling of coincidence intensified as the film started. A film of intrigue, danger and love. A forbidden love because the heroine, Ilsa, was married.

Wrapped up in the plot, Sandra didn't want the film to end.

The story finally came to its conclusion with Rick telling Ilsa, his eyes glistening with love, that they both knew that she belonged with her husband and that she must leave with him. Sandra couldn't bear the heartache but she knew it was the honourable thing Ilsa must do. A lump grew in Sandra's throat and as she sniffed, Brad fidgeted and brought a handkerchief from his pocket. On the screen, as sentimental music played in the background, Rick's final words to Ilsa were, 'Here's looking at you, kid.'

Sandra gave a huge sniff to stop tears rolling.

As the couple emerged from the cinema into the cool night air, tears spilled from Sandra's eyes down her cheeks and she brushed them away with a hand. To her embarrassment and shame Sandra couldn't stop. Her tears weren't just for the couple on the screen but for all that had happened – and not just to her – over the past months. Suddenly it seemed a tap had been turned on and couldn't be stopped. She cried because she had been a hair's breadth away from being raped, because of the horror of being thrown out of the Kirtons' and having nowhere to live, then Frieda's plight, the ever-increasing fear for her family left in Germany. Most of all the tears fell because she hadn't heard from Alf and feared for his safety.

It was still light, and Brad led the way, albeit slowly on his crutches, away from the picture goers swarming out of the cinema entrance, past the magnificent towering abbey to the grassy grounds beyond. Finding a wooden bench, he eased himself down and patted the place beside him.

'Sandra, don't cry, it's only make-believe.'

'S-sorry. I don't usually… It just reminded—'

'Hey! It's okay. Whatever it is, you must have needed to let it all come out.'

The fact that Brad understood and sympathised made a fresh bout of tears start. He put an arm around her shoulders and held her tight. 'I'm listening, if you want to tell me.'

A picture of the curate saying something similar came to Sandra's mind and she was reluctant to tell her woes again, especially to a relative stranger, even if Brad was kind and understanding. The pang of disappointment returned as it always did whenever she thought of Mr Carlton. She wrenched her mind away. What was she doing? This feeling sorry for herself must stop. She sat up straight and wiped her eyes on the handkerchief. Brad, she knew, had been through much worse than her.

'I'm over it now. The picture triggered something and—'

'I understand. This war gets us all down at times. I'm only happy to be here to lend a handkerchief.' His cheeky grin was infectious.

Sandra surprised herself by thinking she was glad he was single and fancy-free. Were her feelings for Brad replacing those she had for the curate? Confused, Sandra brushed the perplexing thoughts aside and tried to just enjoy the moment.

They sat in intimate silence for a while and, as she surveyed the scene in the still and quiet evening, the buildings had a surreal quality. It was as though Sandra was part of a painting. She shook herself to make sure she was real.

Such fanciful thinking – it was time she was back at the hostel and in bed.

She noticed weariness etched in Brad's features. It had been a long and tiring day for him too. She asked, 'Are you all right? You look rather done in.'

'The nurse at Hallington wasn't keen on me having this outing. But I can be very persuasive when needs be. I must admit, though, it's taken more out of me than I expected.' He gave a tired grin. 'It's worth it, though. Apart from the visit to the dance this the only time I've been out of hospital since the crash.'

Sandra looked at the abbey clock. Five past nine. She stood up. 'We best get going if we're going to catch the bus.'

'Can I see you again?' he wanted to know.

'Yes.'

Sandra would like nothing more.

CHAPTER TWENTY-FIVE

Frieda

'Bye, Aunty Doris.' Frieda called.

'Mind you eat that sandwich. It's cheese and tomato, the bread very thinly spread with butter from Mrs Nichol's pantry.'

'I will.'

'Don't go overexerting yourself, I don't want you losing the weight you've gained.'

There was no way Frieda would eat the sandwich now, the paranoid voice in her head said, not if she looked fatter. Then she remembered Antonio's approving gaze at her slightly fuller figure, especially her bustline.

Frieda, now fifteen, worried about Antonio finding out her age. If he did, he would consider her a kid and stop seeing her.

When it had been her birthday, Frieda didn't want to mark the occasion. For special occasions such as birthdays and Christmas reminded her of joyful times she had celebrated with family, and her young heart ached at the memories. Frieda feared she would never see her beloved family again and she was swamped with despair.

Aunty Doris thought differently about celebrations.

On her fifteenth birthday, when Frieda returned from work and walked into the post office, Aunty Doris looked up from the accounts book on the counter and gave a distracted glance.

'Hello, love, hope you've had a good day.' She bent her head and continued with the accounts.

Frieda was surprised her aunt had forgotten her birthday. Just as well, she told herself, she would rather have it that way. Climbing the stairs, her traitorous mind began recounting birthdays in bygone years back home.

As she opened the kitchen-living room door, Frieda gave a sharp intake of breath. Paper chains hung diagonally across the room from the ceiling and 'Happy Birthday' posters drawn in different coloured crayons were dotted around the walls. On the table, set for two, was a small box with a colourful card propped against it.

Inside the card were the words,

The happiest of birthdays to dear Frieda. Did you think I would ever forget?!

Much love,

Aunty Doris

Frieda opened the box. Inside, lying on a rather worn red velvet inlay, was a small silver pin leaf brooch.

'It's second hand.' Aunty Doris's voice came from the doorway and made Frieda jump. 'But I got it at a bargain price.'

In her hands Aunty Doris held a round cake with candles burning brightly on the top. She began singing 'Happy Birthday' heartily.

When she'd finished, she held out the cake for Frieda to blow out the candles.

But Frieda hesitated.

Aunty Doris's expression changed from enthusiastic to serious. 'I know, love. It's difficult but think on, your mama wouldn't want to forget today.'

Too emotional to speak, Frieda nodded. With an intake of breath, she exhaled and blew out the candles.

Aunty Doris set the cake on the table. 'I made it yesterday when you were out at work. I worried you would smell it when you came in and opened all the windows. It's made from real eggs, I saved them for the occasion.'

Frieda swallowed the lump in her throat. 'Thank you. I love the brooch and the cake looks… scrumptious.'

But could she eat any? Frieda thought of the heartache Aunty Doris too endured. She was sad and lonely for the husband she'd lost and all Frieda wanted was to make her happy.

'How about you try just a tiny piece…?'

Seeing hope and expectancy in her aunty's eyes, how could Frieda not oblige?

Aunty Doris cut the thinnest slice that broke into crumbs on the plate. When Frieda put a few crumbs in her mouth she was rewarded with her aunt's broadest smile.

'I just know this is the beginning of you getting better, Frieda.'

The good thing, now that Frieda was eating more, was that she had more energy and didn't fear staying off work and missing seeing Antonio. But to her dismay the ministry in Hexham had recently assigned him to a farm way out in the sticks.

He had told her the day before he left, 'The farmer's horseman, he take sick and I help as it is haymaking time. In morning I leave camp and move into the farm.'

Frieda knew from villagers' gossip in the post office that prisoners of war were sometimes fed and slept on far-out farms. They weren't supposed to mingle and were restricted to a five-mile radius from their workplace.

The move, however, far from being restrictive to them seeing each other, proved beneficial as they were still able to meet up.

It started one night as Frieda walked home from the Nichols' farm, when Antonio, riding a bicycle, had pulled up alongside her in the road.

Frieda couldn't believe her eyes. Her heart thumped.

'Hello, lovely Frieda. The farmer, he take pity on me as I am lonely. He say I can borrow this.' He nodded at the bicycle. 'He say to go to pictures but I meet with you instead.'

So, Frieda took to riding her bicycle to meet with Antonio halfway between the village and the farm when work permitted. In the obscurity of golden cornfields that ran up the sloping hillside, and beneath the big blue Northumberland sky, they carried out their courtship. They had only exchanged a few passionate kisses before but in the seclusion of the fields Antonio's hands increasingly wandered beneath Frieda's clothes to private places. Though uncomfortable, she was afraid to refuse him as Antonio might take this as a signal she was still a child.

The last time, as they lay on the grassy path between two fields and Antonio's hands had slid beneath her knickers, she'd panicked and brushed his hand away. Antonio had groaned as he sat up, a hurt look crossing his tanned and handsome face. 'You no understand. *Ti amo.*' He shook his head in frustration. 'It means…' He touched his heart with his hand and then placed it over hers.

Mama had left a book about such things on Frieda's bed when she was nine. 'These matters are private,' Mama had told her one night at lights-out time. Frieda, in bed, had devoured both the words and illustrations in the book. '*Meine kleine*, keep yourself for the special one you will meet and marry someday.'

'How will I know when I've met the special one?'

'You just will.'

'Like you and Papa?'

'Yes. Do not worry now. You have a lot of growing up to do before these things happen.'

In Frieda's mind, she had now met that special one. A pleasurable thrill surged through her groin whenever she thought of Antonio. But Mama's words reverberated in her mind since the discussion in the bedroom. Antonio wanting them to make love when they weren't officially engaged, let alone married, dismayed Frieda. She was concerned, though, that Antonio might take her refusal as a sign she didn't love him. Alarm shook the foundations of her young heart.

'I love you so much,' she blurted to reassure Antonio.

As they sat on the grassy path with only the caw of black crows soaring overhead, a glimmer of expectancy was in Antonio's eyes. His kiss this time held an urgency Frieda hadn't experienced before and it hurt her lips, but, in a wanton state, she didn't care. The kiss lingering, Antonio fondled her breast and with his free hand he lifted her skirt to her thighs and stroked the soft skin between her legs.

He was the special one, so where was the harm? Frieda eased back onto the pleasant-smelling grass and an ache of pleasure lingered in her private parts. She closed her eyes in expectation of what would come next. Then she froze.

'No!' she cried. She struggled to sit up.

It wasn't fear of reprisal that stopped her surrendering to Antonio but the disappointment she would surely see in Mama's eyes when she discovered Frieda was no longer the innocent child she'd put on the train that fateful March day, years ago. For Mama would know, and if she didn't then Frieda would tell her because there were never secrets between them.

Antonio stood, and, mounting his bicycle, rode away.

Today, Antonio was back at the Nichols' farm. Frieda saw him as she made her way into the byre. Glimpsing his stocky, muscled figure and tousled black curls, her young heart soared.

Since the last time they'd met in the cornfields, her thoughts had swung from heady heights of love when she convinced herself true love could withstand a falling out, to the stomach-churning dismay of doubt that she'd deeply offended Antonio.

Striding towards the tack room, Antonio stared blankly at Frieda. The despair clutching her throat threatened to suffocate her.

Putting pride aside, she wanted to run to him and beg him to listen while she explained and tried to make things better between them. This, though, was neither the time nor place and she'd have to wait until dinner break to catch him alone.

A busy morning followed with never-ending tasks, then Mr Nichol appeared in the yard as she and Sandra were washing their hands in readiness for dinner. He told them in his clipped way, 'You two can help the womenfolk after dinner with the pig.' He nodded and walked away.

Trotty the pig had been killed yesterday and had been hanging from a hook in the ceiling of the Nichols' pantry since.

'What do we have to do?' Frieda asked Sandra.

'Beats me.'

At the thought that blood might be involved, Frieda felt her face blanch.

Sandra noticed and spoke up. 'You're tough. You'll win through whatever's involved.'

Frieda wished that were true of her love for Antonio.

'I'm off to sit in the sunshine and have dinner,' Sandra told her. 'Are you coming? I've brought a piece of chocolate for you. It was a gift.'

The fact that her friend had chocolate, a precious commodity these days, didn't register with Frieda. All she wanted was to be with Antonio.

'I'm not hungry.'

'Are you meeting Antonio?' Sandra looked at her keenly.

'I need to talk to him.'

An anxious look clouded Sandra's face.

'I busy,' Antonio told Frieda as she walked into the stables that held a horsey smell of sweat, manure and hay. He put the bucket he carried down. 'In morning, I see you at breakfast time.' She heard finality in his voice.

The temptation to plead overcame Frieda. She bit her lip. Pride wouldn't allow her. Crushed, she left him to his work.

Making her way back to the yard, she told her doubting mind, *He's busy, that's all. He still wants to see me.*

A ray of hope ignited within her.

Sandra, coming out of the byre, bait tin and lemonade bottle in her hand, gave a little wave. 'Change your mind?' Her expression was hopeful.

'Antonio is busy.'

'Come and join me for dinner, then we'll go to the farmhouse and help with the pig.'

Just about to reply, out of the corner of her eye, Frieda saw someone cycling up the farmhouse path.

She turned and saw Bobby Teasdale from the village. He was fifteen now and had left school to deliver telegrams, earning the poor lad the nickname the Angel of Death. Sandra saw him too and both stood transfixed as they watched him turn into the yard and head towards them. Time stood still. Then a black crow soared overhead and Frieda shuddered. To her it seemed a bad omen as the last time she'd seen one was when she and Antonio had fallen out.

Bobby approached Sandra and her face turned ashen. But he didn't acknowledge either girl as he passed and cycled up to the farmhouse. He dismounted and knocked on the open porch door.

Frieda saw Mrs Nichol peer out of the front window. She disappeared, then re-emerged from the kitchen into the porch doorway, wiping her hands on her white pinafore.

Frieda couldn't hear what Bobby said, but Mrs Nichol couldn't take her eyes off the telegram he handed her. Face expressionless, she went back indoors.

Bobby, cycling past the two girls again, kept his eyes glued on the roadway ahead.

A terrible howl was heard from the kitchen area and, like a trapped animal, it went on and on. Frieda unable to bear it any longer, covered her ears with her hands.

When, finally, she was brave enough to listen she heard hysterical screams.

'Bastards! You took my baby. You took my baby.'

Frieda had never heard either of the Nichols swear before.

Sandra, galvanised into action, told her, 'Go and fetch Mr Nichol. I'll see to his wife.'

Tears blurring her eyes, Frieda ran full pelt over the uneven ground to the cornfield.

Later they lay on their backs, knees bent, feet planted on the grass, under the shade of a tree.

'It too unbearable to think about,' Sandra told Frieda. 'Their only son. All their dreams for the farm… gone.'

Frieda shook her head in sorrow. 'Mr Nichol couldn't take it in when I told him a telegram had arrived at the farmhouse. It was awful. His first words were "Has Mother opened it yet?" When I told him I thought so, I didn't know a person of his age could run that fast.'

'I've never seen a grown man cry before.' Sandra shook her head in sorrow. 'I sensed they wanted to be alone and so I left them. I hope I did the right thing.'

'I don't think they'd have even noticed. There's nothing anyone can do. Anyway, I saw the neighbours arriving to help with that dratted pig… they'll know what's best. I expect when she hears, Aunty Doris will close the post office. She knows how to help in this kind of situation.' She left it unsaid that her aunt had experienced tragedy when her husband died.

They lay in silence for a while.

'I thought at first the telegram was for me,' Sandra said in a small voice. 'I feel guilty that I'm glad it wasn't.'

'Anyone would think the same. It's natural. I know your brother is a source of constant worry for you.'

Frieda spoke wisdom beyond her years and a yearning to protect her washed over Sandra. They both knew that Frieda's family and Sandra's brother mightn't survive the war and they might be left alone in the world.

'The thing most hard to bear,' Frieda said as though she read Sandra's mind, 'is knowing you might never see your loved ones again.'

They looked at one another and tears brimmed in their eyes.

*

'Hallington Hall…' the bus driver called.

Sandra, making her way down the aisle, alighted from the bus and called to the middle-aged lady driver, 'Thank you.'

Sandra peered through the stone pillars and saw a hive of activity on the expansive and verdant lawn. A sweeping drive led to a large country house with extensive gardens and outhouses and walled garden. Wooden recliners spread out on the lawn this sunny summer day, where soldiers in uniform lounged, presumably in all stages of recovery. Nurses in blue uniform and starched white caps mingled between patients, and relatives visiting loved ones watched on.

Sandra ventured in and, as folk stared, she felt like an interloper. Further down the lawn a soldier stood up from a basket chair and waved. Sandra recognised the sturdily built figure as Brad.

When they'd parted after their outing at the cinema, Brad had told her, 'It sure would be nice if you came to visit on Sunday. They say the cast comes off over the weekend. Who knows what state the leg will be in.' His eyes grew both warm and intense. 'Sandra, it would be good to see you.'

Sandra liked that about him. Brad stated what he wanted and there was no mistaking his intentions. Unlike her, who worried she'd offend people and often found herself going places or doing things she'd rather not do.

When she asked Jessie for time off milking that Sunday afternoon, the forewoman had told her yes without hesitation. 'You never ask for time off, not like some who are always requesting time to go home at the weekend.'

Sandra didn't confess to Jessie that the hostel was her home.

If Sandra were truthful, it felt good to escape the sadness of the Nichols' farm for a while. Mr Nichol turned up to run the farm each morning but his emotions were all over the place, and he struggled to stay strong. It was achingly sorrowful to watch, and Sandra felt helpless as there was nothing she could do to help. He had good company in the collie who appeared to know his master's distress and would never leave his side.

Making her way along the lawn to meet with Brad, like a schoolgirl on her first date, Sandra felt butterflies in her stomach.

'Hi, Sandra.'

She squirmed under his gaze and as he bent forward and kissed her cheek she reddened. She looked around, but, too engrossed in their own conversations and affairs, no one was watching. Soldiers reclined back against loungers, some with bandages, or arms in slings; other poor souls had limbs missing, while others, ashen-faced, stared ahead as relatives tried in vain to bring them out of themselves.

Brad sat down again and, lighting a cigarette, he gestured to the basket chair next to his.

As Sandra sat, he told her, 'These lads have had it rough but they don't complain.'

'I would have brought you something' – she'd noticed the brown paper containing, no doubt, sweeties and goodies the other visitors had brought – 'but the village shop shelves were bare of anything that—'

'Sandra, it's enough you've brought yourself.' His eyes met hers and his genuine look melted her heart.

They spent a companionable afternoon in the sun talking and getting to know each other better, Brad leaning forward, intent on her every word. Sandra didn't feel able to be open about her past as she felt embarrassed about her lowly background with someone as worldly as Brad.

Brad had no such reservation. He talked about his life in Florida which seemed a far cry from the experiences Sandra had known.

'Pop owned a drugstore in Jacksonville and we lived in a little house with a white picket fence. It's the only home I've ever known. The drugstore was open seven days a week and Mom helped serve drinks behind the counter.'

'Drinks? What kind?'

'Cherry coke is the favourite.'

'Is it true it's terribly hot in Florida?'

'You kidding me? The only way to keep cool is to be neck deep in water. Which was what me and the boys did in the Atlantic Ocean, in summer when school was out. I tell ya, we practically lived at the beach. Miles of golden sand as far as the eye could see and whopping great waves to dive in and little sandpiper birds that strutted about and we liked to chase – but never caught.'

'It sounds idyllic.'

Brad smiled as he reminisced. 'It was.'

'Does your dad still run the drugstore?'

A shadow passed over his face. 'Pop had a heart attack in his early fifties. He'd always wanted me to follow in his shoes and, being an only child, I wanted to please him. Going to pharmacy school seemed the right thing to do. When Pop took ill and it was obvious he wasn't coming back, it seemed natural that I took over the drugstore.'

'He must be proud.'

'Then the war in Europe started and seeing all the Army and Navy recruitment posters in the windows, I wanted to be in the action. Pop had ingrained duty in me and being loyal to customers.'

'They must have loved him.'

'They sure did. The feeling was mutual; Pop treated them like family.' Brad rubbed the back of his neck. 'Thing was, I was torn. Pop instilled in me that duty comes first – but he meant to our customers. Everything changed after the Japanese attacked the naval base in Pearl Harbor. I reckoned that I owed my duty to my country. So, I got someone to take over the drugstore and enlisted and, after a long stint training in the army air force… here I am in England.' He gave a corner of the eye, roguish look. 'And boy, am I glad.'

Feeling awkward at the implication of his words, Sandra changed the subject. She looked down at his leg. 'How is it now you've had the plaster cast removed?'

'It sure looks puny and wasted.'

Sandra gave him a sidelong glance. Surely nothing about Brad's stocky figure could look puny.

*

Later, as Brad leant on a stick, slowly making his way over to the house, he thought about Sandra's visit. He reckoned there was a good fifteen years between them, and though she appeared naïve for her age there was some inner perceptive quality that attracted him. Though he'd sworn after his heart had been broken that, from now on, he'd love and leave women, instinctively Brad knew that wouldn't be true of Sandra.

Why, he didn't know. She wasn't his usual type, but since the day of the crash when she'd appeared like an angel, she'd been on his mind.

He wasn't smitten, he reassured himself. He paused for a moment before entering the doorway of the dim building and lit a cigarette.

His conscience pricked him. He should have told her. But why? He was only having a harmless flirtation during war time.

Wasn't he?

CHAPTER TWENTY-SIX

The hostel was silent when Sandra arrived back late afternoon after visiting Brad. Many of the Land Girls had gone home for the weekend but would be back soon.

Munching a Spam sandwich, Sandra made her way along the corridor to the bedroom. She found a note on her bed, presumably from Evelyn.

Perplexed, Sandra tried to make out what the note said. She spelled out the easy words in her mind.

Such a... night. Ruby and I... a few... bike ride. I've got... some news. See you later x

Opening the window in the airless room and sitting on her bunk, Sandra wondered what the news could be. She'd been up since five thirty and, overcome with tiredness, she felt her eyes droop. It would do no harm to have a nap, then wander up to the church after. Of course, it would be closed but even if she touched the church and said a prayer for Alf, surely that would count.

As she lay, light coming in through the window, scenes played behind her eyes of the pleasant afternoon she'd spent with Brad.

She must have slept because suddenly she awoke with a jump. In the drowsy state between reality and dreams, she still flew on a fluffy white cloud looking down at the earth where Brad was riding a bicycle.

Her brow hot and sticky, Sandra told herself it was only a dream. She looked around but couldn't see in the claustrophobic darkness. The blackout curtains were drawn. Sandra felt beneath her pillow for the torch and, switching it on, looked at her wristwatch. Two o'clock. She shone the torch's beam on the bunk below where a hump in the covers confirmed that Evelyn was in bed asleep. She then shone the beam over to where Ruby slept. Sandra must have been tired as she hadn't woken when the others came to bed. It was an unwritten rule that Land Girls didn't disturb others as, working such long hours, they all needed their rest.

Sandra switched off the torch and, replacing it back under the pillow, she snuggled beneath the blanket. Then as a thought struck, panic rose within her. Sandra sat bolt upright again. She'd missed going to church again.

The next morning, after a night of fitful sleep, Sandra was rudely awakened from below by a not-so-good rendition of 'You Are My Sunshine'.

She remembered missing church yesterday and the thought rendered her sick with fear.

The singing from the bunk appeared to get louder.

Sandra, in no mood for early morning cheer, threw her pillow. 'Stop that racket.'

The singing stopped.

'Can't a person be jolly, for goodness' sake?'

'Only if a person has something to be jolly about,' Sandra snapped, swinging her legs off the bed.

Evelyn's beaming face appeared. 'A person has.'

'What?'

'I got a letter from Gordon. He's alive and well… and what's more, he wants us to get engaged.'

Feeling guilty that she was spoiling her friend's wonderful news, Sandra decided to buck up. Where was the harm in visiting church one day late? she asked herself. She would go straight after breakfast and before she went to work.

Sandra got up and noticed the others had left for breakfast. 'Sorry I'm a grump.'

'I noticed.'

'I'm so glad Gordon's safe. Eee! Hearty congratulations. That's marvellous news.'

Evelyn sat on the edge of the bed, eyes shining in delight. 'I told the others last night but didn't want to disturb you. I'm thrilled. The only thing is Daddy's going to be proved right, blast him. My life is mapped out.'

'When did you receive the letter?'

'It must have arrived on Saturday afternoon. The one day I didn't check.' Evelyn clicked her tongue. 'I found it yesterday when I arrived back from work. I wanted to tell you but Jessie said you had the afternoon off.' She rolled her eyes. 'Methinks you met with the aeroplane crash man…?'

Sandra couldn't help the blush that rose from her neck.

Evelyn laughed. 'By the glossy look in your eyes, I'm right.'

There followed a time, as the pair of them got washed and dressed, of joyful banter. Evelyn was in such high spirits and who could blame her. For such wonderful news was a rarity and had to be savoured.

Making their way to breakfast, they sat at the long table next to Ruby.

'Isn't it jolly news,' she remarked.

Evelyn chipped in, 'Gordon said in his letter he couldn't wait till he came home to propose.'

'That's so romantic.' Ruby looked starry-eyed. 'I don't blame him. It doesn't pay to wait. These days me motto is, grab your chance at a bit of happiness while there's time.' Her expression changed and turned infinitely sad.

'I agree.' Enid, the other side of Ruby, leant forward and joined in the conversation. 'I'm up at the Robsons' farm and the ministry's sent a new man to help with the horses.' She gave them a brazen look. 'Don't be shocked, but one of the Italian prisoners has taken a fancy to me. He's dreamy-looking and I intend to play along while it suits.'

The hairs on the back of Sandra's neck stood up.

'You won't get to see him much when he's in POW camp,' Ruby commented.

'Mr Robson allows him to sleep in the granary. We'll see each other at night after work.'

Ruby looked rather taken aback. 'I thought you had a sweetheart.'

'I do. But mum's the word as I wouldn't want Dan to find out.' She shrugged. 'I don't see why I should miss out on a bit of fun.'

Ruby rolled her eyes. 'It takes all sorts.'

Sandra spoke up. 'What is this Italian prisoner's name?'

'Antonio.'

At supper that night, Sandra didn't join in with the nattering girls around her. But their chattering away helped drown out the nerves of her reading lesson ahead. Later, as she knocked on the vicarage door, she felt her heart quicken. She had allayed her fears a little about Alf by going to church that morning before work as she'd promised.

The door opened instantly, as though the curate had been waiting behind it. Sandra wondered if something seemed different about him.

'Miss Hudson, come in.' He stood aside. 'I hope you've not been ill.'

'I'm so sorry I missed the lesson last week, but I was… To be honest something came up and I simply forgot.'

'No matter. You're here now.' He seemed rather tense as he led the way to the front room. 'I thought we'd sit in the garden. It's such a lovely evening it's a pity to be indoors.' Opening the French windows, he gestured towards the garden outside. 'After you.'

Sandra looked around. 'Isn't Mr Fairweather here?' She almost added *to chaperone*. She inwardly smiled as she wondered what the vicar thought they might get up to but knew such propriety was called for under the circumstance.

'The vicar decided to stay indoors… he's listening to the wireless in the other room.'

The curate was indeed acting oddly and for some reason Sandra felt protective towards him.

She stepped out onto a small patio and gasped. A black wrought-iron table with two matching chairs occupied a space. On top of a white tablecloth was a vase with a single rose from the garden in it and a jug and glasses. She was touched that he'd bothered to make such an effort.

'Why, how lovely.'

'It's only water with a few leaves of mint, I'm afraid, but it's refreshing.' His cheeks reddened with pleasure and his boyish face reminded her of a schoolboy on his first day of school. But there was still something else, an edginess, as if something was afoot.

She sat and poured herself a drink. 'I need this after the day I've had, including chasing after sheep.'

His lips pressed together, smothering a laugh at the image. She'd noticed before that Mr Carlton had a keen sense of humour which he tried in vain to hide. Sandra checked herself; it was best not to think too deeply about the curate, about his endearing character traits – it stirred up unwanted emotions.

'Why were you chasing after sheep?'

'Mr Nichol and I were bringing them in to drench them... which is to give them medicine for worms. As soon as I opened the gate a group of them made off up the path.'

'Where was the sheepdog?'

'Tyne can go deaf when he wants.'

'Ahh!'

There was a somewhat awkward silence.

'Ahem... Miss Hudson, I've been to see the bishop and...' He seemed to run out of steam.

In the slight pause, Sandra thought the poor man must be feeling uncomfortable and was trying to make polite conversation. She decided she'd save him the trouble.

'I really do feel bad about last week,' she butted in, 'I was with the airman I told you about.'

Feeling awkward, she stiffened. Why had she brought up the subject of Brad?

The curate sat very still for a moment as if collecting himself. 'The one that crashed?'

'Yes, he's out of hospital and convalescing at Hallington Hall.'

'At Hallington Hall... He came to see you?'

Under his intense gaze, she felt scrutinised. She blurted, 'We met at the village dance.'

Sandra seemed to have lost control. Why did she insist on babbling about Brad? Was it some kind of defence mechanism?

'At the village dance...'

She wished he would stop repeating what she said. What was wrong with him tonight? Perhaps he was absorbed with church matters or those of one of his parishioners. It made her wonder who he shared his own problems with. Sandra knew it wasn't done to question a curate.

'Brad – that's the American's name – wanted to thank me for what I'd done. He asked me out and we went to the pictures in Hexham.' It was as though her voice had mind of its own.

'You went to the pictures—'

'Brad is a gentleman,' she interrupted before he copied again. 'Not like some you hear of—'

Sandra cringed as she realised what she'd said to a man of the cloth. He wasn't naïve and must know what she meant. And he was attractive in a sensitive kind of way. He could get married one day and so he must have… sexual feelings.

Appalled at her thoughts, Sandra's mind snapped shut. Breathing deeply, she attempted to gain back some control.

She simply stated, 'Brad and I mostly talked about life in America.'

Mr Carlton straightened in his seat and likewise took a deep breath. 'This Brad does sound nice.'

Lips pressed firmly together, she nodded noncommittally.

In the silence that followed, the urge to tell him what was bothering her was overwhelming. She trusted him. He was the only person she could confide in and he was so easy to talk to. Sandra valued his advice.

'Before we begin the reading lesson, I'd like your thoughts on something, if that's all right?'

His limpid eyes softened in a supportive way – but there was a hint of reservation too, as though he was worried about what she might say.

'I'd be happy to be of service in any way I can.'

She told him about how Frieda had a crush on Antonio, and how he was now consorting with a Land Girl. She concluded, 'I don't know what to do. If I tell Frieda she mightn't be strong enough for the hurt involved. I'm worried the lass might stop eating and become ill again. But if I don't tell her then she is being deceived and that's wrong too. What am I to do? She's infatuated with the man.'

Mr Carlton stood up and held his hands together in front of him in that way of his. He thought long and hard before saying,

'It is a dilemma, indeed. I can't tell you what to do but what I would ask, Miss Hudson, is this. If you were Frieda what would you want from a friend?'

Sandra thought and then the resolution became clear. 'I'd be upset if I knew my friend had known all along and hadn't told me.'

Mr Carlton smiled reassuringly. 'She may hold it against you for a while, but you have the strength to cope. And I would say, Frieda has strength too. It takes great willpower to stop eating for whatever reason. Frieda is stronger than you think.'

'Thank you, Mr Carlton. You've been such a great help. The matter of what to do was getting me down.'

The curate looked at her with a serene expression. 'I'm glad to be of help. But it was you who worked the answer out for yourself.'

'Oh!' She suddenly remembered. 'What was it you wanted to tell me earlier about the bishop?'

The curate gave a curious, sad smile. 'No matter. The subject doesn't apply any more.'

*

Later, when Sandra had gone and her presence still lingered in the room, Matthew pondered over the conversation. He tried to guide parishioners when they sought his advice, but the final decision belonged to them.

He thought of how she'd talked about the American and how her face had become animated. Matthew, a keen observer of the human state, noticed such details as it had helped on numerous occasions while dealing with the distraught or bereaved. Sandra might not be aware of it yet, but she had strong feeling towards the American.

Love wasn't always about finding the right one, and being with them, Matthew knew. Caring for someone also meant doing what was best for them and in this case if that meant losing Sandra to someone else, then so be it. All Matthew's generous heart wanted was for her to find happiness and someone to be close to, even if it wasn't him – she deserved no less.

But Matthew was worried, not for his own sake but hers. For though she was tough, because of her disadvantaged background, Sandra was also vulnerable and alone and clearly inexperienced. He couldn't help but feel guarded at her attachment to this Brad – an American soldier likely to return home – whose motives he didn't know or trust. It was the same scenario as what Sandra experienced with her friend, though she couldn't see it that way. She wanted happiness for Frieda, but she had reservations about Antonio.

Matthew hoped his fears were unfounded as he couldn't bear the possibility that Sandra's heart might be broken.

*

'I wanted to talk to you,' Sandra told Frieda above the noise of squealing pigs.

Sandra was in the pig shed where she'd broken up a bucketful of cooked potatoes with the blade of her shovel. As she tipped the potatoes into the trough, a scuffle of hefty, pink-skinned pigs, climbing over each other, wrestled to be first at the food.

Frieda chucked a fresh covering of straw over the pigs' sleeping quarters. 'What about?'

Sandra hesitated, but she was determined to be outspoken. 'This is uncomfortable for me to say but I—'

'What does it concern?'

'Antonio.'

Frieda blanched. 'There is nothing wrong with him?'

'No – it's nothing like that.' Sandra gulped. 'I found out that he is seeing someone else. I thought it right you should know.'

Frieda reeled. Sandra saw the shock etched in her face.

They were silent awhile and all that could be heard was a snuffling noise as the pigs gobbled food.

'Who? How do you know?'

'One of the Land Girls at the hostel. She works up at the Robsons' farm. She was talking about how she meets with one of the prisoners, an Italian called Antonio.'

'You think it was my Antonio?'

'It would be too much of a coincidence if it wasn't.'

Ashen-faced, Frieda began to rake the straw.

Sandra, at a loss what to do, watched the pigs gobble down their food. She cursed Antonio for causing her friend such confusion and unhappiness.

'Antonio didn't show at breakfast time when he promised.' Frieda looked lost and alone. 'He had talked of us having a future together…'

Sandra was so furious she would personally have liked to have sent Antonio back to the prison camp and not let him put a foot outside for the duration of the war. Frieda, young and vulnerable, had had enough loss to cope with in her short life. Another ordeal like this might send her over the brink, and she'd become ill again. Sandra knew that platitudes – like telling Frieda it was puppy love and she would get over it – wouldn't help. But finding the correct words was difficult. She wished Frieda had confided in her aunt, as she was worldly and would know how to handle a problem such as this.

She decided to be honest. 'It's difficult to know what to say when you're inexperienced at being in love like I am.'

Frieda relaxed a little. 'I do love Antonio and I thought he did me. How could he flirt with someone else?'

'My friend Evelyn says that these things happen with soldiers too. I suppose we all crave company and want to escape the war. But Antonio shouldn't have acted in this way.'

'He made me happy, Sandra. I began to believe good things could happen. When I was with him the world didn't seem such a dangerous place and I began to hope for… everyone's future.'

'You must go on thinking like that.'

Frieda's face flushed as though she was ashamed. Her head lowered, she looked from beneath dark and curled eyelashes up at her friend. 'The last time I was with Antonio he wanted to, you know... I don't know what words to use.'

'I know what you mean.' Sandra could imagine.

'I worried that if I didn't, I would lose him. I wanted to but I knew Mama wouldn't approve. Now I've lost my chance with Antonio. He's found someone else. He doesn't love me any more.'

'I know enough to say that it wasn't love, Frieda. If it was, Antonio would have patience and would have respected your wishes.'

Sandra knew she was on a moral high horse, but she was so enraged for Frieda's sake, she couldn't help herself.

'I'm not strong like you. I was so happy. I wanted to get well for Antonio's sake.'

Sandra thought of Mr Carlton and quoted him. 'You do have strength. It takes a lot of willpower to stop eating, and even more to begin again and get well, as you have. You can get over this, I promise you. One day you'll meet someone special and it will be meant to be and you will put this behind you.'

Frieda, open-mouthed in astonishment, replied, 'That's what Mama would say. She told me there was someone out there special for me.'

'Your mama was right. But Frieda, I suspect you won't get over Antonio overnight.'

Frieda, big-eyed, nodded as though Sandra's words were now gospel truths.

'I still love him, but I also feel humiliated.'

CHAPTER TWENTY-SEVEN

The time dragged and there was still no news from the Red Cross about Alf. Sandra's nerves were on edge. She had at least got a letter thanking her for her correspondence. The letter stated the department responsible for Prisoners of War had been informed of her enquiry, but she'd heard nothing since.

The news on the wireless dominated everyone's lives these days.

'The allies are gaining ground,' Enid announced one supper time, her voice high pitched with excitement.

'Surely, the end of the war can't be too far away.' Ruby, who sat next to Sandra, gave a heavy sigh.

Enid piped up, 'In her last letter, Mum said the feeling at home is that people aren't too hopeful and are convinced Hitler will have a crack at us before he goes under. She says people are depressed at the thought of another winter of blackouts, rationing and all the other upsets and tragedies war brings.'

Sandra glanced at Ruby, but the lass didn't flinch and appeared to be coping with the conversation well. At weekends Ruby stayed at her boyfriend's home. She and the family – including Roy's sister – now got along and they had seen Ruby through the first months of heartache after her parents were killed. Ruby had reported that her future plan, after the war, was to live in with Roy's family until they got hitched.

Sandra was over the moon for her.

*

The summer days were spent mostly working at the Nichols' farm milking cows and harvesting the fruits of the Land Girls' labour. The days were long and Sandra often worked as late as ten o'clock in the dusk – and bed was the only thing she was interested in when the work was done.

The atmosphere on the farm was sombre as Mr Nichol, grey-faced and a shadow of himself, immersed himself in his work. He looked, though, like a man with a guilty conscience. Sandra wondered if his wife held him responsible for the death of their son. She sincerely hoped not. These days Sandra never clapped eyes on Mrs Nichol as, at mealtimes, she locked herself away in the bedroom. Goodness only knew what state the poor woman was in, but the local doctor was often seen calling on her.

'Mother isn't up to seeing folk yet,' was Mr Nichol's clipped explanation.

Antonio returned to the farm unchanged and still his extrovert self. Unaware that he'd been rumbled, he couldn't understand why Frieda was so aloof.

'He keeps asking me to meet with him,' Frieda told Sandra, her face troubled.

The pair ate dinner together in the field behind the shed. Frieda's meal was two cream crackers with a smidgeon of butter, a tomato, followed by a fallen apple from the tree in the farmhouse garden. Her cheeks were pink, her dark hair had a lustrous sheen; the lass looked healthier than Sandra had ever seen.

'Do you want to?' Sandra tried to take a leaf out of the curate's book, letting Frieda make her own decisions, while she kept her opinions to herself.

Frieda pulled a tortured expression. 'If I am honest, yes. But you help keep me strong. I know I'll be hurt further if I allow my feelings to get the better of me. Antonio deceived me and I know he is a…' She raised her eyebrows as she searched for the word.

'A two-timing cad?' Sandra helped out. She wanted to both laugh and yell 'Hurrah for you!' and she would have done if the moment hadn't been so serious.

Instead, she nodded encouragingly.

Sandra continued to meet with Brad on Sundays after work and a visit to the church and it never ceased to amaze her how her heart rate quickened at the thought of seeing him. However much she was worried about Alf, or exhausted from work, being with Brad restored her strength. Her mood, from the moment she clapped eyes on him, instantly became brighter.

'Hey, Sandra. How are you doing?'

She cycled up close to where he was waiting in the road on his bike – they'd begun cycling together, which was helping his leg become strong again.

He brushed her forearm. 'Still pedalling that black monster.'

Her arm tingled at this touch. 'No hills today, remember. Not everyone has the luxury of gears.'

'I've looked at the map and planned a route. We're off up the shire.'

The little dark shadows under his eyes now gone, Brad looked tanned and carefree, and though he still had fine lines etched at the corners of his eyes and grey in his hair, he looked younger than when she'd met him at the dance.

The day was clammy and hot, with a blanket indigo sky. As she cycled behind Brad, Sandra noticed a haversack on his back. They cycled along narrow roads, the sun dazzling her eyes. Passing workers in the fields, they rode up a steep hill where Sandra viewed the breathtaking collage of colourful fields for miles around.

Brad stopped to look at his map. 'See that building…?' Sandra shaded her eyes and looked up to the brow of the hill where there was a church with white painted windows. 'According to this map, there should be a track on the right just before you reach the summit.'

'So much for no hills,' Sandra grumbled. Then squinting, she pointed. 'There it is.'

Brad folded the map and mounted his bike. All Sandra could think of as she followed him along the narrow track was, *Who on earth built, let alone attended, a church in this isolated countryside?* Then she remembered there had been lead mines in the area and, according to the elder villagers, the area had crawled with workers.

Cycling on, under the blissful cool of the overhanging trees, they came to a glade where a flowing stream torrented over high rocks and filled the deep and inviting pool below.

'It's what I imagine a fairy glen to look like.' Sandra's eager tone echoed her delight.

Lush grass surrounded the pool and the pounding from the waterfall intensified the magical feel.

'How about we take a dip?' Brad laid his bicycle on the grass.

Sandra did the same then moved closer to him, noticing beads of sweat on his brow. The masculine sweaty smell of him aroused her. Flustered, she let out a laugh. 'I don't even own a bathing costume.'

Her thoughts turned to the one she'd once worn when she went to the beach at South Shields on her afternoon off when she worked for the Kirtons. It was woollen, and when it got wet it hung down to her knees. Not very romantic.

Brad rummaged in his haversack. He brought out two towels. 'I noticed on the map the track ends abruptly. In England that usually means there's a little stream.'

He handed her a towel. 'Slip your things off.' He gave a cheeky grin. 'I won't look.'

Sandra was appalled. Then she looked around, at the wonderful setting, the sound of the waterfall, and felt the heat of her body, her clothes clinging to her skin. The man standing before her had a soppy grin on his face. How often in life did an opportunity like this present itself?

'Promise you won't look?'

'I promise.'

Brad turned his back towards her. Sandra undressed to her knickers – no way was she removing them – her clothes slipping to the ground. She stood by the water far away from the waterfall and dared herself to go in. She sat on the edge and plunged into the pool. The icy water reaching above her groin, Sandra gasped in surprise at the cold.

'Ready or not, I'm coming in. Close your eyes.'

In a flash Sandra dipped down and immersed her shoulders in the icy depths. After the initial shock, she found she quickly acclimatised to the silky waters.

There was a terrific splash and then a stillness of water, then Brad's head emerged in front of her. His hair pasted to his head, droplets of water running down his face, Brad's eyes locked with hers. He moved towards her and ran his tongue over his lower lip. Sandra couldn't help herself. She bent forward and kissed him on his full lips.

Their naked bodies entwined, she knew before she got lost in the kiss that she'd fallen in love with Brad Carter.

CHAPTER TWENTY-EIGHT

Nothing that Monday morning could dampen Sandra's spirits. Not the nights getting dark quicker, nor the fact the weather had turned muggy and wet. After the day spent with Brad yesterday, Sandra was still in a euphoric daze.

Cycling along the road to the farm in the awakening light, her mind drifted to the kiss in the pool and a quiver of pleasure that had rushed through her. Afterwards, Sandra had swamped herself in the towel as she wasn't confident enough to show Brad her naked body. Her skin tingling and refreshed, she had looked over to where he was drying himself with his back towards her – and Sandra's eyes had been drawn like a magnet to his tight and firm naked buttocks.

Brad had turned and his prolonged gaze held a questioning look. One nod was all it took and, swiftly, he moved towards her, seizing Sandra in his arms. Their bodies pressing together, his skin cool and soft against hers, she realised without shame that the towel had dropped to the ground. Brad's kiss was long and sensually slow. He teased her bottom lip with his teeth. A pleasing sense of warmth flooded through her. Shocked, Sandra realised her throbbing body wanted more.

As they stood like that, a scene had played in her mind's eye. Frieda telling how Antonio had wanted intercourse but she knew she wasn't ready.

Abruptly, Sandra had pulled away from Brad. 'I'm sorry I can't do—'

'No... no, I don't want you—'

'I'm not ready to—'

'I understand. Sandra, I'm not being fair.'

Neither was she. Was she really comparing Brad with Antonio? Suddenly, and without quite understanding why, she thought of the curate. Surprised, Sandra wondered why she was concerned about Mr Carlton. She had this sense that if she went the whole way with Brad, somehow she'd be letting him down. Just as Frieda had felt when she thought of her mama's reaction.

She had brushed the thought aside. All Sandra knew was she ached for Brad.

As she'd dressed for work that morning, the thought occurred to her that if she and Brad made a go of things, it would mean she'd have to move to Florida. That was expected of girls who married American servicemen. How exciting – a new start in a foreign country. A small frown corrugated Sandra's brow as she pondered the matter. She would regret leaving the life she'd built here, the friends she'd made. But she'd be with Brad. That was all that mattered, wasn't it?

Cycling the last few yards to work though the drizzle, a pink hue adorning the grey sky, Sandra acknowledged that she could understand Frieda's predicament. For the thought had crossed her mind that Brad, an undoubtedly experienced man, would have no more to do with Sandra now he'd found out how immature she was in matters of sex.

What was she thinking? Brad was too worthy a man to have such dishonourable thoughts. His final words as he'd left her at the bottom of the hostel path proved the fact; he was trustworthy and wasn't just after one thing.

'Here's looking at you, kid. I've had a smashing time. Same time same place next week.'

He wanted to see her again.

But as she left her bicycle in the yard and made her way up to the byre, she frowned again.

Why had Brad said yesterday, 'I'm not being fair'?

*

For the rest of the day Sandra didn't have time to think. A harvesting gang of Land Girls sent by Jessie had arrived in the yard.

'I think it's lovely people rallying to help,' Sandra told Mr Jeffries in the byre.

Mr Jeffries had rounded up local farmers to give Mr Nichol a hand. The farmers' wives had arrived carrying food provisions for the day.

The old man removed his pipe from his mouth. 'Aye, it's the neighbourly thing to do when folk have troubles.'

The people of Leadburn went up a hundredfold in Sandra's estimation.

When Mr Nichol appeared in the byre, he looked shrunken. With red-rimmed eyes and gaunt face, he gave the impression he hadn't had a wink of sleep. He adopted an attitude of being in charge but Sandra could tell, by the way he kept giving a deep swallow, that at any minute his emotions would get the better of him.

'When you're done milking give a hand in the field,' he told her in a gruff voice.

Sandra supposed the best thing for the poor soul was to immerse himself in work. She didn't dare explore what Mr Nichol was going through – it was too unbearable even to contemplate.

She didn't get to speak to Frieda during milking time to find out how she was, and afterward the lass was off on the milk round with Mr Nichol. But Sandra had done her habitual daily inspection and felt reassured that, though still bony, Frieda hadn't lost any weight and her skin still had its recent healthy sheen.

After milking, Sandra spent time with the harvesting gang, which included Evelyn. Her job was to help cut out an area at the entrance of the field with a scythe.

'Why are we doing this?' Sandra enquired of Evelyn.

'I should think it's obvious,' Evelyn replied with her usual candour. 'It's so that the reaper and binder can get in.'

A feeling of being a 'daft townie' washed over Sandra, but then she thought of all the skills she'd acquired recently and felt proud.

The damp morning changed into brilliant sunshine and it was a case of making hay while the sun shone.

After a satisfying dinner of corn beef hash served up by the village women, Evelyn appeared with – surprisingly – a box camera. 'Gather round, everyone, and smile please.'

Six of the Land Girls, carrying bound corn sheaves, four at the back and two kneeling in front, posed for the camera.

'Say cheese,' someone called.

'*Cheese*,' they all said in unison, followed by a great guffaw.

Evelyn clicked the camera. 'When you're old and grey,' Evelyn told them as she put the camera in its case and hung the strap over a shoulder, 'your grandchildren won't believe you were once young and worked on a farm.'

Sandra sobered. *If we survive this war,* she thought.

Her thoughts turned to Alf. She wondered what he'd do after the war. She couldn't bore folk by incessantly talking about him and so Sandra liked to delve into her mind and have these little imaginings. It helped her feel she was keeping him close, and lessened the pain of worrying how he was faring when she didn't hear from him.

Before she could wander into an ideal future, a whistle pierced the air from the vicinity of the farmhouse.

She saw the village women carrying trays across the field.

Evelyn looked at her watch. 'Half five. They're late bringing the sandwiches.'

'Blimey, the time's raced.' Sandra couldn't believe the afternoon had gone so fast.

'My back's breaking with all the stooping.' Evelyn headed for the field entrance. 'I'm ready for a sit down.'

Sandra followed and sat with the rest of the workers on the grass between the farmhouse and the cornfield. The women set the trays on the ground and Sandra eyed the tempting pot of tea and plates of doorstep Spam sandwiches and scones.

A farm labourer with a grimy and sweaty brow turned towards Sandra as though he was about to speak. Something caught his eye as he gazed over her shoulder.

'Is that the post office lassie?'

Sandra, her back to the farmhouse, turned.

Frieda was hurrying across the path from the farm and she came across to where the company was sprawled on the grass.

She held something in her hand.

A telegram. A cold shiver ran through Sandra's body.

The chattering stopped and only the distant sound of a dog barking could be heard. Frieda passed the workers one by one and the relief was plain to see on their faces.

She stopped in front of Sandra. 'I wanted to bring you this myself.' Her voice breathless, she held out the telegram.

Sandra stared at the yellow envelope Frieda handed to her. A feeling of foreboding crept over her and she had the uncanny sensation that she was moving in slow motion.

Everyone was staring at her. Sandra didn't want to open the telegram here and have Frieda read it out loud. And she was too impatient to stumble over the telegram's words herself.

There was only one place Sandra would feel secure, one person who she could rely on to read the telegram dispassionately but still be there for support if needs be. She brushed aside thoughts of how awkward she'd felt since she'd talked to him about Brad. This was too important to let personal matters get in the way.

The sound of the knocker as it banged on the door echoed along the passageway.

Staring at the telegram in her hand, which she held as if it were a grenade ready to explode, Sandra felt sick.

Mistakes do happen, she told herself. But she realised she was only trying to make things better. Like she did with Frieda. How many times had she told her to look on the positive side, to believe that her family in Germany would survive? Sandra knew now how empty and trite the words were.

Suddenly, she wanted to shout her anger at the gods, scream at them for allowing her precious brother to be in danger.

A hand touched her shoulder and Sandra nearly passed out with fright.

She turned to see Mr Carlton astride his bike, back to exuding friendliness again. 'You're early. I didn't expect you'd make—' His eyes travelled to the telegram in her hand. His features softened. 'You'll want to know what that says. Follow me.'

There were no preliminaries, just deep concern in his voice.

He leant his bike against the red brick wall and, leading the way, took her around the side of the house through the wooden gate and into the back garden. He nodded to the seat by the table and they both sat down. She passed the telegram to him.

He expression non-committal, he read the words out loud.

Report just received through the international Red Cross. Your brother Sgt. Alfred Hudson has been reported as escaped from internment by the Swiss government. If further details or information are received you will be notified at once.

Sandra's body trembled with relief. Then fearing for his safety, anger erupted inside. 'Stupid boy. Why didn't he just stay put where he was safe?'

'Maybe your brother felt it was his duty to try and get back to Britain.'

Sandra's anger subsided as quickly as it came. She crumpled and burst into tears. 'Where can he be?'

'I wish I could tell you.' The curate's tone was grave.

Cycling back to the hostel, she made straight for the dormitory bedroom. Sandra didn't want to be in company as the least sympathy would reduce her to a helpless wreck.

Much later, Evelyn came into the room and found Sandra on her bed staring at the ceiling.

'What did the telegram say?' Evelyn's tone was anxious.

Sandra sat up in the bed. Telling her friend that Alf had escaped made the telegram seem real for the first time. She vented her frustration at her brother for leaving the relative safety of the Swiss ski resort where he'd been interned.

Evelyn frowned in concentration. 'I agree, but we don't know the circumstances or how much being kept in captivity and out of the war affected Alf.'

Mr Carlton had said more or less the same thing and Sandra knew both he and Evelyn had a point. Alf would think it was his patriotic duty to be free and continue to fight the aggressor.

Sandra, frustrated at her ignorance, not knowing the layout of the countries involved, was forced to swallow her pride and ask, 'How difficult would it be for Alf to make his way back to England?'

Evelyn thought for a while, looking into space. 'The two ways that come to mind are across Vichy France and over the Pyrenees into Spain, then into Gibraltar, which is British territory; or through France to the Channel coast and maybe smuggled in a boat to Britain.' She climbed up to the top bunk and sat alongside Sandra. 'I read about a soldier who escaped like that. The French resistance helped him.' Her face creased in concern. 'I must tell you, though, both ways have their dangers as they're occupied by Germans.'

Sandra went weak at the thought.

*

The next morning, with clouds passing over the weak sun, Frieda caught up with Sandra as she pushed her bike into the farmyard.

'I couldn't sleep for worrying what the telegram said.'

Sandra put the bike on its stand. Even in her distraught state she observed that Frieda's cheeks were becoming fuller.

'The Red Cross reported that Alf has escaped.'

'Oh! Sandra, that is disturbing. But your brother is alive and there is hope. Aunty Doris told me last night that the news might not be bad and to look on the bright side.'

Her emotions mixed, Sandra didn't know what to say. Of course, she was thrilled Alf was alive, but she couldn't breathe easy because he was still in mortal danger.

'I told Mr Nichol about the telegram. He understood why you ran off.'

Sandra gave a grateful nod. She hadn't given her quick exit from the farm another thought. She thought of the Nichols, what they were going through, and felt shame. What they would give to have their son alive and escaping capture.

She told Frieda, 'I'm sorry I didn't fully understand what you were going through before and talked a load of twaddle that was no help.'

'I don't understand? Twaddle?'

'It means nonsense.'

'You did help, you've always been there for me, especially when I'm down.' Her pretty face became intense. 'You were right. Our lives do mirror each other's.'

Their eyes met and there was confirmation in them, as if they both knew that their meeting was fated.

The enormity of recent events caught up with Sandra. 'Let's promise we'll never give up hope.'

Frieda's eyes misted and she nodded.

*

'There's enough of us here to complete the job,' Jessie told Sandra that afternoon as she helped with threshing the corn. 'You can finish in time for supper.' She strode off.

The only explanation Sandra could think of to cause the forewoman's lenient attitude was that Mr Nichol had told Jessie about the telegram. That the farmer thought of her in a time when he was going through his own distress caused Sandra to well up.

She wasn't sure being alone was the wisest choice but neither did she relish the complication of working alongside a lot of people. Collecting her bicycle, she made off along the country lanes, the thought of food in her present state of mind loathsome.

It was early evening, and if she were in a better frame of mind, Sandra could lose herself in inventing shapes out of the marshmallow clouds drifting across the sky – something she used to do with Alf when Mam had washing to collect and Sandra looked after her younger brother. The pair of them would lie in the backyard of their downstairs flat and stare up at the cloud-filled sky. 'I can see an elephant,' Alfie would exclaim, when no such thing was apparent.

Her heart tugging, eyes scratchy, Sandra smiled at the long-forgotten memory. She needed to go on a long bike ride to tire herself out in order to get some sleep tonight.

She hadn't anywhere special in mind, or so she thought, until she was surprised to find herself pedalling along a single track road that led to Hallington, over five miles away.

Why not? she thought. Seeing Brad was the lovely distraction she needed right now.

CHAPTER TWENTY-NINE

Dismounting her bicycle, Sandra peered through the two stone pillars that were the entrance to the hospital. There were few people sitting on the lawn this time and Sandra was hesitant to enter as she knew hospitals had strict rules about visiting.

She scoured the people sitting out on the lawn. Then she saw someone with salt-and-pepper hair smoking a cigarette sitting on a basket chair.

Brad did a double take when he saw her. Stubbing out his cigarette in an ash tray on the grass, he stood up and waved her over, the book he was reading falling from his lap.

'Hey, Sandra!' He beamed as she approached. 'What are you doing here? Though I'm mighty pleased to see you.'

'Am I intruding? Are you allowed visitors?'

'You're fine out here. Come, sit down.' He fetched a vacant chair.

She discovered she didn't want sympathy. She wanted her time with Brad to continue to be magical, to pretend the outside world didn't exist and she could be free of anxiety for a while.

Brad leant forward. 'Gee, Sandra. Am I allowed to know what's up?'

She sighed; so much for hiding her feelings. 'I had a telegram yesterday. My brother Alf was interned in Switzerland but he's escaped.'

Brad slapped his good knee. 'What a guy! I'd do the same.' He had the grace to look sheepish. 'But it sure is tough on you – you must be worried about him.'

She didn't feel it necessary to fill in any details.

His gorgeous blue eyes held hers. 'Thanks, funny face.'

'What for?'

'That it's me you came to see.'

He made her feel better already.

A young nurse in uniform came then and handed him some pills and a glass of water. He swallowed the pills and gulped the water, returning the glass to the nurse with his broad smile.

'Not long now, nurse, before you send me packing.'

'Mr Carter, you've been a model patient.' She gave him a lingering look and then hurried away.

Brad pulled a decisive face. 'How about we get out of here and take a bike ride. It'll help you take your mind off your troubles for a bit.'

'But I only—'

'No buts, Sandra.' His expression roguish, he told her, 'I promise there won't be any pools involved.'

Twenty minutes later, they were following single track roads in the open countryside.

'Where are we headed?' Brad called over his shoulder.

'I don't mind.'

Brad laughed, a deep pleasing sound. 'Not that we'd find anywhere when there aren't any signposts.'

Signposts had been removed to confuse the enemy if there was an invasion.

'You can't forget it, can you, the war?' Brad called. 'I expect the English people have forgotten what normal life is like.'

Normal life. Was there such a thing? Sandra didn't know. If there was then she certainly had never had one. Choices were for the rich and not for the likes of her. But what was she complaining about? Sandra wouldn't have life any other way. She had Alf and if he came home safely that's all she asked – except, God willing, maybe marriage and babies. Money and riches didn't count.

They passed through villages, some only consisting of a few houses.

'I'd at least want a pub.' Brad slowed to let her catch up with him.

'I prefer it like this with no bustle, plenty of greenery and—'

'Village gossips.' Brad laughed.

They stopped to rest awhile on a grassy knoll off a narrow track. Brad stretched out, hands behind his head, looking up at the sky. Sandra joined him, sitting up with her arms circling her legs.

'My body is telling me I shouldn't be cycling up steep hills any more.' Brad reached into his trouser pocket and wiped sweat from his brow with a handkerchief. 'I'm sorely out of condition.'

'All this cycling and you're still convalescing.'

He sat up and searched her face. 'The thing is I'm not officially an invalid any more. They're gonna discharge me any day soon and then it'll be back to duty.'

Sandra's pulse quickened. 'At the aerodrome?'

'Might be. I'm only up here on rest from ops.' He shrugged. 'Who knows what will happen next.'

Sandra knew better than to ask any more questions.

'Hey, Sandra, why so glum? You thinking of that brother of yours?' Brad lifted her chin with his index finger and the kiss he gave her was tender.

The tears came then, unbidden. Brad put an arm around her shoulders and cuddled her in, her head nestled against his chest, his heartbeat thumping through his shirt.

They sat like that for a long while. Something relaxed in Sandra and the future didn't seem so bleak.

'I can always get a pass and hitch a ride from Cambridgeshire.' Brad's voice was hoarse.

She turned up her face to look at him. 'I'd like that very much.'

A car passed by in the road and hooted its horn. The ancient Austin moving away, Sandra wondered if it was someone who recognised her. Disentangling from Brad's embrace, she wiped her eyes with her fingertips.

'I think we should head back. It will start getting dark.'

Cycling along the dark narrow roads by dimmed torchlight, they travelled via the reservoirs. Reaching higher ground and seeing the disturbing scene in the distance, they stopped and dismounted their bicycles. For way ahead in the darkness, searchlights criss-crossed in the sky over the Tyne showing anti-aircraft action.

'Poor souls, someone's in for it tonight.' Sandra shivered. 'It's true you really do have to live for the moment.'

Brad lowered his bike to the ground and moved over towards Sandra, taking her in his arms. His kiss this time was more demanding, his tongue pressing against her lips, parting them and exploring hers.

Every nerve in her body tingling, Sandra wanted more.

*

The sky had cleared now and the moon was shining an eerie light. Brad, cycling back to the hospital, wished he hadn't listened to Sandra. Hell, he should have accompanied her back to the safety of the hostel, no matter what she said. It was his duty to do so. But Sandra sure was one independent dame.

She'd insisted she would be fine and would only spend the night worrying if he made it back to the hospital or not. Damn it, he regretted his decision now. Furious with himself, he pedalled back to Hallington in record time.

The thing was, Brad thought, as he pulled into the entrance of Hallington Hall, he felt bad he hadn't been honest with Sandra. When they met at the dance, he never dreamed it would get this serious and there had been no need at first, but now he knew differently. Sandra had got under his skin and he'd never thought he'd feel like this about a woman again.

They'd arranged to meet next Sunday and Brad promised himself he'd tell Sandra everything then.

Though he wondered what her reaction would be, it was his duty to tell her the truth.

CHAPTER THIRTY

September 1943

Sandra

A week later, Sandra waited patiently at the end of the hostel path for Brad to arrive. She stood for half an hour and when Brad didn't show, she didn't know what to think. She ruled out the idea that he'd stood her up as their relationship had gone far beyond that kind of behaviour. But uncertainty filled her with self-doubt.

Sandra knew her judgement of Brad was correct. He wasn't the Jack-the-Lad type like Antonio – Brad was a true gentleman. And Sandra had fallen in love with him.

Different scenarios flitted through her mind. Maybe he was ill or had been sent back to the aerodrome. If he was unable to get a pass he had no way of telling her.

Sandra couldn't possibly go back to the hostel without knowing. There was nothing else for it; she headed for Hallington.

She left her bike by the entrance. Peering into the grounds, she searched the few invalids sitting there but there was no sign of Brad.

Then she glimpsed him sitting with his back towards her. Above the back of the chair, she saw his salt-and-pepper hair and sloping shoulders. Her heart lifted in joy. Sandra made towards him. But the man, as she approached, swivelled his head and Sandra found herself looking into the face of a perfect stranger.

'Can I help?' A voice came from behind her.

Sandra turned and looked at the young nurse she'd seen the last time she visited Brad.

'I'm looking for the American, Mr Carter.'

'I thought you might be. He was discharged on Thursday.' She gave a regretful smile. 'A nice gentleman. He's missed. I'm glad he fully recovered from his accident.'

'Did he go back to the aerodrome, d'you know?'

'I'm afraid I don't.'

Even if she did, Sandra felt the nurse wouldn't say.

'Sorry I can't be of any more help.' The nurse moved away.

Sandra walked slowly back to the entrance, feeling flat and downhearted. There was a simple explanation, she told herself. She trusted Brad.

Sandra had an overpowering need to escape everything and everyone – except, perhaps, for one person. But the curate was off-limits to her. The situation was awkward, she'd feel embarrassed confiding her fears, and she felt guilty for not having attended reading lessons recently. Mr Carlton had been her confidant and her supporter so often in recent times, but however much she wanted to, she couldn't turn to him now.

With heavy heart, she pedalled towards Leadburn.

Entering the hostel, Sandra automatically checked for post. A letter addressed to her in Olive's handwriting lay on the table. A warm glow of expectancy surged through her. Making her way to the bedroom and finding it empty, she sat on one of the bunk beds and read Olive's letter as best as she could, slowly spelling out some words letter by letter.

Dear Sandra,
     Kenneth's home from A-B-R-O-A-D because he's I-N-J-U-R-E-D. He got shot in the S-P-L-E-E-N. Part of me

is glad because he's out of the war, H-O-P-E-F-U-L-L-Y
till it's ended. As Tommy says the lad's done his bit.

Sandra continued reading, getting the drift of the news of what
was happening in South Shields in her friend's colourful language.

There hasn't been A-N-O-T-H-E-R major raid since the
one when you were here. Which was rotten luck. Still it
got that L-A-S-S-I-E Frieda out of herself and talking. Tell
her I'm asking about her.

The letter went on to describe that Jerry planes had dropped
metal containers scattering a load of pamphlets (this word took
ages to understand) in the street and Sandra couldn't understand
what they said – something to do with lies about the amount of
loss of British ships – then Sandra gave up trying.

Look after yourself. I pray every night that you hear about
the W-H-E-R-E-A-BO-U-T-S of that brother of yours soon.
       Your loving friend,
       Olive xx

Sandra stared into space. Loneliness washed over her and she
was overwhelmed with a longing to see Olive.

CHAPTER THIRTY-ONE

'I'm off to the pub tonight. How about you?'

It was Saturday night and Evelyn was standing by Sandra's bunk bed, removing metal curlers from her hair. She had washed it that morning and worn the curlers, covered with a turban-style headscarf, all day at work.

'Who's going?' Sandra wanted to know.

'Almost everyone's gone home for the weekend so there's only a handful of us left.'

'You can count me in,' Enid called from the other side of the room. 'Ruby says she's going too with Roy, and Harriet says two of them are going from their room. She says RAF boys are usually there on Saturday nights.'

Sandra, lying on the bed, didn't want to spend another evening alone wondering about her brother or Brad – and why he hadn't told her he had been discharged – which was what she did whenever her mind wasn't distracted. A futile occupation which led to more questions than it ever did answers.

'I'll think about it.'

'Don't think too long. We're going straight after the evening meal.'

Wondering what on earth she could wear, Sandra went for clean jodhpurs, thick socks, stout shoes and her heavy coat as the nights were cooler now. Her hair was glossy after being freshly washed, and she'd put a dab of flowery-smelling perfume behind her ears.

As she entered the Fox and Hounds, with its low ceiling and rustic beams, the pub was a blast of noise. Folk gathered around the piano for a good old singsong and, at the other end of the room, local farm workers were having a game of darts. Sandra scoured the smoke-filled room for a vacant table.

'There's one.,' Evelyn made a beeline for the table at the far end of the room by the tiled fireplace embellished with ornamental brasses. The rest of them followed.

The music stopped and a voice was heard to say, 'Crikey! More sodbusters.' Sandra looked to the next table where soldiers sat with some ATS lasses. The girl who'd spoken looked peeved. She was the same lass from the dance in the village hall.

With a pang Sandra remembered that had been when Brad introduced himself.

From the corner of her eye Sandra saw Evelyn stand up from her seat, indignation written all over her face. 'Not again!'

At that moment, Ruby and Roy mercifully entered the pub and came over to join them.

'What a time we've had getting away,' Ruby exclaimed as she removed her coat and sat down. 'Roy's sister arrived with the bairn. Did I tell yi' she'd had one?' Ruby prattled on and the moment passed. Sandra gave a sigh of relief as she saw the ATS lass carry on talking to a serviceman sitting next to her.

He was wearing an American air force uniform.

Sandra stiffened; she thought she recognised him. Adrenalin raced through her. He was the same Yank who'd been at the dance with Brad. He looked up and she saw a glimmer of recognition in his eye. Embarrassed that she was staring, Sandra averted her eyes.

Ruby, centre stage, was telling a tale about a mouse. 'I was stacking sheaves of corn into stooks and I must have disturbed a mouse and it ran straight up me dungaree leg. I started dancing around 'cos I was scared the damn thing went up to me nether regions. Then some cheeky bugger farm labourer suggested I took me dungarees off.'

Everyone was hooting at Ruby's perplexed face.

'What did you do?' Enid guffawed.

A voice spoke up beside Sandra. 'Miss Hudson, isn't it?' She turned and looked up to see the American standing at her side.

'Yes, and you are?'

'Hal Miller.'

'Pleased to meet you. You're a friend of—'

A roar of riotous laughter exploded around the table and Hal cupped his hand around his ear. 'Pardon me.'

'You're a friend of—'

More laughter.

Frowning, Hal looked around the room, then pointed to two vacant chairs by the fireside. He went over, sat down and Sandra got up and followed him.

Tall and fair, with wide apart eyes, Hal had an assured air. The idea he might know something about Brad sent a wave of nervous anticipation through Sandra.

'Would you like a drink?' he asked.

Sandra wracked her brain trying to think what Evelyn had bought her the last time.

'Cider. Please?'

'You're sure that's all you want?'

Sandra wasn't because she didn't know what else was on offer. 'That's perfectly fine,' she answered primly.

Hal made his way to the bar where a busty barmaid fluttered her eyes at the American.

Sandra felt daft. *Perfectly fine* sounded so typically English, but she felt uneasy in his company. He knew Brad and probably knew about her.

Surely she hadn't been wrong about Brad. He wouldn't see her as a conquest to talk to his mates about, would he? Maybe now he thought of her as someone out of sight and out of mind.

Hal returned with her cider and a small glass for him.

The piano struck up again and servicemen, arms around each other's shoulders, began to sway and sing uproariously.

Hal leant towards her. 'I guess I feel I know you. I've heard so much about you.' His voice was raised so she could hear him.

She felt the heat in her cheeks. What had Brad said about her? 'From Brad?'

'Yep. Pity the guy had to go.'

'After he left the hospital, you mean?'

'Didn't you know?'

She shook her head.

Hal looked puzzled. 'Brad and I… we go back some and talk about things that matter. He's overboard in love with you. He was told to report back to Cambridgeshire. Last I heard he was going to write to tell you.' Looking uncomfortable, Hal took a swig of his drink.

'Well he didn't.' Sandra's voice was sharper than she intended. 'There's something you're not telling me, isn't there?'

'Gee. It's not my place.'

Sandra wasn't going to allow this conversation to end there. 'It's been weeks since I saw Brad and he hasn't had the decency to be in touch. I need to know now what this is all about because it's obvious he isn't going to say.'

People sitting at a nearby table looked on as if they were witnessing an argument.

Sandra, her mind in turmoil, was past caring. She glowered at Hal.

She could see he struggled with his conscience.

Visibly reluctant, he told her, 'Brad's married. According to him it's over. I know he meant to tell you and get it off his chest.'

The next day as they walked home, telling Frieda was difficult, but Sandra knew if she wanted to be able to look herself in the mirror again this must be done.

'So, you see, Brad hoodwinked me just as Antonio did you.'

'Hoodwinked?'

'It means deceived.'

Frieda touched her friend's arm. 'I am so sorry, Sandra, I know how devastated you must be.'

'I'm just sorry I wasn't more understanding about Antonio. I know now all you wanted was someone who'd understand and listen, not some clever clogs who thought she knew better.'

'You were right about Antonio. And you were worried about me.'

Sandra sighed. 'Once again we are sisters of the same fate.'

'I wish I was your sister.'

Sandra smiled at Frieda. She felt the same.

They walked for a while in silence, deep in their own thoughts. The chilly, blustery evening signalled that summer was over and autumn was truly here.

'Sandra… I would ask Aunty Doris this question, but I haven't told her about Antonio…'

'Go on, what is it you want to ask?'

'Do you think I will love anyone again as much as I did Antonio?'

Sandra searched her own feelings for an answer. How could she have been so wrong about Brad when she had believed he was special? Yet, he'd lied to her. Sandra felt used and cheated. She now understood Frieda's predicament. It wasn't easy to fall out of love even though the man involved was a scoundrel. Despite this, she steeled herself. Brad was married and off limits. Sandra must put him out of her mind.

Frieda deserved an honest answer. 'I don't know. But now I know what it feels like, I sincerely hope so for both our sakes.'

As they approached the path leading to the hostel, they stopped and without a second thought, Sandra hugged Frieda close.

She spoke in her ear. 'No matter what life throws at us we've got each other to rely on. Night night.'

Frieda seemed too emotional to speak.

As she hurried up the path, Sandra heard her voice ring out behind her. 'Night night. God bless.'

There, beside two other letters on the hostel's occasional table for post, was a crumpled-looking envelope addressed to her. The writing was Alf's. For an instant she felt like rubbing her eyes to make sure she wasn't seeing things. Hands shaking, she tore the envelope open.

There was a letter inside. She pulled the slip of paper out of the envelope and her fingers touched a small object. Bemused, she shook the envelope and the object fell into her hand. A chain and round disc with Alf's name inscribed on it.

Alf was alive; the proof was in her hand.

She wanted to share her wonderful news. Sandra couldn't help wanting to share it with Mr Carlton. She owed that to him for all his caring; besides, she needed to apologise for not attending classes.

*

When Matthew answered the door, Miss Hudson stood there looking rather hesitant. She didn't meet his eyes. He worried that something was wrong.

'Mr Carlton, I'm sorry I haven't been turning up for reading lessons, lately…'

He wondered if her nervousness was anything to do with the American. But the affair was a private matter and none of his business.

Matthew concentrated on what he did best – helping those in need. His attitude was one of genuine concern for one of his parishioners. For that was what Miss Hudson now was.

'That's perfectly fine.' He knew he sounded stiff and starchy but being formal was the only way he could handle matters with Miss Hudson. 'I doubt you need any more instruction. You should be extremely proud of yourself.'

'Thanks to you.' She hesitated. 'I have some good news and I wanted you to be the first to know.' A radiant smile transformed her face. 'I've had a letter from Alf!'

Matthew found himself grinning. 'Come in, we've just finished tea. Mr Fairweather will want to know the good news.'

He led the way to the dining room where Mr Fairweather was pouring a cup of tea.

'I heard,' the vicar said. 'Sit down and tell us all about it. There's milk but we've run out of sugar.' He handed over the cup of tea to Miss Hudson, who took it and, distractedly, took a sip.

Matthew felt glad at seeing Mr Fairweather be so charming to Miss Hudson.

'Is this the brother that was interned in Switzerland?' Mr Fairweather asked.

'Yes, but he's escaped and is now in Spain.'

'He's in Spain?' Matthew repeated.

'I'm so excited, I've only skimmed the letter and can't take it all in. Would you read it to me please?' She turned to Mr Fairweather. 'I'm sorry. I hope you don't mind. Forgive me for interrupting.'

'No… no, child. You need to know what your brother says. Read the letter out loud, Mr Carlton.'

Matthew watched Sandra fish the letter out of her dungarees pocket and hand it to him.

He unfolded it and read out loud.

Dear Sis,

I'm in Spain! At the British Consulate in Barcelona. The official has agreed to my request to send you this letter. I'll be brief.

After a long journey which included a hike over the Pyrenees, I arrived here. After the formalities, I was informed I'm to be driven with two RAF pilots to Madrid, approximately some four hundred miles, to the British embassy. From there I'll be sent to Gibraltar and repatriated to England by sea or air. Apparently, it could take some time but the hope is I'll be home for Christmas.

Meanwhile, I wanted you to have my necklace. Keep it safe till I see you.

Sorry to cause you worry.

Your loving brother Alf

'Child, you must be so relieved.' Mr Fairweather's round face pictured his delight. 'May I see this necklace?'

As Sandra brought the necklace out of her pocket, Matthew detected her chin wobbled.

He kept decorum. 'It's good to see things turned out so well.' *And it does my heart good to see you radiating with happiness,* a traitorous voice in his head said.

He'd talked about his feelings for Miss Hudson with the vicar. And told him that she was attracted to someone else. Matthew had needed guidance on the matter. After discussion, the vicar's final words had been, 'I will pray for you, Mr Carlton, that you're able to be at peace about this matter.' His look had been perceptive. 'You are only human.'

The clock struck the hour and Matthew's attention was drawn to the fact he'd need to leave if he was to be punctual for the WI meeting, where he was taking part in judging jars of homemade jam.

'I'm afraid I must go. I have an appointment.'

Matthew rose and left the room, purposely avoiding Miss Hudson's gaze.

CHAPTER THIRTY-TWO

November 1943

Frieda

Terrific assault by the RAF on capital of Nazi-land [...]
*Hun must regret the ruthless attacks on London, and
Coventry* [...] *Berlin will be eliminated as Germany's
war centre.*

It was breakfast time, and Frieda, swallowing a spoonful of
porridge, felt her stomach plummet as she read the article in
yesterday's newspaper that lay on the table.

But what about the innocent people? her mind cried – Mama,
Papa, her brother Kurt. Her appetite lost, she pushed the bowl
of porridge away.

Aunty Doris bustled into the kitchen. 'Morning.' She looked
at the table and clicked her tongue. 'Sorry. You weren't supposed
to see that. I meant to hide the paper before I went to bed.'

Hiding the truth doesn't make any difference to the truth, Frieda
thought. But she knew her aunt was only trying to protect her.

'Come on, love, eat some breakfast.'

Frieda heard the anxiety in her aunt's tone. She wanted to
please Aunty Doris but the resolve not to eat was stronger. She
pressed her lips firmly together.

'What would your mama tell you if she were here?'

Her vision blurred, Frieda sniffed. 'She would be worried and say the same as you.'

In the dark, drizzly weather on the way to the Nichols' farm, torch pointed towards the ground, Frieda tried to conjure up Mama's face. When she couldn't, she panicked.

Was that a sign that something was wrong?

As she splashed through the puddles, images of bombs dropping on her neighbourhood in Germany played in her mind. Willing the horrifying scenes away, Frieda tried to think of something pleasant.

She thought of Sandra, the wonderful news that her brother was alive and would be making his way home from Spain one day. It was just the glad tidings Sandra needed right now as the American's betrayal had hurt her deeply.

It had been the same for Frieda for a long time. But now she felt magically cured of lovesick yearnings for Antonio. Perhaps it had been a crush, after all. Or, maybe the new farmhand who had started at the Nichols' farm a fortnight ago to help with the horses had something to do with it. Blond, with baby blue eyes and thick, perfectly shaped eyebrows, Colin Gibson was the same age as her.

Her stomach curled with pleasure at the thought of Colin, his sweet and caring personality that made her feel special whenever their paths crossed.

For a moment, Frieda forgot the horrors of war-torn Berlin.

*

Since she'd received Alf's letter, a weight had lifted from Sandra and she refused to allow her broken heart over Brad to bring her down.

But the state of Mr Nichol preyed on her mind as she cycled home by torchlight, the darkness all around her oppressive.

'Poor man's worried sick about his wife,' Doris Leadbeater had said when Sandra visited the post office earlier to buy a stamp for Olive's letter.

'I never see her these days,' Sandra had admitted.

'She's turned her face to the wall since her son was killed.' Mrs Leadbeater gave a heartfelt sigh. 'The same thing happened to me when my husband was killed on his motorcycle. I've never got over Jack's death.' She shook her head as she passed over the stamp. 'But I've learnt to live with it.'

A noise caught Sandra's attention and, looking to the left, she saw the red glow of a cigarette in the darkness.

A male voice spoke in the shadows. 'It's me, Sandra – Brad.'

She stopped her bike and shone the torch in his face. It looked eerily white.

Adrenalin racing through her veins rendered Sandra weak. 'Go away. I've got nothing to say to you.'

He moved towards her. 'I sure don't blame you after the way I treated you. Please hear me out. I've only got a two-day pass, then I'll be gone. I want to set the record straight before I go.'

There was finality in his voice and it left Sandra wondering what he meant. *Gone from here, or gone from England for good?* She didn't care, she told herself.

'Nothing you could say would make things right. You lied to me. You're married.'

As anger and blame hung between them, the atmosphere tensed.

'Hal told me you knew. I didn't lie, Sandra. I just hadn't told you the truth yet.'

'It's the same thing in my book,' she retorted. Yet, in her heart she wanted him to wrap his arms around her, tell her it was all a big mistake. She steeled herself. The man was a cad.

'It matters that you understand. I know I'm a scoundrel, but I couldn't go without telling you the truth.'

Despite the fury she felt, an inner voice told her to hear him out. Brad could have walked away and never come back.

'An hour, Sandra, that's all I ask.'

Sandra sat in the pub at a corner table by the fire where no one could see her – not that anyone was in the pub this early. Brad was talking to Ina Turner, the bar lady, a rather plump, plain-speaking woman whose husband was serving abroad. Mrs Turner kept looking at Sandra as Brad spoke, then she nodded.

Brad came over and, placing a pint of beer on the table, he took off his leather jacket and sat opposite her.

'I told the landlady that you've missed your meal at the hostel and she's agreed to make you a pot of tea and sandwiches.'

Sandra childishly refused to be swayed by the kind gesture. 'I'm not hungry, thank you.'

There was an uncomfortable silence. Brad appeared unable to start the conversation. He stood and moved to the fire and warmed his hands.

Sandra decided to make it easier for him; she wanted this over and done. 'Why didn't you just tell me you were married from the first?'

'Gee, Sandra, that's a hard question to answer.'

'Try me.'

He came to sit at the table and the nearness of him made her pulse race.

'At first, I didn't think there was any need. Then I got serious about you, and I guess… I was afraid I'd lose you. I figured I had plenty of time. Then, when I was discharged from hospital, I was posted back to Cambridgeshire. I had every intention of writing but I decided that was the coward's way out. I thought it best to wait and tell you to your face.'

Sandra's torn heart wouldn't allow leniency. 'So, did your wife know about me?'

He shook his head. 'There was no need. The marriage was over.' Like a man who needed it, Brad took a swig of his drink.

'Maybe it's best if I told you from the beginning. Betty and I were crazy head over heels in love and got married when we were young. Jeez, we were skint and with me still studying we moved in with Mom and Pop. When Pop had his heart attack, he and Mom decided to move to somewhere smaller near the ocean, while Betty and I took over the house. She was employed as a hairdresser while I worked all hours at the drugstore.'

'Did you have a family?' Sandra asked, despite her determination not to show any interest.

'I was keen to start a family but Betty kept putting it off. Don't get me wrong...' Brad rubbed his hand over his mouth. 'I was a stick in the mud type and all I did was work. While Betty... she wanted more out of life before she settled down.' He took another swig of his drink. 'Time went on and then Betty decided she wanted to try for a baby but nothing happened. After that... we drifted apart.' He looked Sandra straight in the eye. 'It wasn't Betty's fault. I realise now I was married to the drugstore.'

'Then you joined up after Pearl Harbor,' Sandra hurried the story along.

'I sure did. I was posted abroad in March forty-two.' His amazing blue eyes looked meaningfully at Sandra. 'Up until then, me and Betty were man and wife in every sense of the word.'

Why was he telling her this? She didn't want to visualise Brad and his wife making love.

At that moment, Mrs Turner came over. 'Here you are, love, get those Spam sandwiches down you. That'll do yi' the world of good after being out in the fields this time of year.'

'Thank you.'

Mrs Turner didn't move and appeared to want to chat. With the tray in her hands she looked from one to the other of them, then seeming to sense the strained atmosphere she made a hasty retreat.

'Shout out if you want anything,' she called over her shoulder.

Sandra looked at Brad. 'Spare me the details,' she told him, as she poured tea into a cup.

'Sandra, I want to be honest. It's important you know what went on between me and Betty.' He handed her the milk jug. 'I guess you know the rest, me being posted to England and all.'

Sandra lifted the cup to her lips. 'What's the point of this?'

He took a breath. 'In the spring Betty sent me a letter saying she'd met someone else and the marriage was over.'

Sandra, cup still in the air, blurted, 'Blimey. That must have been a shock.'

'I guess not. Deep down I knew we'd reached the point of no return.' He gulped the last of his drink and Sandra watched his Adam's apple go up and down. He put his empty glass down on the table. 'I won't deny I had flings and lived it up… but then I had the plane crash and I met you.' He stopped as a couple passed the table and made for the bar.

'Why did you leave it till now to tell me all this?'

'I sure as hell wanted to. I made up my mind I would the next time we met but then I got posted. Then all leave was cancelled. I knew you'd think I'd let you down. So, despite wanting to tell you face to face about Betty, I wrote a letter explaining.'

'I never received it.'

His troubled eyes told her to prepare for the worst. The 'but' she'd expected all along.

'I was ready to post it but… Betty got in touch.' His face altered, looked pained as if he didn't want to hurt her. 'There's something else… Betty and I… before we separated… we made a baby.'

Sandra's free hand cupped her mouth and she gave a sharp intake of breath. Brad took the cup out of her hand and put it down on the saucer.

He rubbed his forehead with a finger as if eliminating a pain. 'Betty admitted she hadn't wanted me to know. She wanted to get on with her life. The new guy played along for a while. But after the baby was born, he couldn't handle bringing up another man's son. He left Betty in August to manage on her own.'

Sandra sat perfectly still and let the bombshell explode in her head.

Brad's expression was that of a man burdened with guilt. 'Betty wants us to give the marriage another go, for Howie, the baby's sake.'

'And you?' Dread tingled in her throat.

His face had gone pale, she noticed, and there were dark circles under his eyes. 'I have a son, Sandra. It's' – his voice cracked – 'my duty to look after him.'

Her mind went blank as if she was incapable of thought.

'Sandra, I swear I didn't want to hurt you.'

She came to her senses. 'The baby… he's definitely your son?'

Brad sighed. 'Betty is a lot of things but she isn't a liar. Besides, Howie's age tallies. He is my kid.'

Sandra felt numb. She stood, her limbs seemingly trembling, and shrugging into her heavy coat without looking at Brad, she moved towards the door.

'Thank you for making the trip to tell me.' She opened the door and left.

As she walked away from the pub, she heard his footsteps running after her in the dark.

He caught her arm. 'Sandra… Jeez, I'm sorry it's ended like this. I didn't want to give you up or give you heartache. You didn't deserve this.'

She shrugged him off. 'Don't, Brad.' She hurried away before she broke down.

'I'll always remember you,' he called.

'And I you,' she whispered.

Life went on as before. But for Sandra, who had fallen in love and then lost love for the first time, life could never be the same again. She joined the local Women's Institute with Evelyn and Ruby because on these cold winter nights, there wasn't much else to do and Sandra didn't want to stay at the hostel with nothing to do but think.

The November weather was cold, and frost sparkled like diamonds on paths and rooftops. When she'd finished milking, her breath a small misty cloud when she exhaled, Sandra, bundled up in her coat, mittens and hat, trekked the uneven ground to the sheep-dotted field. She checked for those sheep whose long woolly coat may have frozen to the ground overnight and would need help to stand. She then ensured the sheep had plenty of food and the drinking water wasn't frozen. For nutrition was the key to keeping the sheep healthy to withstand the cold.

Her thoughts, as she made her way through the gate and back to the farmhouse, returned inevitably back to Brad.

She'd talked with Frieda and told her about her meeting with him. Her friend had helped to clarify Sandra's thoughts.

'I pity him. I wouldn't like to stay married if there was no love and the trust had gone.' Frieda had shaken her head to verify the fact. 'Women don't have any other option when it's men who supply the money to live. Aunty Doris says all that's changing with this war when women are doing men's work and putting food on the table.' She frowned. 'There is talk in the village that things might revert back when the menfolk return from the war.'

Sandra, still reeling from Brad's visit, didn't want to get into that particular argument.

Frieda seemed to sense her friend's mood and changed the subject. 'It was hard enough finding out Brad was married, but him admitting he had a baby and was going back to his wife must have been a terrible shock.'

Sandra had thought long and hard about the situation.

'I loved Brad but... don't ask me how... but somewhere deep inside I knew I didn't have a future with him. The first niggly doubt was when I realised that if Brad and I made a go of it together, I'd have to move to Florida. Though moving to America sounded wonderful the thought pulled at me heartstrings. This is the first real home I've known and I've grown fond of the village and the folk.' She raised her eyebrows. 'Well, most of them.'

Frieda laughed. 'I know the ones you're talking about.'

'This is where I want to settle.' Sandra swallowed over a lump in her throat. 'I know that now. I've spent too long already in a different country to Alf, I wouldn't want to be so far away from him when he comes home.'

Now, as Sandra trudged up to the back door of the farm for breakfast, feet cold in her wellingtons despite her thick woollen socks, she wondered what the weather in Spain was like. Excitement surged through her at the thought that sometime soon her brother would be coming home.

But a fearful voiced warned in her head to be careful of being too optimistic. It didn't pay.

As she opened the farmhouse door, Sandra made a mental note today was Sunday. She would visit church.

*

In the afternoon, Matthew, sitting in the front pew waiting for the boys to show up for choir practice, was making notes for the article he was writing for the church's monthly magazine.

He heard the church door open but didn't turn as past experience taught him it might be a parishioner who needed privacy.

Absorbed in his work, time passed and then Matthew was aware of footsteps walking down the aisle. Miss Hudson stood at the end of the row of pews he was sitting in.

He noticed her bright and shining eyes and how her pink and cream complexion had changed to rosy in the cold weather.

He spoke, attempting to keep his voice neutral. 'It's a pleasure to see you. Have you heard any more from your brother?'

He hoped she hadn't had bad news. He couldn't bear that for her.

'No. But I'm not worried now I know Alf is in Spain and will be repatriated to England. It's only a matter of time before he'll be home.'

'Where is that?' he couldn't help but ask.

'Why, here in Leadburn, of course.'

A wave of unsurpassed joy surged through Matthew.

*

Sandra missed having Mr Carlton in her life, she realised as she looked at him. Maybe all it would take to get back to the easy-going relationship they'd shared before was for her to confide in him.

'How is the reading coming along?' he asked.

Did he really want to know or was he just being polite?

'I can read most of *The Land Girl* magazine bar a few difficult words.' She struggled for something else to say. 'How is Mr Fairweather keeping?'

'Bothered with his arthritis, I'm afraid.'

'Tell him I'm asking after him.'

'I will, Miss Hudson.'

The stilted conversation was unbearable.

She wanted to tell Mr Carlton about Brad and what had happened so they could get their friendship on a more natural footing again. But the awkwardness between them held her back.

She could *try*, a voice in her mind said.

'If you've got the time to spare I—'

At that moment the church door opened and three lads came in.

'Choir practice,' Mr Carlton explained, looking rather crestfallen.

As she hurried up the aisle Sandra thought that the interruption was probably for the best. Then why, she asked herself, did she have this feeling she'd let herself down?

CHAPTER THIRTY-THREE

December 1943

Sandra

The Sunday before Christmas when Sandra awoke, she brought her arm from beneath the blanket and checked her wristwatch. Startled, she sat up in the bed. Crikey. Half one in the afternoon?

Earlier that morning she'd been to work and, after she'd milked the cows and fed the animals, Mr Nichol had told her, 'You and the lass can take the rest of the day off until afternoon milking.'

It had been too early to have dinner, and bone-tired as usual, Sandra had reckoned she had time for a lie-down. Fully clothed, she'd slipped beneath the blanket on the bunk bed.

Dinner would be over by now, she thought, but snacks would be left by Cook on the hatch.

With only six days until Christmas, the Women's Institute had arranged to decorate the church hall for the festivities and would be arriving at the church at two o'clock. Sandra decided it would be fun to join them. She'd been surprised at how many young lasses were members of the WI and all the good works they were involved in.

Shivering in the chilly air, she padded over to the window, the cold from the linoleum flooring coming through her woollen stockings. From its high vantage point, the window looked out over the view at the front of the hostel to the seemingly velvety hillsides. Staring up at the powder blue sky where a dazzling golden sun shone low in the sky, it was difficult to believe the heavens could hold such terrors at night.

Feeling a sense that all was well with her life, Sandra pulled on her boots and, fastening the laces, made for the common room. She picked up a cheese sandwich and, smothering margarine and jam on a slice of bread, she put them on a plate. Pouring milk from a white jug into a cup, she made for one of the long tables.

It felt strange being in the common room without hustle and bustle or the clatter of cutlery or the din of rowdy voices as they talked over one another. Just Sandra, in a silent world of her own.

The door squeaked open.

As though some primal instinct warned her, the hairs on her arm bristled and Sandra was afraid to turn around. Footsteps came closer and then a figure came to stand beside the table.

She looked up and saw Hal Miller.

His face sombre, he took off his hat. 'The warden let me in.'

Sandra went cold inside. She didn't need to hear the words, she knew.

'It's Brad, isn't it?'

He sat opposite her at the table. He met her eyes, regret in his. 'I'm afraid so, Sandra. Prepare yourself for a shock.'

Such a silly phrase, her mind rambled. How could she prepare? Her muscles had already gone weak. An ache started somewhere in her chest.

'Is he dead?'

His guard dropped and his face etched in sorrow. 'Yes.'

She shook her head in disbelief. Brad couldn't be dead.

From a tunnel, it seemed, Hal's voice spoke. 'I'm stationed back in Cambridgeshire but had some leave due. I hitched a ride as I wanted to tell you myself.'

'That's good of you,' she heard herself say.

'It's what Brad would want me to do.'

Sandra gazed around the empty common room. She wanted time to revert back ten minutes to when the world still had Brad in it.

'How did it happen?'

'We were on a mission. Brad was escorting bombers over enemy territory. I saw him in a dogfight with an enemy fighter. The Messerschmitt went down in flames and the last I saw of Brad's plane was it turning back, heading for home, smoke trailing behind.'

'He didn't make it?'

'Apparently Brad sent a radio message to base; they answered but there was silence.' His expression sorrowful, Hal heaved a great sigh. 'Over four hundred planes left that night. Bad weather conditions meant that many of the airfields were covered in fog. Over fifty planes didn't make it back. Brad's was one of them.'

All those families, Sandra thought, *left broken-hearted*. As she was. She'd said goodbye to Brad once and though it hurt she had been glad he was somewhere out in the world carrying on with his life. She couldn't bear the thought of him at the bottom of the sea or in some foreign field amongst wreckage.

'If it helps, Brad once told me he was doing what he loved. Flying aeroplanes.'

Sandra nodded. He'd said the same to her but, she admitted to herself, it didn't help.

Brad's amazing, transparent blue eyes, stocky figure, slow smile as he looked at her, played in her mind's eye. She mourned all that could have been in his life and a sob escaped her.

Hal, still standing, brought a letter out from his uniform pocket.

'He told me to give you this if anything should happen. His parents will receive formal notification.'

Sandra took the letter.

Poor souls. Her heart bled for Brad's parents. What they must be going through. She remembered that they had their grandson to remember their son by. She hoped it would give them some comfort.

'Is there anything I can do?' His chair scraped back and he stood.

Sandra shook her head. 'No, thank you. Thank you for coming to tell me.'

'Can I get someone?'

'I'll be all right. I... have friends I can talk to.'

'If you're sure?'

She nodded, not trusting herself to speak, staring blindly ahead of her.

'Goodbye, Sandra... and good luck.'

She heard Hal's footsteps retreat and the common room door close.

She opened the envelope.

My darling Sandra,

I'll keep this short for both our sakes. Because if you're reading this, I'm dead and I don't want to dwell on my demise and neither, I imagine, do you. But it's necessary you receive this in the event.

Let me begin by asking, do you remember me saying that I was a stick in the mud? Well, that was true but not any more. Because I found happiness and adventure, first by training to fly aeroplanes, a job that I love and secondly coming to Britain because, Sandra, I met you.

I loved you, never doubt that. The best moment was when I opened my eyes after the crash and saw an angel talking to me. The moment causes me to smile every time I think on it. My beautiful angel, Sandra.

I have two regrets. One that I won't see my son grow to be a man – be there for him as a dad. The other leaving you as I did. Nothing in my life was so difficult. I wanted to

*stay but I could never live with myself if I did – I couldn't
turn my back on my duty as a dad.*

*I promised to keep this short, so before I go, I'll end now
with what is in my heart.*

*Darling girl, I will never regret the short time we spent
together, because I know now what it's like to love someone
heart and soul.*

*Never look back. You're young, find someone to love.
I wish you a full and happy life.*

Here's looking at you, kid!

Your Brad

XXX

Sandra folded the letter and clutched it to her heart.

A panicky feeling overcame her. Without thought – of either
muffling up in warm clothing, or that she hadn't eaten – she shot
from the chair and made for the front door. She hurtled along
the path as though the devil himself was chasing her.

She didn't think where she was going and was surprised to
find herself at the church hall door. Entering the empty hall, she
saw, at the far end of the room by the stage, the little Christmas
tree, donated by one of the farmers. It stood green and proud
waiting to be embellished with ornaments and brought to life.

For some reason she never quite understood, the scene reduced
Sandra to shoulder-heaving tears.

*

Matthew, going to see that all was ready for when the WI arrived
to decorate the hall, found Sandra. She was standing in front of
the tree and, turning at his footsteps, eyes pink and glistening,
tears dripping from her cheeks, she looked the picture of distress.

Alarmed, he hurried towards her. 'Whatever's the matter,
Miss Hudson?'

She shook like a leaf. 'It's Brad.' The words came out jerky. 'His plane didn't return. He's dead.'

He couldn't bear to see her so distraught. He was skilled at dealing with such matters but now, at the sight of her, Matthew was lost for words. He tried but he couldn't think what to say.

'I'm sorry.'

He told himself to leave. This was a private matter and she hadn't requested his presence. Besides, Matthew admitted, he was too involved.

'I'll make you a cup of tea in the kitchen.' His response was inadequate, he knew. 'The women from the WI will be here soon.'

He made to move away.

'Please stay,' she managed to say through sobs. 'I would rather be with you.'

What else could Matthew do? He rifled in his pocket for the clean handkerchief he kept for such occasions.

She wiped her eyes on it.

'I'm so sorry for your loss.' Matthew was genuinely regretful Miss Hudson's sweetheart had died. He only wanted her happiness.

'Me and Brad had finished.'

Before he could think of a reply, she hesitantly went on to tell him, as best she could through her distress, how the American was married and had gone back to his wife.

She wiped the tears from her face. 'I've learnt these last few months' – her expression had changed, become resolute – 'to trust my inner feelings. Though I didn't want Brad to go, there was a familiar feeling about him leaving. Do you know what I mean, Mr Carlton?'

'That it was ordained?' Matthew put it into words he understood.

'You could say that. I'd never been in love before and I couldn't see a future with Brad.'

'In America?'

'I suppose, but that would have been difficult.' She frowned. 'The strange thing is I never told Brad my background.' She added quickly, 'It wasn't that I didn't trust him. It was more we lived in a world of our own when nothing else mattered but that we were together.'

It occurred to Matthew as Miss Hudson spoke how much more confidence she had now than when he'd first known her, how much more inner strength.

She gave him a quivery smile as if she knew he was thinking about her. 'It's strange but I've always felt comfortable confiding everything to you. Thank you, Mr Carlton.'

'I'm glad I could be of help.' He inwardly groaned at such an inane answer. There was so much he wanted to say but couldn't.

She looked at him with a surprised look of discovery. 'You've always been there when I've needed someone.'

He saw the tears start and, deciding she must want to be alone, he got up to go.

*

'Please stay,' Sandra told the curate.

It was true she could speak her mind to him and felt neither judgement nor condescension. She could be completely at ease. She could be herself.

In a moment of clarity, an overwhelming sense of knowing she was in the right place at the right time washed over Sandra. A moment of reality, as though the blinkers had been taken away from her eyes.

Sandra didn't want to be anywhere else but safe and secure here.

She had loved Brad heart and soul, but he wasn't for her. Their precious time together was only ever to last those few short months. Sandra knew that now. And Brad had known it too. She thought of him and all the other brave souls who had given their lives that others might live.

Brad's words came back to her. *Live a full and happy life.* She owed that to him. But could Sandra love again?

She said a silent prayer. *Sleep peacefully, Brad Carter. I'll never forget you.*

She looked at Mr Carlton, who gazed back at her with his warm eyes.

She felt awkward with him as she saw not the cleric but the worldly man with... tenderness in his heart.

What an idiot she'd been, not seeing what had been right in front of her all this time.

Gazing at the curate, the simplicity of the man, his beliefs, honesty and goodness, Sandra realised with an absolute certainly she'd known only a few times in her short lifetime, that yes, one day she could learn to love again.

CHAPTER THIRTY-FOUR

January 1944

Frieda

Christmas had come and gone and Frieda felt bleak because, though everyone around her was optimistic about the prospect of a second front, all she could think about was the distressing news that British bombers had conducted their heaviest raid yet on Berlin.

Sitting opposite her at the kitchen table making up Comfort Fund packages, Aunty Doris leapt from her chair and switched off the wireless.

Aunty Doris was glued to war news, the same as everyone else, but Frieda knew her aunt was worried about her becoming too involved in the situation in Berlin and wanted to protect her.

Frieda couldn't help being obsessed and listened daily to the news and read all the newspapers on the subject. She imagined the devastation in Berlin, toppled buildings reduced to rubble, the dead lying on the ground. The fear that her relatives were amongst them reduced her to a state of despair.

But Frieda hadn't succumbed to the voice of will that wouldn't allow her to eat. Sandra's method of experimenting daily with morsels of different kinds of food and gradually increasing the helping size had been successful and she knew her attitude to food had changed as a result. She still worried constantly about getting fat but she had regained a certain standard of health she wanted to maintain, and she wasn't so exhausted any more.

It was dinner time and Frieda was home early from the farm as Mr Nichol had said she could help Aunty Doris in the post office because Mrs Teasdale was off sick and her son (who was a Boy Scout) was doing firefighting training in Hexham.

More himself these days, Mr Nichol's ghastly grey pallor had changed back to its normal ruddy complexion. Frieda suspected that Mrs Nichol's improved health had helped with the transformation.

The farmer had warned his workers when Mrs Nichol began to be seen downstairs again at mealtimes, 'Don't mention our Wil— the laddie, as Mother's heart isn't strong enough to handle the grief.'

Frieda felt sad for Mr Nichol, because just thinking about his son made him well up.

She finished a dinner of mince, half a potato and peas and pushed back her chair, taking the dirty dishes to the sink to wash them.

'Thanks, love. You're a great help.' Aunty Doris resumed packing parcels at the table. 'These long dark winter nights at home cooped up with only the wireless for company give me the hump. Which reminds me, how did the panto go last night? I couldn't keep my eyes open.'

'I really enjoyed it. Lots of funny jokes about the village.'

Mrs Curtis from the shop was a Guider and had written a pantomime for the Guides to perform on stage in the church hall. Frieda thought the Guides brave as the idea of being stared at terrified her. Memories from her schooldays came back to her, when she was singled out and bullied by the other children for being a Jew.

What was wrong with her today? She felt as vulnerable as eggshells inside. Deep down Frieda knew why. Another year had passed without any word from her family. News had filtered through about what the fate was for Jews left in Germany. And, in her weak moments, she feared the worst.

Guilt-ridden, she still wondered why she had survived.

'Did anyone forget their lines?' Aunty Doris gazed at her with that intense expression she used when she suspected Frieda was experiencing a moment of mental torture, and wanted to bring her out of it.

Frieda took more deep breaths. 'No. Sandra didn't have to prompt.'

Some of the Land Girls had volunteered to help the production by painting scenery or improvising with clothes to make costumes. Sandra had volunteered to act as prompt.

These days Sandra was never far away from the church. It hadn't escaped Frieda's attention why that was. She'd noticed surreptitious, lingering looks between her friend and the curate. But she hadn't pried. She knew her friend would tell her when she was ready.

That time had come yesterday morning, when the pair of them were cleaning out the pigs' shed together.

Leaning on her rake, eyes shining, Sandra told her, 'I've had a letter from Alf. He says the reason he isn't home yet is him and the RAF boys he was travelling with were arrested by the Spanish police and imprisoned for two months for entering the country illegally. He says he's been released and is now in Gibraltar in an RAF camp. He expects to be flown home at any time.' She beamed. 'Oh! Frieda. I'm so relieved and happy.' Then she had looked stricken. 'How thoughtless of me with all you're going through.'

Frieda was busy putting a woven willow fence across the shed side opening to keep the pigs outside.

She had assured her friend, 'It's wonderful to hear good news. It gives me hope, I couldn't be happier for you.' It was the truth. 'I was so worried about you when the American died.

Despite everything I would have felt the same if anything had happened to Antonio.'

Raking the muddy straw from the entrance into a heap, Sandra paused. She frowned in concentration as though trying to find suitable words to reply. 'While I don't regret a single moment I spent with Brad, I realise now he was never mine to have. He should have told me he was married from the start. But he showed me how to love. He'll always have a corner of my heart, but only as a first love.' Her eyes widened in amazement. 'Frieda, I've got something to tell you in strictest confidence.'

Frieda guessed what the secret was but turned and looked suitably expectant.

'I've fallen for Mr Carlton.'

Frieda knew it. 'And does he feel the same way?'

Squeals came from the outside fenced-off area – it would seem the pigs were excited too – and Sandra hesitated.

'Would you believe, yes. Apparently, he approached the bishop some time ago about the matter of us courting.'

'He must have been smited—'

Sandra laughed. 'Smitten.'

Frieda giggled. 'Smitten by you from the first.'

'Isn't it incredible? All that time and I never guessed. It just seems right, as if I've always known him. I think because he was a curate I held back.' She shook her head in amazed wonder. 'He says the bishop insists that propriety is important, so we're to court in secret.'

'So, no holding hands in public,' Frieda replied playfully.

Sandra went pink. 'Until the event of an engagement announcement, no.'

Frieda beamed. 'Sandra, this kind of thing only comes once in a lifetime. Enjoy each moment. Though' – she pulled a mock horrified face – 'personally I would find keeping a secret as big as this difficult.'

'I don't mind. I'm just so happy.' Sandra looked pensive. 'I'm prepared to wait as long as it takes. Matthew insists being involved with him is a big step for me and he wants me to be sure.'

Frieda leant the fork against the shed wall. 'The curate's a good sort. I would imagine he would put your feelings first.'

'He does. He would jeopardise his own happiness if he thought I'd be unhappy.'

Frieda crossed her heart. 'I promise I won't tell a soul.'

'I had to tell you. You're family to me.'

Maybe the only family I've got, Frieda thought.

Thinking of family, Frieda said, 'Why don't you write and tell Mrs Goodwin the good news about Alf and that you've found happiness with Mr Carlton? It will make her day.'

'Better still, I've written and told her I've got next weekend off and will spend the night. I intend to tell Olive in person.'

'Oh! She'll be thrilled. I wish I could come with you' – Frieda gave her friend a mischievous grin – 'but someone has to milk Gertie. Give Mrs Goodwin my love.'

'I will.' Sandra laughed. 'I bet she's started baking already.'

Frieda, delivering the afternoon's post before she went back to work at the farm, brought out the last letter from the sack.

She passed an opening where a wrought-iron gate would have been had it not been taken away to make munitions earlier in the war.

Posting the letter through the brass letterbox, she retraced her steps back to the post office. She passed the little white bridge over the gushing stream, swollen now with the recent torrential rain. Walking along the stream's grassy banks, the sun peeped through a cloud and the village was drenched in sunlight.

In the absolute silence, she gazed around the village, empty of people except for an elderly man who sat on a wooden bench on the other side of the stream, smoking a pipe.

As she made her way back to the post office, Frieda knew, with a clarity that comes only a few times in a lifetime, to prepare herself because something momentous was going to happen.

'Yoo-hoo,' a voice called, as if on cue.

Aunty Doris was standing at the end of the garden path, behind the stone wall.

As Frieda approached her aunt held out a letter, an anxious look in her eye. 'I put this aside so you would see it.' She handed over the letter. 'Did you not see it by the post bag?'

Frieda hadn't.

'It's from the International Red Cross, probably sent on from their headquarters in Geneva.'

A cold sensation shivered up Frieda's spine.

'Come and read it inside.' Aunty Doris led the way up the path.

Dreamlike, she followed Aunty Doris and, as the post office bell gave its familiar ting, she wondered if, after opening the letter, life would ever be the same.

Throwing the empty post bag on the counter, she wondered if this was what Sandra must have felt when she received Alf's telegram.

She stood in the deathly quiet post office where only a clock ticked. She could procrastinate no longer. She tore the envelope open.

The letter was written in German, something Frieda struggled with after so long, but she got by enough to manage.

November 1943

Dear Frieda,
    Sorry I ran away that day.

Her heart raced; it was from Kurt!

I found the good friend and I am in hiding. Our parents and grandma were arrested and taken to the camps.

The Red Cross helped find you. I hope you are well, my beloved sister. I wished to write in case the worst should happen but in my heart I feel that one day we shall meet again after this war is done. I miss you. I'm sorry I didn't protect you and Mama.

    Your loving brother,
    Kurt

Her throat aching, Frieda read the letter again. Though she stared at the words she couldn't quite believe that they were real.

Time slipped away, and Frieda was transported back to the crowded station in Berlin, staring into her brother's mutinous face.

I won't go. Papa told me that I'm now the man of the family until he returns.

She relived in her mind's eye Mama's drawn, white face, the acute shock when Kurt jumped ship, the loneliness and fear of the sea journey.

She had survived. So had Kurt. As the enormity of the moment sank in, tears fell from her eyes. She brushed them hastily away with a hand. This was not the time for tears. As the joy of knowing Kurt was alive filtered through every fibre of her being, happiness overcame her.

'Frieda, for goodness' sake, tell me what the letter says.'

'My brother Kurt is alive.'

'Oh, my goodness. That's wonderful news. I'm so glad for you.' Tears of joy brimmed in Aunty Doris's eyes. 'Does he say where he is?'

Frieda read the letter out loud.

'Who is this good friend? Do you know?'

Frieda's brow wrinkled in thought. 'I can only think Kurt means Herr Unger. Papa always referred to him as *my good friend.*' She remembered something else. 'Herr Unger has a cellar. Maybe that's where Kurt is in hiding.'

Aunty Doris's expression became grave. 'You realise it would be too dangerous for them if your brother was to say any more.'

Frieda nodded.

Aunty Doris gathered her up in a hug. As they held one another there was an expectant silence and she knew Aunty Doris was wondering about the rest of Frieda's family. But Frieda couldn't face the subject of her parents right now when all she wanted was to bask in happiness.

The post office door tinged open.

Her aunt kissed Frieda on the brow. 'I'm over the moon your brother's alive. Just trust in the future, love.'

Frieda knew her aunt understood. Though it was good news she was still worried about Kurt, who, presumably, was in hiding in war-torn Berlin.

Aunty Doris moved behind the counter, a smile of welcome on her face.

Impatience grew in Frieda like a balloon ready to burst and she didn't know what to do, how to handle the jumble of emotions inside.

Then she knew. Of course! She would seek out Sandra, tell her the news and they could wonder together at how their lives mirrored each other's yet again.

She too had a beloved brother who'd survived.

She raced from the post office, down the road towards the farm and her friend – out of her lonely world into one of hope and expectation.

A LETTER FROM SHIRLEY

Dear Reader,

I want to say a huge thank you for choosing to read *The Outcast Girls*. If you did enjoy it, and want to keep up to date with all my latest releases, just sign up at the following link. Your email address will never be shared and you can unsubscribe at any time:

www.bookouture.com/shirley-dickson

The book was the inspiration of my editor, Christina Demosthenous, who suggested that I wrote about another orphan from my debut novel *The Orphan Sisters*. I'd always wondered what became of Sandra as the two sisters lost touch with her. And so I decided to explore Sandra and her brother Alf's story, and it was like meeting up with old friends.

Frieda, originally, wasn't going to play such a big role but her story was so utterly heart-breaking, how could I not give her a major part. I'm so glad I did. The friendship and moving similarities between the two girls' lives became the focus of the book.

Once again, the setting is the lovely north-eastern town of South Shields – the place where I was born – and the beautiful Northumberland countryside – where I now live. The Land Girl hostel mentioned in the book still stands although it is now a youth hostel. Although Northumberland is rich with quaint and lovely villages there is no such place as Leadburn.

And, as far as I am aware, there were no Americans stationed in Northumberland. I have taken the liberty with bombings for the sake of the story, but the 1943 bomb in South Shields did take place with loss of life.

If you enjoyed *The Outcast Girls* and have time to leave a review, I would be most grateful. It makes such as difference to an author and I do love to hear what readers think. Or maybe you could mention my book to family and friends as it could help fellow readers to find me for the first time.

I would love to hear from you on my author page or on Twitter. Your support is most appreciated.

Happy reading!

Thanks,
Shirley

shirleydicksonbooks

ShirleyDWriter

ACKNOWLEDGEMENTS

Huge thanks to my husband, Wal, for his endless support and keeping me fed when I'm working, helping search for facts – I'd never find them myself – and for just being there when I need an ear. I couldn't do it without you!

As ever, thank you to my wonderful publisher, Bookouture, and the amazing people behind the scenes: Kim, Noelle, Peta, Alex, Jennie, Lauren, Natasha, Becca and each one of the dedicated team. Thanks also to the wonderful Bookouture authors for being informative and hugely supportive.

I'm indebted to the brilliant Vicky Blunden for making *The Outcast Girls* so much better than I thought possible. Special thanks to my editor Christina Demosthenous for your ideas – yes, it was you who instigated the story – the work, support and belief in me – I'm truly grateful, Christina.

My thanks and gratitude go to Katy, David and Mary Carr for taking the time to share their knowledge of farming. Also, Howard and Margaret Forster, Brenda and Eddy Carrington. To Mr Kennedy for taking the time out of his busy schedule to inform me about matters of the clergy. To Mel and Val Douglas for showing me around their house which became the home of the Kirtons. I'm indebted to Cindy and Karl for their hospitality showing me around the former Land Girl hostel. To my friend Prue for advising me on a solicitor's working day. And Mavis Jones for sharing her experience as a Land Girl with me. To Jo and Christine for advice on German and Tracy on all matters concerning pigs, to Andrea and

Gary for help with IT. And Tom Burnakis for help with pharmacy information.

To my lovely family – Tracy, Andrea, Joanne, Phil, Nick, Gary, Gemma, Dale and Robbie, Laura, Tom and Will – that make it all worthwhile.

To you, my readers, none of this would happen if you didn't buy *The Outcast Girls* – and not forgetting the reviewers and book bloggers – a massive thank you.

Made in the USA
Coppell, TX
30 March 2020

18004400R00192